THE SECOND
MRS. ASTOR

THE SECOND
MRS. ASTOR

SHANA ABÉ

KENSINGTON
PUBLISHING CORP.

www.kensingtonbooks.com

KENSINGTON BOOKS are published by

Kensington Publishing Corp.
119 West 40th Street
New York, NY 10018

ISBN-13: 978-1-4967-3205-7 (ebook)
ISBN-10: 1-4967-3205-7 (ebook)

ISBN-13: 978-1-4967-3204-0
ISBN-10: 1-4967-3204-9
First Kensington Trade Paperback Printing: September 2021

10 9 8 7

Printed in the United States of America

For Wendy McCurdy, with my deepest gratitude,
for taking a chance on this haunted fairy tale

PROLOGUE

August 23, 1912

My Darling Jakey,

I gave you his name. He gave you his eyes and that swirl of fair hair. I suspect your chin is mine, however, and I suppose that's as it should be. Your father towered, remarkable and alone, over everyone we knew and certainly over my heart. There can be no true living reflection of such a man left, not even you.

As I write, you're nestled in your bassinet, so tiny and tranquil. Whenever the breeze from the nursery window swells the lace curtains, scented of horses and muggy summer rain, your lips purse into something I fancy is a smile—one that strikes me to the bone. I am filled with both astonishment and despair to think that you will never know Jack, nor he you. Even these four months later, the truth of it will still steal up on me, as surprising and damning as a blow from behind: Jack will never see that dimpled smile, or celebrate your first steps, or fall in love with the shape of your toes or the burble of your laughter. And you, my own brilliant miracle of a son, will never have a single memory of him.

Yet my mind overflows with memories. I am a waterfall of memories of Jack; I drown in them; and so for your sake, and perhaps for my own peace, I will write down what I can for you now. Someday—some faraway day—I will hand these pages to you, and my memories will become your own.

I won't begin with our ending, which everyone in the world knows anyway: that jet satin night, the slight rumbly tremble that shook me in our bed—like it was nothing, like the ship had briefly and inexplicably sailed over a field of stones. The groggy minutes spent getting dressed, my body heavy with five months of you and the unyielding desire for more sleep.

Making our way abovedeck. Watching the panic begin to wheel, stronger and stronger, through the masses, until the shoving and screaming had consumed everything the North Atlantic had not.

Being helped through the slant of that promenade window, teetering at its brink. Your father's hands, hard and certain, pushing me along. Women moaning, crying, stretching out their arms to their men left behind on the ship. Trying to find a place in that lopsided little lifeboat—

Well. I suppose I've begun with our ending, after all. But as I said, everyone already knows it, has shed their tears over it and offered their (copious and entirely uninvited) opinions about it. Our beginning, however, belonged only to us.

And it was sublime.

He had been noticing me for weeks. I felt his gaze whenever we happened to be at the same garden party or concert, or riding through the same park or visiting the same club. Colonel Jack Astor was likely the richest man in America, and difficult to miss. Missing the force of his gaze was more difficult still—a calm lucid gray, clear as a winter dawn.

(I made the mistake once of telling him so. He laughed, bussed me on the cheek, and called me infatuated. I do think I was more subtle than that. I did say *winter*.)

Your grandmother drifted about in spasms of hope. Your grandfather was more pragmatic but no less optimistic. It didn't seem to bother either of them that Jack was divorced and nearly thirty years older than I.

"He would be fortunate to have you," my father said.

"Do not contradict anything he says," commanded my mother.

"He has said practically nothing to me so far beyond *how do you do*," I pointed out, but we all three knew it was merely a matter of time and opportunity for that to change. I was young, but not *that* young; I'd already been escorted to picnics and teas by a clutch of interested fellows. I knew what that clear, steady gaze of Colonel Astor's meant.

He invited us for a weekend at his cottage in Bar Harbor, even though we summered at our own—far more modest!—residence in town. It was a penny-bright August in Maine, and everything was scented of honeysuckle and cut grass and the salty strong sea. We were not the colonel's only guests during those few days, but it seemed by the attention of the servants and splendor of our rooms that we were the ones who mattered.

There was a dance to attend, and seven-course meals, and a trip around the harbor upon Jack's steam yacht *Noma* (I did get seasick, but I believe I managed to successfully hide it). We played games of whist and croquet, poker for the gentlemen. The hours spun out, lazy and golden, and nearly all of them remain a blur to me except for one singular moment.

Mother and Father and Katherine were resting after Saturday's luncheon. The colonel was to take us on an automobile ride along the coast later on, and Mother had wanted to look her best for it— because even then, we were shadowed by the press. I considered myself already at my best, and lying about in bed in my corset and all my hairpins for an hour sounded interminable. I'd slipped away as soon as she'd started snoring.

And so I was seated alone in a corner of the brass-and-mahogany citadel of the cottage's library, flipping through the pages of what I suspected to be a book of Grecian poetry. I was the successful product of a proper finishing school, but Latin was my strength. Beyond the most basic alphabet, I did not speak or read Greek. I was instead studying the strangely emphatic flow of the letters, the structure of the stanzas, guessing at sounds and meanings, when I sensed that he had entered the chamber.

Thinking back on it, I realize now he must have been stalking me a bit, waiting for the perfect instant to encounter me alone, and normally I would have been both flattered and prepared. He was, after all, the reason I was there. But as soon as I realized he was walking toward me, all I could think was, *Oh, no.*

I wished, with all my heart, that I had any other book in my hands but the one I did. If he asked me about it, I'd either have to lie and say, yes, indeed, Grecian poetry was so divinely brilliant . . . or else admit that, like a toddler, I was merely entranced with the pretty shapes.

I looked up as he approached, tall and angular and so sharply handsome, his pale brown hair combed flat against his skull, his moustache neatly trimmed.

"May I?" he asked, gesturing to the burgundy leather chair opposite mine.

"Please do." I closed the book and turned it over, so that the title and author were hidden against the folds of my skirt.

He sat. He crossed his legs. The sun-pebbled sea in the window behind him shot platinum along his hair and starched collar and the taupe serge of his lounge coat.

As I said, he was older than I, but in that moment, with light gleaming so bold and blinding behind him, he might have been a young man on the verge of his first brush with courtship.

He cocked his head, met my eyes directly.

"How lovely you are, Miss Force."

I looked down at my lap as I had been taught, and murmured, "Thank you."

"And how opaque."

That made me look up again. *Opaque?* Was it a compliment?

The colonel smiled. "Like no woman I've ever known before. Your mind is a mystery to me."

"Oh," I said, "sometimes it is to me, as well! But I'm not really very mysterious, I'm afraid."

He leaned back his head and laughed. I felt the sudden spark of the power of that, of making a man like John Jacob Astor laugh in genuine amusement. Of making him *react*. It rushed like lightning through my veins, hellish and bright.

I think, from that instant, we were both doomed.

CHAPTER 1

June 1907
Newport, Rhode Island

The first time she saw him, she was essentially invisible: thirteen years old, a schoolgirl on holiday, her hair dripping from the sea, sleek wet mermaid curls clinging to her arms and back. She was nestled, legs tucked under her, in the coarse silvery sand of Bailey's Beach, her ruffled cap tossed beside her. Her nose was tingling hot and she didn't care, because it was breezy and warm, and the sun was a high glorious pinpoint, and if it were ladylike in the least to stretch out all the way in her bathing costume to make a sand angel, she would have.

But Madeleine was not five; she was thirteen. And as it was just after eleven in the morning—the hour that only ladies were welcome to swim in the red algae-choked waves—Mother was bobbing nearby. She was *always* nearby. Maddy's removal of her cap was transgression enough.

Gulls screamed and darted overhead. Madeleine lifted her chin and followed their loose circles, ragged-tipped wings, dragon shadows dipping and spinning against the sky.

A gaggle of girls a few years younger than she stood shrieking at the shoreline, kicking froth and sand at each other, too timid to venture all the way in but too aware of their bare shins and feet to resist the cool water. They were nearly louder than the birds.

Like Madeleine and every other female on the beach, the girls wore black. Black bathing bloomers, black shirtwaists with fat blossoming sleeves, everything from their necks to their knees down to the bones of their wrists thoroughly concealed. It was as though each and every summer noon, the exclusive strand of Bailey's Beach became haunted by covens of fashionable, water-soaked witches.

A pair of carefully plodding bays hauled a carriage past the long arabesques of seaweed that marked the tideline, stopping at the very last stretch of dry sand. Blue-liveried footmen leapt free of the carriage; large, mysterious bundles were liberated from their leather straps in the back. Maddy twisted to watch as the men—who weren't *technically* allowed on the beach right now, but they were only servants, so that was all right—swiftly erected a saffron-striped tent, complete with rug, wicker chair, and folding table, and then returned to the carriage to assist a solitary lady down to the sand.

She was white-haired, stooped. She squinted crossly at the sudden hard light but was so quickly guided inside the tent that Maddy barely had time to take note of the glimmer of jet beading on her dress and the garnet brooch pinned to her bosom. As soon as the lady was seated, a wind-tousled maid began unpacking a hamper for her meal.

"Ha," breathed a voice in Maddy's ear, accompanied by the sound of a body dropping down onto the grit beside her. Madeleine darted a look at her older sister (grinning and capless and somehow not at all sun-scorched), then looked back at the saffron-tent woman.

"Are you not awed?" Katherine drawled, leaning back on her arms, examining nothing but the unflagging sea rolling in before them. "Are you not suitably cowed?"

"Should I be?" Maddy asked.

"Yes, you certainly should be, little girl. *That* is Mrs. Astor. *The* Mrs. Astor. Dare to stare her in the eyes and you'll turn into stone. Or is it burst into a pillar of flame? No, wait! You'll be struck from the social register and die a shriveled old maid." She gave an exaggerated shudder, still grinning. "The horror!"

Madeleine knew, of course, who Mrs. Astor was. Everyone knew. It was just that she had never seen her in person before; the Forces and the Astors didn't move in the same social circles. Maddy had always imagined the matriarch of the venerable Knickerbocker set as a woman grown wiry and vicious and strong, with a smile of sharpened daggers and the fingernails of a warlord.

Not this. Not this stout, elderly creature who shied from the sun and had her lobster cut into cubes for her by her maid on her gilded china plate.

"And who is that?" Maddy asked, tilting her head toward the hatted man who was crossing the sand in long, leggy strides toward the tent. (He was definitely not a servant, but no one stopped him.)

"Ah," replied her sister, in a tone of both confidentiality and superiority. She flicked a strand of drying kelp from her thigh. "*That*, my dear, is her son, the colonel."

Oh, Maddy thought.

He was comely. She'd heard that he was, but only through school gossip, and *comely* in schoolgirl parlance might as well mean *not so drippy-nosed*, or *not quite yet bald*, or *not so fat as his horse*.

But Colonel John Jacob Astor, gentleman, inventor, and war hero, *was* comely, in an older, hawkish sort of way, rather like her father . . . but on second thought, not at all, because the colonel was fair as her father was gray, mustachioed as her father was not; fit and tall as . . . well, as only himself. Because he moved so quickly, she only just managed to get a good look at him, but what she noticed—what she would remember for the rest of her life from those few warm breezy seconds on that rough Rhode Island beach—was that he was smiling as he walked toward his mother.

That he was easily conquering the sand, graceful and determined. And that, for the smallest inclination of a moment, he turned his head and caught her eyes and noticed *her*, there on the sand not so far off.

And then, for an instant, he was smiling at *her*.

It was as though a dart of light from the summer sun had pierced Madeleine's heart. A dart, sweet and wonderful and terrible, right through her heart.

Then he was gone, swallowed by the interior of the tent. Someone untied the flap of the entrance and it fluttered closed, and then there was only saffron and white, and the gulls still calling out overhead.

"Maddy," said her sister, placing a hand on her arm. "You look so queer. Are you all right?"

"Yes," Madeleine said. She sat up straight, wiped a hand across her brow. She licked her lips and tasted salt and sand, relentless, pervasive in her every crease and pore. "Right as rain."

The next time she saw him, she was not invisible. She was seventeen and draped in greenery: ropes of ivy, braids of ruffled roses, daisies, bright clouds of candytuft (the closest the stage manager could come to rue, sadly unavailable) woven through her dark brown plaits. She was singing, mad, twirling at times across the stage so that her skirts would lift to reveal the smart new boots she'd bought especially for the play.

She was Ophelia—tragic, bereft Ophelia—and had practiced singing her mad, sad lines until her voice had gone hoarse and she'd had to rest it for two days just to speak again without a rasp.

"He is dead and gone, lady, he is dead and gone; at his head a grass-green turf, at his heels a stone."

After weeks of rehearsals, the Junior League society had the honor of presenting *Hamlet* in Bar Harbor for two nights only (the Casino's theater was ever-popular and only borrowed, after all), and this was the second. The previous night's opening had left Madeleine shaking with nerves, but tonight she felt better; she was a creature composed of flaming hot candle-lanterns and greasy face paint and flowers, saturated in poetry and song. The heels of her boots struck the stage so lightly, she felt at times she might actually be floating.

Beyond the lights lining the edge of the proscenium, beneath the darkened stained-glass chandeliers, sat the hushed, breathing beast that was the audience. Except for the occasional muffled cough, the subtle twinkle of diamonds in earrings and collars, the beast was unseen, unheard. It was there and not there, anonymous. At least until it roused itself into applause.

But—

On her third twirl *("You promised me to wed. So would I ha' done, by yonder-sun—"),* she saw him. She had no idea how she'd missed him before; he was in the front of the house, very nearly center. A demon or a ghost could not have materialized more suddenly out of the shadows. Colonel Astor kept his focus fixed exactly on her, his hands folded in his lap. In the half-light cast from the stage, the planes of his face gleamed dim and harsh.

The toe of one boot scraped the stage; Madeleine stumbled. She stopped and turned in the abrupt silence, then looked upstage and realized the other members of the cast were all staring expectantly at her.

It must be her line. Her mind was a fizzy blank.

She stared back at them helplessly, the roar of her blood louder and louder in her ears.

In the back of the house, someone sneezed once, twice.

Dorothy Cramp, who had been so bitter with envy that Madeleine had won the part of Ophelia that she'd threatened to renounce the League, glared at Madeleine from beneath the tin of King Claudius' crown.

"How long has she been thus?" Dorothy said again, biting off every word.

The fizziness in Madeleine's brain cleared; she remembered her song, her wild dance, what to do. She got through her next lines and then swept off the stage in a storm of petals and leaves, and spent the rest of the show watching him from behind a slit in the stage right curtain.

After the curtain call, which included a pelting of bouquets, backstage was a jumble of cast and crew, everyone talking and laughing. Props teetered in precarious piles; willowy young women in wigs and trousers jostled back and forth, abandoning their wooden swords and bulky vests, hugging and kissing and telling each other how perfect it all was, how spectacular, and how next year they would tackle Molière or Marlowe and all the world would bow at their feet.

Madeleine accidentally bumped shoulders with Dorothy and smiled—part apology, part dare—but Dorothy ignored her and walked away.

By the velvet-swathed entrance to the house stood Mrs. Ogden Mills, a matron so prominent and formidable that Madeleine could not recall seeing her even once without at least four strands of pearls around her neck, no matter the time of day. Amid all the bustle and mayhem of the play's aftermath, she remained as motionless as a graveyard statue; even caught up in the giddy *we-did-it* silliness bubbling around them, none of the Junior League débutantes dared to venture too close.

"Miss Force," Mrs. Mills said, lifting her brows and tilting her head toward the man standing, also unmoving, slightly behind her. "Have you met the colonel?"

Of course Madeleine hadn't; she wasn't even officially out yet. There was no reason at all for someone like John Jacob Astor IV to have taken notice of her.

She was still in her mad weeds. She dripped with wilted petals and curling leaves. Her hair was fraying from its braids; candytuft dribbled down her shoulders, teeny white starbursts at a time. A stolen glance in a small rectangle of a mirror tacked to a flat revealed her eyes, pale blue smudged with kohl, her skin plastered white, cheeks and lips still painted red as blood.

The colonel glanced where she did, noticed the mirror. The skin along her cheekbones began to prickle with heat.

"Jack," continued Mrs. Mills, oblivious, serene, "I would like to introduce you to Miss Madeleine Force, daughter of William and Katherine Force of Brooklyn and, of late, Manhattan. You saw her as our Ophelia tonight. Madeleine, Colonel John Jacob Astor."

There was no choice but to extend her hand. He accepted it, his fingers folding firm and warm over hers.

"How do you do?" she asked faintly.

"How do you do," he echoed, soft.

It was as though her vision failed and she could not see him, in spite of the fact that he was right there in front of her. She didn't see him so much as feel his presence; the warm, tanned glow of his skin, the knowing curve of his mouth, the air of a man who knew what he wanted and was not bothered by the wanting, because everything he touched was already his.

Madeleine felt thirteen again, back on that rock-scrubbed beach—that moment when their eyes had met, and his smile seemed just for her.

From somewhere near her left shoulder, a pop of light flared, died, but she didn't turn her head to see what it was.

"You were excellent tonight," the colonel said, letting go of her hand.

She stopped herself from wiping her tingling palm down her dress. "I could have been better, I'm afraid."

"I don't see how," he said, and with a nod to Mrs. Mills, angled away. A moment later, he was gone, devoured by the crush.

Mrs. Ogden Mills sent Madeleine a pointed look. Madeleine smiled tightly, murmured her thanks, and retreated slowly, gratefully, back into the Junior League crowd.

* * *

It was only much later—hours later, as she lay sleepless in her bed and stared out her window at the cascading, moon-silvered clouds—that Madeleine realized the pop of light backstage must have been a magnesium flash from a photographer, stealing for himself that moment when Colonel Astor had first taken her hand.

CHAPTER 2

Your father's courtship of me began with a daily delivery of fresh hothouse flowers, starting the very morning after we were first introduced.

Someday I will teach you the language of flowers, my darling. Of how you, as a gentleman, will initiate your wooing with a floral message aimed only *just* slightly sideways, signifying nothing beyond the suggestion of *yes, I have seen you.* Yellow bud roses in fern, perhaps, or a spray of violets. A simple corsage, something modest and easily pinned to a bodice, should the young lady so desire. At this stage, always choose a bloom both sweet and candid, one to which no respectable mama could take offense.

Only after that (no fewer than four weeks of teas and picnics and cotillions, and before you groan, believe me, I know how tedious that becomes) may you move on to the flowers more opulent. Gardenias, pearled and intoxicating. Carnations, peach and lemon and cherry. Too many people (Europeans, really) consider carnations to be nothing but a vulgar American indulgence, but in my opinion, there is no blossom more intricate, more deliciously, thickly, fragrantly lavish, than a carnation.

So. After months of courting, you are at last allowed to consider sending red roses, but *only* if your intentions are sincere. Red roses have but one meaning. You will not be forgiven for mistaking it.

After the roses—after the conquest—what is left? Orchids.

In the fullness of time, I trust, the woman you love will tell you of those.

July 1910
Bar Harbor, Maine

The brick-and-cedar prison that was the Forces' summer residence might easily have been a metaphor for Madeleine's entire life: cramped, elegant, strictly contained. Although not one of the sprawling "cottages" famously dotting Millionaires' Row, there was no aspect of the house that was not perfectly proper, and perfectly predictable: the handful of Old Masters paintings on the walls, the trompe l'oeil fresco in the dining room (Persephone accepting a pomegranate seed in her palm), the Aubusson rugs, the immaculate gleam of the teak handrail topping the banister that guarded the stairs. The windows were small but ocean-facing, never inviting much of the light or wind inside.

Everything in the Force household, and in Madeleine Force's world, was exactly as it should be, and everything was exactly as it always would be. Not a single enhancement had been made in all of her memory, except for the Louis XVI ormolu chairs her mother had brought back from Paris three years ago because the cranberry satin cushions matched the runner in the foyer.

It was a wonder that Madeleine herself had managed to change, to expand from infant to child to young woman, within these walls. She *thought* she had grown; despite the evidence in her mirror, sometimes she wondered. The rooms and hallways did seem more claustrophobic than they had years ago, but otherwise her world seemed always, always the same.

Yet the globe did spin on its axis, and the seasons did flow from one to the next like water along the smooth, certain bed of a stream.

It was the height of summer, the weeks long and shimmering with heat, and the cottagers had descended upon Bar Harbor in a whirlwind of yachts and straw hats and billowing white linen. Drowsy shops, hungry for customers all winter, suddenly bustled with patrons; up and down Main Street, jolly banners snapped in the breeze, announcing fresh clams or imported cigars or exclusive Parisian tea-gowns. Newport, of course, had its matrons ossifying in their marble palaces—but Bar Harbor's balmy months boasted a slightly franker, more daring crowd.

And, as had been true ever since Katherine's debut, breakfast at the Force home (whether in Bar Harbor or New York) was punctuated by the arrival of flowers, which their butler placed strategically, jewellike, all around the dining room.

Pink sweet peas by the chafing dish of buttered eggs. Rubied dahlias at the other end of the credenza. Zinnias, marigolds, and hyacinths positioned between the pearlware figurines along the fireplace mantelshelf. Twin clusters of roses (one cream, one canary) in crystal bowls by the saltcellars.

Each delivery was accompanied by a small pasteboard card, which would be carefully collected and handed to Madeleine's sister, who kept them in a stack by her water goblet for the duration of the meal. And even though not a single one of her beaux ever called before noon—Madeleine imagined they weren't awake before then, anyway—Katherine dressed as if one might emerge unexpectedly from the side hall or the drawing room at any moment, ardently demanding the next dance.

Katherine at breakfast was a vision in lace and chiffon, powdered and perfect. Katherine at lunch was a vision, and Katherine at dinner was fairly staggering. Katherine, in short, was always a vision, and it was no surprise to Madeleine that the florists in town were kept so busy on her behalf.

So although she was glad of the scattering of fresh flowers that brightened the lead-shadowed room, Madeleine was used to them. She barely looked up any longer whenever some clever new arrangement appeared nearby.

A single, ivory-colored card was placed by her plate. *Her* plate.

She looked at it aslant, her cup of *café au lait* paused halfway to her lips.

"Miss," murmured the butler, and stepped back into the gloom.

Madeleine set her cup upon its saucer.

"Who's it from?" Katherine inquired, taking a sip of her own coffee.

In deep indigo script, the card read:

> *Pansies, for thoughts.*
> –JJA

For a heartbeat, she could not move. For a heartbeat, she only swooped inside, the heady and helpless feeling of falling from a very steep height. Then she blinked and looked around until she found it: a small nosegay on the sideboard, captured in one of the few rays of sun to pierce the chamber. The mauve edges of the petals glistened so sheer and crisp they looked dipped in sugar.

"Maddy, who is it from?" Katherine asked again, focusing on her eggs.

"Colonel Astor," Madeleine said.

Katherine's eyebrows climbed; Father lowered his newspaper; Mother inhaled sharply. Wordless, she held out her hand for the card. With a sense of breaking free from invisible chains, from gravity itself, Madeleine rose, walked around the table, and gave it to her.

"My heavens," her mother said, turning the card around and around, as if there might be a hidden message somewhere in the margins. "What's that supposed to mean?"

"It's from *Hamlet*. It's a reference to something Ophelia says." She took a breath; did the air taste of sugar, too, or was it only her sudden and unbounded imagination? "I told you we met last night, remember?"

"You *told* me you were simply introduced to him in the crowd backstage. I assumed he was there to congratulate everyone on the performance."

Madeleine shook her head. "We hardly spoke. We shook hands. That was all."

"Hardly all," Katherine said, leaning far across the table to steal the card from their mother. The chiffon folds of her morning dress drooped dangerously close to her eggs. "That must have been quite a handshake."

"I suppose he's sending flowers to all the girls in the cast," Madeleine said. Her own dress was ecru muslin—thin, fetching, everyday. She rubbed a pleat between two fingers. "Perhaps he's only being kind."

Katherine tapped the edge of the colonel's card against the gloss of the tabletop, then slid it back toward Madeleine. "Little sister. Even you are not that naïve, surely."

No. She was not.

The art of stillness—that classic and stultifying hallmark of a true lady, at least according to Mother—had never been one of Madeleine's best skills. It seemed to her that remaining frozen in time and place really only suited hunted creatures. When she'd said so aloud one day during deportment lessons at Miss Ely's School, her teacher had retorted that there was surely no creature more hunted than a young, pretty heiress.

Point scored.

And yet, in Madeleine's hidden heart, she could only marvel at the obedience of her peers, those girls who could sink into such quiescence that their voices never rose, their skirts never twitched with a restless foot as they sat; their hair was never mussed and their jewelry never fiddled with. She wondered if they fell asleep like that, facial expressions composed and pleasant, hands arranged neatly over their bellies and legs pressed together.

She wanted a gallop, not a trot. She wanted the sun burning her face, the wind ripping at her hair, rather than the soft, safe comfort of salons and tea parties and early evening soirées.

And yet.

The al fresco dinner at the cottage named Beau Desert had been on the Force calendar for weeks. It was one of the more coveted invitations of the season; barring actual death, Madeleine knew there was no avoiding it. The afternoon layer of low, lustrous clouds streaking abalone across the sky had at last dissolved away. This close to sunset, the horizon glowed empty and clean, an incandescent heaven melting into the darkened bay. The Porcupine Islands in the distance bristled green and ochre and velvet black above the water.

Beau Desert's splendid garden itself, so neatly composed of shell-and-gravel paths, nodding flowers and fragrant herbs, had been enhanced for the evening with silver-trayed offerings of champagne and cold canapés, and a string trio playing from a gazebo nestled amid the pines. Paper lanterns crisscrossed the sky overhead, radiant embers, whimsical fireflies, swaying gently on their wire lines with the breeze.

The dinner tables, dressed in damask and wisp-thin china, had been arranged atop the scattering of grass rectangles and ovals and squares framed by the paths. (Anticipating a spongy lawn, Mother had insisted they all wear slippers with low heels.) As twilight began to descend in earnest, women in pale silken sheaths and men in white tie glided through the trees and flowers, meeting, breaking apart, ghosts with soft chattering voices and bursts of muted laughter.

Despite the paper lanterns, the garden supplied plenty of shadows. Mother and Father stood sipping champagne with their hosts by a trellis frothing with honeysuckle, but Madeleine had lost sight of her sister not five minutes after their arrival. The last she had seen of her, Katherine had been headed toward the rose maze with an admirer on each arm.

Katherine, confident queen of both admirers and dinner parties, knew she'd have at least another twenty minutes of venial sin before they'd be seated for the meal.

Madeleine was hardly queen of anything. She stood alone in

the sifting crowd and felt surprisingly unmoored, even though she had known this party and these people most of her life. She looked around, searching for (*not* him, certainly not him) anyone from the League—Carol or Nathalie or Leta—but either none of her friends were here yet, or else, like Katherine, they were taking quick advantage of the secret corners of the estate.

So she became one of the ghosts. She sipped from her own flute of champagne and rambled down a path of crushed oyster shells that gleamed before her like an ashen ribbon, unwinding into the dusk.

The air began to cool. It wasn't long before she regretted her own silk sheath, floaty layers of coral edged with lace and very little else. She handed her glass to a passing footman and shivered, just for a moment, as the wind skimmed along the exposed skin of her chest and neck and upper arms. It ruffled through her hair, wayward strands already coming loose from her Psyche knot, and turned the pearls at her throat into stone.

The string trio began a new piece, the barcarolle from *The Tales of Hoffmann*. She paused beneath a gold bobbing lantern, closing her eyes to take in the notes, imagining how she would dance to it, the placement of her feet, the man who would hold her in his arms—

When she opened her eyes again, she saw, utterly without astonishment, a second shadow overlapping her own.

"Miss Force," said the colonel, just behind her. "Pardon me. I hope I don't startle you."

Madeleine turned to face him. "Not at all."

He was elegant and black-clad and taller than she, enough so that she had to tip back her head to meet his gaze. It was a strange sensation, and an unfamiliar one; Madeleine was tall for a girl, and most boys her age looked at her straight on.

She thought, *This is what it's like to feel dainty.*

They studied each other, motionless in the hitch and trick of the swaying gold light. He seemed almost exactly as he had the night before, his hair precisely cut and combed; his ebony tailcoat immaculate; his expression a combination of gravity and absolute focus, as if nothing else existed in the world other than her.

She remembered that day on the beach in Newport; how she'd thought him comely. But *comely* wasn't the right word for him, she thought now. It was too simple, too shallow to describe him. It was true that he had little of the muscular charisma of the young men she'd spy down at the docks, sunburnt and joking, sons of lobstermen grown to be lobstermen themselves, hauling in their daily catch. But neither was he one of the pale, paunchy gentlemen of her father's circle, who golfed leisurely and dined voraciously, and spoke only of market fluctuations and real estate prices and the abundant promise of industrialization.

When she had been still in pinafores, Colonel Astor had out-fitted an entire regiment in the Spanish-American War and then gone with them to do battle down in Cuba. He was a scion of the most blue-blooded family in America, head of a massive fortune, and distant cousin of President Roosevelt himself. He had traveled the globe purely because he'd wished to do so, visited lands her imagination could not stretch to encompass, and in the hush of the moment, Madeleine could very nearly catch the scent of those wild, exotic adventures still lingering upon him like a perfume—gunpowder and sharp spice and the dust of faraway trails.

Faint lines fanned outward from the corners of his eyes, crin-kling his tan. Deeper lines bracketed his mouth, that long mous-tache, and she found herself looking at them and admiring them and thinking, *How well his face suits him.*

The diamond in his stickpin sparked a sepia rainbow.

The colonel cleared his throat. "I was just contemplating what a pleasant evening we're having. How fine the night is, the gloam-ing, when I saw you here. I didn't mean to intrude."

She smiled. "You're not intruding, Colonel Astor."

"Ah," he said. "Very good."

A pair of crickets began to exchange songs, hesitant at first, gradually throbbing stronger. Madeleine clasped her hands over her elbows, then dropped them again when she realized she was wrinkling her dress. "I was listening to the music. I think I got a bit lost in it."

He cleared his throat again. "Do you like opera?"

She thought, surprised, *He is nervous.*

She said, "We saw *The Tales of Hoffmann* last year, in Paris. Have you seen it?"

"Ages ago. I don't remember most of it, I'm afraid."

Her smile turned rueful. "I didn't understand most of it," she admitted. "But I enjoyed the production."

He nodded, looked away. Behind him, the diaphanous ghosts lingered in the dark, drinking their sparkling wine, chortling. Above them both, the stars began to wake, a handful at a time, right above their heads.

The colonel seemed in no hurry to speak again, but neither did he leave; Madeleine cast about for something more to say. "This is the first time I've seen you in Bar Harbor, sir. I don't believe you visit often?"

"No. I've been here before, naturally. Friends and extended family, all that. But Newport is . . ." He paused, frowning.

"Yes, it's—"

"My customary summer home." His gaze angled back to hers. "Yours is here, however?"

"Ever since I can remember."

"And you . . . like summering here?"

"Well." She lifted an open palm to the air. "It's all I've ever known."

"Of course."

Silence again. She regretted now giving away her glass of champagne, because at least then she'd have something to hold in her hands, something to do besides stare up at him and feel gauche.

She said, "I'm sure it's nothing so excellent as Newport, though. I've heard the cottages there are all fashioned of marble and gold, inside and out, like the temples of the gods crowning Mount Olympus."

He ducked his head and smiled at last, rubbing a thumb along the line of his jaw. "Some of them are, perhaps. Certain families seem to take pleasure in that sort of thing. But I think most of the homes are more limestone than marble. Plaster and brick. And *cuivre doré*—only gold leaf, I'm afraid."

"But even so—like heaven, all white and blue and gold."

"I suppose that was the idea," he said seriously.

"How resplendent it must be."

"Yes," he said, as if he'd never considered it before. "Yes, Miss Force, it is."

Beyond the trees and shrubs and heavy-headed flowers, a dinner bell chimed. They both glanced toward the brighter heart of the garden, where all the tables were laid, then back at each other. Without a word, Colonel Astor offered her his arm.

Madeleine took it. Her gloved hand lay small and curved against the black of his sleeve. Her head reached just above his chin.

"Speaking of the theater," he said, walking slowly beside her, "I appreciated your performance last night."

"Oh?"

"You were . . . enthusiastic."

"Oh." She laughed, mortified. "I know I'm not terribly skilled, but I don't seem to ever lack enthusiasm. Things were going all right, I think, until I forgot my line."

"Did you? Forget a line?"

"You must have noticed. *Everyone* noticed."

They stopped. He turned to her without releasing her arm.

"What I noticed was how committed you were to your role. How you made me believe in her tragedy. Her great loss. It seems to me that's the most valuable skill one might have on the stage, the ability to convince the audience that you inhabit the truth."

She searched his face for any sign of teasing, but he only looked back at her with that unwavering focus, in shadow now, the gloaming he had admired before fading into a darker, deeper night.

The wind pushed again and her skin tightened and Madeleine

wished very much for a shawl, or a witty thing to say, or for her sister's infinite poise.

"Forgive me." The colonel shook his head, scowled down at the path. "I, ah—I'm not expressing myself well."

"No, you are. I'm glad for your honest opinion, thank you. And for the pansies," she remembered to add. "They were lovely."

"Miss Force," he said, his lashes lifting, and through the dusk she could see only that his eyes were darkened too, fixed on hers. "Please never doubt I'll give you my honest opinion."

"Colonel Astor," she replied, "please believe that I shall never doubt you."

It seemed, astonishingly, that she had found the right thing to say after all, because his smile returned, now easy and slight, filling her with a warm buzzing wonderment.

The dinner bell chimed again, three melodious peals. Neither of them moved.

She thought, *This is what it's like to feel understood.*

They strolled on, and every glittering soul they passed stopped talking, and stopped drinking, and eyed them askance as they went by.

They were not seated at the same table. They were not seated, in fact, anywhere near each other, but on separate islands of grass, in separate sections of the garden, with beds of larkspur and poppies between them, and a solitary weeping birch that draped its long branches like a curtain off to the side.

She could still see him, though. Past the birch, past the other guests, through the shadows. Sometimes she thought she heard him, too.

She had been placed between the ginger-haired son of a *nouveau riche* shipping and forwarding importer—not coincidentally, the same profession as her father's—and a giraffe-necked boy from an old and affluent Philadelphia family. On the other side of the ginger-haired boy sat Leta Wright, one of Madeleine's better friends, who was brash and spirited and not in the least afraid to speak her mind.

"Harold," she was saying to the ginger-haired boy. "Did you forget to do something this morning?"

The ginger boy sat up taller in his chair, looking nervous. "Um . . . did I?"

Leta smiled at the air straight ahead of her, a sweet and dangerous smile, as she picked up her claret. "You attended the play last night, did you not? You saw me as Queen Gertrude?"

"You know I did, Lettie! You know I'd never miss seeing you onstage!"

"And did you admire my performance?"

"Of course I did. Naturally!"

"That's what I thought." She took a sip, aimed the smile at him. "So imagine my surprise this morning as I was receiving posy after posy from all sorts of lovely boys to congratulate me and I realized, Harold, dear, that *none* of them were from you. Not a single sorry petal."

"Um . . ." said Harold again.

"Ollie sent flowers. Morris sent flowers. Ernest and Walter Owens sent flowers, and you know they hardly even like me! Valentino Louis sent daisies, my favorite." She faced him directly. "But nothing, *nothing*, from you."

"Lettie, good God, I'm so sorry, I just—"

"Maddy," she said, leaning around him, "don't you agree it's nice to get flowers from boys who say they admire you? Don't you rather *expect* it?"

"Well—"

"I'm sure *you* got flowers this morning from admirers of your Ophelia, didn't you?"

Madeleine pressed her lips together, embarrassed, then admitted, "Yes."

"You see, Harold? It's not such a terribly onerous task. Who sent yours, Maddy? Please do not tell me it was our boy Harold here."

Madeleine looked down, tapped her fish fork against her plate. She'd hardly sampled the bouillon, or now the salmon tartare; she felt simultaneously out of breath and out of room inside, as if her corset was too tight. "No. It was Colonel Astor."

Leta paused. "It was *who*?"

"John Jacob Astor."

"Gosh," said Harold after a moment, sounding impressed.

Leta clapped her hands together in delight. "How exciting! What sort of flowers were they?"

"Pansies."

Her friend made the connection instantly; her brown eyes widened. "Wonderfully perfect! Were you thrilled?"

"I was . . . surprised."

"Well, then, was your *mother* thrilled, at least? What did she say?"

Madeleine poked her fork at the tartare. "Not very much. But I suspect she's already grappling with the agony of who will design my wedding gown."

At this, the Philadelphia boy stirred at last, turning to stare at her with hooded eyes. "What's that? You and Colonel Astor? You can't be serious."

"Why not?" Leta challenged. "Maddy's good enough for a king, much less a colonel."

"But not a Knickerbocker," he said. "Trust me. Anyway, he's too old for her, *and* he's divorced."

"He's not so terribly old," Leta said.

"And lots of people get divorces," added Harold. "My uncle and aunt did, and it was fine."

"Because they are not Knickerbockers," said the other boy, patient. He swallowed a bite of the vinegary salmon. "I don't expect you to understand, I suppose."

"I think I understand snobbery quite well," Leta retorted. "There's nothing wrong with Colonel Astor sending Maddy flowers. I think it's romantic."

"I think it's onion-headed," the boy said.

Leta gave an incredulous laugh. "So that's it for you, then? You'll never fall in love with someone unexpected? You'll never marry anyone outside of your own little world, never ever?"

The boy shrugged, returning to his fish. "It's simply not done."

Madeleine sat back in her chair, hands on her lap, and secretly wished for the Philadelphia boy to choke.

All around her conversations bloomed, swelling and falling like the constant waves that scored the harbor. Beyond them rose the murmur of the breeze through pine needles and leaves, and the canticles of the crickets tucked beneath shrubs, and the dulcet notes of the string trio floating beneath the arc of the luminous blue night.

Through it all, she listened for the singular baritone of that older man, that king of the Knickerbockers, who had sent her purple flowers, and had escorted her to her table, and who'd told her not to doubt.

And she was out of breath.

CHAPTER 3

Pansies.
Cosmos.
Delphiniums.
Asters.
Snapdragons.
Bellflowers.
Tulips.
Forget-me-nots.

Upon reflection, it strikes me as somewhat macabre that the joining of my life with your father's began with flowers. It ended with flowers, as well. To be clear—it ended on that frigid, starry morning atop the skin of the Atlantic. But as I sit here at my desk, all I can smell is lilies: thousands of lilies, ornamenting his casket, lining the church, crushed beneath the wheels of the undertaker's wagon, the hooves of the black horses, as somber-faced strangers standing alongside the roads watched and tossed ever more flowers at the procession passing by.

Even on the train that carried his body from Rhinebeck to Manhattan: lilies.

That stench. That overwhelming, sickly sweet stench.

I don't think I can bear to be around lilies ever again.

July 1910
Bar Harbor

The handle of the racquet bit into her palm, the leather strap wrapped around it digging rough into her skin. But it was a good kind of rough, necessary, and as Madeleine swung her arm and the catgut strings connected with the ball, the force of that connection bounced back through her, powerful and jarring, through muscle and bone, lungs and heart, all the way to her feet.

Her momentum kept her leaping forward, great huge strides that she checked by twisting sideways, a swift and dangerous dance in long skirts, ignoring the pain of her corset biting into her.

The ball streaked low across the net. Her opponent lunged and swung and missed.

"Game and set," called out the chair umpire, "to Miss Force!"

A mustering of applause lifted up to the overcast sky.

Madeleine bent her head to wipe the sweat from her eyes, then turned and sketched a quick curtsy to the Swimming Club spectators, arranged in pastels and parasols in the lawn chairs lining the length of the tennis court. As she crossed to the net, she swapped her racquet to her left hand to shake with her right.

Her palm smacked into the other girl's.

"Well done," Stella Mitchell puffed, still breathless from her final sprint.

"And you."

Stella was the sort of girl Madeleine always privately envied, because she was the sort of girl that Madeleine feared she would never be: refined and chic and creamy cool, no matter the circumstances. She looked like a Gibson portrait of a girl, a poet's idea of a girl, one who would be perfectly content to pass the span of her days reading upon a chaise lounge, or embroidering samplers, or contemplating the number of tumbling, adorable children she would someday produce. And perhaps she *was* those things—Madeleine had known her since Miss Ely's, and heaven knew they'd both embroidered enough samplers—but in tennis, Stella became ruthless. Beating her today was the figurative feather in Madeleine's cap. It hardly ever happened.

"I was lucky this time," Madeleine said, stepping back.

"Perhaps it was that your lucky charm lingered nearby," Stella said, with a significant look past Madeleine's shoulder.

Madeleine wiped her eyes again, hoping that her face didn't look too red, that the pins in her hair had held and that her armpits weren't showing their damp through her shirtwaist. Because, yes—there he was, standing at the end of the row of chairs, a walking stick slanted to the ground in one hand; in the other, the end of a leash connected to a large, tan dog.

Their eyes met. She nodded, and the colonel nodded, and the dog looked at her and furrowed its brow.

It had been over a week since she'd seen him last, and even then it had only been in passing, as they rode in opposite directions past the Mount Desert Reading Room. Yet the daily arrival of flowers had not ceased, each one accompanied by a card bearing simply his initials.

Even though he hadn't come to call in person, every morning Mother practically hummed with anticipation.

"They're just flowers," Madeleine had said at breakfast three days ago.

"Colonel Astor is neither blind nor imbecilic," Mother had responded, examining the fresh arrangement of mums he'd sent with something close to hunger. She kept each new delivery beside her plate—as though they were for her, instead of her daughter—and throughout the meal she would gaze at them as raptly as if they whispered the answer to a puzzle that had long perplexed her.

Madeleine said, "I just don't think we should get our hopes up. That's all."

Mother looked up. "Maddy, my love. Do you mean your hopes, or mine?"

Madeleine shrugged, uncomfortable.

"Because in this instance," Mother went on, "*your* hopes are the only ones that matter. I trust you know that."

"I have an idea," Katherine had said. "Why don't we just go and call on *him*?"

"Don't be ridiculous," Mother had sighed.

"Well, why not? It's the twentieth century now, after all. I don't see why we can't at least drop by and leave our cards. Ask him what he means by sending all these silly flowers every single day. One would think he might have moved on to chocolates and jewelry by now."

"Katherine . . ."

"My point is, we're no longer bound by all those archaic rules hammered out by Mrs. Astor a generation ago. In fact," Katherine finished, inspired, "there *is* no current Mrs. Astor. Not one who matters, anyway."

And Mother had tilted her head to examine Madeleine, and Madeleine had examined her back and knew what exactly what she was thinking:

Yet.

"Miss Force," the colonel greeted her now. He lifted the hand with the walking stick to tip his hat.

Madeleine strolled toward him sedately, casually, swinging her racquet by her hip in a slow, contained arc, the way she'd seen Stella sometimes do when talking to a beau. "Colonel Astor. I see you have a friend. Is it your dog?"

"She is. This is Kitty. Kitty, meet Miss Force."

Madeleine had to laugh at the name. She came close and bent down, lifting her free hand. The dog leaned a little nearer and sniffed her fingers.

"Hello," Madeleine murmured. "Hello, pup called Kitty."

The dog—an Airedale, she thought—sat back on her haunches and gazed up at her with wary eyes.

"An outstanding game," the colonel said. "There seems to be

no end to your skills. Actress, athlete. What else do you have up your sleeve, I wonder?"

"Dog charmer, I hope," she said, and smiled. "And you, sir?"

"Tennis dilettante." He looked down and stroked Kitty's head. The dog lifted her chin and began to pant. "Yachtsman. Adventurer, I'd like to think."

"An interesting description. I've not met many adventurers before you, Colonel Astor."

He arched an eyebrow. "But you have met others, Miss Force?"

"No," she said, as placidly as she could manage with her corset pinching, her lungs burning, perspiration creeping down her back. "Actually, I have not."

Another moment between them, stretching long and strange and lovely somehow, filling her with both elation and dread, because Madeleine understood then that, despite what she'd said to her mother, she knew she stood at the edge of a very steep cliff, and falling off of it would mean either flight or annihilation.

A lance of sunlight speared the clouds. From the corner of her eye, Madeleine saw a pair of figures approach. She turned to them in relief.

"I'm afraid my mother and sister are swooping in," she said, returning Katherine's wave. "Mother has been . . . quite keen to meet you. Do you mind?"

"Not in the least."

"She's very impressed with your flowers," Madeleine said under her breath, and the colonel slanted her another look.

"Only she?"

"No. Not only she."

Madeleine made the introductions. She heard herself making them, saying the correct words, using the correct tone, and everyone shook hands correctly as she watched from slightly outside of herself, still suspended in the fleeting light. Still standing at the edge of that cliff, wondering what would come next.

From the saltwater bathing pool walled off from the bay came echoes of splashing, of children shouting and nannies chiding, and cormorants screeching for scraps.

People were beginning to stare at them again.

Mother was speaking. Katherine was trying to catch Madeleine's eye.

Colonel Astor tested the bottom of his stick against the grass and shifted on his feet, the wind flipping his jaunty striped tie this way and that. For the first time, she caught a hint of his cologne.

Sandalwood, rich and heady. Amber. Bergamot.

"I didn't think dogs were allowed at the Club," Katherine was saying.

The colonel's eyebrows quirked. "Oh, aren't they?" he asked innocently. "Alas."

As if on cue, Kitty yawned, showing miles of tongue and teeth. Madeleine and Katherine burst into laughter, spontaneously, loudly, and both at once.

It was one of the hallmarks that branded them as sisters, their matching laugh: low and full-throated, bubbling up without reservation. It remained the despair of their mother (who feared it revealed a shade too much a bourgeois background) but was as natural as breathing to Madeleine and Katherine, who both brimmed with appreciation of anything absurd.

Throughout their childhood, Mother had dressed them identically, to the frustration of them both. Chocolate-haired and blue-eyed, the sisters might already have been twins, except that Katherine was always a little taller, a little merrier, more sparkling.

Even so, the colonel's attention kept returning to Madeleine, instead of fixing upon the brighter star.

"Miss Force! Colonel Astor! A photograph? To commemorate Miss Force's win in the tournament?"

It was a young man in a boater and tennis whites, already setting up his camera and tripod on the spread of lawn just ahead of them. He must have been a member of the Club, although Madeleine didn't recognize him.

The colonel looked at her. "Would that be all right?"

"Yes," answered Madeleine's mother, and tucked a loose lock of hair back behind Madeleine's ear before moving to stand beside her.

Katherine grinned. Madeleine pushed more hair behind her other ear, and they all four faced the photographer, gathering closer, pulling the dog into the frame. The colonel's sleeve brushed lightly against her own, electrifying; she clamped her arms to her sides, hoping she didn't stink of tennis and the fried cod she'd had for lunch.

The young man removed his hat. He stooped behind the camera and lifted a closed palm to them, his fingers opening one at a time to count *one . . . two . . . three . . .*

Madeleine would have many years to reflect upon this moment. She would study it, pick it apart in a dozen little ways and wonder how things might have turned out differently had she been daring enough to overrule her mother. To say, *No, I'd rather he didn't take our photograph, please. I'd rather we all just turn around and walk the other way.*

Set a precedent, as it were.

In her darker musings, she would wonder why Jack himself hadn't said something. Offered her a whispered warning about what it would mean, a sidelong glance, *something*. After all, he had to have known what would happen next. He had to have at least suspected. He'd asked her if it would be all right, and maybe that was all the warning he thought she needed.

But the Madeleine of that particular afternoon was scarcely a month past her seventeenth birthday; she was teenaged and untested and sweaty and bedazzled. She didn't speak the subtle code of the magnificently rich, not then.

To be honest, it likely wouldn't have made any difference anyway. In the space of just that single conversation—the sea light, the clouds, his gray eyes and his dog—she had already made her choice. She was already plummeting off that cliff, ready to soar.

And so the shutter had snapped, capturing them in their untidy, sunlit line, about to become the cynosure of the world's avid attention.

When the grainy image showed up on the front page of the scandal sheet *Town Topics* three days later (COLONEL JOHN JACOB ASTOR, 46, AND MISS MADELEINE T. FORCE, 17, AND FAMILY, CELEBRATING AT THE SWIMMING CLUB, BAR HARBOR), it showed the dog yawning again and Mrs. Force beaming.

After that, she started to notice them: men—it was always men—lingering at the edges of events, their hats pulled low over their foreheads, sometimes toting cameras, sometimes not. There was something about the stalking, the staring, the incessant sprinkling of her name in gossip columns that unnerved her. When they noticed her noticing them, they'd touch their hats and nod, and Madeleine would turn away, because she didn't want to look any of them in the eyes for too long. She didn't want them to memorize her face.

She became better at the art of stillness; she had become the hunted, after all.

Two weeks went by, and she didn't encounter the colonel again. The flowers still arrived every morning, and he still never called, and no one in the household now said a word about it, not even Madeleine herself. She began to spot the journalists less and less.

America's richest man had apparently packed up and moved on, taking the ravenous appetite of the public with him. Which was fine with her; certainly it was fine; it was madness to think the brief attention he'd paid to her had been anything more than a superficial kindness—perhaps even a gentlemanly sort of pity— all this while. He'd sent her a single posy, and she'd thanked him, and now they were trapped in a loop, where he felt obligated to continue with the flowers because she'd been so grateful.

John Jacob Astor was reported to be in Newport aboard his yacht.

In Manhattan at his Fifth Avenue chateau.

Abroad in the West Indies with his son.

At his mansion in Rhinebeck.

Back in Newport.

But he wasn't back in Newport. On that point, the tabloids were entirely wrong.

She was standing with her father against the railing of the Robin Hood Park Raceway one afternoon, waiting for the horses to thunder past. Katherine and Mother had decided to take luncheon at the Club instead, but Madeleine and William Force, both dedicated riders, appreciated the energy of the races, the earthy must of the track and clods of soil flying, and the rising excitement of the swaying, cheering crowd with every go-round. It was as raucous as it ever got among Bar Harbor's society proper, and Madeleine enjoyed adding her small voice to the chorus.

Like many of the ladies in attendance, she wore a picture hat, tied in place by a scarf that wrapped around the crown and brim, tugging against her head with every burst of wind. The cream silk scarf was wide and opaque, and it was easy enough to knot it so snugly beneath her chin that it concealed half her face.

Perhaps that was why she didn't see him at first, or perhaps she was just distracted. One moment he wasn't there, and the next he was. As before, in the audience of *Hamlet*, he seemed to simply manifest between two beats of her heart.

"Miss Force. A pleasure to see you again."

He was standing next to her on her left. As her hat gave another quick, hard tug, the long tails of the scarf lofting, she reached up to brush them back into place, and he bent his head to meet her eyes past the panels of silk framing her face.

"Colonel Astor! Forgive me! I didn't realize you were there." *I thought you were in Newport*, she almost said, but stopped herself in time.

He smiled broadly, removing his bowler. "Quite all right. I've been told I'm stealthy as a cat sometimes."

She was flustered, and surprised at being flustered. She'd thought of him every single day since their last conversation—of course she had; he'd made certain that she would with the daily flowers. Newspaper reports or not, she'd searched the summer fashionables for him every time she ventured out. But here he was again, without warning, like a genie's wish unexpectedly granted.

He stepped back, lifting a hand to the person standing silently on his other side. "May I introduce my son, Vincent. He's decided to summer here with me for a while, no doubt to keep me in line. Vincent, Miss Madeleine Force."

They shook hands, their palms barely touching. One quick shake, up-and-down, before he pulled away.

Vincent Astor, she knew, was her age, or not much older. She'd seen his face in the rag sheets, his name linked to one blue-blooded socialite after another amid constant speculation of some imminent engagement, even though he was only just starting his studies at Harvard.

It was said that his mother, the scandalous Ava, had been a great beauty in her day, but she spent more time abroad than not, so Madeleine had no idea if it were true. It was probably true. Her son had the brooding, heavy-browed look of a man already in his twenties, not his teens, and he certainly didn't resemble his father much. But he was attractive, if unsmiling, and his eyes had met hers steadily, almost defiantly, in that moment that their hands clasped.

His eyes were gray, like the colonel's, only darker. More dire.

Careful, warned a voice inside of her, clear and sudden. *Careful with this one.*

From over her shoulder came a diffident cough.

"Oh," said Madeleine, blushing. "Sorry! I don't know where my head is today. Colonel Astor, Mr. Astor, please meet my father, William Force."

She leaned back as they all greeted each other, keeping her eyes on the hem of her dress, on the shiny black tips of her shoes. She was afraid to look up again and afraid not to look up. She knew they were all three waiting for her to speak, but her mind was empty. If only Katherine were here—she always knew the exact right thing to say, something droll and smooth and gracious.

Then be Katherine, directed the voice. *Play the part.*

She lifted her lashes. Across the racetrack, a photographer had raised his camera, pointing the lens straight at them.

She turned around, set her back against the railing. She imagined herself a Gibson girl, cool and perfect, and smiled up at the colonel.

"How pleasant you're both here for the season. Do you have any special plans? I'm told there's going to be a regatta among the yachts in Frenchman Bay this weekend. Unofficial, of course."

Thank goodness, it worked. Straight off, everything returned to normal. Well, as normal as it could be with Jack Astor and his heir standing with them, chatting about nautical miles and tides and who in Bar Harbor had the fastest ship.

A horn sounded in the distance. Madeleine turned again to the track. The ground beneath her began to tremble seconds before she saw any of the horses, but then there they were, streaking past in percussive, rolling beats, and for a very brief moment the steeds and their jockeys were the entire world, the massive engine of their competition churning by, the heat and essence and pulse of it engulfing her senses.

In a flash, they were gone. She gazed after them, her hands gripping the metal railing with the excitement of it all, bits of sod now clinging to the front of her dress by her ankles. Father craned his neck to peer down the course, and Madeleine let go of the railing, opening and closing her fingers.

Colonel Astor leaned closer to her ear. "A zealous fan of the ponies, Miss Force?"

She glanced up at him and then it was as if the rest of the world were gone, too, not just the sweating horses and their jockeys, their thunder; everything else was gone but the colonel, smiling down at her, his eyes bright, his lashes long, the shadow cast by the brim of his bowler a soft painted darkness along his cheekbones.

She hesitated, weighing the consequences of truth against what she knew she ought to say.

"I would rather be the rider than the observer, honestly."

"A young lady of action. I appreciate the sentiment."

"Or, merely a young lady who is easily bored."

"Are you? Easily bored?"

She sensed a line crossed, some moment of politeness missed, and tried to think of a way to go back but couldn't. "Maybe. My mother might say so."

"I hope," he said quietly, after a moment, "that I do not bore you."

Madeleine studied her toes once more. When she answered, her voice was even quieter than his. "Colonel Astor, I cannot imagine any man more stimulating than you."

As if they'd planned it, they dropped their poses and faced each other as the crowd around them milled and the horses battled close again. The wind pushed, recapturing the tails of her scarf, lifting them to float between them. She saw his gaze follow that, the cream silk dancing.

Without meaning to, she licked her lips. "How is your dog?"

He watched that, too, and the horses rumbled by, and it was another long moment before he answered her. "Restless, I think. Like you, she prefers to be in the thick of action, rather than observing from afar."

"A good pup."

"Very." He looked away. She felt that, the physical and mental distance he constructed between them as he took two steps back and slipped both hands into his jacket pockets. He aimed a wry smile down at the ground, then turned to her father.

"Mr. Force. I wonder if I might be so forward as to invite you and your family to spend the weekend at my cottage here, sir. We're slightly starved for company, you see, and if there *is* a yacht race, we'll have an exceptional vantage of it from the back lawn."

"Ah," replied Father, bland as rice pudding. "A kind offer, Colonel Astor. Most kind. I must consult with my wife, of course, but I think I can say we are free." William Force glanced at his daughter. "I admit I do enjoy a good regatta. We would gladly accept your hospitality."

"Wonderful." The colonel gave a nod, not looking at Madeleine or her father again but instead at the trampled, empty track that stretched before them.

The thunder of the race began once more to swell near.

Vincent Astor said nothing, only staring bleakly off into the stands.

The photographer was persistent, and he got his shot anyway: that carelessly unguarded moment of intimacy, of Madeleine and Jack gazing at each other as the wind teased her scarf, her head tipped back, his bent toward hers, both of them standing a shade too close for propriety.

However, because of her hat and the distance, the frustrated newspaper editor could only safely caption it as COL. ASTOR, DIVORCED, AND YOUNG BEAUTY ENJOYING THE RACES.

CHAPTER 4

I thought I had witnessed splendor before. Luxury.

I had been schooled alongside Knickerbocker girls who would not willingly share a single molecule of oxygen with me if they could help it. Who acted as if I did not exist whenever we dined or studied in common areas, and who spoke to me in classrooms only when our lessons mandated they do so. I had heard about the gulf between their world and mine, but until that weekend at your father's Bar Harbor cottage, it had all seemed so . . . contrived. Invented. A convenient construct designed to help those splintery, unpleasant young women feel better about their lives. About who they *admitted* into those lives.

Nevertheless, I remember how flummoxed we were when our History teacher one day chalked out upon the slate that scorching fragment of a sentence from the Declaration of Independence:

. . . all men are created equal . . .

It was, perhaps, the one topic the Old Money Girls and the New Money Girls could agree upon.

Of course, we're not all equal.

You see, little Jakey, there's equal—in the sense of human potential and dreams and the rule of law—and then there's *equal*. As in, *who are your people, my dear?*

I guess you'll find out about all that soon enough.

So: that weekend.

Jack's leased cottage overlooked the bay, expansive and bright, light and breeze gracing every chamber. Gilt and granite, beeswax and mahogany. It was so easy to waft from one sun-soaked room to another.

The water below us, the forest behind. All that land. All that empty *openness* unfurled in the midst of one of the nation's most exclusive towns, upon one of the nation's most exclusive islands, majestic beyond the harbor. Beyond the sloping grounds, houses crowded closer and closer together; the town streets cut more and more tapered. All of it rippled down to conclude in a thick huddle of wooden shanties on stilts at the water's edge.

Lobster boats and tour boats and ferries jounced in the bay. They looked barely a dirty smudge against the splendor of the yachts spread along the waters beyond.

On the grounds of this fair cottage, there was a garage and stables and gardeners and game attendants and maids and footmen ready to leap into action at the lift of a finger.

Would you like your tea refreshed? More lemon, less sugar? Yes, miss.

Have you lost your croquet ball in the shrubbery? I will find it, miss.

Do you need your wrap, miss? The taffeta or the pongee? I will send a girl for it at once.

The butler (I recall his name was Baird, and that he was leased along with the mansion) seemed to ooze out of the woodwork whenever needed.

Those ordinary workers who circulated their way through the estate each and every day and night . . . I have no doubt they also understood that we were not all equal. Far from it.

That golden-limned summer of 1910, the cottage—indeed, maybe even all of Bar Harbor society itself, so giddy in love with the colonel— seemed to exist only to serve your father, Jack Astor.

August 1910
Bar Harbor

Sunday morning arrived with cerulean skies and a salty wind skating in off the Atlantic that stung her eyes. Madeleine squinted against it, then turned her shoulder to it, keeping a careful hand on her hat. From this distance, the vessels dotting the disk of the harbor moved in sluggish lines, breaking the navy waves into arrows of white.

It was the same harbor, the same ships and boats as could be glimpsed from practically anywhere in town. Yet it *felt* different here, in this uncommon and enviable space. The slant of the sunlight struck her skin a warmer tone; the clouds soared higher, plumper, a Renaissance painting hanging just above her head. Even the sea looked different, sheer as a sheet of colored glass. If Madeleine could take wing with the host of sparrows fluttering above the bay, she might peer all the way down into blue infinity.

Katherine stood beside her on the colonel's back lawn. With their arms linked and their skirts whipping, they watched the yachts slowly maneuver into their starting positions.

"What do you plan to do with him?" Katherine asked, not taking her gaze from the ships.

"I plan," Madeleine said, "to watch this race with him. And then eat lunch. And then attend the dance he is hosting tonight."

"Don't be stupid. You know what I mean. Will you marry him?"

"Katherine!"

Her sister unlinked their arms. She wasn't smiling. "Will you, Maddy? You'd better figure it out sooner rather than later, because *that's* what all *this* means. Don't imagine you're not on trial here. So is he."

The colonel's weekend guests stood in clusters along the rolling lawn, some watching the yachts tracing their desultory paths, others chatting. Colonel Astor himself lingered on the terrace in deep conversation with a trim, sallow man he'd introduced as William Dobbyn, his private secretary.

The colonel spoke quickly, gestured calmly, and occasionally took out his pocket watch to check the time. Mr. Dobbyn would only nod, repeatedly nod. It was hard to imagine Jack Astor receiving a *no* from his secretary very often. Or from anyone else, for that matter.

The sun gleamed razor sharp; whenever the wind stilled, the air sank into a briny, humid heat. The curious slanted light picked out in detail the threads composing Madeleine's lace gloves, showing every tiny twist and knot. Despite her best efforts, tomorrow she was likely to wake with its pattern outlined on the backs of her hands.

"Look around you," Katherine murmured. "Look at everyone. There are—what? Perhaps fifteen, twenty guests staying over? Maybe more coming in tonight. Newport cottagers, mostly, plus a few of our own. But none of your friends or mine. The only one here our age is the charming Vincent. This is all for you."

"Us," Madeleine countered.

"I am merely a necessary bystander."

At the southern end of the docks, a pair of lobster boats began to ring their bells, sending seagulls whirling up and away. They gazed at that for a moment, the lofting, the dispersal, before Madeleine admitted, very quietly, "He found me in the library yesterday, after luncheon. He told me I was lovely."

Katherine only sighed. "And you still think we're not here because of you?"

Madeleine threw up her hands. "Had he come across you yesterday instead, sitting there with a book in your lap, he likely would have said the same thing."

"You can't possibly believe that."

"I have no reason not to believe it. You're—you're better than I am in every way. You're smarter and prettier and more stylish—"

"Better," Katherine interrupted, her eyes narrowed. "You mean, better for him."

"Yes! Better for *him*. And if I can see that, surely he can, too."

"I wonder about you sometimes. I truly do."

"You know I'm right."

"What I know," said Katherine coolly, "is that when we are standing side by side before the colonel, I become your shadow. I become smoke, a foxed mirror. I'm invisible, because that man cannot tear his gaze from you."

The wind picked up, sticky with salt. Katherine lifted her face to it, closing her eyes and holding back her hair from her cheeks with both hands.

"If you won't believe in your own worth, Madeleine, at least have the sense to allow other people to believe in it."

"Good day, Miss Force, and Miss Force."

They both turned. Mrs. James Cardeza and Mrs. August Heckscher approached, clad in sturdy beige and diamond-link chains, and enormous straw hats that left their faces speckled with sunlight. Fearsome dragons, both: Madeleine had met them only once, and only briefly. They had attended a charity tea for the Traveler's Aid Society in Manhattan months past, had made a single pass among the tables to assess the stature of the chamber's occupants—and left as soon as they could.

Mrs. Cardeza dabbed at her temples with a handkerchief. "How very unexpected to find you here. I didn't realize your parents were acquainted with the colonel. I don't believe I've seen either of them in Newport in years." She looked to her companion as if to confirm it, and the other woman nodded thoughtfully.

"Nor Rhinebeck," Mrs. Heckscher said.

Katherine glanced at Madeleine, who stood mute, then took the lead. "No, ma'am. We've summered here for ages."

"Of course. Your family summers in Bar Harbor," Mrs. Heckscher said, with just enough delicate venom flavoring the words *Bar Harbor* to make her meaning clear.

"We find it delectable." Katherine lifted a hand to take it all in, the grounds, the Renaissance sky, the huge mansion. "Don't you think?"

Mrs. Cardeza cocked her head, birdlike, and the sun-speckles jerked bright and dark down the folds of her neck. "Tell me. How do your father and Colonel Astor know each other? Do they have business dealings together?"

"Oh, no," Madeleine heard herself say, "I introduced them." And then made herself smile as the silence ballooned.

"I see," Mrs. Cardeza said slowly, trailing the handkerchief down her temple, her cheek, her chin.

A hot sense of recklessness took hold of Madeleine, a clenching in her chest that felt like anger and release entangled. If Katherine was right, if this was indeed a trial, she had no doubt it was going to be one of fire. Might as well burn.

"Colonel Astor saw me dancing on the stage, you see, and sought me out after."

"*Hamlet*," clarified Katherine. "A truly superior production put on by the Junior League last month, right here at the *Bar Harbor Casino*." Katherine tapped her chin with one finger. "I forget. Was that when the colonel began sending you flowers?"

Madeleine flushed and did not answer.

"Flowers," Mrs. Cardeza said. "How . . . extraordinary."

"Yes, I'm sure that's when it began," Katherine continued. "Maddy played Ophelia, and I must say, she did a bang-up job. Colonel Astor thought so, too. Did either of you manage to catch it?"

Mrs. Cardeza's nostrils flared as her mouth formed a downward curve, lending her the aspect of a disapproving sheep. "I'm afraid we did not."

The pair of them swept off, pushed eastward by a fresh gust of wind.

Katherine shook her head. "A damned shame they missed the performance. I bet it's about to become the talk of the town."

Madeleine couldn't even act shocked over the swear word. She could only watch the women leave, their shadows swaying long and righteous along the shorn grass. The clenching in her chest abruptly loosened, giving way to a dismal heaviness, and then nausea.

What had she done? Once Mother found out . . . Or—worse— Colonel Astor . . .

Her sister linked their arms once more, drawing her close, and kissed her on the cheek.

"Cheer up. You'll dance again tonight, love, this time with him, in front of all of them. Let them look down their noses at *that*."

It wasn't a ball, it was only a dance. And it wasn't in any sort of official ballroom, like the one at the Swimming Club or the Casino or even the auditorium at the Building of Arts. It was·held inside the cottage itself, in a parqueted chamber that might have managed concerts, or theatrical productions, but tonight contained a small orchestra and tables of pastries and punch and garlands of crimson roses—dozens of them—draped along the ceiling and beveled glass doors, even around the brass chandeliers.

The other guests moved past the garlands as if they did not exist, those hefty red chains, as if they didn't notice at all that they walked through clouds of perfume, a scent that seemed to diffuse from the opened blooms and then simply hang in the air, weighted and weightless at once, sweetening all that it touched.

Madeleine noticed. She stood by the champagne table as the colonel's guests mingled and stared; she took deep, deliberate breaths of that perfume, and let her fingers drift along the petals of a particularly extravagant blossom.

She wished she wasn't wearing gloves. She wished she could feel the texture of it against her uncovered skin.

The colonel and his son had greeted the Force family as they'd entered, so that was done. She hadn't caught sight of him after that, and the orchestra was already on its fourth piece. Father was caught in a tangle of gentlemen lingering in one of the corners, sharing stock tips and snifters of brandy. Katherine had been twirled away early on at the behest of a strawberry tycoon from California (*Thousands of acres*, Mother had whispered happily, *right along the coast!*), and Madeleine was on her second glass of punch. She had not danced once, not even with the naval cadet across the room who kept throwing her flagrant glances. It was as if she wore some sort of sign, a placard yoked around her neck, unseen by her but read by everyone else: Do Not Touch.

"Here he comes," Mother warned. Madeleine lifted her head.

The colonel was a few paces away, shaking hands with a rust-bearded man in an admiral's uniform . . . but his eyes were on her. He spoke a few final words to the admiral and then broke away, closing the space between them in rapid steps.

"A capital night," enthused Mother, as soon as he was near. "Dinner was so delightful, and now this!"

"Thank you. I'm glad you're enjoying it."

"Maddy," said Mother, "don't you think it's a capital night?"

"Most capital," Madeleine said, stroking her hand along the garland by her hip. "And what lovely flowers."

Colonel Astor frowned at one of the garlands. His shirt was ivory linen, immaculately ironed and starched; beneath the chandeliers, the ruby studs tracing a path down his chest flashed all the colors of the roses. "Do you like them, then? I feared they might be too much. I had Dobbyn arrange things somewhat on the spot, poor fellow, so I can't blame him for the excess."

"Everything is perfect. American Beauties are my favorite."

"Are they really? They were my mother's favorite, as well."

Which, of course, Madeleine already knew. It had been mentioned in the papers more than once. She was not *entirely* without wiles.

"What excellent taste your mother had."

The colonel opened his hand. "Will you dance with me, Miss Force?"

"I would be so happy to," she answered, sincere. She passed her punch glass to her mother and accepted his hand.

She was wearing a Fortuny gown of dove silk with glass beading along the shoulders (brand new, perhaps a *little* much for the evening, but Katherine had declared it perfect), and the long, tiered folds of the overskirt floated above the floor as they walked, rippling and falling like the wings of a slow-skimming moth.

They turned to each other. She had the sense of eyes watching them, of conversations broken off, but it didn't matter. He lifted his chin, lifted her hand. Then, with a dip of his shoulder, he led her into the next measure of a waltz.

She was a good dancer; she knew that. But he was equally as good. Madeleine couldn't count the number of times her toes had been mashed by some awkward partner, boys who'd blushed bright as beets at having to go so far as to place a hand at her waist. But she and the colonel glided across the polished wooden floor as if they'd rehearsed together for years, their steps at once perfectly matched, their timing synchronous. She felt a flash of understanding of that old chestnut *they moved as one*, and in her mind the phrase transformed a little, became even better: *they moved as one beneath his lacework of roses.*

Madeleine couldn't help grinning up at him. Colonel Astor grinned back, and the room was crimson and gilt and teal plastered walls, and it was fine that they sailed practically alone across the elaborate parquet as everyone watched. It was fine, because they were touching, they were dancing, they were together.

He handed her a fresh glass of punch. It tasted more of champagne than of the fruit it had an hour before, and that, as it happened, was also fine with her. The music played on, and the people danced on, but Madeleine and the colonel had retreated past an open set of French doors to a balcony silvered in moonlight, where the breeze felt cooling now instead of chilly, and the soft, persistent scent of roses was washed away clean.

They weren't really ever alone. There were people wandering in and out, spying the balcony, admiring the view, going back. There was a pair of servants, footmen in black jackets and crisp ties, who stood unobtrusively at either side of the doors, awaiting the colonel's next instruction.

The balcony jutted out over a bluff. Thick cedar braces dug into the rock face beneath them, rugged pink granite that crumbled gently down into the woods. Looking out straight ahead showed her only more forest, mysterious and dense. Golden, flickering lights occasionally glinted past the trees—torchlights or cabins or lost spirits, Madeleine couldn't say.

They stood in silence. She tried the punch again, savoring the bubbles popping along her tongue.

"Might I ask a favor of you, Miss Force? Would you call me Jack?"

"Yes," she said, "if you will call me Madeleine."

"Not Maddy? I've heard your mother and sister calling you that."

She laughed, feeling warm and bold. "No, please. I've tried for years to get them to stop. It's so undignified. *Maddy*. I'm not a child anymore."

"It is a lovely name. *Madeleine.*" He said it again, under his breath. "Madeleine."

"Thank you. At least I am grown to someone."

He smiled at the trees, a wistful smile, one that tugged at her unexpectedly, that lodged itself in a tender place somewhere near her heart.

"It can be difficult sometimes for our families to accept us as people separate from who they are. As separate souls. When we're young, we're taught to behave as our parents do—to cherish what they cherish and believe what they believe. And for a while, that's as it should be. But as adults, sometimes we have our own desires, our own hopes, that are at odds with how our parents view the world."

"Is that how it was for you? You grew to be at odds with your parents?"

His jaw tightened; he took a longer breath. "Oh, for a while, yes. It was inevitable, I think. My father and I used to lock horns on so many things. Where I would attend school. What I would study. My companions, my ambitions . . . He was so determined that he knew the best path for me. And I, of course, was determined that he was wrong." He shook his head. "All these years later, I see that we were both right, and both wrong. I wish I could tell him so now."

An owl began to call from below them, earnest and deep. Another answered, closer to the sea. The golden lights in the woods winked and glowed.

"But your father must have been so proud of you," she said. "No matter how you locked horns. Look at you. Look at all you've done."

"What have I done, do you imagine?"

"Why," she said, astonished, "you're John Jacob Astor. You're—you're incomparable, really. Everyone in the world has heard of you. Every man and woman in the world admires you."

"My money, do you mean?"

He said it mildly, and without looking at her, but she felt the nick of it anyway.

"Not just that. Certainly *that*, but not just. You've invented things, useful things. I've read about them, the road improver—the—that special brake, for stopping bicycles. You volunteered to go to war when you didn't even have to. You've funded all sorts of charities, for people and places that need things so desperately—"

"Stop," he said, now on a laugh. "I beg you. You're making my head swell."

"You've written a book," she went on. "An entire book."

"A passing fancy."

"A book of fiction about exploring the solar system. Men in spaceships, landing on Saturn and Jupiter. Finding new life. Only someone tremendously clever would think of that."

He leaned forward, braced both hands against the balcony railing as if to assess its strength, then shook his head. "It was a while ago. A lifetime ago, it seems."

She tasted the punch again—it really was delicious!—then lowered the glass. "May I read it? Would you mind?"

"Oh, it's not very good, I'm afraid. Just a clutter of ideas I had when I was younger."

"But I want to know your ideas. I want to read your words, your book, because I might find a part of you inside those pages. A part I won't have a chance to know any other way. And I would love to know every aspect of you, Jack Astor. Do they have it here at the library in town?"

"No," he said, after a long, dumbfounded moment. And then, "Yes, I suppose they might. But I'll give you a copy. You needn't borrow it."

"Thank you."

He looked at her then with those winter gray eyes, and she looked back without shrinking. Around them rose the warm spill of light, of music, of every splendid fantasy she'd ever nurtured about him suddenly, wildly possible.

Then he straightened, turning away once more. When he spoke again, it was with deliberation, as if he were testing out the words before he said them.

"We live in a marvelous age, Madeleine. A magnificent age. We are witness to innovations and ideas never before imagined upon this earth. Science, philosophy, the arts. We're fortunate enough to be cast amid these times, destined to be amazed at man's ideas and innovations. Destined to be improved by them."

"How beautifully you've captured it. You've rather swept me away."

He ran a hand down his hair, then sent her a look she could not read, small and slight and maybe abashed.

CHAPTER 5

There are certain people in this world who have the ability to make you feel as if you're the only person in the universe who matters to them. Whether it's moment by moment or enough years to count up to a lifetime, they look you in the eyes and smile at you, direct and sincere—and you're smitten.

They draw you into their realm, into their rendering of events and ideas and rituals. Everything they say becomes vitally important. Every action of theirs becomes truth. Sometimes these people are innocents—this is a charisma they were born with; they did not earn it; it's simply their birthright—and sometimes it is a craft they practice, a manipulation. They *set out* to entice you, to seduce you, simply because they can—or because they want something in return.

It's hard to tell the difference sometimes.

Your father had that gift, and I believe it was inherent. He never meant to seduce me or anybody else. To this day, I don't think he had any nefarious intentions about anything in his whole life. He would simply pin you with his gaze and tilt his head and smile his wry, charming smile . . .

It wasn't merely that he was *so* rich, or *so* worldly, or *so* intelligent. It was that when he spoke, his deep voice melted over you like molasses. When he touched your skin, even for just a handshake, you felt important. You felt as if you mattered, whatever your name or fortune or background.

That was Jack Astor's talent: his presence. His attention.

Those canny winter eyes.

That was one of his talents, at least.

After that weekend, he suggested a picnic.

I suggested tidepools, the Shore Path, an afternoon at the beach.

He motored to the house to pick us up, the first time he'd ever come by.

He brought Vincent. And the dog.

August 1910
Bar Harbor

"There is a strange man outside," Katherine announced, standing by the parlor window, her pinkie parting, very slightly, the Youghal lace curtains.

Mother looked up from her embroidery, alert. "The colonel? He's early."

"No. Not him. The colonel would not be strange. This gentleman is lurking across the way, beneath the Pattersons' old red oak. He is pretending not to notice me noticing him."

Madeleine, walking into the room, crossed to the window and opened the curtains wider.

Mother sent her a frowning look. "My dear, have you finished dressing?"

"I have."

"That's what you've chosen to wear? I think you'll be too cold in muslin today. Why don't you go put on the green ocher satin?"

Madeleine leaned cautiously closer to the panes, searching the tree-dappled shadows lining the lane. "It's a picnic, Mother, not an evening at the opera. I'd look ridiculous in satin at the beach."

Katherine lifted a finger to point. Madeleine found him then, a broad-shouldered man leaning casually against the trunk of a tree. He wore a charcoal-colored suit and bowler and had turned his side to the Force home as if it were of no interest to him. He lifted a cigarillo to his mouth, inhaling slowly, breathing out a long, blue twist of smoke. If he carried a camera, Madeleine couldn't see it.

"That's not Ned Patterson?" she asked.

"Definitely not. Ned's shorter. And he dislikes tobacco."

Mother stood up, tossing her embroidery to the chair. "I wish your father was here. I do hate it that he is gone on the weekdays."

"How did he know?" Madeleine wondered. "How did he realize Jack would be coming by?"

Mother didn't hear her, but her sister did; Katherine shot her a covert smile. "*Jack* now, is it?"

Madeleine lifted a shoulder.

"I can think of two possibilities," Katherine said finally, returning her attention to the lurking man. "Either someone in the colonel's household shared information they should not have . . ."

Madeleine waited for her to finish, that sense of heavy tightness in her chest descending upon her once more, almost like drowning.

"Or else he *didn't* know. Doesn't. And he's just . . . here. Because you are."

"That seems much worse."

"Yes," said Katherine. "It does."

"I'll have Matthews send him off," Mother said from behind them. "It would be pleasant to offer Colonel Astor a measure of privacy, at least here in our own home."

Madeleine and Katherine exchanged a look. Matthews, their butler, was genteel and efficient and about a thousand years old.

"Too late for any of that." Katherine released the panel of lace. "The colonel's here."

The sound of an automobile roaring up the lane, powerful and rough, was impossible to miss. The man beneath the oak pushed away from its trunk, flicked his cigarillo to the grass, and crushed it beneath his heel. Madeleine began to pull on her gloves.

"Maddy," Mother said sharply. "We are a civilized household. Allow Colonel Astor to come to the door."

"No," Madeleine said. "We'll meet him outside. Otherwise, the next thing you know that fellow out there will be tapping at the windows to get his story, and soon everyone will be reading about the color of our walls and the arrangement of the furniture. Are you ready, Katherine? Yes? Let's go."

Mother sighed. "Poor Cook has spent half the morning preparing *choux à la crème* for him. She'll be so crushed."

"Tell her I'm sorry, I really am. We'll have cream puffs by the ocean, anyway, I imagine. Or sandwiches. Or something. We'll be back before you know it. 'Bye, Mother."

She didn't even wait for Matthews to reach for the door, didn't pause to pacify her mother further or to see if her sister followed. Madeleine finished with her gloves, adjusted her hat, opened the front door, and walked outside into the sunlit day as if she had every right to do so.

Because she did. It was her home, on her street, and she did not have to be intimidated by a stranger beneath an oak. She didn't. She *wasn't*.

She chanced a swift glance at the man—he had abandoned his nonchalant pose to scrawl something in a notebook—but after that looked only at the colonel, still seated behind the wheel of his touring car in his driving cap and duster, breaking into a smile as he caught sight of her.

In the high back seat, Kitty was clambering to stand upright on the cushions beside Vincent, her tail tracing a wide, cheerful loop in the air.

"Great," Katherine grumbled, hurrying to catch up. "I suppose I'll have to sit in the back with Sir Surly so you can be next to *Jack*."

"Keep the dog between you. She'll be better company."

They followed the coast for miles, with the engine of the shiny yellow Atlas a grinding, uneven roar in Madeleine's ears as Jack shifted gears and slowed, shifted gears and sped up. Conversation without shouting was impossible. She kept one hand locked around the strap on the door and the other on her hat, watching the shoreline, the surf, the colonel. A distant haze blurred the horizon where the ocean kissed the sky, but closer in, both shone vivid blue. The air rushed by fresh and warm, almost tropical.

Every now and then, Kitty would poke her head over the front seat, eyes wide and tongue lolling, and Jack would reach over and rub her ears without taking his gaze from the road.

As far as Madeleine could tell, they'd left the man with the cigarillo behind; no one raced after them. They passed two plodding buggies and an elderly woman driving a one-horse shay, but that was all.

He took them to a cove she didn't know and never would have guessed existed, its entrance half-hidden from the roadway behind a thicket of pine and wild sarsaparilla. A handful of chickadees scattered up to the topmost branches as they rumbled past, and a single brown hare leapt daringly right in front of them across the gravel, clearing the wheels by inches.

Madeleine watched it melt safely into the shadows of the woods, a fleet, secret life, there and gone.

The road narrowed, narrowed, until eventually it was little more than a footpath, choked with hobblebush and wintergreen and slabs of rock.

They left the Atlas parked off the side of the path—in case anyone else came by, although the odds seemed slim—and the colonel carried the heavy wicker hamper of food with both hands, leading the way to the sea. His son, just behind him, carried the blankets.

Kitty raced ahead, doubled back, raced ahead again.

Madeleine and Katherine, in their elegant layered skirts and modish heels, moved at a more moderate pace. As the trail grew rapidly more rocky and vertical, they picked their way along; the sound of lapping water made a low, lovely counterpoint to the crunch of stone underfoot and the birds gossiping above them.

The path curved, the trees opened, and all at once they were at the shore: a secluded wedge of sand framed by rugged pale rocks, glassy ripples of salt water rolling up along the slope of the beach to dissolve in sparkles and foam. More rocks broke the surface of the water farther out, sun-bleached and jagged, a giant strand of shark's teeth protecting the cove, shattering the strongest of the waves.

Vincent began to unfold the woolen blankets. Kitty plunged into the water, prancing. She came out, threw herself at the colonel, shook the wet from her coat, then bounced back into the sea.

Katherine stood with her arms crossed while Madeleine laughed, and John Jacob Astor IV merely brushed the damp sand from his waistcoat before bending down to unpack the hamper.

As predicted, there were sandwiches: shaved ham and cheddar between thick slices of buttered bread, garden pickles on the side. There were also clusters of red grapes and green; cold chicken salad and smoked salmon on wafers. No cream puffs, but an assortment of blackberry tartlets, their crusts golden and crumbly. The hamper also produced two corked jugs of lemonade, still nicely cooled, and one of a very pale ale, which only Vincent drank.

They sat on the blankets and dined on Limoges porcelain so translucent Madeleine could see the shadows of her fingers through it. Kitty had given up her play in the surf to collapse between Madeleine and the colonel, half on the sand and half off, panting and eyeing the tartlets with interest.

"Watch out," advised Jack. He'd shucked off his jacket and now sat with his legs straight out, ankles crossed, leaning back on his hands with his face tipped to the sun. He'd loosened his tie, as well; with his sleeves rolled up and his collar undone, he might have been any country gentleman relaxing beside her, his mouth smiling, the sea light complimenting his tanned face and neck, that tantalizing glimpse of the base of his throat between the open wings of his collar. His hair was mussed from the wind and his driving cap, but she liked that about him right now, that informality that made him more human than myth. It suited him here on this small hidden beach, this fine intimate day.

He *might* have been any ordinary gentleman regarding her from beneath those gilded lashes, but he wasn't.

He definitely wasn't.

Jack tipped his head toward the dog. "Kitty has a sweet tooth, and I regret to say she's a shameless thief."

Madeleine moved the tin of tartlets farther from the Airedale. "It seems unfair that we get all the delicious things to eat, while she has none."

Vincent, who had hardly touched any of the food, gave a derisive grunt, then scowled at Madeleine's glance.

"It's only a dog. It can go hungry for a few hours."

"But why should she?" Madeleine asked. "When we have so much extra?"

He smiled, dismissive. Like his father's, his shirt was wrinkled, and his hair was unkempt, but unlike Jack, it didn't suit Vincent. He looked hot and uncomfortable, the pomade he wore giving off a heavy, tarry scent.

"It's not even your dog," he said, not looking at her. "I don't know why you think you should care."

Jack warned, soft, "Vincent."

His son stared out at the sea.

Madeleine glanced at Jack, then down at the tin. "I was only thinking—one tartlet. But I don't want to presume—"

"You're not," Jack said, sitting all the way up. "But we can do better for her than that. Cook boiled her some chicken; I forgot about it. It's at the bottom of the basket. I should have served her first, I suppose."

"It's not starving." Vincent turned back to him suddenly, dark-haired, dark-eyed, ferocious; the waves danced into bright confetti behind him. "You coddle it. You spoil it. It eats all the time."

"And now," said the colonel, "she is going to eat chicken."

Into the silence that followed, Katherine said tranquilly, "I've always thought the best way to get the measure of a man is to observe how he treats his animals."

Jack found the tin, unwrapped the waxed paper, and emptied the diced chicken onto his own plate before setting it down in the sand before the dog. Kitty scrambled to her feet. Beads of water dotted her fur, dribbled down to the ground as her tail went around and around. The chicken vanished in seconds.

Very deliberately, Jack leaned across the blanket to take the lone tartlet—one bite gone—from his son's plate. Just as deliberately, he presented it to the dog, who stretched out her neck and swallowed it in a gulp.

Vincent stood, his color rising, slapping at his trousers. "The jam was too sour, anyway." He shoved his hands into his pockets and walked away from them, climbing back up the trail.

They watched him go, all of them, until he disappeared behind the spiky green branches of the pines. A fresh batch of teeny birds scattered skyward as he passed. The rolled glass waves behind them stretched and sighed and retreated.

The colonel studied his lemonade, lifted the tumbler, and gave it a slow swirl in his hand. There was a hardness to his jaw that wasn't there before, an edge of temper. He raised the tumbler to his lips.

"I believe," said Katherine, also rising, "that I glimpsed a tidepool over yonder, past that knot of chokecherries. I so enjoy tidepools. Nature, starfish, and all that. Please excuse me."

"I apologize," Jack said, as soon as Katherine was out of earshot. He set the tumbler aside but did not look away from it, running a finger along the rim.

Madeleine waved away a hovering fly. "No need to apologize. It's such a beautiful day, isn't it? Maybe he didn't want to have to spend the afternoon being our chaperone. Who could blame him?"

"I'm usually more careful with him. He's had a difficult time."

"Has he?" she said, thinking about wealth and privilege and physical beauty, and about how Jack Astor's son seemed to swim in all those things.

Jack reached for his jacket, shook it out, refolded it carefully before laying it flat against the blanket once more. "He's so much like his mother. Clever. Impetuous. Quick to temper and slow to forgive." He drew a long breath, at last meeting her eyes. "The divorce last year was punishing for him. For all of us. Ava was so unhappy, you see, and that just . . . bled through us. All four of us."

He paused. She nearly murmured something banal and appropriate, *I'm sorry*, or *how awful*, but the light was brilliant and the ocean was sparkling and the way he was looking at her, both troubled and distracted at once, lost in those bad days, lost in the immutable fact of divorce, stilled her voice. So instead she leaned toward him, silent, laying her hand atop his. His expression didn't change, but he turned his palm over to lace his fingers through hers.

They were holding hands. They were *holding hands*, and he didn't even seem to *notice*, but oh, she did. His warm skin against hers. His long fingers, the slight, bony pressure of them tucked between her own. For a delirious moment, palm to palm felt even more intimate than a kiss. She hardly dared breathe; she felt swooping, silly, and had to force herself back into the moment, to listen to him still speaking, still telling his story, his voice so low and melodious beneath the *shuss, shuss* of the sea.

"Alice—my daughter—is only eight. She lives with her mother now, and that was the right decision, I think. Ava wanted her, and Alice wanted to go, so . . . But Vincent." He sighed. "Vincent noticed all the unpleasantness that Alice was too little to understand. It changed him, I think. Made him . . . bilious. Resentful. He knew there were problems, and he knew he was powerless to fix them, any of them, so I fear he's still just carrying them all bottled up inside of him."

"How painful for him."

"I would help him if I could. I've tried, I swear I have. But he's eighteen, with a will of his own. He's starting school soon, and I have hope that it might steady him, but the truth is he's too old to coddle, and too young to set free."

"A separate soul, you might say."

"Indeed he is."

The fly returned to flit past him and land on one of the sandwiches. Jack uncoupled their fingers to shoo it off (she leaned back again, feigning serenity), then began to break the bread apart, meticulously dividing the meat from the cheese.

Kitty, following his movements closely, gave a hard *wuff!* through her nose.

"So Vincent is adrift," Madeleine said. "I'm sure it's only temporary."

His smile was slim. "Are you? I wish I shared your certainty. This distance with him, this unhappiness, seems to drag on and on. I cannot change our history, the divorce, everything that's happened. I can only *try*—" He paused. "*Try*, I suppose, to be a better father to him." His voice thinned. "And I *have* been trying, God knows. I have."

Madeleine pressed her finger against a crumb on the blanket, flicked it out to the sand. "I think that . . . sometimes it's easier to understand a problem when standing outside of it, rather than from within. So here I am, on the outside. I don't know your son very well, but it's clear he looks up to you. If you remain his anchor now, I bet he'll find his way again."

A measure of the tension hardening him lifted; his gray eyes softened. "Words of wisdom, Miss Force?"

"Oh!" she said, embarrassed. "Words, at any rate."

The colonel examined the wrecked sandwich in his hands with an expression of vague surprise, as if he hadn't quite realized what he'd been doing all this time. The Airedale placed a hesitant paw on the blanket, a question in her glance, and he dumped the entire mess in front of her, then whisked his palms clean.

"Thank you, Madeleine."

"For what?"

"For listening. It's been a long while since—well. It feels good to be heard. Truthfully, I'd forgotten how good."

She shifted and the giving sand shifted with her, and she pushed her feet out from beneath her skirts, stretching her legs before her as he had done. The Maine summer day gleamed around them both, perfect as a postcard.

"You are most welcome, Jack."

CHAPTER 6

Bar Harbor, you will discover, isn't a terribly large place. First of all, you're on an island, water on all sides, which is crackerjack in some ways but not so crackerjack in others. You're on this island—a *lovely* island, yes, a *bucolic* island—in this little bijou of a town, and for all the summer months, everyone is as trapped as everyone else (except for the papas, those hustling businessmen who all flock back to the city on Sundays to pay heed to their various vocations, only to trickle back to the island again on Thursdays or Fridays, girded once more for their wives and offspring). So everyone knows everyone else, and where to go, and what to do, and they all do it at practically the same time, in the same way, day in and day out, until it's time for everyone—the summer colony, at least—to trek back to their respective urban homes to hunker through the wintertide.

(No one in their right mind wants to winter on the island, not if they can help it, with the Arctic wind screaming down and the snow blowing horizontal and ice caking thick as planks over the houses and walkways and spiky dead gardens.)

Anyway, everyone knows everyone else, the locals and the cottagers alike, and everyone has their own familiar routines, from the person nibbling lobster rolls while idling in a hammock, listening to the wind stir song through the birches; to the person who brought the lobster rolls to the person in the hammock; to the person who brought the lobster to the cook; to the lobsterman himself. There really aren't any strangers in Bar Harbor proper.

That's why when the newspapermen began to drift in, everyone noticed.

August 1910
Bar Harbor

She wouldn't quite remember the program of music played by the Boston Symphony that one particular evening at the Building of Arts; Madeleine had meant to keep the card detailing the program, to treasure it, preserve it between the pages of some special book, to be discovered and admired later on, but at some point during the concert she had misplaced it, and hadn't noticed until it was too late to procure another.

She did remember the air outside as she'd walked beside her mother up the path leading to the grand marble entrance, how mild and tender it felt, not quite cool but not too warm, either, because sunset was only a half hour or so away. She remembered how the light turned the enormous Ionic columns that braced the roof from pale gray to peachy gold; how it reflected off the windows in great blinding squares; how all the other concertgoers greeted each other in friendly tones, everyone gratified with the air and the sun and the turnout.

She remembered their seats, somewhat near the back third of the interior hall but not unreasonably so, her own right at the end of the aisle. Sitting there with Mother, fanning herself with the program card, wishing she could peel off her gloves.

Mother was smiling and scanning the audience, because the purpose of going to a concert at the Building of Arts was not, of course, to actually listen to the music. It was to see and be seen, and on this occasion, she would be seen in her new evening gown of palomino crêpe, which had arrived only that very morning from Redfern in Paris.

Madeleine was there to be seen fixed at her side, her gradually-becoming-notable daughter, a shining ornament in human form, casting her meager glow upon the sophisticated Mrs. Force.

Katherine, sensing the trap, had refused to come. Father had escaped back to New York days ago. Jack was—

Jack was here, standing before them. He stood with his hat in his hand, his tanned fingers distinct against the black beaver brim. He smiled down at her as if he hadn't been gone for days, as if he hadn't just materialized from the air as he always did. She glanced to his left and right, but his son wasn't in view. Only the man himself, bowing his head to her mother, lifting his gaze back to Madeleine, bidding them both a good evening in that quiet, pleasant voice as people pushed by him along the aisle.

"Good evening, colonel!" said Mrs. Force. "We hadn't heard you were in town again."

"My final meeting was canceled—the fellow missed the train in Pittsburgh—so I was able to sail a little sooner than I'd planned. I did hope to return in time for the concert. Madeleine mentioned you might be here, so it's happy luck I've found you. How well you look tonight, Madeleine. That shade of green suits you."

"Thank you," she said, acutely aware of how quiet the members of the audience in their immediate vicinity had become.

"Where are you seated, Colonel Astor?" inquired Mrs. Force.

"Oh," he said, gesturing with the hat, "I'll be standing in the back. All the other tickets had sold. It's the price I pay for my tardiness."

"Nonsense!" said Mother. "You must take my seat."

"Madam, I could never take—"

"I insist! Look there, right over there, is my friend Mrs. Silas Reynolds. Her husband could not attend at the last moment, and so she has an empty seat right next to hers."

Mother turned and waved to a woman stationed at the far

other end of the hall, who lifted her hand and returned the wave so instantly, Madeleine knew they had planned the entire maneuver. Heat climbed up her neck, flooded her cheeks. No one, *no one* could possibly be fooled, least of all a man as sharp as Jack.

"There, you see? I shall have her empty chair, and you shall have mine, and everyone will be happy."

Madeleine couldn't bear to look up at him. She couldn't look at anyone. She kept her gaze trained on her hands, fingers and knuckles clenched in a white satin ball on her lap.

"Are you certain?" Jack was asking gravely, as if she were sacrificing her arm or her heart's blood.

"Positively. I would never be able to enjoy the music knowing you were stuck back there with the hoi polloi. You'll be wonderful company for Madeleine. She's mentioned she missed you very much, you know, even though it's been only days."

Madeleine closed her eyes. Her face felt on fire. "Mother, *please.*"

"Well, you did. And now you don't have to." Mrs. Force came to her feet.

Jack said, "At least allow me to escort you to your friend."

"I wouldn't want to bother you . . ."

"It's no bother at all. Now *I* insist."

Mother brushed past and Madeleine stood to let her by, and then she and Jack were looking at each other straight on. He was smiling, really smiling, but in a way that looked like a secret: his lips pressed closed, the corners tipped. There was merriment behind his eyes, but she couldn't tell if he was amused at her, or at her mother, or at the whole scheme, so clumsy and obvious.

Sorry, she mouthed.

And his smile grew. He looked back at her mother, offered his arm. "Mrs. Force? Shall we, before the musicians file in?"

They slipped away, Jack a full head and a half taller than Mother, who always walked with the straight dignity of a ballerina, no matter how transparent her intrigues.

Madeleine resumed her seat. After a moment, she summoned enough pluck to lift her chin, finding the thick card of her program again and using it as a fan, casually, easily, as if she had not a single care.

From the edges of her vision, she felt their stares, all the people seated around her appraising her, whispering behind their hands. She felt their curiosity, their disdain and titillation shivering along her skin.

He returned just as the lights were dimming, once, twice, thrice, to let the audience know it was nearly time to stop gossiping and preening and at least imagine, for the next hour or so, that they had gathered together as one to be uplifted by the magnificence of the performance, by the hard work and mastery of the musicians and conductor and composers.

She made herself look up at him as he settled against the velveteen cushions. She'd abandoned the program as a fan but couldn't stop herself from twisting the slim bangle on her left wrist around and around, a band of silver firm as a manacle against her glove and bones.

"I'm afraid she's not very subtle," she said.

Jack tugged his waistcoat straight. "I'm quite accustomed to ambitious mamas. Yours was obliging enough to read my mind, at least."

"Did she?"

That secret smile returned; he gave her a sideward look. "She did. And I thanked her kindly for it, too."

Madeleine sat back, relieved and yet still mortified. The burning bulbs in the chandeliers above them sank away into cherry, into cinders, into ash.

She hesitated, then whispered, "If you encourage her, though, she'll never stop trying to throw us together."

"Madeleine," he replied quietly, leaning his head toward hers, "what on earth makes you think I want her to stop?"

* * *

This was why she would not remember the music played that night by the accomplished musicians of the Boston Symphony Orchestra, nothing beyond the first few dramatic notes of Bach's *Fantasia in G minor*: because in the newly fallen darkness, Jack reached over and took her hand—deliberate this time, nothing absent-minded about it—and he held it the entire while, the entire performance, while Madeleine's cheeks went warm again and her heart bloomed like a savage flower inside her chest.

It was the habit of the audience of the Building of Arts to wend slowly outside again once the affair was done, the play or music or lecture, where they would discover vendors in rolling wooden carts parked in the grass, selling sarsaparilla tonics or hot frank-furters or oysters or roasted corn by lanternlight. Any children in attendance would immediately begin tugging on their parents' arms, pleading for pennies, only to run amok once they'd claimed their prize, darting from cart to cart to decide which treat looked best. And although most of the ladies, in their fine gowns and gemstones, declined to handle the mess of a shucked oyster or a buttery ear of dripping corn, a small slice of cake might be accept-able, as well as a glass of lemonade.

As a child, Madeleine would have been delighted with the corn, with the sweet tonic or a sharp mustardy frankfurter. But, as she'd said to Jack before, she wasn't a child any longer; she was a young woman wearing white satin gloves and a dress of jade silk, and so when Jack Astor turned to her beneath the evening sky and asked if she would like anything, anything at all, she glanced around the carts until she found the one selling cider doughnuts, because they were easy to eat and always came with a thick paper napkin to hold the crumbs.

"Perfect," he said. "My favorite."

"Really?"

"Really. Mrs. Force, for you?"

Mother shook her head. She would not risk her new gown, not on its very first wearing.

The doughnuts had been fried during the day by the wife of a fisherman and were sold at night by her daughter, a freckled girl of about fifteen, and they were always moist and dense and tangy with apples. Madeleine took her first bite and closed her eyes in pleasure. She opened them again to find Jack watching her, his own doughnut untouched.

A pair of boys stampeded between them, clutching stick candies and yelling for a friend. A cool breeze followed on their heels, scented of sugar and the promise of rain.

"You . . ." Jack said, and paused. "You, ah, have a . . ."

He took a step closer, lifted a hand as if to touch her face. Before he could, Madeleine raised her own hand and brushed away the crumb from her lower lip and that was when the light exploded only feet away, startling her. She immediately turned her face aside as Jack did the opposite, pivoting toward that blinding burst.

"Sir," he said, a word edged with exasperation. "Some warning, if you please."

The smell of sugar and rain vanished, replaced with an acrid, chemical stink.

"Beg your pardon, colonel," said the photographer, grinning. "It was a nice moment, though."

Jack moved to stand between Madeleine and the photographer. There was now a giant pale spot in her vision that she couldn't blink away.

"Very well, you've gotten your moment. My companions and I would like to get on with our evening, if you don't mind."

"One more of you and Miss Force, colonel? One more, with fair warning?"

Jack glanced back at her; she gave the slightest shake of her head, but perhaps he didn't see. "One more, *if* you agree to leave us in peace afterwards."

"Deal," said the man, swiftly adding powder to his handheld trough, lifting his camera again. "Look this way, Miss Force. There you are, *thanksverymuch*. A wee smile, please, miss? I promise it don't hurt a bit."

Flash!

But it did hurt. A petty little wound, this photograph, that photograph, this mention in the papers, that one. Each one chipping away at any thought she might have had of privacy, of control of her own face or figure or destiny.

Two years from this *nice moment*, Madeleine would be a widow and a mother, the most famous widowed mother on the entire planet, and by then she would have developed her own flinty ways of dealing with the press.

But that was still two years away. For now, in the short months to come, Jack would teach her *his* rules on how to interact with them:

Learn their names, so you can get an idea of how they write about you.

Learn where they work, because some papers are more discreet than others.

Never say more to them than absolutely necessary; words are easily misquoted.

Don't get caught in a lie; a good newspaperman will always sniff it out.

Don't lose your temper, no matter how they goad you. Spectacles always sell sheets.

And finally, if truly pinned, negotiate. Offer them something they want, a very limited something, so that you can have something *you* want. If it helped, he would tell her, kissing her hand, she could think of it as a tiny sacrifice for the greater good.

That sultry August evening after the concert, Jack's idea of the greater good was simply the freedom to walk with her, to enjoy apple-flavored doughnuts with her, to speak of flimsy nothings while quietly learning the unspoken things about each other: how they harmonized, how they linked, how even the silences between them were light and lovely.

And it worked, more or less. After the photographer had gotten his shot (Madeleine pasty and smiling nervously; Jack at ease; Mother cropped out entirely), the man had tugged at his cap and let them alone. But the next morning, there were two more of them camped out across the street from Madeleine's house, underneath that sturdy red oak.

They were only the beginning.

CHAPTER 7

BEWARE *LA FORCE MAJEURE*!
—Special to *Town Topics*
September 1, 1910
Bar Harbor, Me.

Mother Force has her heart set upon adding a certain army officer to her list of kith and kin, and nothing will stand in her way. Mr. and Mrs. William H. Force, favored with two stunning jewels in their family crown, would happily bestow either upon this newly eligible suitor, no matter his recent marital woes.

Sources have caught sight of both of these freshly polished gems being squired about this Mount Desert town by the fickle man himself. The question becomes, what will this fortunate fellow choose to do with such generous offerings?

The papers, even the scandal sheets, had been able to unearth only the barest-bone facts of the luscious Ava Lowle Willing Astor's divorce from her lanky, obscenely rich husband. The details of the petition and decree remained sealed by the court, which meant there was nothing to rein in the breathless rumors: that he had been unfaithful, or she had. That they had fought incessantly; that they lived apart; that the only reason the divorce had not happened sooner was that they'd been forced to await the passing of the colonel's puritanical mother. No doubt had the dissolution of their marriage happened in her lifetime, the disgrace of it would have stopped Lina's heart.

A year ago, Madeleine had paid little attention to the talk regarding the Astors. Gossip was a ceaseless fact of society; there was no getting around it, she knew that firsthand. Tittle-tattle flitting through school would catch flame in the dormitories, in the hallways. Madeleine had seen perfectly pleasant girls ruined by slander, and perfectly horrible girls elevated by it. She'd managed her final few years of finishing school by keeping her head down, mostly, and her comments close.

Graduating from it all last June had been a relief. The ceremony itself had been conducted out-of-doors in an amphitheater dotted with flowery hats and lace parasols. The one-and-three-quarters hours of speeches had been tedious and wilting and crammed full of phrases like *fair womanhood* and *gentle hearts* and *our future wives*.

And here I am, anyway, Madeleine thought now, the ink-smudged sheets of the tabloid crushed in one hand. *Being gossiped about, someone's future wife—at least according to the papers. Maybe nothing ever really changes.*

"You shouldn't let it upset you," Father said. It was twilight; they sat together on the swinging bench hung from the rafters of their back porch, watching the sky darken above the trees. There was a bite to the air tonight that hadn't been there even this morning; the breeze from the bay nudged by with an undercurrent of woodsmoke, pungent and crisp. Soon birch leaves would litter the ground scarlet, and the grass would dry into straw, and the days would grow clipped, with violet shadows reaching longer and longer.

Soon they'd have to close up the house and leave, to head back to New York.

Where there were even more reporters.

"How is Mother handling it? The papers calling her—that?"

"Don't tell her I said so, but I think she's secretly flattered. *La Force Majeure*. It implies influence, doesn't it."

"It's rude."

"It is the nature of our lives, Madeleine. If you dance in the limelight, it's only natural that people will look at you. You can't expect otherwise."

The black iron candle-lanterns decorating the porch remained unlit, but a wan orangey glow from the lamps inside the house spilled over the windowsills, outlining Madeleine and her father both but only very softly, and only along their laps. She hoped that if she kept to the shadows enough, she'd remain a smudgy nothing to anyone observing from the darkness beyond. Of late, there were always strangers skulking nearby, walking slowly up and down the lane, watching the house, watching for her.

"Maddy," said her father in a new voice, one she knew all too well; it was the graveled voice of lectures, of authority, of imposing family rules. Madeleine braced herself.

"Yes?"

"You *are* young yet, but God gave you intelligence—"

"Why, thank you," she said, dry.

"—and a sensible head on your shoulders. I want you to think very carefully about the path you're treading now. About where it's going to lead you."

She turned her face to his. In the deepening dusk, his silver hair became phantom gray, barely discernible. "I promise you, Dad, I think about it every day."

"No doubt." He lifted her hand, the one with the tabloid, taking the crumpled pages from her fingers, smoothing the paper flat again against his leg. "You understand, don't you, that all I've ever wanted for you is your happiness?"

"Of course," she said, surprised.

"But the *quality* of that happiness . . . I've devoted a great deal of thought to that subject lately, something I likely should have done years ago. The quality of happiness. The shape and texture of it. The endurance of it. Believe it or not, I remember what it's like to fall in love for the first time. To be young and fearless, when the future is spread before you in every color of the rainbow, everything bright, everything impossible suddenly made possible. You're invincible then."

She nearly laughed. "I don't think I'm invincible."

"Don't you?" He nodded. "Good. That's something, to understand that we humans are creatures of marl and earth. Forgive me now, child, but I am your father, and being a father comes with certain prerogatives, so I'm going to ask if you love him."

She was silent. The sky was deepening, clouding, blue on blue, a wide, curved sapphire at the bottom of a lake.

"Because love is a tremendous gift, Maddy. A gift and a burden. Marriage especially is more than just hope and luck and a handshake. Marriage is work, enormous work, because it's a living entity that needs everlasting attention. It will push you and bend you and test you, and if you're not prepared for any of that, it will shatter you. I imagine the colonel could tell you something about what that's like."

She stared at the black tall trees, the swimming blue light.

"Being in love makes all that work easier, but it does not make it go away. There will be necessary sacrifices. There will be pain. So I'll ask you again: Do you think you're in love with him?"

She sighed. "I could be. He's—oh, he's wonderful in so many ways. I could be in love."

"But you're not certain."

Madeleine scowled down at her lap, trying to explain. "When I'm with him, I feel like I'm practically a different person. I feel so . . . *noticed*. I'm not sure how else to describe it. He looks at me and it's almost as if he's given me a magical ability, the ability to be *seen*. Almost like being on stage again, all lit up, but even better, because it's only the two of us." She plucked at her skirt.

"But then, when we're apart, I'm just me again. And I think, well, maybe it was all pretend. My imagination run riot."

"Will you marry him?'

She felt that heated jolt rise through her, that hot confusion of mortification and hope; she wanted to spring up, she wanted to jump from the swing and leave, but she didn't. She remained sitting, pressing her palms against the slats of the bench.

"Katherine asked me the same thing, back at his cottage."

"Katherine is far more savvy than the rest of us, I suspect."

Madeleine crossed her legs and kicked up a foot, up, down, trapped and restless, and the folds of her dress hissed with each kick, and the bench rocked and creaked. "He hasn't *asked* me to marry him."

"He will, though. Unless he's an absolute scoundrel—and despite the tales, I don't believe that's true—he will ask."

"Maybe," she said. "Maybe he will, or he won't. I don't know. I want him to, but I don't know why he would."

Father's eyebrows raised. "Don't you?" he said again.

"I don't," she said fiercely. "And I realize you're my father, and you'll tell me all sorts of reasons of why I'm so special, why Jack *should* want to be with me, but in the end, it's not up to you or me, is it? It isn't. It never is. The man holds all the power in courtship, and always will. So I can't—I can't let myself worry about marriage now. If he does ever ask, I'll worry about it then."

Father paused, looking at her. The swinging bench creaked slowly back and forth. "You have power too, Madeleine. You have the power to walk away."

"But I don't want to," she whispered.

"Then I fear marriage *is* a worry for today, not tomorrow. John Jacob Astor is no ordinary man. He carries a storm on his back wherever he goes, a tempest of unremitting scrutiny." He tapped the battered tabloid against his thigh. "The rumors, the journalists, the gossip sheets . . . it's important for you to comprehend that we stand at the beginning of it all still. Aligning yourself with the colonel, with his family—with all that would entail—means this storm will never end for you. Ever."

"I'm not afraid of that," she said, willing it to be true. Because it was Jack, wasn't it? Jack, who could smile at her over a cider doughnut and make her feel like the luckiest girl in the world, like she'd only been waiting to be discovered until *he* had discovered her.

So it *had* to be true.

Dad patted the back of her hand. Rheumatism was beginning to take his joints; his fingers hardly flexed against hers, his skin cool. "All right. But you will allow me my fatherly prerogative, I hope. You will allow me to be afraid *for* you."

He gazed out into the night, at the scattering of stars just beginning to prick the lining of the sky, and said it again, muted.

"Allow *me* to be afraid."

The bite to the air grew sharper. The leaves began to change, slowly at first, and then seemingly all at once, and everywhere she looked were great splashes of copper and vermilion and plum atop spindly trunks, and the bright annuals in the Village Green flowerbeds faded into beige. It rained still, black-pearled days of misty rain, but it wouldn't for much longer. Soon the rain would turn into snow, and all the cottagers would flee back to their city homes, to the solid comfort of life amid every winter luxury to be found.

Madeleine wanted to leave, but then on the other hand, she didn't. Jack had decided to stay a while longer in Bar Harbor, and so remained the rest of this small, glimmering society, like barnacles attached to an anchored ship's hull. Yet she couldn't help thinking that being back in Manhattan might be better, somehow. More anonymous. Their brownstone was much smaller there but the city itself much, much larger. It would be easier to blend in with crowds, to walk and shop and dine without always fretting about being followed.

But the colonel stayed, and so the Force family stayed. And everyone stayed. Madeleine began to wonder if they would be there long enough to see the lakes freeze, and the locals driving their motorcars and ice boats across the thickly glazed water. She'd seen daguerreotypes of that, bundled figures skimming along on skates, the autos parked far from the safety of shore.

At Jack's invitation one brisk September evening, they dined at the Swimming Club. He'd booked the entire dining hall of the clubhouse, and the mood was festive, with wine freely poured before the meal and the colonel's guests laughing and chatting without taking their seats, a few of the ladies occasionally tugging their gloves higher to better cover their arms.

As Mother had begun to mention more and more, they had not *shopped* for this weather—and while stranded so far from the elite modistes of Manhattan, they were unable to do so. Looking around the room, Madeleine thought that hardly any of the ladies had prepared for the cold: the lightest of crêpe de chine and tulle were still being worn, gentle swirls of pastels much better suited for the months that had come before than for this one.

The seasons seemed all atilt. Summer had dissolved into something new, something not quite *not* summer, but not yet definitely anything else.

It was all because of Jack.

"Would you have ever guessed there exists a man with the power to change the orbit of the planet?" Katherine asked lightly, standing beside her sister near the chamber's only hearth as they watched the colonel greet yet another patrician couple.

"Is that his power?" Madeleine asked.

"We hang like icicles here by the andirons, Maddy, trying to thaw. It feels like we'll be thawing for an eternity yet—why won't the Club's harebrained manager build up the fires? Anyway, no. That is not the colonel's power. It's far more straightforward than that. It's the power of wealth."

"Which is also his," Madeleine noted.

"Yes." Her sister rubbed her arms. "His preposterous, ridiculous wealth."

Leta Wright strolled up, a cashmere shawl wrapped tight over her shoulders.

"May I join your little cloak-and-dagger conference over here by the fire?"

"It's not cloak-and-dagger," Katherine said. "We're just trying not to freeze to death."

Leta nodded. "It's worse across the room. Look at Henrietta over there, talking to William Dick. I think her lips are blue."

As he was shaking yet another hand, Jack turned his head, finding Madeleine across the busy chamber. They looked at each other in the flickering light, steady, connected, *two-three-four*, before he turned away again, smiling, bending at the waist to reply to something a diminutive white-haired matron had said.

"Maddy," said Katherine in a low voice. "Fix this."

Madeleine came awake. "What?"

"Fix it."

"Fix what? The fire?"

"No, silly. Fix *this*." She made a sweeping gesture to take in the chamber, the finely dressed people attempting to smile past their clenched teeth. "We are pinned here in Bar Harbor like bugs to a board because of your beau."

Leta snorted a laugh; she smothered it with a hand clapped over her mouth. Madeleine glanced at her, her merry dark eyes above the fabric of her glove, then back at Katherine.

"Don't be absurd. I don't have the means to—"

"Of course you do," Leta interrupted. "You have the means, the ability, the wiles—all of it. Any of it. We are entirely at your mercy, anyone at all could see *that*. You, the sublime Miss Madeleine Force, hold us hapless, commonplace mortals hostage, captured in the heart of your hand, because God knows our own mothers don't have the sense to yank us out of the cold. Not as long as Colonel Astor dallies nearby. Make use of it, *please*, I *beg* you, and send us all back to civilization. I swear I can't eat another bite of lobster, or clams, or lobster mixed with clams." Leta lifted the flats of her palms to the fire and gave a groan, tilting back her head so her neck showed long and taut. "*Lord*, I miss dining at the St. Regis."

It had been weeks since that al fresco dinner party in Beau Desert's ripe garden; Madeleine and Jack no longer sat tables apart. He had placed her on his right, within easy distance for conversation and lingering looks. Despite the fire popping in the hearth and the gas chandelier quietly hissing above their heads, the walls loomed dark and the light spread thin, and it felt something like dining in a chilled, stylish cave.

Madeleine cut the side of her fork into her lobster rissole. The pastry flaked apart, paper-thin slivers falling pale against the plate.

She took a breath, prepared to tell the first, the smallest of white lies, which surely did no real harm to anyone, did it, but which might actually accomplish some greater good.

"Mother is talking about going back to New York in the next week or so," she said, not loud, and brought the fork to her lips, tasting butter and marjoram and cream.

Jack looked at her, arrested, then recovered. He sliced into his own rissole, severing off a sizable chunk.

"Then let's go back," he said.

CHAPTER 8

December brought my debut.

Officially it happened one gray frosted afternoon, at the coming-out reception my mother hosted for members of our circle at our Manhattan home. I wore white, of course. We had tea and punch and sandwiches and éclairs, and all my friends attended, along with their various minders attached. In the span of just a few weeks, there was a flurry of receptions for the Junior League, and it seemed we chased each other from house to house to house to fit them all in. Inevitably we'd arrive shaking the weather from our hems, smoothing the snow or the sleet or bitter drops of rain from our meticulously managed coiffures.

Each new gathering, each new luncheon or dinner held in our honor was conducted in rigid ceremony. Our mothers and grandmothers seemed to be warning us, *Yes, once and for all, your childhood is over. Womanhood means you must not ever laugh or burp or break wind again. This is how you will marry well.*

I could not wait for the formalities to end.

And then came the Christmas Ball at the Murray Hill Hotel. It took place a few days later and was my first real appearance as a young woman deemed Acceptable for Marriage by the *beau monde*.

That spangled, icy night. Alabaster satin, ostrich feathers, a narrow bracelet of diamonds sparkling against one wrist. That morning, Jack had sent over an entire box of pink roses, their color so creamy and delicate the petals might have been carved from the inside of a seashell. Nestled in with the roses was a cable of pearls of the precise same tint, heavy and long enough that I wore it like a bandolier of bullets around my body.

I danced for hours.

In a small, empty antechamber off the ballroom, your father and I shared our first kiss.

The papers would later call me a Christmas present for all of New York society. I don't know about that; I think really they meant for themselves. Young Miss Force, freely and openly presented to the world, fodder for the tabloids, her face (soft and demure and in profile; Mother had paid a small fortune to the photographer and that damned docile image followed me *everywhere*) published as often as they could find an excuse to use it.

I was now officially fair game.

February 1911
Manhattan, New York

The air in Manhattan had a different tang to it than that of Brooklyn, although Madeleine couldn't define exactly how. It smelled less stale, perhaps; less sour, since most of the streets snaking around and across Fifth Avenue were no longer hard-packed macadam. The air here was scented more of stone than tar, and (in the summer) more of trees than grass. Since the clouds above the city had bubbled into their thick, slaty-blue gloom and the snow had only just begun slanting down, Manhattan was now also blanketed in the particular odor of burning coal and damp iron and, for Madeleine, the pungent miasma that was the exhaust rising from the back of the family's chauffeured limousine.

Whenever the auto stopped or paused along the streets, fumes seemed to seep through the very seams of the chassis, coating her skin and the back of her throat.

It was making her nauseated. Madeleine began to pry open the window beside her.

"Maddy!" Katherine slapped her hand away, leaning over her to shut the window again. "You're wearing *brocade*. Do you want the reporters to see you all spotty?"

"No," Madeleine said, chastened and queasy. "Of course."

The motorcar bounced along a mudhole and passed a wagon; the staccato strike of horseshoes against cobbles rang in her ears. She set her jaw, closed her eyes.

"Madeleine." It was Mother, seated on the other side of Katherine, soft-voiced, thinly urgent. "Chin up. We're nearly there, and you look so peaked."

Madeleine opened her eyes. She wondered if she might vomit, and if she did, if any of the cameramen lying in wait for her would capture it for all of humanity to relish.

Absolutely they would. Without question, they would.

Katherine put her mouth to Madeleine's ear. *She* smelled of orange blossoms, spicy sweet.

"Think of the colonel," she whispered. "Think of his face. Think of his smile the instant he first sees you. How it brightens him. Illumes him. Think of how that smile is for no one else but you."

Illumes. "You should be a poet," Madeleine muttered past her teeth.

"Maybe I will," Katherine responded, cheery. "No doubt all the gentlemen would swoon over my verses."

"All but one," said their mother.

"All but one," Katherine agreed. "But with so many laudable gentlemen to choose from, I can afford the loss of just this one."

Madeleine had a brief and wholly convincing vision of Katherine stepping from the motorcar as they pulled up to Jack's French Renaissance mansion; Katherine lifting her gloved hand to him, accepting his short, elegant bow, magnesium bursts flaring; Katherine sailing onward and upward into the life of the new Mrs. John Jacob Astor IV, trailing gemstones and velvet and tears in her wake.

"Madeleine," said their mother again, in an even more urgent tone.

"I'm *fine.* I'll be fine."

And she would be. It was only the stupid newspapers making her so nervous, that was all it was. Not even the newspapers that would come out *tomorrow,* columns and columns that would be, no doubt, dedicated to tonight's upcoming, phenomenal gala. No, she was disquieted over the papers that had already been printed, that had taken care to mention her name alongside Jack's with a sort of vicious delight, that had underscored the fact that she *wasn't* going to be his hostess tonight, that she *wasn't* the only young socialite of looks and means invited (which made sense, as there were over five hundred of New York's finest invited, but anyway) and that there was still no ring at all to be seen on Miss Force's left hand, not even a speck of one, after seven months of trying.

Implied, if not yet directly printed: What a dear girl she was; what a solid, faithful girl, the kind that one might suppose may be always counted upon to be waiting in the wings. How very different this girl was from Mrs. Ava Astor, so divinely gifted and charming, who'd never had any problem obtaining whatever she desired, even a divorce.

The colonel's dinner party and cotillion tonight was predicted to be the spectacle of the season. Or perhaps, Madeleine mused, *she* was going to be the spectacle, the Girl Who Clung to Hope.

The auto smacked into another pothole. She swallowed hard, wishing for water—no, wishing for wine, for whiskey (which she'd only ever tried once, on a dare in school; it had been like drinking fire), because even false courage was courage of some sort.

She had been seen at Jack's side for all this while, all these months, over and over. Restaurants, theaters. His box at the

Metropolitan Opera House, number seven (*Lucky number seven,* she'd said, and he'd smiled and replied, *It seems so now*) in the famed golden horseshoe. The Christmas Ball.

The word was out—according to these anonymous writers, penning their poison columns from their grimy little desks, in their grimy little newspaper offices—that tonight would surely be the night that Colonel Astor would announce his engagement to the adolescent Miss Force. That it had to be tonight or never, because how cruel would it be otherwise, as he was having over two hundred for dinner and another three hundred more for the dancing to follow, and every lion of society would surely turn up to hear the news?

Except, of course, as both Madeleine and Jack (and definitely Mother) knew, there would be no announcement of their engagement, since there had been no proposal. Not yet.

She didn't want to care so much about it. It was foolish to care so much. Why did it matter what a bunch of muckrakers printed?

But oh, the idea that he was only toying with her, that he might not ever ask . . .

She'd constructed sandcastles of reveries around him, his lucid eyes and his lined face and his tanned, competent charm. She dreamed of him: the hook of his nose; the way his hair gleamed honey in the open sunlight and his irises took on a cast of faraway blue, but his moustache always stayed the same brown; how when he walked, he squared his shoulders and jabbed the ground with his stick, as if the *tap-tap* of his pace should be heard and marked by all, men and beasts and even the tiny insects sleeping beneath the sidewalks.

She'd let him kiss her practically in public and had felt herself floating like a lark in his arms.

Color and shade rippled past the motorcar. As they ventured farther up Fifth Avenue, the mansions grew taller, more stately, sketched in bold layers of snow. Row after row of gabled and copper-roofed palaces sprouted from the plain pavements and dirt, blotting out the sun, the moon, the sky.

At the age of eight, Madeleine had voyaged to France for the first time with her family. After a week submerged in the delirium of Paris—and over her mother's protests—they'd removed to a vineyard so ancient and idyllic that the ground had melted up all around it, submerging the river-rock base of the crush house, the thick weedy bottoms of the vines, their stalks and stakes. The rich black soil was soft and sucking with Madeleine's every step, pulling at the soles of her boots. All the wild trees leaned, branches akimbo, toward that living dark earth. Everywhere she roamed that summer, the vineyard had seemed to whisper, *I am older than ages. You are a spark of nothing compared to me.*

Manhattan's Millionaires' Row was man's rebuttal to that vineyard's earthen grace. Warlike, glorious, every inch of the chiseled marble and limestone and wrought iron was hard and unyielding. The soil here would never rise. Nature would never regain the ground it had conceded.

"One more block," Katherine said, and Madeleine took a steadying breath.

"Do I look all right?"

Katherine smiled, lifting a hand to adjust one of the diamond-and-topaz clips nestled in her sister's hair. There were three of them, two smalls and a medium, fashioned as shooting stars. Her Christmas present from Jack.

(She had gotten him a cigar cutter fob, gold to match his watch, with her initials engraved on the back. He'd worn it every day since.)

"Better than all right," Katherine said. "You're luminous. Utterly prepared to illume."

The Astor chateau spread its massive shadow along the street; the automobile began to slow. A line of motorcars idled in front of the mansion, and a handful of pressmen huddled along the sidewalks, long-coated figures powdered with snow, hats and umbrellas turning white. The nearest one noticed the Forces and his camera jerked upward, and then they all did, one after another, as though linked by a puppeteer's string.

Their limousine came to a stop, still seven cars away from the main doors.

"We're sitting ducks out here," said Katherine.

Mother leaned forward. "You're right. Let's get out now, before they surround us entirely."

A pair of footmen had noticed them, as well, trotting up to the automobile's doors.

"You are a queen," Mother said to Madeleine quickly, in those last few moments. "Head high. Show them all you belong here."

Swathed in ermine, Mrs. Force stepped out of the limousine.

Katherine gave Madeleine a wicked smile, then followed. There was a sporadic dazzle of lights, but most of the flashes, Madeleine knew by now, were going to be aimed at her.

She gathered her skirts. She slid across the squabs and raised her right hand to the footman awaiting her, exiting the auto in a slither of mink and ice-blue brocade, trying to show as little ankle as possible.

The flash-powder explosions began, hot lights surrounding her, men shouting her name.

"Miss Force! Look this way, please!"

"Miss Force! Over here!"

She kept her gaze cast down, focusing on her feet, the slippery folds of her gown. The wet gray slush of the pavement.

Think of Jack.

The footman released her hand, keeping an umbrella positioned above her head.

"Miss Force! Did you help plan the menu?"

"How many dances will you share with the colonel?"

"Any surprises in store for this evening?"

She had to look up to orient herself, to make certain she was heading for the *porte cochère*. It was a mistake. Within seconds, she was blinded, and the only thing to do then was to pause and wipe all expression from her face until her vision cleared.

"Miss?" It was the footman, paused with her but politely concerned, and Madeleine gave a nod and moved forward again, this time with a serene, slim smile, as if she'd meant all along to let them fix her there, frozen as a deer in the road.

"Miss Force! Miss Force!"

And then she was past the open doors, past the inner bronze entrance gates and into the glass-domed hall, her heels striking wood and stone instead of concrete. The air swept by her more temperate, and the snow disappeared, and she did not have to picture Jack any longer because he was there before her, smiling at her, taking up both of her hands in his own.

"Madeleine," he greeted her, his tone low and intimate. He bent his head to place a kiss upon her knuckles. She felt the warmth of his breath through her gloves.

In that moment, it was all of it, every bit of it, worth it.

Did you help plan the menu?

No. Wives planned menus. Or, in this case, personal secretaries.

How many dances will you share with the colonel?

Any of them, all of them. As many as he wished.

Any surprises in store for this evening?

Only Jack himself knew the answer to that.

The portrait of Mrs. William Backhouse Astor, Junior—Lina, *the* Mrs. Astor—hung with frigid magnificence upon a buff-plastered wall of the Fifth Avenue residence. It dominated the reception room, looming larger than any of the other masterpieces arranged nearby. It had been done by Carolus-Duran during the acme of Mrs. Astor's tight-lipped beauty; her painted flesh gleamed like the pearls around her neck against the russet background and the black satin of her gown.

Beneath the portrait was a leopard-skin rug, one upon which the living Mrs. Astor used to stand to greet her guests, so that anyone fortunate enough to have gained entrance into these hallowed halls would be presented with the delight of double Mrs. Astors, both smiling grimly in welcome.

Madeleine took careful note of that painted smile, along with the pearls and the diamond-decorated fan and the impressive ruby so discreetly, yet openly, displayed upon the ring finger of Mrs. Astor's bare left hand.

Behind her, the Knickerbocker guests of Lina's Knickerbocker son drained cocktails and conversed as they waited for the dinner to begin. Bankers, Wall Street speculators, railroad barons, timber barons, plantation owners; potent, important men with interests in tobacco and politics and steel . . . and all their stiff-backed wives, all very much the age of her mother. The nape of Madeleine's neck crawled with their attention.

They'd swiveled and smiled at her as she'd entered the chamber on Jack's arm. Smiled with such pleasantly blank expressions, and took her hand and looked her not quite in the eyes, and the whole time Madeleine had marveled, *I thought they'd be more terrifying.*

But then Mrs. James Cardeza was in front of her, Charlotte Cardeza, that war dragon, who regarded first the colonel and then her with that same bland, genial air, and Madeleine came back to herself with a start.

She thought, *Are they* all *pretending?*

All those tittering scandal sheets were still being read. Madeleine's lack, the scant merits of her blood, her family's fortune, were still being weighed against theirs. Even Jack couldn't protect her from that.

Katherine approached, carrying two coupes brimming with champagne.

"Those sleeves," Madeleine murmured, without turning from the painting.

"That *expression*," Katherine murmured back, handing her one of the etched crystal coupes, spilling a little on her glove. She lifted her glass in mock salute. "She looks as though she feasts upon orphaned children gone astray in the woods."

"Hush! Everyone will hear you."

"Never fear. I shall spend the evening as orthodox as a nun."

"That would be a first. How much champagne have you had?"

"Honestly? Not nearly enough."

Night had fallen, and it was still snowing outside, stronger now, thick and fast, cushioning all the outside sounds. The windows shone sable with curling fringes of frost, and all up and down the chamber shadows clung to the floor and ceiling and furniture and walls, a slightly milder sort of black than the black outside, sliced with patches of light.

Jack's Manhattan residence was made of stone. Beneath the caramel oak woodwork, beneath the many rugs of wool and silk and royal tiger and polar bear, beneath the towering marble columns and archways and imported Italian tiles, was stacked block after block of sober hard stone. So with the snow keeping outside noises outside, and the stone trapping inside noises inside, everything in the chamber echoed, amplified, voices and footsteps and breathing; the splashing of the water in the fountain out in the entrance hall; laughter and veiled looks and the smell of floor polish and beeswax.

Gray, antique tapestries undulated with the draft against the walls, labored and slow, like the respiration of old elephants, but even those didn't dampen the sound.

It was a concert hall of a house, a colossus twisting of a house, crammed with rare and beautiful things yet at the same time composed mostly of hollow air, of wraiths. It seemed impossible that anyone with a pulse could actually reside here, much less thrive.

She had dined at the Fifth Avenue mansion exactly three times before—informal dinners, family dinners, nothing like tonight—and on each occasion, she'd sensed how very easy it would be to be pulled apart by the history and expectations of this place. The life she would be required to live just to survive here.

Mrs. William Backhouse Astor, Junior, had designed the whole of her home to ensure that everyone but herself was made small in its rooms. And right now, Madeleine definitely felt small.

She should turn around. She should mix with the other guests.

She should confront their stares and tilt her head and smile, as grim and unapproachable as the famed woman in the painting.

"I only wish it was over already," she said under her breath.

Katherine opened her fan, hiding the lower half of her face behind a spread of feathers as she drained the last of her champagne. "Who knows? Tonight may be the night he musters his nerve."

"May," Madeleine said.

"May," her sister concurred, matter-of-fact. "But either way, you'd better buck up. Even in the midst of clouds and doom, we must remain sunny. Mother will wring our necks otherwise." She snapped her fan closed. *"Sunny,"* she hissed. And then, much louder: "Excuse me. I see Mother conversing with the Pulitzers, signaling me with her eyebrows that I need to come over."

And, fan and coupe and all, she was gone.

Jack came near. The volume of conversation in the room dipped considerably before picking back up again. Madeleine sent him a brief, welcoming glance, then returned her gaze to the portrait. She deliberately avoided looking at the ruby ring.

He said, "She would have been fond of you, I think."

Madeleine couldn't help it; she allowed herself a dubious pursing of her lips.

He noticed. "No, sincerely. She was formidable in her way, of course, but also fair. She valued virtue. Goodness."

She thought of the stories she'd heard—of débutantes melting into tears at Lina's smiling insults, of grown women fleeing town in shame over her snubs—and bit her tongue. From the corner of her eye, she could see Jack rotating the signet ring on his pinkie, almost fretful, and wondered that such a man could have been carved from the flesh of a woman like that.

His nails were short and glossy, evenly filed. She liked the shape of his hands, the blue tracing of veins just visible beneath his skin. She liked the *experienced* look of those hands. Here was someone, surely, who could teach her how to banish whatever specters haunted these halls.

Madeleine said, "Your mother was a remarkable woman. I'm sorry we never met."

"Yes. Yes, so am I."

But he sounded distracted. It gave her the nerve to face him, angling herself so that the light from the candelabra nearby fell full upon her features. With her face upturned and the diamond stars in her hair, the blue of the gown that matched her eyes and set off the cream of her cheeks, she knew how she looked. She *should* know; she'd planned it down to the last detail.

That was the sum and skill of her life now, it seemed. How to make herself alluring to this magnetic, just-out-of-reach man.

His brows drew downward, his lashes lowering. He seemed almost pained.

She remembered their kiss, their only one. His lips had been silky soft, his moustache scratchy. He'd tasted of mint and cigar and everything forbidden and unknown that she longed to explore, to sink her teeth and fingers and soul into. She'd felt herself expand with his kiss, her spirit swell and spill out of her like Katherine's champagne overflowing from its shallow glass, and she couldn't imagine that he looked at her without remembering it, too. Without craving more, as she did.

Without *dreaming* of more, as she did, waking up sweaty and breathless in the middle of the night.

Jack turned away from her, just enough to break their connection.

"Those ink-stained villains out there," he said now, shaking his head. "I'm sorry about that. I can keep them off the property itself, but they've got free rein of the sidewalks and streets."

"I know. It's all right."

"I despise how they harass you. I despise that it's because of me."

"Really. It's all right." She tried a smile. "I'm following the patented Astor method for dealing with them, you know. I won't break."

He exhaled, slow, quiet, beneath the ebb and swell of chatter filling the chamber.

Now, she thought. *Ask me now.*

Maybe he read her mind; maybe he only read her hope. When he spoke again, he sounded almost weary.

"You're seventeen still, Madeleine. You're so young."

A surge of anger flooded through her, but she kept her tone carefully neutral. "So everyone keeps telling me. *Young* is not an unpardonable offense. *Young* does not mean I cannot make rational decisions, or abide by them."

Her ire had revealed itself, after all. They gazed at each other in surprise.

"I beg your pardon," Madeleine said. "I am young, I suppose, but I don't feel especially young inside."

"That's curious," he said somberly, "because people call me old, you know." His lips twitched. "At least, they do behind my back. But when I'm with you, I don't feel especially old."

As quickly as it had washed over her, her anger evaporated. "Then we're a pair, I guess."

"I guess we are."

With Lina looking coldly on, Jack took a step toward her, reached for her hand, and she let him, unmoving, barely breathing, feeling the scrutiny of two hundred of New York's elite gather and center on them both.

"It's going to be this way, you know. Forever and a day, we'll be watched and followed, studied and analyzed. I fear you'll know no peace with me."

"Peace," she scoffed, light—but her heart was pounding, fierce and strong. "What a tedious notion. Who requires peace, when one may have Colonel Jack Astor?"

He smiled at her, the corners of his eyes crinkling in that way she admired. And then, even though everyone around them was now blatantly watching, he touched her on the shoulder, running his hand down the cap of her sleeve, lingering on the exposed skin of her arm just above her glove. He did not look up into her eyes again, but kept his attention fixed there—his hand, her arm, the satin of her glove. The skin of his palm burned against her.

His next words were spoken so softly she had to strain to hear him.

"I'll talk to your father tomorrow."

"Good," Madeleine said, and meant it.

CHAPTER 9

We kept our engagement private. It was important to your father that it not be publicly announced until after I turned eighteen, which by then was only four months away.

Four eternal months.

I understood his reticence, I did, but the burden of holding that secret inside me was like enduring a lump of hot lava burning behind my breastbone every day and night. My parents knew, naturally, and there was never any hope of hiding it from your Aunt Katherine. But your father didn't even tell Vincent, not for the longest while, for fear it might end up reaching the ears of his former wife. And I know he definitely didn't mention it to anyone else, because believe me, if he had, the papers would have exploded with the news.

As, of course, they eventually did.

July 1911
Newport, Rhode Island

Accounts of that February night had trickled out to the tabloids in dribs and drabs, but as there was no announcement from Colonel Astor regarding a betrothal, it wasn't the juiciest of tales. Just the usual tattle, who had attended, what they ate, what they wore, how expensive were the favors. Most of the press still took care to refer to Madeleine as *fair*, or *accomplished*, or (especially) *youthful*.

A handful were starting to call her *determined. Ambitious.*

She wondered if they weren't running out of even remotely polite adjectives. If they might not soon move on to *oblivious*, or *obstinate*, or *desperate.*

The Forces still summered at Bar Harbor, at least officially. The house was opened, aired, and occasionally they *did* stay there, a few weeks at a time. Jack would come to visit on the *Noma*, living aboard the yacht instead of leasing another cottage, and whenever he was in town, they would carry on as they had the summer before, tennis at the Swimming Club, picnics, dances at the Malvern or the Casino. But Madeleine (always accompanied by at least Mother or Father or both; appearances were strictly maintained) began to slip away, more and more, to Newport with him.

To Beechwood, Jack's red-brick mansion overlooking the sea.

Lina Astor's hand was visible there, as well. She had not commissioned the original cottage but she had erased the soul of it, that blocky, commonsense New England retreat, and subsequently replaced it with a fairy-tale translation: cream-and-butter chambers of rococo gilt filigree and larger-than-life mirrors, floors so thickly varnished it was as if one walked on water. Crystal chandeliers with curling branches and beads that dangled from the ceilings like prismatic, upside-down flowers. Frescoes of Poseidon brandishing his trident, bare-breasted Nereids, mythical creatures frolicking in waves. Marble statues posed in nooks. Palm trees grew in Satsuma pots, their fronds sharp as knives against the turquoise view.

Everywhere Madeleine looked was some fresh wonder, some astonishing new sight to take in. Beechwood was a waking dream, one that she wafted through in these warm summer days with her eyes wide open and her heart bursting full.

She took breakfast on the pillared back patio whenever she

could, to let the sun and sea tease her with the promise of the day to come. The painted iron benches and chairs were not as comfortable as the furniture inside, even with cushions, and her hair always ended up tearing loose, but that was fine. It was worth it to watch the waves fold into their long, slippery lines in the distance, and to listen to the wind clatter through the copper beeches, and to drink coffee that was never allowed to grow cold.

A ginger tabby was slinking its way across the lawn, intent on the bed of hydrangeas that traced the border of the patio. Madeleine took a bite of toast and watched it creep toward the plants, fragrant globes of azure and amethyst, the tip of its tail twitching.

She hoped there wasn't a bird in there. She hoped the cat hunted only shadows.

Footsteps clipped behind her, too firm and fast to belong to the footman keeping an eye on her meal.

Vincent emerged from the house, pausing near the open doors to eye her up and down. He hadn't slept at the cottage last night, so he must have only just arrived, still dressed in his traveling suit and a rumpled maroon necktie.

"Oh," he said, unenthusiastic. "Miss Force. You're here. Again."

"I am." She took a sip of coffee, her demeanor as bland as those Knickerbockers back in Jack's New York reception room. "If you're looking for your father, he's gone into town for a while. He said he'd be back in a few hours."

"All right." Vincent noticed the cat, still hunting, and for about half a minute they watched it together, a pocket-sized tiger stealing closer to the mass of swaying flowers. A trio of sailboats crossed the waters beyond it, triangles of white slicing lazily through the blue.

There *was* a bird, Madeleine realized, squinting. A bird or a leaf shaped like a bird, a smudge of brown amid the branches.

She placed her napkin on the table, tucking a corner beneath her plate so it wouldn't blow away, prepared to intervene.

"Only a few years past," Vincent said quietly, "my grandmother wouldn't have even acknowledged your existence. And why should she? She'd be rolling in her grave if she knew you were here now."

The blood drained from her cheeks. She managed to pick up her cup again without spilling it, forming her reply just above the rim. "How fortunate for me, then, that we live today, when your grandmother is gone, and her son finds me wholly acknowledgeable."

"It's laughable that you think you're on par with us. With my mother. Believe me, you're just another girl to him, and he's had a great many girls."

The coffee went sour on her tongue, but she remained so bland, so brutally neutral. "But they're not around anymore, are they?" She turned in her chair and looked up at him, dark and sneering, a patch of stubble on his chin that he'd missed on his morning shave, whenever that had been. He'd nicked his neck, too, right above his winged collar. A rusty red stain blossomed down from the brim.

"Exactly my point. They didn't last, and neither will you. You're cheap tinsel, Miss Force, and tinsel always tarnishes."

Madeleine pushed out of the chair, moving to face him. The wind lashed by, and the edges of her napkin fluttered, and her lips curved into a smile that was not a smile. "We'll just have to see what happens then, won't we?"

"Mr. Vincent Astor! What a happy surprise! Whenever did you get in?"

It was Mother, chirpy, walking out to the patio in a rustle of steel organza and a chilly gaze.

Vincent gave Mother a curt nod. "Mrs. Force. Excuse me, I must get on."

Some demon made Madeleine call out to his retreating back, "So pleasant to chat with you again, Mr. Astor."

Mother took a seat at the wrought-iron table, smoothing her skirts. She accepted the cup of coffee Madeleine poured for her, adding cream and a measure of sugar so meager that Madeleine always wondered why she bothered with it at all. The silver spoon clinked, clinked against the china as she stirred, a little harder, Madeleine thought, than she usually did.

"It won't do you any good to antagonize him."

Madeleine plopped back into her chair. "As my very being seems to antagonize him, I don't see what difference it makes."

"Pouring salt over the wound, my dear." Mother finally stopped stirring. "I have heard, from various sources, that the consequences of divorce can be even more devastating for the children than for the parents themselves." She gazed out at the sailboats, still making their way along. "As difficult as that may be to believe."

It was the first time Madeleine had ever heard her mother say the word *divorce*.

"So, I should just ignore Vincent's jibes? Offer him kindness for rudeness, all because his parents didn't get along, even though I had nothing to do with it?"

"Offer him compassion," Mother said, "even though you had nothing to do with it."

Madeleine huffed a sigh, thrust out of the chair again to check on the cat. It had vanished entirely, not a hint of tiger stripes crouched anywhere beneath the hydrangeas that she could see.

"I would not want the world to be cruel to you because of anything your father or I had done. I would not want you to suffer for our transgressions, be they real or imagined. For the past few years, that boy has endured a very public humiliation, one that should have been very much private. On top of that, you and he are of the same age, and now you're going to be his stepmother. Think on it. On how difficult the mere possibility of that must be for him."

"It really has nothing to do with him."

"From his perspective, it has everything to do with him. How could it not? His family, the foundation of his life, has been rent. And it is about to be transformed yet again."

Madeleine shoved her hair from her eyes. "What of Jack? Or

even Ava? Don't we all deserve a chance at happiness, no matter the mistakes made before?"

"A question for the ages, I think. Oh, I *do* want you to be happy, Maddy. I want you to enjoy fine health, a good marriage, a safe home. A superior man for your husband and gay children of your own. And you have those things now, or soon will, which—" She paused; for an instant, Madeleine caught a hint of her fragrance, delicate vanilla, before the breeze stole it away again. "Sometimes I wake up at night and think it's all just a fantasy, a reverie in my head I invented for you, drawn from the depths of my fears. All my fears. My terrible nerves. I swear to you, when I awaken like that, it leaves me shaking."

"No," Madeleine murmured, and found her hand.

"I would not have the world be cruel to you," she emphasized. "I would not have Vincent Astor be cruel to you. But if—when— those things happen, I would not have you be cruel in return. Kinder hearts are stronger, I think."

She squeezed her daughter's fingers and pulled her hand free; they sat without speaking. Madeleine pushed at her loosened hair again; no matter how many hairpins she added, none held up for long out here. She buttered another slice of toast, added jam— a dense, tangy apricot—then placed it on her mother's plate.

A hummingbird darted up to them, examined the red-painted anemone on the glazed coffeepot. Flew off.

"Do you think it's true?" she asked finally, concentrating on the toast. "That he's had a great many girls?"

Mother frowned. "I think you shouldn't listen to bitter young men who try to stir up trouble just because they can. Colonel Astor will always be the flame that captures the fascination of *all* the moths, of *all* sorts. He was born to be both famous and infamous, poor creature, and those are facts he will never be able to escape, try as he might."

Poor creature. Her mother might be the only person on earth to look upon John Jacob Astor with pity.

"But, Maddy, here is something that I do not think, but that

I *know*. In all my life, I've never seen a man look at a woman the way he looks at you."

Madeleine stilled.

"Such devotion. Such—*relief*, I would say. As if you are his own secret sun, warming his innermost soul."

Madeleine dabbed a clot of jam onto her plate, smearing it around in slow circles with the bowl of the spoon even though she had no more toast. "I hope that's true. I want it to be true, so, so badly. There have been times I've thought—you know, like you—that maybe this is just a dream." She glanced up, worried. "How can it be real? How can *he* be real?"

Mother tilted her head, considering it. "Very well. If this is a dream, then I say let us allow it to *be* a dream, for as long as good dreams may ever last. A forever dream, filled with beauty and joy and light. Just like you, my sweet child."

The sun climbed higher. The sailboats slipped from view, and breakfast became crumbs. On their way back to their rooms, they passed the mirrored doors that led to the ballroom. Madeleine stopped, retraced her steps. She touched a hand to one of the latches; the door swung open on soundless hinges and she gazed inside, silent, drowning in the gold and cream and white of it all, the serene vista in the windows beyond that showed only more light, more ocean, more colors.

It was her favorite chamber in the Newport cottage, even more so than the guest bedroom she'd been given, which was lovely in aubergine and lilac, and fairy tale enough by itself.

Mother gestured toward the windows. "There is the colonel back from town, out there on the lawn. He's looking for you, I presume. Don't keep him waiting, love. Go on. Go be his sun."

Madeleine crossed the herringbone floor of the ballroom and opened another set of doors, the ones leading to the outside world, letting in the salt air with the light.

As if he'd expected her to emerge from the ballroom instead of anywhere else, Jack turned. Saw her there paused, framed in all that sunny rococo elegance. He did not smile at her. He only watched her come to him, her steps sinking one by one into the prickly lush grass.

The wind took her dress and molded it against her body, turning the chiffon tail of it into a primrose flag that snapped along behind her. Sheep Point Cove, indigo and foam, pitched ahead, the source of the wind and the salt, and when the last of her hairpins surrendered, she only let it happen, feeling the weight of her chignon give way, unscrolling down her spine. Feeling the freedom of that.

Since he didn't smile, neither did she, but only approached him like one of the painted nymphs in the ballroom, a mythical being unbound by rules.

This was, after all, still a dream.

When they were near enough to touch, she stopped, her hair blowing into heavy dark tangles between them. A bent hairpin tumbled to the grass.

"You've come undone," he said, still serious.

"So I have."

"It suits you."

"Does it?" She shook her head and lifted her arms to the sky, then let them fall again, her hands reaching for his.

Their fingers met, slipped together and then apart.

She took a step closer. Placed her palms upon his forearms.

"Did you have a fruitful trip into town?" she asked, and without answering he took her into his arms and kissed her, right there on the vast lawn that opened up to the cove with anyone in the world to see, the Vanderbilts in their mansion on one side, the Oelrichses on the other, and all the servants, and all the fishermen, and all the angels in heaven up above them.

Vincent, the dog, the cat.

Their second kiss.

From somewhere back inside the cottage, Kitty let out a piercing bark.

He put her away from him almost hastily, and the look on his face let her know she was no longer trapped in a dream: he looked baffled and hungry, his breath tugging uneven. Just like hers.

He smoothed a hand along his hair—also windblown—and then his moustache. There was a hint of color staining his cheekbones that wasn't there before.

"I've brought you something. I hope you like it."

She said nothing, still ragged around her edges, uncertain of her voice.

Jack unbuttoned his jacket and reached inside, pulling out a small black leather box stamped with silver. He gazed down at it a moment, a line between his brows, then handed it to her.

"I thought—something simple. Sophisticated. Peerless, like you."

She accepted the box, opened the lid.

It was a ring, a white oval diamond the size of a filbert catching the sun, instantly smarting her eyesight. She had to look away from it to see clearly again, just as she did for the camera flash explosions that followed her now.

He waited. She blinked a few times, loosened the band from the slot that kept it fixed in place.

"Would you put it on my finger, please?"

He took it from her, the platinum band bright, the diamond utterly blinding, and Madeleine lifted her left hand and opened her fingers. The metal pushed cool against her knuckle, smooth and heavier than she'd expected.

"There were others," he said, hesitant. "I know the fashion now is nothing so plain. I could exchange it for something more embellished. Or a ruby, if you like. An emerald. Perhaps a diamond stack—"

"No," she said. "This is the one. This one is mine."

She held out her hand between them and they admired it together, rainbow fire and white sparks dancing along her dress and skin.

The hummingbird darted by again, a jeweled trilling song traced across the sky.

Someone let Kitty out of the cottage. She bounded across the lawn in enormous loping strides, barreling toward them with her tongue flipped sideways and her paws a blur.

Madeleine wore his ring to sleep. She could not wear it out in public yet—not yet—but she could do this, at least. All night long she felt the weight of it against her finger, a sensation both alien and comforting. Twice the prongs holding the diamond caught in the lace of her nightgown, and she'd rouse enough to free it, then sink back into her slumber.

When she awoke the next morning, her finger had swollen and she had to work to get the ring off, using cold water and lotion and soap. Even so, the red indent from the band remained crushed into her flesh, not fading until well after noon.

CHAPTER 10

Colonel J. J. Astor Seen About
—Special to *Town Topics*
July 30, 1911
Newport, Ri.

Colonel John Jacob Astor is busy this season at Beechwood. He has entertained frequently at his mother's summer home, with the finest of society's luminaries passing through his doors. But the young woman now most often in his company is still that fresh Force rose. She, along with, we fear, *La Force Majeure*, seem entirely unaware of their fine surroundings, so taken are they with the life of the *beau monde*. There is no better view, we've heard, than that to be had from the colonel's own backyard, where he and the eager Miss Force were recently witnessed having a *very* intimate *tête-à-tête*.

William Force telephoned the colonel the next morning.

By then, Madeleine and her mother had already returned to

their brownstone in New York, their planned visit to Newport concluded, so when the tabloid was published, the entire family, everyone, *everyone*, read it the same day it was being hawked by the scabby-kneed newsboys shouting from street corners.

Madeleine read it last, probably, because Katherine had tried to hide it from her, then, red-faced, had offered the paper over with a snap of her arm, looking as steely as Madeleine had ever seen her. Mother was out paying calls; Lord knew what she was hearing.

Angels and servants *had* witnessed the kiss, that deep and scandalous thing; they'd missed, however, the ring that had come just after it, the blinding white vindication decorating her left hand.

Madeleine discovered her father in his study, staring at the Hughes watercolor of a black-haired shepherdess standing atop a knoll, one he'd acquired even before marrying her mother (who had since expanded the collection into far weightier pieces). It had always been one of his favorites, and without even trying to summon the memory from her childhood, Madeleine could still hear him explaining to her why: *Acknowledge the lucidity of the air and the clouds. The play of shadows. The light behind her eyes. She is alive, isn't she, Maddy? Right there on the paper, behind the glass. Caught in this singular moment forever by a great man, she lives on just for us. Isn't that something?*

"Father."

"Madeleine." He turned his head and looked at her, still distracted. "My girl. You realize I have to act now."

"Yes. I don't think it will be a problem. For him, I mean."

"It had damn well better not be," he said bluntly, abruptly focused, and Madeleine crossed to him, sank to his feet as she'd used to do as a little girl, relying upon his strength and kindness and strong arms. She rested her cheek against his knee. A sunbeam was tracing its way across the hardwood floor, the worn Venetian red rug, splashing light against the far wall.

"Should I be there when you talk to him?"

"No," said Father. "This is a business I must manage alone."

* * *

There is the matter of a young lady's reputation, Father said into the telephone's mouthpiece. *There is the matter of offensive gossip. Innuendo.*

The household telephone was stationed prominently in the foyer, inside a small alcove (possibly meant for a bust) inset by the front door. The tiled floor and wainscoted corridor made it impossible to converse with any expectation of privacy. Every little sound carried.

The device itself had been installed three years previous, so Katherine and Madeleine already knew from experience how easy it was to overhear at least half of a conversation. They hovered together in the drawing room a few steps away, just out of view, right behind the cracked door. They held hands as Father spoke.

You understand, he said, *that I will act in my daughter's best interest. It is my unshakable obligation, one I must and shall fulfill. I will tell you quite frankly, sir, that I will no longer be put off. You have a daughter yourself. You must understand.*

A pause.

Excellent. It's good to hear you say so.

Pause.

No, I'll do it. I'll make the announcement from my office later today. It will be more appropriate, I think, coming from me, at my place of business. To lend it all a more . . . official air. The press will channel their attentions here, on all of us here as a family, rather than on any of your . . . other retreats.

Pause.

I shall tell them we have not yet decided the date. I'll keep it as vague as possible, while still making matters clear.

Pause.

We are agreed. I will inform Madeleine. Goodbye, Colonel Astor. I trust I will see you soon.

Pause.

If you insist. Jack. Goodbye, sir. Goodbye.

* * *

It seemed the gates of hell had swung open and disgorged a mass of tweed-jacketed men at their front steps. Madeleine stopped counting at thirty—thirty! in just the two hours since the announcement!—and stood on the other side of the door, caught between amazement and dismay. The incessant knocking had at least died down, as Matthews had sternly instructed the crowd that Miss Force was not at home at the moment, nor was she likely to be any time soon.

She felt flushed and hot and disconcerted. She looked at her mother, who looked back with an iron face and ordered the hall boy to stand guard at the top of the steps, a gangly child of no more than fourteen, perspiring and jittery and full of awe at his abruptly elevated position, instructing the rabble that they must *respect the house*; they must *stay back*.

It didn't deter them, though, those grown men out to hook this shiny fish of a story caught in their net. Neither did the sun, the lack of shade, the airless waves of heat shimmering off the pavements and buildings. August had arrived, gummy and funky with the rot of wilting garbage. It had been so long since Madeleine had spent a summer season anywhere but by the ocean. She'd forgotten how stifling the city could be.

Mother, attempting to take command of the situation at her door, had already sent the hall boy a glass of iced tea and issued a brief statement from the safety of the entranceway: Yes, her youngest was engaged to Colonel Astor as of a few days past. Yes, the two of them had first met in Bar Harbor a year ago. And yes, the wedding was likely to be small, quiet, and for close family only.

It wasn't enough. A couple of the journalists peeled away to file their reports, but a great mass of them remained, sweltering and determined to speak to Madeleine herself.

"I won't," she said now. "I don't want to. I don't know what more to say to them that you and Father haven't already said."

Mother settled into the appliqué chair by the telephone, cooling herself with a Chinese fan. Matthews approached with more iced tea. She accepted it with an eloquent, languid hand. "Just let them see you. Give them a smile. Tell them how happy you are."

"No. My happiness is none of their business. I have nothing to say to them."

"Madeleine—"

"They pick apart every little thing I do! If I smile at them, they call me insipid. If I don't smile, they call me aloof. Remember that article in the *Caller* last month? They said I was *brazen* just for waltzing with Jack twice at the Olyphant ball."

"Twice in a row," Katherine pointed out. "You harlot."

"Kat!" snapped Mother, then closed her eyes, holding the glass to her forehead. She sighed. "Dearest, try to remember what the colonel said. It's a stratagem of give and take with the press, so you must be prepared to give them something. Anything. They'll never decamp otherwise."

"I'll wait for Jack. He's coming by tonight, after all, and he can deal with them then. If I try to talk to them now, they'll just muddle me, and for what? All they do is print lies about me, anyway."

She heard how churlish she sounded even as she said it but she didn't care, because it was too hot, and everything smelled, and she was *right*. Her happiness belonged to her, to her and Jack, a sweet and fragile thing she wanted to nurture, to hold close, not turn into some cheap public display. Most frustrating of all, she didn't have better words than the ugly ones she'd already said; she had nothing more sensible or mature or articulate to offer beyond, *No, I won't, I won't, this fresh joy is all mine, and I won't let them take it from me.*

Mother lowered her glass of tea, shifting to sit upright. "Madeleine Talmage Force, this is your *job* now. It is a job for a woman, not a petulant child, and I trust you will remember that. I thought you understood these terms. I thought the colonel himself had made them clear. No doubt he'd say the same to you were he standing here right now, and may I say I am very glad that he isn't."

Madeleine dropped her eyes, shamed and angry, and angry

about being ashamed. Her mother rose from the chair, lifted her daughter's chin with the tip of the fan. She held her gaze a moment, searching, then gave a ghost of a smile.

"You can do this," she said, a gentle, forgiving tone: the tone of Madeleine's youth, of her many mistakes, of her mother's unshakable faith in her and the universe at large. "You know it, I know it, and certainly Colonel Astor knows it. Show those men out there that you are the lady of grace and poise they hope you will not prove to be."

Madeleine wet her dry lips, then nodded. She took the tea from her mother and sucked down a long, heavy swallow.

"Choose just one to talk to," suggested her sister, leaning against the cool plastered wall. "The tallest one, the handsomest one. The one closest to the urn of petunias. It doesn't matter which, I expect."

The knocker sounded again, three brisk raps. Matthews, already standing by, waited for Mother to nod her head, then opened the door a fraction.

"Ah," he said, and the door swung wider; outside shone ragged crowns of trees against a milky bleached sky. "A delivery of flowers, madam. For Miss Madeleine."

He accepted the box in his arms, turning to place it on the chair before moving to close the door again.

Madeleine spared the box a glance then stepped forward, lifting her hand—her left one, Jack's ring flashing—to stop him. Matthews looked once more at Mother, then at Madeleine, then bowed his head and moved aside.

Madeleine handed the tea back to her mother. She approached the doorway, the baking day. All the men below the steps, pink-faced and quiet, jostling closer at the sight of her.

Cameras began to lift.

One of the reporters broke apart from the others, climbing all the way up to the entranceway. Not the tallest, not the handsomest, but certainly the boldest.

The hall boy eyed him edgily.

"Miss Force, *Chicago Tribune*, how'd'you do. May I offer my congratulations on your engagement."

"Thank you."

"Would you care to make a statement?"

"I . . . I am greatly happy."

"Would you show us the ring, please," called out a man from the back. "May we see the engagement ring?"

It felt odd to simply hold her hand out to them, but she did, and the camera shutters began to snap and snap, a host of clicking insects.

"What did the colonel say when he gave it to you?" called out another fellow.

"It was a rather private moment," she said, but made herself smile.

"When will the wedding take place?"

"We have not decided yet. This fall, perhaps," she improvised. "Or later."

"Where will it be?" asked the man in front of her, scribbling quickly across a notepad. Sweat ran down his face, collected in drops beneath his chin. "Manhattan? Newport? Rhinebeck-on-the-Hudson?"

Madeleine laughed and shook her head. "I really don't know. It's all—honestly, it's all happened so quickly."

"Are those flowers from Colonel Astor?" He was peering past her, his eyes scanning the entrance hall.

Madeleine looked back at the box, long and white, precisely balanced across the kingwood arms of the chair. "I don't know. I haven't even opened it yet."

The reporter gave a scant smile. "It must be overwhelming. You're seventeen, aren't you, Miss Force?"

"Eighteen," she corrected him, her humor fading.

"Eighteen," he repeated, making a show of writing it down. "And tell me, do you feel confident stepping into the role the former Mrs. John Jacob Astor has left for you, as the leader of the society of Newport and New York?"

"Um, I hadn't really—"

"Do you think you can make good on her social record?" cut in another man, who had come to stand beside the first, pushing back his hat. "As Mrs. Astor the second?"

"I'm sure I will do my best," she said stiffly.

"So, in your opinion, divorcés should be allowed to wed again?"

"I beg your pardon?"

The Chicago man leaned closer, reeking of musk. "Isn't it true that the terms of the colonel's divorce stipulate that he cannot remarry during Mrs. Ava Astor's lifetime?"

"I don't have any idea what—"

"How does Colonel Astor plan to void that provision? Will he purchase a remedy to it somehow? With all his money, will he just buy his way out?"

Madeleine drew back. "Excuse me. The heat. I must return inside."

The front door was again shut. The reporters were (according to Katherine, stationed at the drawing room window) rapidly scurrying away.

"Like cockroaches," she called out cheerfully.

Madeleine untied the grosgrain bow atop the flower box, allowing the ribbon to fall aside. She lifted off the lid.

Inside were three dozen blood-red roses, American Beauties, long-stemmed and flawless.

Jack's card read:

> *For my own beauty. Thank you for being mine,*
> *today and forever to come.*

CHAPTER 11

∽✦───────✦∽

A Budding Social Queen?
—Special to *Town Topics*
August 1, 1911
Manhattan, Ny.

Col. J. J. Astor's fiancée, seventeen-year-old Miss Madeleine Force, is convinced she can reign over the cream of society as well as her illustrious predecessors, Mrs. John Jacob Astor the first and Mrs. William Backhouse Astor, esteemed mother of the colonel.

Standing on the steps of her family's modest brownstone and sporting a massive diamond engagement ring nearly too large for such a slender hand, Miss Force laughed away the thought that she might be too young, or too inexperienced, for the task. "I will do my best," she said breezily, "and certainly that will be enough!"

Miss Force also appeared untroubled by the suggestion that the colonel's previous divorce might cast an unsavory stain upon her upcoming union. "Nonsense! What's done is done, and all of that business is firmly in the past. I am greatly happy to be wedding the colonel now. We shall be married as soon as possible."

Miss Force has been described as a lithe horsewoman, an adequate pupil, and overall a handsome, jolly girl with an affinity for dancing and other sports. Fine qualities, certainly, for a future Queen of New York and Newport, but it is surely that rarefied society itself which will judge her fit or no.

Letters and cards began to arrive daily at her home address, which had been published too many times to count. At first it was only a few warm, congratulatory notes from family and friends.

In no time at all, however, it became a paper avalanche.

Miss Force,

Please excuse my presumption in writing you, as we have not met. I wish to congratulate you on your engagement to Colonel Astor. What gladdening news to read in these Troubled Times! Our Lord God has exalted you, among all women, with His Divine Favor. May your loins prove fertile, and may you have a long and satisfactory life together and be gifted with many sons. Best wishes.

Dear Miss Force,

My name is Ola Pounds, from Formoso, Kansas. I am writing to tell you what an inspiration you are to me and my bosom friends. We are all of us so happy that you are to marry Col. J. J. Astor. Would you please write me back, and thank you.

Miss Madaline T. Force,

Congratulations on your upcoming nuptials to Mr. John Jacob Astor the Fourth. Allow me the honor of introducing myself. I am the Rev. Scott V. Lurie, of the First Church of His Name in Reno, Nevada. A lady of your discriminating taste will no doubt be interested in our annual fundraiser . . .

Dearest Miss Force,

I am Winnie Yeats aged nine years of age and I wish to correspond with you because i admire you so. Please write me and tell me about you I wish to know every-thyng because you are pretty and my mother says you will be the wife of the President soon so that is important and i would like to be your friend.

Maddy,

How long has it been? I hope you can forgive my extended silence since our chummy days at Miss Spence's School. How tragic we've fallen out of touch! But no doubt you are a very busy bee! I've just returned from the most tremendous tour, Algiers, Marseilles, Monte Carlo, with my new husband, Claud. You remember Claud, I trust? I believe the three of us did bump into each other once or twice after graduation. It's the most terrific coincidence, but Claud also dabbles in hotels, just like your fiancé! Anyway, we would absolutely adore the chance to get together so we can tell you all about our trip. Do let me know when you and Colonel Astor might be free . . .

CHAPTER 12

※

Planning a wedding, even a simple one, takes time. Both your father and I were keen to proceed, but there were so many details to consider. Even with the masterly duo of Mr. Dobbyn and my mother helming the thing, matters seemed to be crawling along.

The thorniest problem to resolve (and really, the only complication that truly irritated Jack) was the difficulty finding a rector willing to preside over our union. The divorce had been *that* tricky and not even two years done. Episcopalian nerves were soundly rattled.

Clergyman after clergyman refused to wed us—and then flocked to the press to smugly explain why:

Divorce was reprehensible.

Remarriage after divorce was reprehensible.

Colonel Astor was reprehensible.

Miss Force was . . .

And on it went.

In the meanwhile, conjecture about the wedding date, the location, or anything at all to do with the ceremony, consumed the masses. Newspapers speculated about what I would wear, the color of my bouquet, who would be invited, what manner of exquisite foods would be served at the meal after. Yet for every inch of column space rapturously dedicated to the bride-elect or the service, there would immediately follow some dour, dire write-up by A Person of Virtue denouncing me, my parents, my education, your father, the entire world itself as corrupt and beyond redemption.

It was ghastly.

Within days, it became impossible to step foot out of my house without being followed and badgered. Everywhere I went, I dragged with me an unwelcome entourage. Your father took to bringing Kitty with him whenever he came to call, perhaps to act as a buffer between Us and Them (although, to be honest, Kitty was such an affable soul that she never managed to rebuff much).

Kitty, in fact, became one of the photographers' favorite subjects, maybe because all decent people love dogs, and it truly seemed like she was nearly always smiling. Even when I would toss away the articles about me, I would save the clippings that featured her, usually captured in some pose close to your father's side, walking or sitting or gazing up at him with worshipful eyes.

Those clippings must still be around here somewhere. I left them behind when we departed for Europe, but surely someone packed them away for me. I must remember to look for them so you can see for yourself how devoted she

When the lack of privacy became crushing, the only solution was to flee. Since both the Fifth Avenue mansion and my own home on East 37th were so plainly situated in the public right of way, the newsmen simply waited to ambush us, following us every step of the way wherever we went.

So we began taking the *Noma* to Beechwood more and more, or else to Ferncliff Farm in Rhinebeck, with its hundreds of protected acres of meadows and forest. Or we'd simply seclude ourselves on-board, Jack and I—as well as my parents, and sometimes Katherine, too—and just sail and sail wherever we wanted to go. No journalists, no photographers, no one to gape. Only us, the crew (who were far too well-paid to gape). The glory of all that deep open cobalt surrounding us, endless.

We ate and drank and laughed and caught what must have been bushels of fish. My hair became licked with mahogany; my skin began to turn brown.

Back then, the ocean was a friend. Back then, being out at sea felt like freedom.

So many precious days and nights your father and I spent tossed about the waves together, both before the wedding and after. How strange it seems now that I never had any sense of what was to come.

August 1911
At Sea

"Madeleine. Wake up."

"Father?"

The night had been rough. The *Noma* had been weathering a bruising purple gale for hours on her way from New York to Newport. Even as the yacht bucked and tossed, Captain Roberts had assured Jack and everyone else that there was nothing to worry about, that it was more a windy wet storm than a proper squall, and the *Noma*, so sleek and sturdy, was more than enough of a ship to handle it.

The captain had actually winked at Madeleine as he'd added that last bit. *Winked.* It was so patronizing and out of character that her anxiety instantly increased.

After a dinner of swordfish and salad, she'd retired to her cabin with her stomach pitching; she fell asleep at last with her fingers knotted in the sheets. Even so, she had dreamt of the storm, of being thrown from her feet with black heaving waves washing high over her, over the deck of the yacht, over Jack and Father and everything. She heard teakwood cracking apart, brass fittings and rails twisting and groaning. The smokestacks collapsing, gurgling with water. The wind, screaming and screaming, the *Noma* ripping into pieces, and still she couldn't get to her feet, she couldn't fight the greedy cold ocean—

It had been real enough that when her name was spoken above her head, she snapped awake at once, sick with certainty that they were all about to drown.

"Maddy, get dressed. Come up to the deck."

"Is it the storm?" she gasped, sitting up, grabbing her father's hand. She'd left a single electric sconce glowing on the far wall, just in case.

"The gale's blown south, and we're not in danger, but there's trouble afoot. Another boat, nearly gone over."

She realized the yacht was no longer rocking quite so wildly, and the noise of the engines had fallen to a low, rumbling hum. Water slapped the topsides; footsteps—many footsteps—thumped back and forth along the deck. Rising thinly above it all was the harsh, uneven clanging of a bell.

She flung back the covers. Father went to the door.

"We're in the midst of a rescue. The colonel thought you might like to see."

The *Zingara* had floundered, her sails shredded by the storm. The sloop had nearly capsized, her hold filling with water from the powerful black waves (*so much like her nightmare, so very much*) surging over the wreckage and the five men clinging to the debris. From Madeleine's vantage up on the bridge, the men looked anemic, slight as paper cutouts, turning their faces away in misery from the searchlight aimed at them from the *Noma*.

"Are they okay?" Madeleine asked, tugging her polo coat tighter around her chest. Jack rubbed a hand up and down her back, peaceful, unhurried strokes. She found herself leaning against him and he took her weight readily, not even shifting on his feet.

Kitty paced uneasy circles around them both, her nails *tick-tick*ing against the wood.

"Roberts will get them aboard, if anyone can. He's the best there is. Don't fret."

"What luck to have come across them at all," Father said.

They watched as the *Noma*'s lifeboat was lowered, slowly and smoothly, down to the water by the crew.

"Ahoy there!" called out an oarsman to the listing sloop.

"Ahoy," came the response, much weaker.

"Blind luck," Jack said. "They should count their blessings the gale cleared out when it did, and we came this way. On a night like this, we might just as easily have passed them by. They saw our lights, and Roberts heard them calling, if you can believe it. That was all that saved them. They didn't even shoot flares."

The lifeboat maneuvered through the crests and troughs of the waves, a misty smudge shaped like an almond, pale against the dark.

"Will we tow the wreck?" asked Father.

"I doubt it, although it's up to the captain, of course. She looks too far gone. We'll probably just wire her position back to shore and hope for the best."

"How long do you think they've been stranded out there?" Madeleine asked.

His hand still at her back, Jack peered up at the inky vault of the sky. At the stars burning above them, diamond chips scattered in ribbons in the aftermath of the storm. "It's after midnight. Hours, I'd say. Three or four. Must have seemed like an eternity to those wretched souls."

Madeleine remembered her nightmare. The icy, suffocating pressure of salt water slamming over her, filling her lungs.

"How cold is the water?"

He looked down at her, his expression guarded; she had the sense he was trying to read her face, to gauge the level of her distress.

"Honestly," she insisted. "How cold? Might they be in shock?"

"They might," he said slowly. "It's the middle of the summer, but it's still the Atlantic. This far north, the water never truly warms."

She tucked her hair behind her ears. She'd only had time for a swift, loose braid that hung in a rope down her back, and it was already unraveling. "I've read about maritime rescues, but I've never seen anything like this. I've never even thought . . . I'll go below to see about coffee for them. Some food and blankets."

Jack looked at her sideways; she had the swift and unpleasant realization that this was not her yacht, not yet, nor was the food hers to offer, or the blankets.

"Would that be all right?" she asked, uneasy. "I only want to help."

"Sweet girl," said the colonel, breaking into a smile. "That would be a godsend, I am sure. But those pitiful men will think they've drowned and ascended to heaven after all when they encounter the indomitable Madeleine Force serving them hot coffee."

She was becoming better at the cotillions, the dinners, the teas. She was becoming better at meeting coolness with coolness, with artificial smiles and softly spoken barbs. The Newport crowd loved to talk, it seemed, and they especially loved to talk about the colonel.

What they loved about Madeleine was to dissect her. They did it from a distance; they did it to her face; and when she and Jack turned a corner along a scrupulously swept sidewalk on their way to luncheon at the Muenchinger-King Hotel, Madeleine could only brace herself as an auburn-haired matron in slate silk and feathers strode toward them, lifting her hand in greeting.

"Jack," called the woman, in a clear and carrying voice.

"Margaret."

The three of them came to a halt, facing each other. Jack tipped his boater. Madeleine felt her fingers tightening on his arm—a nervous reaction, one she was starting to loathe about herself—and forced herself to unclench them.

The woman noticed, a quick indirect look (no flicker of expression to betray what she thought of that, of Madeleine's gleaming white knuckles) then returned her attention to the colonel.

"Dobbyn told me you were back in town," she said.

"*Dobbyn*," replied Jack with emphasis, "isn't supposed to talk, even to you."

"You're going to have to forgive him. I have such a sweet-talking way with men, I swear. He never knew what hit him."

The woman shifted her gaze to Madeleine. Before Jack could introduce them, she stuck out her hand. "You must be Miss Force. I've read all about you, I'm afraid." And she laughed, her onyx earbobs swaying.

"Oh," said Madeleine, uncertain, extending her own hand.

Unlike nearly every other Newport matron Madeleine had met, instead of looking wearily to the side of her, or icily straight through her, this woman's eyes bored into her own, greenish-gray and directly assessing. She had a strong face, not plain and not fair, exactly, but something of both, with even features and laugh lines around her mouth and very dark eyelashes. There was an air about her of barely repressed mirth, as if she knew some happy, hilarious secret she was determined to keep to herself.

The feathers of her hat drooped in graceful curves down to her chin. Madeleine resisted the urge to straighten her own hat, a simple French basket of navy-dyed straw; like everything else about her, it was the best she could do, even if it was not quite *right* enough for the Rhode Island set.

"You're far more beautiful than the papers give you credit for," said the woman in a pleasant tone; her handshake was forceful and brief. "But then, I never give the papers much credit to begin with."

"Madeleine," said Jack, also smiling. "May I introduce Mrs. J. J. Brown, an old summer friend."

"Margaret," the woman corrected him. "Please. I hope you don't mind if I call you Madeleine. I feel as though I know you already."

"Not at all. Um, Margaret."

"I read that you had quite an adventure the other night. A midnight rescue at sea! Is it true, Madeleine, that you helped lower the lifeboat yourself to help save those unfortunate sailors?"

"Oh," said Madeleine again. After months of serenely murmured slights (the lifted, plucked brows; the faux looks of concern; *my dear, are you really quite at ease here? Perhaps you'd feel better playing games with the children on the porch rather than trying to converse with us dreary old folks*), Margaret's open friendliness was rattling. "Hardly. I got them drinks, really. Some sandwiches."

"More than that," said Jack, covering her hand with his. "You were their beacon. They told me so themselves."

Madeleine shook her head, embarrassed. She'd wondered at the time if she *should* have done more. Once aboard the *Noma*, the rescued men had essentially shrunk into sodden, vacant-eyed hulks, even wrapped in blankets and fortified with steaming mugs of coffee (laced with brandy; Jack had poured it himself), their fingers brushing dead cold against hers. After that, both Jack and her father had assured her there was nothing more to be done. Everyone was safe, and they'd be back to shore by morning. She'd returned to her bed and tumbled into a dark, dreamless sleep.

Across the street, a fleshy man in a battered jacket had stopped to observe them, pulling a pad of paper from his breast pocket and a pencil from behind his ear.

"We're on our way to luncheon," Jack said now, nodding toward the hotel ahead, glass windows glinting, men and women ambling in and out of the main doors in crisp linen and gauze and more silk. "Might I tempt you into joining us?"

"Why," said Margaret Brown, "there is nothing I would enjoy more."

She sent Madeleine another smile—if there was any animosity behind it, Madeleine truly couldn't tell—and fell into step beside them. None of them looked at the man across the street.

As they approached the entrance, Margaret asked, "What were those fools doing out on a sloop in the middle of a gale, anyway?"

"Bankers," answered Jack, succinct, and Margaret laughed again as they walked inside.

CHAPTER 13

Your father wanted me to like Newport. Oh, he wanted me to love it as he did, and I swear to you, I did try. But it's difficult to love that which not only does not love you in return, but regards you with little more than thinly veiled contempt. For all of his efforts, for all of Jack's dinners and dances, the tennis games at various clubs, the Astor Cup, the polo matches—Newport remained stiff and hoary toward me. We *were* invited places; after all, no one directly insults an Astor, not without risking certain consequences. But besides Margaret Brown, I found no genuine friends.

The warm and sunny days of my girlhood were back in Bar Harbor. I suppose they always will be.

The only thing I miss about Newport is Beechwood itself. The cottage belongs to Vincent now, and that's fine, too. I had my days there. I had that one special, magical day there, and no one could ever ask for more than what I was given then.

It was a short, brilliant ceremony held in the ballroom. Ivory and mirrors and gilt. Chilled, motionless air. The ocean crashing, a rainstorm rolling in. Red roses everywhere, everywhere.

My mother wept; my father, sister, and I did not; and for once, your brother kept his dark opinions to himself.

I had awoken that morning aboard the *Noma* in my little cabin as Miss Force.

I fell asleep that night aboard the *Noma* in a different cabin, with a different name.

And I was uncoiled.

And all the world was new.

September 1911
Manhattan; At Sea; Newport

Everything was kept as secret as possible. Which meant, naturally, that hardly any of it was secret.

It was predicted that the terms of the colonel's divorce meant he could not be married again in a church, or that he could not marry again while Ava lived, or that he could not marry again in the great state of New York. Only that last guess was actually true, which left them with Beechwood or Bar Harbor if they wanted to keep the thing small and in the family, which they did, according to every single person except Jack himself. But he was willing to do whatever it took to hasten the ceremony. They hoped, all of them, that after it was done, the publicity, the notoriety, would begin to fade.

Madeleine had her doubts. But it seemed easier to go along with her mother and Mr. Dobbyn's plans, to allow herself to be swept up and away by them rather than resist, flotsam atop a tidal wave of other people's ideas about flowers and cakes and dresses and vows.

She didn't care. She didn't. She wasn't one of those girls who lived for the explosion of excess lavished on one single day, Consuelo Vanderbilt, May Goelet. Even as a child, she'd never spent hours daydreaming about her wedding; it all seemed rather silly to her. Surely the most important part of it all wasn't that *day*. It was every day after.

And now, on the brink of that ritual that would change her

name, her family, her home, Madeleine knew in her heart that all she truly did care about was the end result. Becoming his wife. Heart to heart, flesh to flesh.

Jack's attorney had managed at the last minute to wrangle a Congregationalist pastor for the ceremony, who was quietly shuttled in from Providence, and then just as quietly shuttled out afterwards, a thousand dollars richer. It seemed a strange miracle that none of the newsmen lurking in town had picked him out of the crowd, but then, there were so many frantic rumors regarding what was going on, who was where, when was what, that perhaps it was just the benefit of chaos.

Colonel Astor and Miss Force were to be married in Connecticut in a week. No, Boston in a month. No, Robins Island in the next few days. The *Noma* was being provisioned and coaled for a short voyage north, or a long one south, or maybe she was preparing to head all the way to the Bahamas. The crew wouldn't say.

To throw the press off the scent, Madeleine and her family had spent the days leading up to the ceremony back in Manhattan, popping in and out of the brownstone on so many errands the reporters had to trot to keep up, and split into groups, and hurl their questions on the fly. Jack was still able to fend them off with a laugh and a quip, but Madeleine had given up attempting to be cordial. When a man demanding to know the details of the antenuptial agreement actually *stepped in front of her* to prevent her from entering a jewelry store uptown, his black eyes gleaming, his sour breath in her face, she found herself recoiling. She found herself clenching her fists.

A white-hot pressure spiked through her that felt very much like murderous rage. An animal rage, barbarous and untamed, and it felt feral and boiling and *good*.

Her fists had raised, all on their own. Who knew what she would have done next, in those flowing, perilous few seconds with that pressman blocking her way; Madeleine had never struck anyone in her life but was certain, *certain*, that she could, that she should, and that it would feel even better than good if she did.

The man's eyes had widened.

And then, thank heavens, she found herself ushered inside by the store's burly security guard, who gave the reporter a sharp elbow to the side in the process, one she sincerely hoped broke some ribs.

Don't lose your temper, no matter how they goad you.

And how they did like to goad.

Father had had worse luck. On his morning walk (the opposite direction Madeleine and Katherine would take a quarter hour later; their lives had become maneuvers within maneuvers), he'd been trapped by a photographer, who ended up getting away with a snapshot of an exasperated William Force shaking his cane at the lens.

Town Topics published the image with glee.

The *Noma* floated, lights dimmed, off the coast of Long Island amid gentle swells and a lavender-smudged dusk. Madeleine, her father, and Katherine had slipped aboard that afternoon as the ship remained moored off Eightieth Street; their luggage had been smuggled on first, and then them, and then Jack, and somehow, it had all worked out. By the time the reporters had gathered en masse at the water's edge, the yacht was already beyond them, steaming rapidly out to sea.

So far, not one of the papers had dared to charter a boat to follow them.

So far.

They would reach Beechwood by dawn. Mother and Vincent and a handful of guests would meet them there.

The full moon hung behind the drifting clouds, round and pale, encircled with mother-of-pearl mist. The long, slender bow of the *Noma* sliced through the waves as easily as a sword might a soufflé; on this evening, the deck hardly rocked beneath Madeleine's feet.

In the water all around her crested night castles of foam, white-maned horses, sinuous mermaids with splashes of tails and wild flowing hair.

It was cool out; it felt always cool to her on the ocean after dark, no matter the daytime weather. But the wind skimmed by with that first bite of fall to it, briny still, sometimes pungently fishy from a gust pushed from shore.

The season had changed yet again, and this time, Madeleine was going to change with it.

"Penny for them," said Katherine, standing at her side on the foredeck, gazing out at the broken reflection of that great fat moon.

"Only that everything is changing."

"True enough." Katherine sent her a wise look. "By this time tomorrow, you'll be a new woman. I do emphasize *woman*."

"Stop. You're making me blush."

But she wasn't blushing. When she thought of Jack, of whatever tomorrow would bring, she didn't feel afraid, or ashamed, or bashful. She felt impatient. Her blood seemed turned to champagne, fizzing and euphoric.

She cupped her hands around the edge of the railing and thought, *What will this moon look like tomorrow night? Will it be different, because I will be?*

"How grown up you are now, little sister."

"Am I?" She smiled, dry. "Most of the time I don't feel so. At least, not lately."

"More than I am, I think, because there isn't a man alive who could drag me to the altar yet. From now on, I shall have to call you *missus*, and you'll have to wear your hair in a curly pile on top of your head, along with pounds of pearls around your neck, and when young ladies walk by, you'll cluck at them and think them saucy just for the sparkle in their eyes."

"Good gracious. I sound horrible."

Katherine snuck her arm through Madeleine's. "But I'll still love you, even though you'll have become so unbearable. And you'll let me borrow your pearls."

"What's mine is yours."

"How reassuring."

They fell quiet again. From back inside the main saloon came the sound of the dinner service being cleared by the stewards, china clattering, the occasional silvery chime of crystal meeting crystal. The last, lingering fragrance of the asparagus hollandaise, the veal cordon bleu, wafting past the door.

Katherine said, "Do you remember that Easter back when we were fourteen or fifteen, when we went to supper at the Mackays', and there was that boy staying there, that handsome, handsome boy—"

"Alasdair something," Madeleine said, flashing on a set of bright green eyes, a golden mane of hair, a roguish smile.

"Yes. Alasdair . . . something. A cousin come to visit all the way from Scotland, with that gorgeous accent."

Madeleine nodded at the water. "I remember."

"I never told you this before—I never told anyone—but he kissed me that night."

She turned. "What?"

"He kissed me in the portrait gallery off the dining room, in the shadows, in the dark. And it was lovely. He kissed me more than once. And then he told me that he wanted to marry me—in retrospect, I'm sure he'd gotten into the Riesling—and for *that*, I let him kiss me a fifth time."

Madeleine's mouth had dropped open. Katherine smiled, pushed the end of her finger against her sister's chin to close it up again.

"Do you know what I said to him, that boy with the soft red lips and the gorgeous accent, who tasted of sweet, forbidden wine?"

"No."

"I told him that I would not marry him, because we were too young, and I didn't want to fall in love with the idea of love.

I wanted *actual* love, not a looking-glass reflection of it. Not stolen kisses, or sotted promises. I wanted the truth of love, the pure molten core of it, because anything short of that was just a cheat."

"My. I had no idea you were so sagacious at fifteen."

"Then he asked me how I knew this *wasn't* the truth, real love, instant love, and I told him that we had only just met, but even still I knew it wasn't because my skin didn't melt from my bones at his touch, and my soul didn't sting, and I didn't have butterflies in my tummy, only the shredded ham and egg salad from supper. I let him kiss me one more time, and then I walked away."

"You slyboots! All this while!"

"All this while," Katherine agreed. "So tell me now, please, just between us, because I love you and you love me, and you're the one person on earth I've entrusted with my confession of those delicious Easter kisses. Is it the truth for you two, Maddy? The truth, or the looking glass?"

"Oh, the truth," Madeleine said softly. "After how far we've come, how could it be anything but the truth? My soul does sting."

They looked at each other, frosted with light, alike and not, a matched pair and not, two halves of a whole as only sisters could be. Two halves about to follow two acutely divergent paths. And even though that hurt a bit, even though it smarted, it was still all right.

"But that's a shame about Alasdair." Madeleine sighed, facing away again. "I seem to recall he was quite rich."

"*Stinking* rich," Katherine said, laughing. "But I never would have been able to stand the Scottish winters, even if his touch did make me melt."

"It's a lot of snow."

"A *lot* of snow, and a lot of days and nights trapped by the snow. No parties or balls. No dancing with anyone but him."

"Did I say sagacious before? I definitely meant wily."

"I will accept your compliment, *missus*."

Madeleine linked their arms again, leaning against her sister's side as the wind brushed by, and the fish smell came and went, and the *Noma* sliced towards the future.

After a while, she whispered, "I wish I were as brave as you."

Katherine was leaning back; they'd found their careful balance. "Isn't that queer? I've always wished to be as strong as you."

The ocean slid past. The moon beamed down, scattered white fireflies across the water.

"Perhaps I'll become a mermaid instead of all that other nonsense," Madeleine said to the view. "Being a *missus*, I mean. Having to cluck."

Katherine glanced at her.

"Mermaids still get to wear pearls, so that part's fine. And they live forever, or very nearly forever, don't they? Enchanted lives that go on and on. No curly piles of hair, however. I'll wear it down, with a crown of sea flowers."

"Do mermaids have husbands?" asked a new voice, just behind them.

They both turned, Katherine giving a swift, startled laugh.

"Colonel Astor! You're not supposed to see the bride before the wedding! It's terrible luck, you know!"

"I just saw her at dinner." He joined them at the railing. "And you've put me in the awkward position of having to point out that the yacht's not *that* big."

Madeleine smiled up at him, his craggy lavender-and-silver face, and he smiled back. Heat filled her up again, that fine, champagne heat, and her soul did sting.

Butterflies, butterflies, butterflies.

No one is going to have to drag me to the altar.

Her sister hugged her arms over her chest. "Yes, well . . . but there has to be *some* sort of a bridal time limit. No seeing her after coffee and dessert, I'd say."

"After our goodnights," he countered.

"Yes," agreed Madeleine. "Not till then, at least."

Katherine paused to take them both in, wise once more. "Hmm. I find I suddenly miss my coat. But I *will* return soon."

Her footsteps faded off.

Madeleine lifted a hand to the lapel of Jack's jacket, running her fingers down the sharp woolen crease. He brought up his to capture her palm against his chest and they stood there like that, connected, gazing into each other's eyes. His were pale as the moon now, just the same soft silver. His heart beat so strong against her.

"How happy you make me," he said, unexpected.

She curled her fingers tighter around his. "Good. Because I've decided that mermaids definitely have husbands. At least, this one will. So become accustomed to happiness, Colonel Astor."

"I will," he said, sounding almost bemused. "I plan to. I will."

They held hands during the ceremony.

She wore a suit of kingfisher blue with a pencil skirt and a cream hat. Her bouquet was a sweet-smelling mass of deeply scarlet roses.

Katherine stood to her left as maid of honor; Vincent served as best man. Her father had walked her down their makeshift aisle, a long, snowy runner laid across the shining floor, vases and vases of American Beauties stationed between the poles lining either side.

A part of her knew that it was cold in the ballroom. That her nose was cold, her cheeks were cold. That the storm brewing beyond the windows, gray and thick and spliced with lightning, might prove to be more than just a little rain. That outside of this chamber, outside of this mansion, waited a phalanx of reporters and photographers, eager for their scraps of fresh news.

But that was all fine. She let the tranquil tones of the pastor wash over her and barely heard what he was saying, and it was all fine.

"Colonel and Mrs. Astor," the pastor said, and Mother and Father and everyone else broke into applause, muffled because they all wore gloves.

Jack turned her to him and bent his head and kissed her, his hands light against her upper arms. Their third kiss.

A change of seasons, indeed.

All of her seasons, from now on, were going to be nothing but splendid.

She knew it in her mermaid soul.

CHAPTER 14

Off we sailed.

For months we sailed, up and down the coast, the *Noma* our own sweet personal paradise.

But every time we went ashore—and we did need to go ashore at times; the yacht ran on coal, not dreams, and frankly, sometimes my joints longed for dry land—they were waiting for us. The journalists. The tourists. The gawkers.

The Four Hundred, those avid and disgruntled beings.

Our marriage had not sated them, not a one. The press wanted more and more of us because the public did, and at least that was something I understood. Our names and faces sold their papers; our names and faces paid their salaries; and by devouring even the most mundane details about us, people around the country could imagine themselves, if only for a few moments, living our lives instead of their own.

But the fashionables! The Newport cottagers, the old Rhinebeck families, with their gnarled ancestral roots sunk deep into a fading Dutch-American history . . . they simultaneously craved us and despised us.

I suppose that, to them, Jack and I represented the elimination of that last crumbling battlement shielding the Old Guard from the New. The thought of our unholy union must have been both fascinating and horrifying.

Oh, my Jakey. My poor, beloved boy, who will have to navigate both of these worlds without your father's guidance.

How I fear for you.

In the end, we humans are creatures of marl and earth. We must return to our own soil.

December 1911
Manhattan

Colonel and the second Mrs. Astor spent their days aboard the *Noma* lazing in the sun or beneath the skating clouds, dazed and suspended between the heavens and the vast heaving ocean. They spent their nights entangled, alone together, learning new ways to dance. Learning the language of each other, rhythm and flesh and scents and kisses, and Madeleine was intoxicated.

They never said the words to each other. They never said *I love you,* because everything was still so wild and tender and new, and their souls were still understanding how to fit together. Or perhaps they never said it because they never had to. It was a silence understood by both of them, dark and secret and precious. Their connection, their union, was nothing ordinary, configured from the ordinary world.

But Madeleine was a bride; she knew what love was. She knew as sure as she knew her own body, her own mind, its measureless, electric thrill. In their sleep, they still touched, her hand on his arm, his arm around her waist.

He draped her in jewels, even as they basked in their splendid, salty isolation. More ropes of pearls, emerald chains for her hair and neck, sapphire drops for her ears. Belts of hammered silver studded with turquoise or malachite. Gold bangles chased with dragons, with flowers, or shaped as buckles or ruby-eyed snakes. At night, sometimes she dined with a ring on every finger, so that when she sipped her soup or sliced her fish, sparks would scatter in every direction, and in the softly lit saloon of the *Noma*, she became a minor star.

Because he liked to see her sparkling, he said.

He loved to see her glimmer.

Eventually, however, their constant movement across water began to wear on her, their shifting from place to place like swallows who could never alight home. Madeleine found, after weeks of her glittering life aboard the yacht, that she missed land. She missed riding horses, going to plays, to concerts. She even missed the rattling tumult of the city, automobile horns honking, the stink, the muck. Vendors in the parks calling out about balloons or hot chestnuts or scoops of fruity ice cream.

What she truly missed, she supposed, considering it, was the stability of solid ground. Which was odd, because she was positive she'd never even noticed before now how mindlessly reassuring it was to have a steady world beneath her feet.

But with that stability came a cost—their treasured privacy. Their cherished honeymoon bubble, annihilated the moment they set foot ashore.

The summer season was over, so they might have been safe (saf*er*) holed up in Beechwood or Ferncliff for Christmas, as only the locals tended to confront the merciless winters. But Jack Astor was a businessman. Although his many, many interests were competently managed by a series of clever men, he was not content to abandon his affairs for too long. He needed to go into the city.

"Just for the holidays," he'd assured her. "Then we're off again, out into the yonder."

And because she was a little tired, and more than a little in love, she agreed.

Breakfast was a ritual at the Fifth Avenue chateau, far more so than it had been aboard the *Noma* or even back at Beechwood. At sea, with a stoical New England chef installed in the yacht's galley, they had dined at their leisure, which was whenever the newlywed couple bothered to peel themselves from the bed and crack apart the curtains to find the sun in the sky. At sea there were johnny-cakes and jam and syrup, fried bacon and eggs, strong hot tea, strong hot coffee, sausage and oatmeal and fishcakes (a particular favorite of Jack's which Madeleine never touched, because it was *fish*, for *breakfast*).

Should the sun be dancing far enough above the horizon by the time they bothered to squint at it, they skipped the bacon and oatmeal entirely and moved straight to luncheon, when it was perfectly all right to have fish—so fresh it had been swimming in the blue only hours before—lightly grilled or sautéed or in sauce, or curried chicken from the stores, or plump scallops, or roast beef. At sea, they made their own timetable and followed their own rules.

But, the chateau.

On her first morning there as the new Mrs. Astor, Madeleine awoke alone, enrobed in a pale shaft of sunlight, her cheeks chilled, her nightgown twisted, and she sat up and glanced around her, bewildered. The chamber was entirely unfamiliar—gigantic and unfamiliar—with the paisley-patterned curtains along the windows pulled back, and that colorless winter light flooding in, falling, absorbed by the Turkish medallion rug on the floor, the sapphire walls that seemed to stretch for miles above her head. There was a fire sputtering in the hearth across the room, but from here it seemed feeble and underfed; no heat reached her past that black walnut mantel.

This was one of Jack's homes, obviously. This was—this was her home now. They had arrived so late the night before, she'd hardly registered any of the chambers or corridors she'd been wondering about for months, all the private, family-only spaces beyond the great hall and reception rooms and salons. She'd been conducted to this bedroom, had undressed and fallen into an exhausted stupor nearly at once in her husband's arms, but there was no sign of him now, no hint of any other human being anywhere nearby, save for the fact that *someone* must have crept in earlier to lay that fire.

Dust motes spun and drifted through the sunlight surrounding her, a thousand winking specks soundlessly lifting, turning, falling.

There was a red marble clock inset in that distant fireplace mantel, just beneath a painting of a pretty girl surrounded by flowers, also inset. Madeleine leaned forward from the mess of her bedding, straining to read the time. It was nearly ten-twenty; no wonder Jack was gone.

Her stomach growled.

The linden floor beneath her feet was a cold shock. It took her a moment to find her slippers, then another moment, much longer, to find the bell pull for the maid. She yanked at it, hopefully not too hard. If it rang, it must have been somewhere deep inside the mansion. Madeleine heard only silence.

She thought about retreating beneath the covers again but worried about how it would look, to be discovered back in her marital bed when obviously she had to rise from it to pull the bell, like she was too spoiled to withstand a little chill. So she shuffled to the fireplace instead, trying to control her shivers, trying not to look as disheveled and uncertain as she felt.

She didn't know this place. She didn't know this room, its customs, or even where her clothes were, and yet she was supposed to be the mistress here. She *was* the mistress here.

Madeleine inched closer to the dying fire.

The inscription beneath the painted girl framed by the mantelpiece read:

Innocent.

So, that first morning in the Manhattan mansion, she washed, she dressed, and then she found her way downstairs to the dining room alone. She encountered no one else, not even a footman, although the silver chafing dishes along the sideboard were still warm, and there was toast (not warm) lined neatly upright in a pair of porcelain racks.

A garland of evergreen, woven with holly, decorated the mantelpiece of the fireplace, a nod to the season.

She took a plate, a pale omelet topped with herbs, bacon, toast, no fishcake. She filled a crystal goblet with water from the decanter, another with orange juice, and found a seat near the middle of the table, covered in yards of off-white jacquard. After a bite of the omelet, she got up and moved to the foot of the table instead of the middle, to the high-backed chair where the lady of the house was supposed to sit.

Where Lina had surely sat, and Ava after her.

She ate slowly, aware of the emptiness around her, the zest of evergreen in the air, the small noises coming from parts of the mansion she could not see, a servant's corridor behind a wall, perhaps, or maids dusting in another room. As she finished the bacon, there came a clicking of toenails against stone just outside the doors; Kitty wandered into the chamber, walked over and lifted her nose inquisitively toward Madeleine's plate, then (with no bacon forthcoming) wandered out again.

Madeleine had never been in this room alone before. Maybe that was why she'd never registered how vast it was unpopulated by Astors or guests, how the marble walls shone slick with light, how the Brussels tapestries told stories of men and gods in shifting tones of green, gray, blue. A clock was ticking somewhere, although she couldn't see where. As she was craning her neck to search the corners, the ticking became a spill of chimes from clocks near and far, a count of eleven that trembled along the floor and walls and slowly smoothed to silence.

Her plate was empty. She stood, wondering if she should move it to the sideboard, if she should ring for someone (where was the bell?), and finally just left it on the table. There would be someone nearby, no doubt, a footman or the butler, perhaps in the great hall. She could let them know she was finished.

As she passed a gilded console table by the fireplace, she noticed a stack of letters and cards on a salver and paused, spying her name (her new name! *Mrs. John Jacob Astor!*) on the envelope on top. This, it seemed, was where the household mail was placed. The letter was a congratulatory note from Leta, bubbly and short, hoping they could meet up soon. Madeleine smiled, flipping through the remaining stack, plucking out the correspondence addressed to her, or to her and Jack, until she reached the bottom of the pile, where a single sheet of paper had been already removed from its envelope. Dark, sloping handwriting covered the page.

My dearest boy, it began, and Madeleine put the sheet back on the salver. She squared the letters in her left hand and then, despite herself, found her eyes returning to the opened letter, the stock thick and creamy, the folds precise, that tilting script leaping out at her.

. . . not too much of a bother, ask him again if I might have the Waterhouse portrait of us. I cannot imagine he wishes to keep it, a reminder of the family he used to have, not when he has obviously decided to begin a new one without us. Whereas I, naturally, will treasure it . . .

"Do you want to see it?"

Madeleine started, the letters she held scattering to the floor. Vincent watched her with his hands in his pockets, unmoving, as she bent and gathered them up again.

"I beg your pardon," she said, straightening. "See what?"

His mouth screwed into a smile, mirthless. "The painting, of course. The portrait my mother wants. She wasn't granted it in the divorce, so she has to beg him for it."

"Oh, I . . . I'm sorry, I didn't know—I mean, I wasn't—"

Vincent turned away. "It's in my bedroom." At the doorway, he paused, still not looking back at her. "Breakfast is always at seven sharp. You've thrown the staff off their schedule, Mrs. Astor."

He left.

All the meals at the chateau followed a strict schedule, as it turned out: breakfast at seven, luncheon at noon, high tea at four (if anyone was home for it), and supper at seven-thirty. The chef heading the kitchen here was from Orléans, Jack explained that night, and was far more thin-skinned than the New Englander on the yacht. Monsieur was prone to sulking if the soup got cold or the puddings soggy.

"We're lucky to have him," Jack said. "My sisters have been trying to poach him away for years."

They sat in the music room before dinner, Mrs. Astor at the piano, Colonel Astor reading a newspaper by the fire, a whiskey sour sweating lightly on the end table nearby. She played carefully, a lullaby she remembered from her childhood, because she was out of practice, and she didn't want to perform poorly in front of him, even this uncomplicated tune.

"I see," she said.

He smiled at her from his place on a rose-pink davenport, the newspaper flat across his knees. "You'll become used to it. Haven't you ever been terrorized by a chef before?"

"No. The cook at our house is from Newark. I suppose she might terrorize the greengrocer some, but she was always nice enough to me."

Against the wall behind the davenport was a bronze of Ariadne, nude and leaning against a rock, a hand covering her eyes. The metal curves of her captured the firelight, rounded hips and breasts and belly.

Madeleine said, "Can't we adjust the schedule?"

"Why?" Jack asked, returning to the paper.

"I don't know. Seven seems early to me for breakfast."

"You'll become used to it," he said again.

She frowned at her hands, at her fingers testing out the notes. She thought of rising at six every morning no matter how late the night had gone before, of crossing that enormous bedroom to the bell pull, of getting dressed in the boudoir, and saw in her mind another woman doing all of those things: Ava happy to wake with the dawn, or before it. Ava happy with the schedule, with the moody French chef.

"I just want it to be a little later, that's all. Will it disrupt the entire household if we push it to eight?"

Jack didn't look up. "You can ask him."

Madeleine focused on the keys, the halting lullaby. For the first time in weeks, she wondered what her family was doing right now; if Katherine was at home in the cozy drawing room with their parents, or maybe out at the theater, laughing and having a fine time, not at all worried about having to rise at six in the morning to avoid cold toast.

The lullaby ended. She sat there without moving, her fingers resting atop the keyboard, as the sound of the fire drank up the quiet.

"Madeleine."

She swallowed, looked up. Jack was studying her with an expression she knew well; she'd puzzled him in some way, and he was going to pick it apart until he understood her again.

That concentration. That scrutiny that pierced straight through her, that boiled through her veins and brought every little insecurity right to the surface of her skin in a hot-and-cold blush.

He said, "How about we try a small reception before Christmas? Nothing too formal, not yet, but maybe a Sunday luncheon for a few important friends? It would be good practice for you for the larger events we'll host later on, the business dinners and balls and so forth. You'll have a chance to learn for yourself that monsieur isn't such an ogre."

She opened her mouth to agree, found her voice didn't want to work. So she nodded instead, pasting on a smile. He smiled in return and flipped the paper back up to keep reading.

"We can have diamond rings as the favors, perhaps."

Madeleine, flabbergasted, found her voice. "Diamond rings? For a luncheon?"

"We've done it before," he said casually. "They were a great success."

We've done it before. We.

Jack dropped the paper once more. "Or a brooch, or a pin. A

gold stickpin with our initials intertwined, to formally mark our-selves as a couple. It wouldn't be difficult to commission. Riker Brothers or Tiffany could do it in a snap. What do you think?"

"I . . . I think that sounds quite brilliant."

"Good. It's settled. I'll have Dobbyn give you a list of who to invite. I don't think we should go above fifty, not this first time."

"Of course," she said, faint.

Madeleine took a few careful breaths, then began a new piece. *Clair de Lune*, with its deceptively simple beginning.

"Has Vincent gone out?" she asked the piano.

"He told me he'd be dining at his club tonight," Jack said, and Madeleine nodded again, following her fingers on the ivory and ebony, the honeyed light that flicked, so tricky, across the keys.

Vincent's bedroom was on the third floor, in a secluded corner that overlooked the back of the property. She knew this because she'd asked the butler that afternoon, pretending she was attempting to memorize the layout of the mansion, as it would be far too easy to become lost in these fields of rooms. And at least that last part was true.

She walked quickly, trying to keep her footsteps soundless against the floor, which was sometimes possible (if there were rugs), and sometimes not (marble and hardwood). There were portraits all along the walls she passed, flat dead faces with flat dead staring eyes, but none of them was the right one. It made sense that Vincent had claimed his mother's image; she should have guessed that if there did still exist a record of Ava in this mansion, it would be secreted in his room.

She did not knock on his door. She assumed it was his; it matched the butler's description, and when she opened it and stepped inside, it seemed like a bedroom. There was moonlight enough coming in from the windows to make out the sleigh bed, the armoire.

She found the switch for the electric lights. The sudden glare of the chandeliers made her close her eyes, open them again.

Another giant chamber. Silk mandarin curtains, broad Persian rugs. A discarded bow tie had been tossed over the back of an armchair; a top hat sat upright at the foot of the bed. They were the only signs the room was occupied. Every other inch of it was just more of the chateau, rich and cold and spotless.

The walls were chockablock with paintings. Landscapes, seascapes, horses, churches, nudes. By fate or intuition, she found the one of Ava at once, because it was directly above the nightstand by the bed, larger than all the rest.

Luminous.

She had been painted as a Roman goddess, standing in a flowing tunic of royal blue, one leg flexed, a copper-red wrap falling gracefully from her white shoulders. She wore a diadem of green stones and held an empty chalice in one hand, gazing directly at the viewer with a subtle, intrigued smile. Madeleine had never seen her predecessor's face before, but there was no question it was she, because her other hand rested atop the tousled head of a young boy who was clearly Vincent, also in robes, looking up at his mother with an expression of reverence. They posed in bright light against a pillar of stone; just behind it stood a third figure in shadow, tall and lean. It was more a suggestion of Jack than a portrayal of him, but there he was, his face angled away, his head bent. The imperfect outline of his shape melted into a background of clouds and sky. Even little Vincent seemed *less* than his mother, fuzzier, a visual device meant to indicate where one should look.

At Ava, of the rippling chestnut hair and cupid's bow lips.

Ava, with her long neck and flawless skin and sloping shoulders, and dark doe eyes that held Madeleine's own with the confidence of the very rich, the very lovely, the very talented and unique.

Madeleine returned that gaze a minute longer, then turned around and crept away.

CHAPTER 15

December 1911
Manhattan

    Mr. and Mrs. Robert Goelet regretfully decline the polite invitation of Colonel and Mrs. John Jacob Astor for Sunday afternoon, December seventeenth.

    Mr. and Mrs. G. W. Vanderbilt II regret that an absence from town will prevent them from accepting the kind invitation of Col. and Mrs. John Jacob Astor for Sunday afternoon, December seventeenth.

    Mrs. Hermann Oelrichs regrets that she is unable to accept the polite invitation of Colonel and Mrs. John Jacob Astor for Sunday afternoon, December seventeenth.

    Mr. and Mrs. William Church Osborn regret that they must decline the kind invitation of Col. and Mrs. John Jacob Astor for luncheon on Sunday, December seventeenth.

    Mr. and Mrs. August Belmont regret that a previous engagement prevents them from accepting Col. and Mrs. John Jacob Astor's kind invitation for Sunday afternoon, December seventeenth.

Mr. and Mrs. John Davison Rockefeller must regretfully decline the kind invitation of Colonel and Mrs. John Jacob Astor for Sunday afternoon, December seventeenth.

Mr. James B. Duke very much regrets that he cannot accept Col. and Mrs. John Jacob Astor's kind invitation for luncheon on Sunday afternoon, December seventeenth.

Mr. and Mrs. Thomas Fortune Ryan regret that a prior engagement prevents them from accepting the polite invitation of Col. and Mrs. John Jacob Astor for Sunday afternoon, December seventeenth.

Mr. and Mrs. John Pierpont Morgan, senior, regret that they will be unable to attend the luncheon of Colonel and Mrs. John Jacob Astor on Sunday, December seventeenth . . .

CHAPTER 16

We were roundly snubbed. I don't mind admitting that to you now, although at the time, it was a reality we danced around, your father and I. A blank space had opened between us, this conclusive fact of our *apartness*, and neither of us could quite think of how to breach it. Or even if it was ours to breach. Anyway, it's not much of a secret these days, that cocoon of isolation the Four Hundred spun around us after we ventured off the *Noma*. I honestly can't claim it came as a surprise—at least, not to me.

But I don't think Jack had ever noticed how many versions of *she's certainly not Ava, is she?* were exchanged behind our backs. The whispers of the Knickerbockers never wormed their way into his ears the way they did mine.

The press delighted in noting our unusual lack of festivities, especially so close to the holidays. Why, the colonel and Mrs. Ava Astor had entertained so grandly in the years before! They had opened their mansion and their wallets and the legendary stories of French champagne and resplendent dinners and costume balls had become etched in the memories of anyone who mattered, and a great many more who did not. It was, after all, an Astor tradition to throw such glamourous parties, those lavish fêtes, just as *the* Mrs. Astor used to do.

How strange that her son and his teenaged bride had shunned the idea of even an informal Christmas reception. Perhaps the new Mrs. Astor wasn't feeling quite well.

And I wasn't. Not really.

The mansion was cold. I was cold. Every single day was cold and raw and lonely, even the ones when my family came to visit, or some of my old Junior League friends (their eyes wide as soon as they walked in, trying not to gawk at the relentless cascade of ostentation and gloom).

Jack told me to give his people some time. "They'll come around," he said. "They must."

But I didn't see why they should. They were his set, not my own. I had nothing to offer them beyond myself, and they had already made their feelings about *that* resoundingly clear.

The jewelry safe in my boudoir still holds nearly forty stickpins of solid gold, untouched, each engraved with our initials, J&M, lovingly intertwined.

I suppose I can always sell them for scrap.

December 1911
Manhattan

The fire was tall and blazing in the south morning room, lending the *brèche blanche* marble hearth an ambered, shifting glow. Even with the logs burning so hot, even with the winter sun outside shining so bright, the chamber remained shivery, the heat lost to the immense corners and lofty ceiling, or eaten up, perhaps, by all the *cuivre doré*, gold and gleaming, that seemed to decorate every last inch of space.

Gold-leafed sconces, pilasters, cherubs, medallions. Gold-leafed tables and chairs, cabinets and commodes. There were still rooms in this hulking home that Madeleine had barely explored, but it seemed to her that Lina Astor had not spared her hand at gilding every lily she'd ever seen.

Sometimes, some mornings (like this one), it hurt her eyes to try to take it all in.

She sank deeper into her cushioned chair by the fire, gathering her cardigan tighter around her waist. Dug her heels into the nap of the rug (woven with little identical birds, wings spread, beaks agape), as if that might help. She wore opals this morning, maybe to counter all of that unrelenting gold. Black opals, eldritch and fiery, stone rainbows captured on her fingers and wrists.

"It's so kind of you to have me over," said Margaret Brown, seated in the easy chair opposite hers. She leaned back, looking completely at home, her legs scissored at the ankles, her toes pointed, like a ballet dancer's. "As I mentioned over the telephone, I could have saved you the trouble and stayed at the Ritz."

"Oh, no," Madeleine said, rousing. "I'm so happy to see you again. It's lucky for us you were on your way through to Newport and the train was delayed. We're glad for the company, honestly."

She heard the tremble in her voice, just barely noticeable, and closed her lips tight to swallow it down.

Margaret lifted her cup of tea, examined the spiral of steam that rose from its surface. "It's a big house, Mrs. Astor."

"Yes. Yes, it is."

Madeleine dropped her gaze to her lap. The wind outside quickened, rotated, became a gust that groaned against the window-panes.

Margaret uncrossed her ankles. "Don't worry. The place will grow on you, I'm sure. It can be rough sliding into someone else's territory at first, even if they're long gone. Ghosts in the walls, I guess. The artwork, the furniture, even the pattern of the china." She cocked her head, smiled at the old-fashioned peonies circling her cup. "Someone else's ideas about living, sleeping, entertaining, manifested all around you. But you're tough, Madeleine. Bright and tough. You wouldn't be where you are right now if you weren't. You'll make this place your own."

"I hope so."

"Hire a decorator," Margaret suggested. "Spread some of your own soul across these rooms. This isn't Europe, after all. We're allowed to stir things up here. In fact, we're expected to. Not everything in America is chiseled in eternal stone."

"A decorator?" Madeleine looked up, around. There was *so much* gilt. "I hadn't thought . . ."

"Well, think it. Change things, invite people over, all those four hundred lovely, *lovely* people, and show them what you can do. Show them who *you* are."

"We were considering a luncheon." Madeleine pinched at the cuff of her thick plum sweater, rolling the wool between her fingers. Why was she always so cold now? It seemed this winter in New York was the coldest of her life so far, and it had hardly even snowed. Just day after day of bitter blue sky, anemic thin sun. That wind. "Nothing too elaborate, of course. Only something close enough to Christmas to be festive, but not enough to intrude on anyone's plans, but . . ."

"Yes?"

"Not many have responded favorably. Quite a few people are already so busy with the holidays."

Margaret raised both eyebrows, said nothing. Tasted her Ceylon.

Madeleine rushed on. "And doubtless many will be traveling, like you. Visiting family near and far. It was all very last minute, anyway. Jack and I have hardly been in town long enough to catch our breath."

Margaret stood, walked to the table that held the tea service. In the giant square of iced light from the window, she waved away the footman who approached, pouring herself another cup.

"Do you know what they call themselves back in Denver?"

"Who?"

Margaret added a thin stream of milk to her cup, lifting the creamer expertly high and then low, her eyes narrowed, before placing it back upon the silver tray. "The elite. The leaders of Colorado high society."

Madeleine looked at her, waiting.

"'The Sacred Thirty-Six.'" She returned to her chair. "The thirty-six best families of the Rockies. The thirty-six who determine who is good, who is bad, and who is merely uninvited. At least here it's only a number, and a bigger one at that. Four hundred. Plenty of room, so to speak. Out there, it's only thirty-six, *and* they had to throw in a *sacred*. To make it all so much more special."

"Are you a member?" Madeleine asked, but thought she already knew the answer.

Margaret smiled; for the first time, the secret mirth about her vanished, replaced with something fiercer, darker. She swirled the tea in her cup. "I was a shop girl. Did you know that, Miss Madeleine?"

"No." She was genuinely surprised. Nothing about Margaret Brown, no matter her plain speaking, indicated anything but a background of culture and education.

"Came west from Missouri as a girl to meet my brother in Colorado. He was a miner, and we were going to make our fortune out in Leadville. But women weren't allowed to mine, not for gold or silver or anything else. It was thought to be bad luck. I ended up in a dry goods store, and I was grateful for it, because it was decent work. Steady work, even though the pay was peanuts. Every day, I dealt with real folks in real life. Folks without a penny left to their names, desperate for a speck of anything to send home to their families back east. Desperate for any brush with Lady Luck. It turned out that Lady Luck, in the end, noticed *me*. I was a poor girl who fell in love with a poor man, and married him. A man who later on became rich from gold. I was nineteen when we wed. He was thirty-one, days from thirty-two." She shot Madeleine a glance from beneath those dark lashes. "Did you know *that*?"

"No," she said again.

"Nineteen. Thirty-two. But it's different out there, you know. Out west. Fewer women by far, at least in the far-flung mountains

and plains. No one raised much of a fuss about it. We were happy
and poor, and then we were happy and rich. And after that . . ."

She drifted off, the tea half-lifted in her hand, forgotten. Past
the closed doors of the morning room, there were maids conversing, very low. There were footsteps, and the muted, solid sound of
well-oiled doors opening, closing. Letting in and out the ghosts.

"After that," Margaret said, "I began to raise my voice. For charity, for laborers. For the rights of the miners, of women and children. To take a little—just a little, mind you—from the Thirty-Six
and send it back to those who'd made their silk-stocking lives possible. The starving men dying in their tents, in the banks of snow.
Their families left behind, left up there at altitude with nothing,
trying to find their way in rags back to any kind of secure base."

Margaret seemed to recall her tea. She looked at it with something like revulsion, then slowly lowered her hand to the arm of
her chair. Without her mask of mirth, she seemed older suddenly,
lined and fatigued.

"Those pinched-nosed biddies in Denver would sooner kiss
the lips of the devil himself than invite me into their homes."

Madeleine sat forward, tucking her feet beneath her. The fire
in the hearth popped, a bright cherry burst.

"How courageous you are."

"Courageous? No. Just saw the truth of things, that was all.
Saw the truth, and tried to change it."

"Did it work?"

"No." Margaret sighed, resting back. "Maybe a little. Not
enough. It's never really enough. That's not how our world turns."

Madeleine felt, shockingly, her eyes begin to burn. A hot band
of sorrow cinched her, constricting her chest. To control it, she
made herself very still, exhaling silently through parted lips, her
fingers curled beneath her legs. She blinked away the tears, scowling at her knees.

The fire. The maids. The hundred doors of this empty, haunted
mansion, opening and closing. Men dying in tents.

It all echoed through her, over and over and over, all the ghosts rising up, taking command.

"Madeleine," said Margaret carefully. "Are you feeling perfectly well?"

She freed a hand to wipe quickly at her eyes. "Oh, yes. A bit tired, that's all."

"A big house," said Margaret again, very soft.

"I miss the heat, I think." She rubbed her eyes again, then pushed the opal rings covering her fingers back into place. She stared down at them, so heavy and vivid, and heard herself say, "I *ache* to be warm. I know it sounds woebegone, it sounds silly, but honestly, I do. And not just warm by the fire as we are now, roasting on your left while freezing on your right, like a chicken half cooked. Warm from the *air*, from the green trees and the sun, surrounded by June. June! It feels as if this winter has dragged on forever, and it's only December still."

"The cold can whittle you straight down to the marrow, I swear. I do know that."

"I just don't—" She swallowed hard against the thickness in her throat—*stop crying, don't be stupid, don't cry*—and when she spoke again, the tremble in her voice had flattened out. "I just don't know when it will be warm again. That's all."

The door to the room swept open on its silent hinges. Jack walked in, still shrugging out of his overcoat, trailed by Kitty and a footman. He tossed the coat back to the footman without looking (who caught it expertly mid-air in a slither of satin and wool), smiling all the while.

"Hello, sweet wife. Good morning, Margaret. Madeleine sent word that you'd come."

He leaned down to kiss Madeleine on the forehead, his moustache prickling. She averted her eyes but lifted her hand to brush his cheek, her fingers falling away as he straightened. "Quite a brisk morning out there! I'm happy to see you both by the fire."

"It does make a difference," Margaret said. "As long as we don't run out of wood."

Jack laughed, headed to the tea service. "No chance of that." He glanced around, impatient. "Wilton? I'd like some coffee, please. And whatever assortment of cakes or pastries the kitchen has on hand. Maybe some of those macaroons from yesterday, if there are any left."

A new footman—not the one with Jack's coat; Madeleine was still trying to remember everyone's names—inclined his head and murmured, "Right away, sir," before backing out of the room.

"Do you know, darling, I've been considering your idea about adjusting the meal schedule."

Madeleine tried to sound interested. "Oh?"

"Breakfast was too early today, I think, because I'm half-starved now, and it's nowhere near noon. Margaret, are you staying for lunch?"

"If you'll have me."

"Certainly."

"Actually, if you'll have me, I'm staying overnight."

"Are you? Wonderful. Madeleine could use the company."

They were nearly her own words, minutes before. Nearly, but she had said *we*, and he had not.

She kept her gaze on the window, the pallid light. She drew the air in past her teeth, blew it out again, slow, restrained, exhaling the tightness in her chest.

Jack planted himself on a cut-velvet settee, slinging an arm along the high, scalloped line of the back.

"What's on the schedule for today, ladies? Shopping? A ride through the park?"

"Jack," said Margaret. "Let's talk about January, instead of today."

He smiled again, tapping his fingers against the wooden scroll topping the settee, and for no reason other than that, Madeleine remembered him in their bed last night, the touch of his hands against her, hard and hungry and eager, burning warm, because the cold never seemed to infect him, not ever.

"January? Is there some momentous event approaching?"

"Maybe." Margaret shot a glance at Madeleine, then back to Jack. "I'm taking my daughter Helen to Egypt. She's never been, and has been pestering me about it for ages. I suppose it's something all the young people want to do now, the Egyptian grand tour. It's become a contest to see who can collect the most postcards from Memphis or Cairo or Thebes. The Sphinx, the Valley of the Kings, all that. I heard even Pierpont Morgan's headed to Khargeh soon to inspect the ruins. Helen's going to be studying at the Sorbonne, so we wanted to get in the trip while we could. Have you ever wintered in Egypt?"

Jack drew up one leg, crossed his ankle over his knee and flicked the cuff of his trouser leg back into place.

(*—and she had stroked that ankle, that knee, dragged her nails up the flesh of his shin, learning his joints, the hard separations of muscle against muscle, masculine and lean, her mouth and body mastering every bit of him, ankle to knee, knee to thigh, thigh to—*)

"I haven't. I've been there on occasion, but only for a few weeks at a time."

"Egypt in winter is the absolutely best time to go." Now Margaret's gaze returned to Madeleine, very direct; Madeleine dragged herself back to the present. "It's warm without the brutal heat of summer. The temples, the stars, the sunsets. The history and art—they'll steal your breath away. There's nothing like traveling to open the eyes and inspire the spirit. We're setting off in January. Why don't the two of you join us? If not for the whole tour, at least for some of it?"

"Egypt," said Madeleine, sitting up, and the word tasted like spice in her mouth, something rare and wonderful and perfumed. She'd never been farther south on the Continent than Marseilles, never traveled anywhere beyond the pearl-chokered salons of New England and Europe.

Egypt.

And then that word, full of spice, transformed itself into a new word, an even better one, resonating down through her bones: *Escape.*

Jack was watching her, his fingers now still. She met his eyes and curved her lips and tried not to look pitiful or pleading. Kitty lumbered over, sprawled along the rug at her feet with a satisfied grunt, soaking up the heat from the hearth.

"Egypt," he said. He rapped another hard tattoo against the wood. "What a marvelous notion."

CHAPTER 17

We took the *Olympic* across the pond. It was a beautiful ship, still more or less new, having only been in service since the summer before. I remember thinking at the time that it was the grandest ocean liner I'd ever been on. There weren't many on board we knew, which was sublime, and no reporters at all, which was more sublime still. We found only a handful of people in first class who were even nodding acquaintances, including J. Bruce Ismay.

Ismay. President of the International Mercantile Marine.

Chairman of the White Star Line.

(Or "Yamsi," as he called himself in the supposedly secret messages wired from the *Carpathia* to White Star's New York offices, attempting to commandeer another ship to spirit him away to England after the sinking. So that he could cower there across the Atlantic, where the United States Senate inquiry could not touch him.)

That bastard. Even writing out his name now makes my teeth clench.

Our entire voyage to Europe, Ismay could not stop boasting about White Star's upcoming newer, better steamship (not yet launched), built as a sister ship to the one we traveled on. He and your father spent countless hours discussing all the technical aspects of both steamers, the tonnage, the reciprocating engines, beams and displacements, deck plans. Jack was always keen on delving into those sorts of details. He was an amazing man of science, in his own way. His inventions won all sorts of accolades and awards.

I'll show you some of the write-ups, his ribbons and certificates and sketches. I'll put aside some of the instruments from his home laboratories. ~~Had he not been born into fortune, I'm sure he would have~~

Your father and Ismay would stay up late into the night in the smoke room of the *Olympic*, holding their sessions, and when Jack would return to our stateroom, he was always starry-eyed and reeking of cigars.

Which, of course, I never minded.

Which now I would give my right arm to smell again.

I don't know. All those rapt, late-night conversations about *Titanic*. I think maybe they seeped into him like a poison.

Yes. Maybe he was poisoned with the thought of that newer and better ship and her maiden voyage; sick with longing to see her all spick and span and untested.

Maybe that was why.

Perhaps Bruce Ismay was right to try to flee. Were he standing before me now and I had a pistol in my hand, I might easily put a bullet in him.

January 1912
Paris, France

France was awash with rain. Not just any rain, but a miserable sleety slush that shifted back and forth from hard stinging drops to wet flaky splats, soaking through even the thickest of oilskins. From the moment they'd reached Cherbourg, it had begun, and had not relented for more than an hour or so a week later. Paris appeared to be weeping, all her famous façades stained with streaks of dirty gray ice. Medieval gargoyles retched watery sludge into leaky lead gutters; puddles and rivulets of melt mirrored the silver, sullen sky.

Whenever Madeleine went outside, her hair frizzed, and her breath frosted into clouds.

The air smelled of gasoline and horses and wet manure.

It was not warm.

There were, of course, history and art aplenty, but the stars remained hidden, and the sunsets descended uniformly gray. At least their suite of rooms at the Ritz-Carlton was well heated, as was the lobby and all the fine restaurants nearby to be found. But she still wore her furs wherever she went—she would wear them to bed if she could—and the tips of her fingers and toes nearly always felt numb. It was the strangest burden, this chill she carried with her. It felt like a fever wracking her, except she shivered instead of sweated.

She must have caught some manner of a flu-ish ague, which was horribly unfair, to be sick on her first trip abroad with her husband. But she was, and all she could do was hunker through it.

Her appetite waned. The sight of food, no matter how elegantly plated, left her queasy; the odors of sautéed meats and rich sauces were enough to make her leave the table. All she could bear to consume was freshly baked bread and softened cheese—which, happily, Paris had in abundance. She gorged on long crispy sleeves of baguettes, sometimes still warm from the oven, their crusts crackling at her touch, tender white insides ready to be devoured. She'd tear into them with her bare hands (if nobody watched), smear them with salted butter and goat cheese, a touch of jam, fig or pear or green tomato.

In all her life, she had never tasted bread so fine.

She drank tea by the gallons until she grew tired of it and switched to water and dry white wine . . . which France also offered in abundance.

"I wish you would try the turbot," Jack said one night, their last night before they were to depart for the Riviera, and then North

Africa. He gazed at her from across the restaurant table, ignoring the anxious waiter and the other patrons (ogling, because in a rising babble of languages, one after another they'd realized with whom they dined) and the constant churn of noise from outside, all the motorcars and coaches and people hurrying past the windows with their collars turned up.

The rain struck the panes in slender clear daggers, always falling.

"Just one bite," he said, setting down his knife and fork, touching his napkin to his lips. Nestled in its little green glass bowl on the table, the flame of a candle bent and trembled.

The turbot lay slick and unpleasant on her plate, drowning in capers and congealing butter. In her mind, she imagined lifting the fork, flaking apart its flesh, and nearly at once her throat closed with nausea.

Jack reached out his hand to her. She smiled at him tightly, their fingers meshed. Along with her diamond engagement ring, along with the other sparkling rings she wore to make him happy, they wore matching wedding bands, plain gold, unadorned.

Madeleine looked from the rings to his face, trying to find the words to placate him. She hated worrying him. Tonight he looked nearly as haggard as she felt. He looked nearly . . . vulnerable, which was a word she had never once associated with John Jacob Astor before. Yes, vulnerable—because of her—and that pained her.

Yet in the end, all she could offer was, "I'm sorry. I can't."

The next morning, figuring the math, she finally understood why.

She hadn't caught a cold.

February 1912
Alexandria, Egypt

The wet weather followed them all the blessed way, from Paris to the coast. The steamer they'd booked in Villefranche had navigated the rain and waves without undue effort, but instead of the limpid beryl sea Madeleine had been hoping to see, for days the Mediterranean remained a cheerless, opaque froth.

As they churned toward the harbor of the fabled city, Alexandria loomed gray before her: drab gray sky, drab gray sand. Gray, dull little houses that resembled nothing more than the massive gray stones stacked in blocks along the shore, slathered in seaweed and foam. Blackened, skinny masts from the myriad boats dotting the water bobbed up and down, up and down, stabbing at the clouds.

In the near distance rose the replica Pharos, that lost ancient wonder of a lost ancient world, now nothing more than a shadowy smear of a lighthouse, shrunk small behind the lens of her porthole glass.

Standing there in her cabin, looking out at it all, Madeleine exhaled a slow, sad breath.

"There, there," murmured her maid, as she fastened the clasp of Madeleine's necklace. "It cannot rain forever, madame."

"Can't it?"

"It won't," said the woman. "You'll see."

Rosalie Bidois, a firmly proper lady's maid taken on back in New York, was the most optimistic Frenchwoman Madeleine had ever met.

She hoped that Rosalie was right, that the rain would soon stop, that the clouds would scatter to the four corners of the earth to reveal a benevolent blue sky.

She turned and caught a glimpse of herself in the wardrobe mirror, a girl washed to gray like everything else, her hair pulled back, her dress and hat darkly sensible. Only her earrings showed any color, Burmese rubies that dangled like fat drops of blood from her lobes.

Her gaze strayed downward. She turned sideways in the glass and ran her hands over her front, trying to feel the tiny lump of her baby beneath her corset.

"Your coat, madame."

"Thank you."

"You will keep it buttoned?"

"Yes."

At least the temperature had risen enough for her to leave off her furs. In Villefranche, she'd been able to switch to a topcoat of gaberdine, a slim harbinger of brighter days to come.

Three sharp knocks rattled the door. The porter, ready for her trunks, Jack standing right behind him in the cramped hall.

"Shall we go? I've already sent Robins ahead with the rest of the luggage. It's going to take some time to wend through customs, I'm afraid. These port towns at the edge of the world. It always does."

"All right."

Kitty, already leashed to keep her in check, pushed past both men, straining to reach Madeleine, her tail thumping against Jack's leg. Her leather collar pulled tight against her neck, but she kept her focus on Madeleine, panting.

"Oh, hello, yes." She cupped the dog's face in her hands, smoothing the coarse brown fur. For some reason, Kitty had warmed up to her tremendously in the past few months, obeying some doggish logic Madeleine could not work out. Kitty followed her around now nearly as much as she did Jack, leaning against her heavily whenever she could. By the end of the day, all of Madeleine's skirts would be coated with dog hair. (The impressive Rosalie would inevitably return the skirts to her closet two days later, pressed and spotless.)

It would have been, as Jack pointed out, cruel to leave their dog behind for so long a period. Besides, he'd spent years taking her everywhere, and Kitty loved to travel.

Which was apparently true. At the very least, Kitty loved to be with her and Jack, so surely that was close enough.

"Hello, my good girl," Madeleine whispered to her. "Are you ready for an adventure?"

"She always is." Jack stole past the porter and the maid to buss her on the cheek, his free hand lightly and briefly gripping her elbow.

Ever since she'd told him her news, back in Paris, the worried cast to his eyes had vanished. He'd gathered her close to him, his lips against her temple. She'd breathed in that bergamot and amber scent of him, closing her eyes, wrapping her arms around his waist. Like the Airedale, like a child, she'd leaned heavily, letting him take her weight.

He'd wanted to know only *was she certain*, and *when did she think . . . ?*

Yes. And, August.

Whenever her husband gazed at her now, all Madeleine saw was a slow burning joy. It practically lit him from within.

She wished she felt the same. She *wanted* to feel the same. She wanted her heart to be as lifted as his, to keep them in harmony, because she adored their harmony and always had. But so far, all she could bring herself to feel about her pregnancy was a thin, distant amazement. Like all the tumbling, strange changes in her life now were happening to someone else, and she was only watching them from afar, observing all their fascinating little facets.

Look at that lucky girl, that newlywed in her coat and lace and jewels. Consider her fine life, her husband, her unborn child, and still all she does is complain about the weather.

She never said anything to Jack about this new, faraway side of her. She couldn't lie to him, not about anything that really mattered, but that didn't mean she had to tell him everything, either. It seemed kinder to let him believe her silence was tranquil contemplation; that her newfound gravity was Madonna-like, not simply detachment.

It occurred to her sometimes that she ought to feel guilty for her lack of feeling. She ought to feel shame, at least. But even those moments would slip away from her, fading off into insignificance.

Kitty licked her hand. Madeleine gave the dog's head another rub, then put on her gloves.

"Let's go find Egypt."

* * *

The New Khedivial Hotel did not, as a policy, allow its guests to house their pets in its splendid apartments. Cats were considered bothersome and dogs dirty, but Jack was so accustomed to circumventing this particular rule that he merely smiled as he handed the wad of cash notes to the manager, who pocketed it without blinking and bowed deeply before conducting them all to their rooms.

They were only stopping for the night before heading to Cairo. She'd passed in a haze through the grand lobby, barely noticing the décor. But once ensconced in their suite, Madeleine had collapsed into a chair and leaned back her head, and all she saw was fussy gilt and silk wallpaper and shiny French brocatelle, and anonymous oil paintings of pastel sunsets blushing behind trees. A few Roman-looking busts gazed back at her, blank-eyed, from veined marble pedestals.

This room could have been anywhere. Any superior hotel room, anywhere in Europe or America, anywhere she'd ever been.

What an awful long way to have come for more gilt.

CHAPTER 18

It rained and gloomed until Cairo.

But I sleepwalked until then, letting your father's meticulous plans buffet me this way and that. I had absolute trust in him to keep me safe, no matter how much I did not or could not see happening around me. I remember falling into my dreams that night in the hotel in Alexandria, relieved enough to be in a downy soft bed that did not rock, relieved even more to have my husband next to me.

(On the steamer from France to Egypt, there had been some mix-up with the ship, or the tides, or the captain or something—I still don't quite know; it was explained in a rapid torrent of French—and in the end, all we could manage to procure in first class were single cabins with narrow bunks.)

I hope it doesn't shock you, me telling you these things. I hope that someday, when you are married, you will read these words and think, "Of course."

I mean for you to know, in every motherly way that I can convey it, that your parents were in love. That we were twin spirits in love. And how special *you* were to us from the very beginning, the spark born from us both.

Anyway, Cairo. We stayed at Mena House, naturally, so close

to the pyramids, with its modern amenities and tram service and stables and swimming bath. We meant to take in the sights and then meet Margaret Brown and her daughter a few days later aboard our rented *dahabiya* for the journey up and back down the Nile.

I went to bed that first night in gray, fuzzy Cairo still asleep. Already asleep.

Overnight, the rain marched out into the desert, evaporating into clouds. The next thing I knew was the dawn.

February 1912
Cairo, Egypt

She opened her eyes. Everything was covered in stars of rosy gold light, a color so warm and intense that it seemed not quite real. The pillow beneath her cheek was scented of lavender and lemon; with the glowing pink stars and the perfume and the rumpled covers all around her, Madeleine sat up, groggy and blinking, and wondered where she was.

Jack was asleep to her left, one arm flung over the quilted silk counterpane. The light poured in from the quartet of floor-to-ceiling windows to her right, festooned in mulberry gauze and masked with carved wooden screens punched through with star-shaped holes, hundreds of them, each one aglow.

From somewhere nearby came a tinkling of chimes, high and delicate.

Cairo. The desert, the Nile.

She slipped out of the four-poster, careful not to wake her husband, and padded to the windows. It took a moment of fumbling to realize the screens didn't open outward or in, but slid on rollers along metal tracks, overlapping each other. She pushed them apart with both hands.

The sunrise flooded over her. She had to squint against it, raising a hand to shield her eyes, and only then did she realize she stood at the edge of a very wide balcony, and the windows weren't really windows at all, but doors left open to allow in the air and sun. She took a single step out and swam in the burgeoning dawn. Her hands and feet and nightgown were rose; the walls were rose; the sky was rose streaked with bronze and copper, a thick band of lapis still lingering low to the west.

Before her, right directly before her, soared the great pyramids of Giza, so towering and perfectly formed, so radiantly orange-pink with dusty blue shadows, that they looked like the painted backdrop of a play. They looked simultaneously both near and far, impossible to touch and impossible not to want to.

The wind stirred and the chimes sounded again, a pretty pair of them dangling above a table set close to the railing, their pipes and tails flashing. A bird in the gardens below began to sing, a low, mellow warble, soon joined by another; beneath them came the sounds of early morning traffic, motorcars and donkeys and roosters and voices, all reaching her from somewhere unseen. The hem of her nightgown ruffled against her shins, and even though she stood there in her bare feet, clad only in a sheath of fine lawn and lace, Madeleine realized she wasn't cold. Finally, at last, she wasn't cold.

"Egypt," she said aloud, letting the breeze steal the syllables from her lips. She wanted to laugh, so she did, making hardly any sound at all. Inside her, deep inside her core, something seemed to unclench.

"Baby," she whispered, cupping her hands over her womb, feeling perhaps the slightest hardness where she had been soft before. "Little baby, here we are."

She felt at once that anything was possible. That she could leap over the balcony railing and clamber down the side of the hotel like a monkey, run across the grounds, across the clipped green grass and in and out of the palms until it all melted into sand. She could run up the pyramids themselves, all the way to the top, giddy with the power of herself. With the power of being free.

There wasn't a single reporter or photographer in view, only a stooped figure in a robe in the distance, slowly pushing a hand mower in front of the far hedges.

"What a view," murmured a voice behind her, and Jack came up, pulling her back against his chest. She sighed, resting against him.

"It's incredible, isn't it? I never thought I'd see anything like this."

"I meant my wife," he said, his jaw against her ear. "My ravishingly lovely wife."

She laughed again. "I was just imagining myself as a monkey. The better to scale the pyramids."

"I thought you were a mermaid?"

"Mermaids do not suit the desert."

"True enough." He lowered his head to her neck, breathed against her skin. "Let's make you a gazelle. Graceful, fleet. A creature of the wadis and steppes, right at home in the heat."

She lifted a hand to his hair, turned her face toward his.

"Perfect," she said.

She did not run up the pyramids. No one ran up the pyramids; one might clamber awkwardly up them, block by enormous block, or else be lifted and tugged and pushed by whichever guides could be hired with enough piastres to carry the tourists practically in their arms the whole way.

Maybe a real gazelle could have managed it. But Madeleine was, in the end, a pregnant woman still worn out from a long series of voyages. Her spirit was willing; her body was not. And she didn't like being lifted by strangers. It felt too much like the pressmen back in New York, trying to touch her, trying to crowd her, trying to get her to react to them however they could so they could write it up and publish it and laugh over it.

She managed seven blocks, then waved away the beaming men attempting to coax her higher. She sat with her feet dangling over the edge with Jack sitting beside her, peeling a boiled egg from the basket of food the hotel had packed for them. Two more guides squatted behind them, ready to lower her down again.

Jack handed her the egg. She took a bite, gazing out at the rippling sand.

"Still happy, Mrs. Astor?"

"Yes." She looked at him sideways from beneath the brim of her Panama hat. "Are you, Colonel Astor?"

Like her, he faced the sands. Below them milled more tourists and guides, and camels adorned with bells and blankets, walking in trudging lines. Rosalie was down there somewhere, too, waiting for them, along with Robins, Jack's valet, but Madeleine couldn't pick them out. All the American and European women carried parasols; everyone, of both genders, was hatted. A line of native women in robes and veils sat at makeshift wooden stalls, selling everything from figs and oranges to crocodile teeth.

It wasn't yet noon, and the sun felt fierce. In the early desert light, beneath his own Panama hat, Jack's eyes paled to silver, and his skin warmed to honey.

"I am," he said soberly, "without question, the happiest man in the world."

At midday, they took a carriage back to the hotel, Madeleine sleepy enough to lean her head against his shoulder. She tried to keep her eyes open but couldn't; it didn't feel as if she slept, though. She still heard all the city around her, the clip-clopping hooves of the horses, the lilting calls of the street vendors, children constantly begging for baksheesh, horns bugling. The pace of the *calèche* along the crowded roads was erratic, surging and slowing, but even that didn't rouse her.

When they reached the hotel, she drifted into their suite, kicked off her shoes, and aimed for the bed. Rosalie barely had time to unpin her hair before Madeleine embraced her pillow and sank into peace.

* * *

That night, that second night, long after dinner, they swam together in the huge marble swimming bath. Fires in iron braziers marked the edges of the pool, casting dramatic dark shadows along the stone and water. Jack told her that later on, after all the guests had retired, the bath would be drained and cleaned and refilled again for the next morning, so that each new day it shone clear and fresh, an aquamarine jewel gleaming at the edge of the desert's dust and heat.

A pair of attendants waited silently in the dark by the cabanas, minding the towels and stars.

The water in the swimming bath felt like her skin, exactly the same temperature somehow. It was certainly warmer than the air, cooled to an arid crispness with the fallen sun, and best of all, they had it nearly to themselves. There was only an older German couple sharing the pool with them, who clung to the steps near the shallow end and had said nothing beyond *guten Abend*, occasionally chortling and splashing each other with the flats of their hands.

Madeleine was a strong enough swimmer not to mind the deep end of the bath. And Jack, of course . . . well, Jack could do anything. It didn't surprise her at all to see him slicing through the water in his tunic and trunks in clean, hard strokes.

"You know," she said, resting her crossed arms along the edge of the pool, kicking her feet behind her, "the first time I saw you, I looked a lot like this."

"Like this?" He swam up beside her, picked up her soaked braid of hair, and wrapped it around his wrist. He drew his arm to his chest to pull her closer, to tilt her head and kiss her on the lips, ignoring the scandalized attention of the Germans.

"Yes. I'd just climbed out of the sea—"

"A mermaid."

"Precisely. And I sat on the sand at Bailey's Beach and saw you walking along. You were going to see your mother. She sat in a tent."

He paused, then unwound her braid to join her with his arms propped atop the marble rim. "Really? When was that?"

"Long, long ago. When I was—oh, when I was a schoolgirl. But even then, I noticed you."

He pushed a hand along his wet hair, slicking it from his forehead. "You never said."

"I think I half-forgot. It was years ago. It's like a dream memory to me now. Isn't that funny? I forget the day, and why I was there. On holiday with my mother, I believe. But I remember you. I remember thinking that you were quite dashing."

"Well." He seemed amused.

"I think that was the moment I fell in love with you," she said.

He sank away from the edge of the pool, treading water, studying her. The Germans were climbing out at the other end, searching for the attendants through the firelight.

"Yes," she said, certain. "That was the moment. I looked at you, you looked at me—you won't recall it, but you did, just for a second—and *ta-dah*. It was done. Love. Just like that."

She dropped away from the marble rim as well, floating on her back with her arms out, gazing up at the night. A scattering of brighter stars shone through the smoke, sometimes there, sometimes not, forming new constellations, cryptic patterns of their own.

The water purled, shattered into ripples of fire as he came to float alongside her. Jack drew his palm along the lines of her— neck, chest, stomach—pausing at that modest roundness where their child grew, before pulling back.

"Do you know the moment I fell in love with you?"

She smiled drowsily up at the stars. "Tell me."

"When you asked to read my book. Do you remember that? That night on the balcony, back in Bar Harbor?"

"Yes," she said, surprised. She turned her head to look at him, water caressing her cheek. "All the way back then?"

"All the way back then," he answered, grave. "You are the only one who's ever asked me about reading it, you know. The only one."

"I really enjoyed it."

"You're a very charming liar."

They laughed together, hushed, and she came upright, treading as he did, feeling the liquid pushing back and forth through her open fingers, buoying her body and legs.

"What a strange mistress Fortune has turned out to be," Madeleine said.

"Strange, and marvelous."

"Yes," she agreed, gliding closer. She wrapped her hands behind his neck so that they bobbed together, their fronts and legs deliciously brushing. "Marvelous."

So they'd said the words after all. And the words had taken nothing away from them, their dark and precious bond. The words had only added another flavor, smoky sweet, like the night.

CHAPTER 19

My first sight of our *dahabiya* came under a searing, cloudless sky, with light and shadows so brittle every line of the vessel shone sharp. She'd been scrubbed and provisioned and freshly painted, forest green and bone white and ochre, a fanciful scrollwork of blue decorating her prow. She was smaller than the *Noma* but not by much, with twin wooden masts and an awning of apricot covering her open top deck.

As I stood at the edge of the Nile and watched the crew queue up to greet us, the overhang of the awning lifted and fell with the breeze, one tassel at a time, as if waving to us.

The name painted upon her side was *Habibti*. Beloved.

Your father stood beside me in the sun with his hands on his hips, taking it all in. When the captain approached, bearded and layered in robes, Jack handed me Kitty's leash and walked with him down to the landing. I stayed back a moment to watch them, your father nodding and asking questions, nodding again whenever the captain gestured to this part of his boat or that.

I didn't need to have the *Habibti*'s virtues described to me. I had no doubt this was the finest vessel to be found on the river. Jack would not have hired anything less.

Here is the moment I remember clearest from that morning: your father beginning to move toward the gangplank, the waiting crew, then stopping, turning to look back at me. As our eyes met, he grinned, boyish, and lifted his open hand to invite me to join him, all alight with the sun.

We stepped aboard the *dahabiya* together, feeling the languid, steady pulse of the Nile rolling gently beneath our feet.

Oh, I hope you have his smile. I hope I get to see his smile again, through you.

February 1912
Abydos, Egypt

They took a hired motorcar to the temple of Seti I, because it was nearly an hour trip from the river even so, and renting horses instead—the more common method of reaching the ruins— would have meant riding in the sun for three hours or longer. As it was, they had decided to camp overnight by the ruins, as the only hotels available were, in the words of Izz al din, their captain, unfit for anything but rats and their fleas.

Madeleine sat in the back of the canvas-topped touring car, crammed against Margaret's daughter Helen, Margaret herself squashed up against the other door. Jack sat in the front with their driver, a handsome young man in a pristine white *galabeya*, who had shaken each of their hands with great ceremony and introduced himself as Thabit, the best dragoman to be found in all of North Africa.

Izz al din had given a shake of his head at that, but as he was the one who had recommended him as a guide from the masses thronging the landing, it seemed he had nothing to say aloud about it.

Madeleine didn't know if Thabit was the best dragoman, but it did seem he had the best automobile in Abydos, which meant that at least it had a roof attached to the chassis. Their tents and baggage and supplies all followed in a second motorcar, along with a few of the crew from the *Habibti*, roasting in the open day. Kitty, too much of a wild card to bring along overnight, remained behind on the boat in the care of Rosalie and Robins, stealing scraps from the galley and napping in the shade.

For a while, they drove surrounded by camphor trees and green fields, sugarcane, barley and wheat, all lush with the abundant water of the Nile. Huge, placid water buffaloes standing alongside the road lifted their heads as they passed; dogs barked at them; children popped out randomly from the stalks and reeds, running dangerously close, their hands outstretched for piastres. Thabit would press the horn and weave around them, hardly slowing. More than once, Madeleine had to hide her eyes.

The trees and verdant fields faded away, gone as the water was gone.

The sands began, long and barren and endless.

Helen Brown, auburn-haired and gray-eyed, and looking like a younger, prettier version of her mother, lifted her chin and closed her eyes and breathed deep, her hands clamped around her knees. Madeleine couldn't tell if she was happy or merely queasy until she spoke.

"Isn't it devastating, Mrs. Astor?" Her voice was nearly drowned by the commotion of the engine.

"Sorry?" Madeleine said loudly.

"The air. The history. One soaks it all in and can't help but be changed by it. A soul-deep sort of change. Shifted. Devastated, but in the best way."

Madeleine smiled, doubtful, but then turned her face to the open window and supposed that Helen was right. They traveled along the heat-shimmered path of ancient gods, on their way to walk over and through the burial sites and shrines of lost kings. So many other souls had crossed this desert land before them, had lived and worshiped and perished here, leaving behind only brick and clay, stone and metal, alongside the fragmented remains of the pharaohs' immense riches.

But *they*, devastated or not, would arrive in their modern motorcar, and tonight would feast on fine food and wine in their tents, and tomorrow head back to the Nile, the river of life, to resume their place among the living.

The kings and temples would remain, standing as long as they could against the sands.

Thabit was shouting something back at them, lifting a hand to point at a row of rocks in the distance. They were the same color as everything else on the ground, buff and dun, bleached and chalky, painfully pale against the neon sky. They looked like nothing at all at first, lines and shapes, but as the motorcar growled closer, Madeleine could see the lines had an order to them, that they connected into a flat roof and pillars. A vast courtyard and wide steps and ramps.

Thabit slowed, still pointing.

"The dominion of the dead," he called back to them, and grinned.

The moment they emerged from the car, they were surrounded by souvenir sellers, men and children mostly, showing off miniature statues, scraps of papyrus, ivory figurines, ankhs and faience scarabs and enameled amulets. One child—a girl, the only one in sight—wiggled between her competitors to present Madeleine with a necklace of polished reddish-orange beads, holding it out to her with both hands.

Madeleine smiled, lifting the string, testing its weight.

"Asalamu alaykum," she tried, one of the few Arabic phrases she had heard repeated enough to have memorized. *Peace be with you*; it seemed to serve as both *hello* and *goodbye*.

"Do not buy it," advised Thabit, appearing at her side. He scowled at the girl and said something brusque, shooing the child away with one hand. "It's likely only glass. If you wish for true carnelian, for jewelry or gold, ma'am, I have a cousin in Luxor with the finest shop in Egypt. First quality. I will get you a bargain."

He lifted his voice and said something else to the crowd, and perhaps it was that the men from the *dahabiya* sauntered up, as well, but the swarm of sellers broke apart, wandering across the courtyard to find easier targets.

The temple honoring the great dead pharaoh was composed of limestone and sandstone incised with cartouches, and armies of small brown birds that winged through the shafts of light and high, dense shadows, perching and hopping and taking flight again. It was much cooler inside the towering stone walls than out, which might explain the murmuring birds, although the floor was mostly uneven chipped stone, so Madeleine had to be careful how she stepped.

Jack held her arm, keeping them both steady.

Both Margaret and her daughter had produced mirrors from their handbags, and they used them to reflect the narrow sun shafts falling from slits in the ceiling into beams of movable light. Everywhere they aimed the mirrors, the walls and columns came alive with color. Thabit trailed behind them, reciting the names of the illumed figures in a quiet, reverent tone, as if he spoke incantations.

Osiris.

Isis.

Seti.

Amun-Ra.

The queen, supplicating the god of the underworld.

The young prince, hunting alone.

Horus.

Ptah.

The goddess Nut, giving birth to the sun.

Seti.

Seti.

Seti.

The friezes were so clear, so fresh, they might have been created only a few years ago instead of centuries. She found herself more than once reaching up a hand to touch them, then made herself stop. These were olden beings, sacred beings. She didn't want to disrespect them. She didn't want them lingering on her fingertips.

Their tent was nearly as large as their cabin back on the boat, lit with both clear and colored glass lanterns, so that the cloth corners became green and violet and tangerine, and the entrance was ordinary gold. The crew had unrolled a large cream-and-carmine rug across the sand, then added a wooden table inlaid with mother-of-pearl, two chairs, and a pair of iron-framed camp beds topped, incongruously, with layers of satin covers.

A bowl of dates and sliced bread (rapidly drying out) sat upon the table, alongside two glasses and a flagon of red wine. Madeleine stood there and nibbled at a date, testing its grainy sweetness.

"Wife," said Jack, from just beyond the open entrance of the tent. "Come out. Come see the moon."

She ducked outside. The stillness of the evening struck her; she heard the relaxed conversation among the men from the *Habibti*, preparing their meal of lamb kabobs and rice over the fire, Thabit occasionally joining in with a chuckle. She heard Helen saying something to Margaret in their tent a dozen yards away, their shadows behind the canvas walls shifting in graceful, elongated lines. But they were the only group camping, the only people within miles, maybe, and beyond those dampened human notes, there lived a noiseless hush, the sound of emptiness that stretched on and on into the ebony night.

Perhaps Jack heard it, too. Without another word, he took her by the hand and drew her away from the tents, from the others and the tantalizing aroma of saffron and charred lamb. They toiled through the sand, sometimes ankle deep, until they stood on a flat, rocky crest far apart from everyone else, facing the ruins in the distance, the moon-frozen courts and shrines and halls.

The dominion of the dead.

Jack reached into his pocket. He withdrew a strand of smooth, heavy beads, reddish-orange, and draped it over her head.

"They were carnelian," he said. "Not glass. I may not own the finest jewelry shop in Luxor, but I know a few things."

He placed his arm around her shoulders. Madeleine lifted a hand to close her fingers over the beads. They stood there saying nothing, only watching, only listening to the aching, terrible silence of the desert, until Margaret summoned them back for dinner.

The next afternoon they returned to the landing, where a series of wooden sailboats were docked, rocking in the blue-green waters. The *Habibti*, larger than the rest, was moored in the shade of a grove of date palms growing close to the riverbank, their fronds rustling with every sultry slip of wind. Their crew meandered along the decks, their long robes floating pale through the light and dark.

Kitty spotted them first. The instant the gangplank was lowered, she tore across it with a happy bark, leaping through the milling sailors and vendors and tour guides to reach them. Jack laughed and dropped down to grab her just as she leapt up to kiss him, squeaking with joy. Madeleine dropped down, too, and the dog whipped out of Jack's arms and into hers, pressing her head into Madeleine's side, whining now, her tail a blur.

"Mother," said Helen, watching the scene transpire, "I want a dog."

"Later," replied Margaret. "When you're done with your studies. We'll get two."

Jack laughed again and straightened, and Robins hurried down to meet them, directing the unloading of the autos, consulting with the colonel about their itinerary and supplies. Madeleine looked around, testing the back of her hand against her neck and cheek, but Jack was still busy, and she was hot, and her legs were cramped from the motorcar ride, so she picked up her skirts and made her way up the gangplank, followed by Helen and Margaret, still debating about the proper time for dogs.

She wanted to change out of her gritty clothes. She wanted to let down her hair and wash and comb it, and drink something cool and tart, and take a nap with the windows open in their cabin so she could listen to the river as she slept.

She got as far as unpinning her hair at the vanity when Jack opened the door, swiftly scanned the room, and said, "You don't have Kitty?"

"What?" Her hands lowered. "No. I thought she was with you."

"She isn't."

Madeleine followed him out of the cabin. They searched every deck, every closet and chamber, even the places a dog couldn't possibly be. At first, it was just the two of them, then together with Rosalie and Robins and the crew, then with Margaret and Helen as well, emerged from their cabins at the ongoing commotion.

They searched the landing and the dirt roads beyond it, Thabit and his auto quickly rehired to help. No one had seen the Airedale. No one noticed one extra brown dog among the many, darting between donkeys and huts.

Kitty was gone, lost to the tremendous, unfolding land.

CHAPTER 20

We searched for days.

We called her name until our voices grew hoarse, until those two small syllables, *Kit-ty*, came out cracked with despair.

You might think it odd to be in such a state over a lost dog. You might, but I hope you don't, because I hope you will be the sort of person who understands what your Aunt Katherine once said to Vincent: You can get the measure of a man by observing the way he treats his animals.

Eventually, we had to sail on. The Browns, especially, were on a schedule, and we had already lingered four days past what we had originally planned.

Before we left, your father offered a princely reward to any of the locals who could find her and get her back to us. It was all that we could do.

I began to slow down. I wanted to sleep more, particularly in the high heat of the afternoon. I still appreciated the unhurried pace of the boat, the scent of the river wafting through our cabin at night. I still appreciated a great many things, in fact, but I just didn't want to venture out for hours and hours any longer to go exploring. No more exhausting day trips, and nothing outdoors overnight. I was content to sit on the deck of the boat and watch the reeds sway along the shore; or the villagers washing clothing and filling urns in the shallows; or the tall, slender minarets of the mosques gliding by.

I was feeling, I guess, sunken. A sunken version of myself. A heavier version, one that wanted, very much, just to sit and eat and admire the moon forging pewter shadows along the dunes.

And, in truth, I could not stop myself from scrutinizing the banks for Kitty. Day or night, I couldn't stop looking for her. Every mangy tan dog loping along made me sit up a bit. (Egypt, in case you are wondering, has a great many tan dogs.) But it was never she.

Carrie Endres joined us in Aswan. She was a nurse of excellent reputation, and your father had hired her as a surprise to me. I don't know why that enraged me so much; it's foolish, in retrospect. Carrie was kind and competent and I am deeply ashamed now, all these months later, that I was so short with her at first. It wasn't her fault that your father had gone behind my back. I doubt she had the faintest idea he had. But springing the foregone conclusion of her upon me in the middle of our honeymoon made me feel like a child being punished. It made me feel like I could not be trusted with my own body, with my own health. It was the first serious disagreement we ever had—it was the only serious disagreement we ever had—and he won it, because Carrie had voyaged all the way from the States to watch over me, and Jack declared up and down that she wasn't going back unless I was going along with her, and that was that.

He never raised his voice. I did.

Our dog was irretrievable, you see, and we were both still raw from her loss. I'm sure that was some of it.

My feelings were bruised. I wept a little, hot helpless tears of anger, although I didn't do it in front of him. That evening as I sulked alone in my chair on the sun deck, Margaret brought me baklava in rose syrup and hibiscus tea and told me that I needed to accept what was done, because it *was* done, and raging against Jack's choices for me (*however highhanded*, she added) would only make matters worse.

Why not, she said, reflect upon his consideration instead of his sneakiness? And then she said something I'll never forget:

"It's plain as day Jack adores you. I think he adores you to the point that the thought of being without you terrifies him to the core. And for a man like Jack Astor, that is significant."

After that, I stopped my complaints.

March 1912
On the Nile

They turned around at Aswan, Madeleine's newly appointed nurse neatly stowed in an upper deck cabin. Izz al din informed them all that the journey downriver would go more quickly than the one up. They needed to make up for their lost days in order for Margaret and Helen to catch their steamer back to Italy. But there were still days enough for Kom Ombo, for Edfu. For Karnak, with its famed hypostyle halls and temples, its pillars built to graze heaven and eerie avenue of ram-headed sphinxes, muscular and staring.

At the feet of the colossal statue of Ramses II, Madeleine and Helen clambered up to stroke the ankle of the much smaller, female figure tucked against his legs: not a wife, as Madeleine had first assumed, but a royal daughter, her features feline and delicate, her lips not quite smiling.

A girl who had lived and died thousands of years past, still standing at her father's feet. Like the shepherdess in the painting in William Force's study halfway around the world, the princess had been captured in a singular moment forever because of a great man. And wasn't that something?

It was.

The *Habibti* left behind the babble of Luxor to make her way downriver again, floating in near silence along the tranquil waters. The weather was turning more summery, still clement, and sitting calm and quiet on her decks became the easiest thing in the world.

One afternoon, Madeleine reclined in her usual chair on the sun deck beneath the apricot awning, reading a book she'd found in the boat's little nook of a library. (It was about the customs and traditions of Argentina, left behind, no doubt, by some well-traveled client.) Carrie bustled nearby, preparing a plate of sandwiches for tea; Jack stood at the port railing, gazing out, restless. Margaret and Helen were playing poker near the stairs, but not very seriously. Every now and then, they would stop moving entirely for minutes at a time. Madeleine would catch them both staring dreamily at the passing view, the fans of cards in their hands forgotten.

Occasionally their boat passed other boats, bulky *dahabiya*s or smaller, lateen-sailed *felucca*s, and when this happened, usually at least someone from the crew would shout out a greeting, getting one in return, echoing across the wide river.

Madeleine could not help glancing up from her book, over and again, at her husband. Against the turquoise sky, he stood tense and tall, his left leg crooked at the knee as if it pained him. He kept his hat clenched in one hand.

She was looking at him when it happened. He lurched abruptly against the scrolled metal railing, leaning out over it, the brim of his hat crushed.

"*There,*" Jack bellowed, louder than she'd ever heard him. He used the hat to point at something below them, something Madeleine couldn't see. "By God, there she is!"

"*Marhaba!*" came an answering shout. "*Al'amirkiu! Hada hu kalabik!*"

Madeleine dropped her book. From somewhere out across the river came a familiar, ecstatic bark.

Everyone rushed to the railing.

Another wooden *dahabiya* surged upriver, its sails stained and puffed, the trio of men on its lower deck cheering at the sight of them, jumping up and down and waving their arms. Kitty stood in their midst, dancing, barking, and had not one of the men at the last moment grabbed her by the collar, there was no doubt she would have launched herself into the water, swimming across the Nile to reach them.

It was difficult for Madeleine to frame her sense of relief into words, into thought. She was able to do so in actions, however. She was able to cover Kitty in praise and kisses, to hug her near and close her eyes and breathe in the musky, not-quite-pleasant scent of a dog lost for weeks to the sand and wilds. She ran her hands along Kitty's ribs and spine and her fingers tangled with Jack's, also stroking, and together they held eyes and smiled and kept telling their dog what a good girl she was, what a good girl.

Although Madeleine's happiness was palatable, Jack's was even more so. Kitty had been his companion through the sticky months of his divorce and all the notorious, lonely days after, when even the *crème de la crème* of society, his own kind, had angled away from him. So she was happiest, actually, for him. For her husband, the hard creases lining his brow now lessened, his gray eyes lightened. He had his friend back. It gladdened her heart.

"Let's just keep her in the cabin with us at night," Madeleine suggested, because they'd been letting her roam before this, patrolling the boat in the silky dark, calling back to the jackals that cried in the distance.

"Yes," Jack agreed. "We'll make a bed for her. She shouldn't put up too much of a fuss."

Jack was right. After her escapade offshore, Kitty seemed perfectly content on her bed of folded blankets, as long as she could keep the colonel in sight. Madeleine thought both human and canine slept easier in each other's company, although she might have preferred a little more private time in the long stretch of night away from a snoring dog in need of a shampoo.

But this was her honeymoon, this time of sun and water and adventure. In its own unique way, this was how her family would knit together, bone to bone, husband and wife and child and companion. They were all here already. Already a unit.

In those final few days aboard the *Habibti*, it seemed to Madeleine that every hour was a raindrop, perfect and enclosed, falling down in a blessing from the sky to the earth.

At night, she would slide into sleep wrapped in Jack's arms, each of them with a hand cradled warm over her belly.

Goodnight, baby, she would think. *Goodnight, my daughter or son, my princess or prince.*

In Alexandria, the sun flirted from behind a flock of woolly white clouds, and their little group broke amiably apart. Jack and Madeleine accompanied the Browns in a horse-drawn *calèche* to the port, waved farewell as Margaret and Helen boarded their steamer to Naples.

"I'll see you this summer in Newport," Margaret said. "You can introduce your new baby to me."

"I will," Madeleine promised, and swallowed the rise of tears in her throat. She still wasn't accustomed to it, these wild emotional swings that would overtake her. Carrie had assured her it was normal for her condition, and eventually her moods would stabilize, but Madeleine wasn't there yet. Margaret Brown, her only ally in the social thicket of Rhode Island, was leaving, and would be absent for months. In just a short while, Madeleine was going to have to endure the icy gazes again alone.

Almost alone. Jack rubbed a slow circle between her shoulder blades with his palm.

"*Bon voyage,* fair ladies," he'd said, and in a froth of lace and netting, Helen had embraced them both, then Margaret, and then they were gone, lost to the bustle of passengers and crew and the gray columns of steam from all the ships, puffing and rolling up into the sky.

They would follow on their own steamer in a few days. They had plenty of time before they had to reach Paris again, and then Cherbourg for the voyage home. Jack had booked their passage to New York on Bruce Ismay's fine new steamship, her maiden voyage, which to Madeleine sounded like a recipe for enduring all sorts of little things going awry, but which her husband was looking forward to with open enthusiasm.

They spent the next few days visiting bazaars filled with spices and lamps and jewelry and blown glass; Pompey's Pillar in the acropolis; the medieval-looking Citadel of Qaitbay, where Moslem princes fallen out of favor had been imprisoned, and the doomed soldiers of the sultan fought off the Ottoman Turks as long as they could. Everywhere she stepped, her feet stirred up the dust of history, hundreds of years old or thousands. She wanted to memorize all of it, so she could carry these days and nights with her back to America. She wanted never to forget the perfect heat, the sand, the stars spread above her in a shifting, infinite river of platinum, stretching from end to end above the earth. The meteors that fell in silence all night, every night, sketching slow blazing lines into the heavy blue.

The rooms they occupied now at the New Khedivial had a very different character than the ones they'd been given during their initial visit.

Notre suite arabe, the manager had said, opening the double doors wide.

The rugs were sage and cobalt; the plaster walls baby blue. The ceiling and all the arched doorways were elaborately tiled, mosaics of interlinked circles and stars, diamonds and chevrons and dots, with punched-brass lanterns—orbs and pagodas and more stars—hanging from chains. Wooden screens covering their windows hid their own enclosed garden, with roses and jasmine and a guava tree, growing right in the middle of the grass.

Kitty began to sniff around its roots with interest.

On their way in, they had passed a celebration in the grand ballroom (*une réception de mariage*, the same manager had informed them from over his shoulder), and even though the ballroom was not near their suite, the music still reached them, muted and elegant, and the lanterns cast slow moving shadows with the jasmine breeze.

In their canopied bed, she lay awake and thought, *How splendid the hours are now. I never, ever want this to end.*

Jack murmured, his arm beneath her neck, "Let's name her Paris."

Madeleine smiled. "If I remember my *Iliad* correctly, Paris is a boy's name."

"Paris," he said, "because that's where we first were sure of her, in the City of Light."

"All right. And if it's a boy?"

"It won't be," he said, confident. "We're having a daughter."

She turned to press her cheek against his chest. "Far be it from me to contradict my husband, but just *in case* you're wrong, I think we need to consider a boy's name, too. We'll keep it in reserve."

"For our next child," he said softly, up to the canopy.

"Yes," she agreed, just as soft. "For the next one."

But the sound of a waltz crept through the bedroom, and while it whispered by, neither of them spoke again, until finally Madeleine admitted, "I'm going to miss it so much. I'll miss the place where we were just *al'amirkiu*, and *ma'am*. Do you know, I don't think I've seen a single camera since we arrived, except for the tourists at the ruins."

"We'll come back," he promised. "Next winter, if you like. Or we could go somewhere new entirely, another place they don't know us at all. How about Japan?"

She considered it. "Margaret raves about Nagasaki. I believe she mentioned wanting to retire there."

"There you have it. It's settled. A few seasons spent at home, a season or so abroad. You and me and little Paris. Or Arthur. Or Joseph. Or Hubert."

"Not Hubert!"

He laughed. "Not Hubert. We'll mull it over. There's time."

"John Jacob," she said.

"How many of us do there need to be? Let's give him a name of his own. Something new."

"John Jacob the Fifth *would* be new."

"I'm afraid not. That one's already taken. A distant cousin in England."

"The Sixth, then," she said, stubborn.

His arm tightened around her, his body warm and close. "Hubert, Grover, Shoeblack. Snarksblood, Muleview, Faradiddle, Muddington—heigh-ho! 'Muddington Astor'! That has a solid ring to it, don't you think? No? Well then, how about Pinky, Pokey, Jokey, Mopey—"

She was laughing too hard to say anything so she pushed up to her elbow instead, leaning over him, stopping his nonsense with a kiss.

CHAPTER 21

The press discovered us again in Rome. Jack had telegraphed both Vincent and Dobbyn the details of our itinerary, and I must suppose that is how the newsmen found us. (I had dashed off a letter to your Aunt Katherine with the same, but she would have never spoken to the press about it.) In any case, one way or another, the information got out, and the next thing we knew, it was published in the papers. We spent Easter hiding in our hotel, which was actually enchanting, watching the sunrise pinken the baroque warren of Piazza Navona from our private roof terrace, cappuccinos in hand. But, eventually, we had no choice but to emerge from our nest to move on to Cherbourg, our departure point in France.

I took comfort in the thought that at least while on the steamship, we would blend in with the rest of the first-class crowd. It seemed exceedingly unlikely there would be a journalist waiting to waylay us on board.

Cherbourg was, naturally, overcast. I couldn't help but think it appropriate, given my mood and the immediate future I was sure awaited me. The journey from Paris on the *Train Transatlantique* had taken no less than six hours. Six hours of smudgy black cinders and chugging motion and nauseatingly uneven scenery flashing by, so weirdly paced I could not gaze out at it for more than a few minutes at a time. Even the train's compartments were small, I thought. Too small to make room for my uncertain stomach, the headache gathering in a knot behind my eyes. By the time we arrived at the quayside terminus, I was in a state well beyond misery.

And then, worse and worse, the ship wasn't even there yet. Our liner had been delayed, we were told, back in Southampton—her first port of call—where she had nearly crashed into another ship ripped loose from her moorings just by the unearthly power of *Titanic's* displacement and wake.

So we waited. A manager from White Star's Paris office circulated among us inside the station, offering apologies and reassurances, and the unlucky man, I felt sorry for him. I did. He wasn't to blame for any of it, but you would think he'd arranged the holdup himself, the way some of our fellow passengers abused him.

The only bright spot was that we ran into Margaret Brown again, also waiting to board. She had received a telegram that her grandson in Denver was gravely ill, and so she had left Helen in Paris to rush back home. *Titanic* was the first available ship headed for New York, and as there were several first-class cabins still open, Margaret had had no problem securing a berth.

It was a relief to see her again, I confess.

In retrospect, of course, I would not have wished that voyage upon anyone, especially a friend.

Wednesday, April 10, 1912
Cherbourg, France

The waiting room of the train station was plainly too small for the number of people anticipating the arrival of *Titanic*. Madeleine estimated there was well over a hundred and fifty of them, and that was just the first- and second-class passengers. There were even more people on the crowded platform outside, mostly booked in steerage, she would guess: men in flowing robes that reminded her of the *galabeyas* of Egypt; women with exotically bright shawls wrapped over their shoulders and around their heads, standing and sitting in clusters, calling out to their children in languages she had never heard before. When the wind blew in past the quay, the many shawls would lift and flutter, and she was reminded of clouds of butterflies, dancing against the gloom.

Porters pushing oversized trolleys loaded with suitcases and trunks wound through the multitudes, answering question after question and somehow keeping their composure amid all the jabbering confusion.

Mr. Martin, the White Star man, had already shepherded the Astor group, Margaret, and an older, ermine-clad matron (nervously pale, constantly blinking) through the concourse to a row of benches placed against a wall, somewhat removed from the maelstrom of people.

"I simply do not know . . ." the matron would mutter, again and again. As she never seemed capable of finishing her sentence, Madeleine had no idea what she did not know. She seemed to be an acquaintance of Margaret's—who kept absently patting the back of her hand, as if in comfort—but Margaret, in her preoccupation, had failed to introduce them.

Kitty had decided to seat herself on Madeleine's right foot. Madeleine leaned forward, careful not to dislodge the dog, and caught the matron's eyes. There was a small smudge of black on her chin, likely from a cinder, but there didn't seem a polite way to mention it.

"How do you do? I'm Madeleine."

"Oh," said the matron, still blinking; she looked as if she could barely hold back tears. "I know who you are, of course! Both of you. How do you do."

Margaret stirred. "Forgive me. Madeleine, Jack, this is Emma Bucknell, a friend from Philadelphia. Emma's been touring Egypt, as well, it turns out."

"How nice," said Madeleine warmly. "Didn't you love it?"

"It was exceptional," the matron said. "But now—now we have this."

"It won't be long until the liner comes," Jack said, crossing his legs. "Martin assured me he means to load the tenders within the hour. We'll be off soon."

"Yes," said Mrs. Bucknell. She blotted her eyes with a handkerchief. "I just—oh, I just have the most frightful feeling about it all. I'm sorry! I'm not usually like this. But I have the most frightful feeling. Just the most *foreboding* feeling about getting on that ship."

Margaret shifted on the bench. "Emma, you've had too much coffee today and not enough food, that's all it is. Once you see *Titanic*, you'll realize everything is fine. We're going to be there in time for supper, I'm sure, and then you'll feel better."

"If it's anything like dining on the *Olympic*," Madeleine offered, "you'll be quite satisfied."

"It will be better than the *Olympic*." Jack came to his feet, brushing at his jacket, Kitty instantly springing up to follow. "All of it, from bow to stern. There's no need to worry, madam. *Titanic* is the safest ocean liner in the world."

"That's right," agreed Margaret, but her eyes were distant once more. "Everyone says so."

The minutes ticked by, the hour Jack had been promised turning into an hour and a quarter, and then an hour and a half, and still the steamship had not been sighted on the sea line, and the tenders did not launch.

Madeleine grew uncomfortable; with her increasing size, it had become harder and harder to sit still in one place for too long. Kitty needed to be walked, in any case, so they left their group behind to take in the scenery, such as it was.

A long, thin jetty stretched out over the chopped water, a stone tower crouched at its end. The two tenders, the *Nomadic* and the *Traffic*, pitched in the waves. They were already heavily loaded with luggage and mail; all they needed now were the paying passengers.

Plus, *Titanic*.

The clouds lowered, lifted, bunched and scattered. Sunlight waxed and waned, sending bright flashing coins across the harbor, and the wind gusted cooler.

"How are you feeling?" Jack asked, as Kitty sniffed at a scruff of grass growing from the muck near the path.

"Tired," she admitted. "A little impatient, I guess. But it's nice to escape that smoky waiting room. I was getting queasy."

"I'm sorry."

"No, for what? I wasn't complaining, I assure you."

"I know. I just . . . I want things to go smoothly. I want you to be careful."

"I *am* careful," she said, irritated.

"And I want to get you a proper meal," he went on with barely a pause, "because you're so grumpy without one."

"I beg your pardon!"

"All right. I pardon you."

She gazed at him, speechless, torn between wanting to be offended and wanting to laugh. Jack slanted a smile at her, lifted her hand in his to kiss her knuckles, one by one, over her kid glove.

"Mrs. Astor. How beautiful you are when provoked."

"You are supposed to tell me I am beautiful all the time, not just when you needle me."

"You are the sole object of true beauty in all the world," said her husband, "no matter your mood. And that is the honest truth."

The White Star manager hustled them aboard the tenders in an optimism of hope, Madeleine thought, given that they were launching out into the harbor without any hint of the liner to meet them yet in view.

The *Nomadic*, like *Titanic*, was essentially new, built especially to shuttle people and mail and supplies to and from White Star's enormous new *Olympic*-class ships, which were far too large to dock near the quay. The tender was spacious enough inside, clean and refined, with tiled floors and carved plaster walls and a long, varnished bar lined with waiting stewards. She'd been on it once before, ten weeks ago when they'd disembarked from the *Olympic*. Back then, it hadn't seemed quite so congested.

Jack guided her to one of the wooden banquettes in the forward lounge, and Madeleine sat again, her maid on one side of her and her nurse on the other, Kitty ducking under the table at her feet, as the colonel and his valet went to see about procuring food from the buffet.

"Waiting for a steward to come to us," he said, looking around at the chattering, restless mob of people, "will leave us *all* old and gray."

They returned with sliced fruit and finger sandwiches, which Madeleine was desperate to eat, but by then, the tender was beginning to battle the rougher waves of the outer harbor, and her stomach rebelled. She tried a bite of apple, chewing as slowly as she could, but in no time, her nausea was worse, and her headache had returned.

She fed a cheese and pickle sandwich to Kitty, who didn't bother to chew at all.

The pretty plaster trimwork decorating the walls began to spin. She shoved to her feet but had to bend over as spots took her vision, balancing herself with all ten fingertips pressed against the rim of the table.

"Ma'am?" Carrie seized her by the arm at the same time Jack said urgently, "Madeleine," taking her other arm.

She wet her lips. "I think I must go above. I—I need to be outside."

Later on, when she tried to remember how she made it from the first-class lounge to the deck, all she would recall was a blur of colors, of voices, and that both of her elbows were caught in two very hard grips. The next clear memory was of sucking in cold, bracing breaths of sea air, half-collapsed against Jack with Carrie hovering nearby, a vial of smelling salts in her hand.

"I'm all right," she said, the words coming out without any actual evidence of truth. She said it again, more slowly. "I'm all right."

The wind scoured her skin, and it felt like waking up from a bad dream. She turned her face into it, blinking. The sun was low now, casting terra-cotta light against the darkening blue clouds, and the water splashed and hissed as it was sliced in two by *Nomadic*'s bow.

She was cold, but it felt good to be cold. It felt like she could take a deep breath again without gagging.

"Come sit here." Jack urged her toward a cushioned chair that a steward had produced from nowhere, and then a blanket, quickly whipped over her lap.

"I'm sorry," she said, holding a hand to her forehead. "I'm so sorry for the bother."

"Nonsense," said her nurse. "It was no fit environment for even the heartiest of us in there, so stuffy and enclosed and choked with all the gentlemen's smoke. I have no notion why they don't bother to take themselves out of doors to enjoy their tobacco, I truly don't. You'll do better out here, ma'am, I promise. I'll stay with you, to make certain you're not too chilled."

"As will I," said Jack. "We'll watch for *Titanic* together. A dollar to the person who sights her first."

"All right," said Madeleine, still savoring her long, deep breaths.

"You have a deal, sir," said Carrie, replacing the salts into her coat pocket.

An hour or so later, Carrie Endres, with her sharp blue eyes and smiling ways, won the dollar.

It came at them as a fortress, as a castle, as a painted feverscape towering above the ocean. It was the tallest, scariest thing Madeleine had ever seen, bearing down on them in a crest of freshly slaughtered saltwater.

Titanic arrived eating up the flat horizon.

Titanic arrived swallowing the waves.

In the gray-foamed disturbance churned to life by the steamship, the gangway between the liner and the *Nomadic* would not cease its uneasy shifting. A group of sailors held it down at both ends, but it popped and bucked as much as it could, groaning with the pressure of the waves. Several other passengers had already defied it to board, Margaret Brown included, but Madeleine eyed the platform with trepidation. The tender's repeated hard collisions against the side of *Titanic* did nothing to lessen her fears, or her nausea. Many of the ladies negotiating the gangway did so with stifled squeals and yelps.

Madeleine made it across, though, with no squealing and her head high (because they were watching already; all those distinguished society people turning in place to watch her), her husband basically propelling her along, Kitty clipping at her heels. She could do no less.

The wind lashed her skirts hard against her ankles in just the eternity it took to hurry along the gangplank, but then it was over. She made it into the vestibule of the liner, her feet finding what felt like firm land, although it wasn't.

But the black-and-white floor of *Titanic*'s first-class entranceway did not shift, not even by a hair. It felt real and solid. She was nearly in tears at the relief.

"Colonel Astor, Mrs. Astor," greeted an officer in a frock coat, inclining his head and gesturing with his hand where they should go. "Welcome aboard. This is the way."

They entered the reception room, Madeleine clinging to Jack's arm. It was an opulent, soaring hall of thick rugs, wicker chairs and tables, men and women dressed for dinner holding aperitifs and listening to a piano and string quartet discreetly playing against a background of potted palms.

Madeleine felt, bizarrely, as if she had stepped back in time. She was back in some mansion in Newport or Manhattan, the same stony people, the same stony expressions. She had plunged right back into the world she had worked so hard to escape. She actually came to a complete halt, her right foot half-lifted, the toe of her shoe dragging against the floor, physically unable to finish her step.

She wanted to turn around, retreat, fly back to the tender and hide ashore.

The stony gazes descended, one by one, to the unmistakable bulge of her stomach beneath her coat and dress.

She lowered her foot.

Bruce Ismay, speaking with a steward against one of the arched windows, caught sight of them and hastened over. He and Jack shook hands, quick and hard.

"So delightful to see you again, so delightful," he was saying. He turned to Madeleine, bowing over her hand in a fluid swoop. "Mrs. Astor. You are as radiant as ever."

Ismay offered a smile from beneath his heavy moustache. Madeleine made herself smile in return, even though she had seldom seen anyone lie with less conviction.

With only the barest undertone of impatience, Jack said, "If you don't mind, Ismay, I'd like to get us settled in our rooms. The delay was rather unpleasant."

"Of course. My apologies. Latimer will show you to your suite; he's our best man." Ismay lifted a hand, and the steward he had been speaking with instantly approached. "The Astor party, C deck, as I recall. Check your manifest." He turned back to Jack. "I trust you'll find everything satisfactory from this point on."

"I trust we will." He paused. "Perhaps later you might offer me a tour of your new ship."

"Colonel," said the chairman of the White Star Line, as the music soothed and the other first-class passengers laughed and gossiped and angled edgewise to look them up and down, "it would be my pleasure."

The comment she overheard time and again on their way to their rooms was always some variation of, *It doesn't seem like a ship at all!*

And it didn't. *Titanic's* interior (in contrast to her sinister dark and sharp exterior, at least what Madeleine had glimpsed of it in those minutes jolting along its base) was more like a fine hotel than anything else, as boldly sumptuous as any of Jack's properties back in New York. The corridors were broad and freshly painted, pungent still, with extravagantly worked wood and plush, plush carpeting that muffled their every step.

There was a wait for the electric elevators, so they climbed the grand staircase instead. It was wide and open and graciously curved all the way to the domed skylight decks above, an inverted cup of lustrous glass and geometric iron fretwork. The repeating curves of the balustrades reminded Madeleine of the math of a nautilus, neatly sliced into pieces.

Their suite consisted of room after room of red-and-mauve silk-papered walls shot with silver, lacquered mahogany tables and chairs, Jacobean plasterwork unwinding in curls all along the ceilings and down the corners. The cushions and coverlets were shiny satin; the lights were either silk-hatted sconces or else ceiling fixtures of cut glass. There were so many chinoiserie vases stuffed with fresh flowers that Madeleine wondered who had thought it a good idea to put them all out. They perched, fragile and expensive, atop the tables and tall, spindly-legged stands.

She stopped in the doorway to her bedroom, taking in the opulence. It was such a far cry from the cabin they'd shared aboard the *dahabiya* that once again she could not move, awash in a sensation of deep tugging loss.

"It's not one of the deluxe promenade suites, I realize," Jack said, coming up behind her. He rested both hands atop her shoulders, pressed a kiss against her hair. "I tried to book either, but I was too late—or else Ismay was simply too greedy. He's taken one for himself. Mrs. Cardeza is in the other."

Madeleine closed her eyes and groaned. "Charlotte Cardeza is here?"

"She is, or will be tomorrow. I didn't see her when we came in."

Mrs. Cardeza, with her cold eyes and cutting words and splendid air of a disapproving sheep, on board with them for the entire voyage.

"It's all right. I envision spending the next few days secluded in this stateroom, no matter what comes." Without turning around, she lifted his left hand, held it against her cheek. His skin felt warm and dry, his wedding band cool. "Do you think they might bring us our dinner here tonight, instead of us having to change and go down to the dining saloon?"

"They will," Jack said comfortably, "if I say they will."

Among its other amenities, the suite featured two four-poster beds, with two fat feather mattresses.

They slept together in one, entwined in its plump middle.

CHAPTER 22

Beautiful boy, I have wrapped you in lace.

Right now it rests lightly over you, an ivory cobweb of slender spun silk, outlining your precious body, folded against your perfect cheek.

Light as a cloud, it was meant, perhaps, to adorn you in church for your christening. Or to be photographed in a formal portrait, for when you are presented to the world. But I decided not to wait that long.

This blanket of Irish lace was purchased from a lace trader who'd slipped aboard *Titanic* in Queenstown, the ship's third and final port of call. As they did with all the liners calling, even by tender, the local souvenir sellers had greased the palms of certain officers to steal aboard, trafficking their wares for a brief while along the boat deck while the captain turned a hard blind eye. In Ireland, it turns out, the lace and blackthorn cane sellers are especially popular.

In that fleeting hour or so of that early Thursday afternoon, before *Titanic* weighed her anchor to sail onward again, Jack had walked among the traders, admiring this and that. By the time the vendors were all packed off again, he had found me a lace jacket and you this.

This blanket was your father's first gift to you.

And it was the last thing I stuffed into my pocket before fleeing the ship.

A number of ill-mannered souls—reporters, of course—have dared, in these latter weeks, to ask me the best thing I remember about *Titanic*. About the ship itself. As if by telling them that, everything that followed might be negated. Rendered *less*.

My usual response is an incredulous stare, then to walk away. I have menservants now to accompany me whenever I go out, so the journalists and cameras do not hound me as easily as they used to do. I've learned, you see, since my days as a dewy débutante on your father's arm.

I have learned that you do not have to speak to the press at all. You owe them nothing.

You don't have to speak.

But I will answer that question for you, my son. Because you were there, and your father was there, and so was I. All three of us together, locked in love for that blink of a moment in time.

The best memory I have about *Titanic* was that she was so large.

So epic.

I never felt any swaying or bobbing or turbulence to interfere with my meals, my sensitive appetite, or my slumber. I never felt any sort of vulnerability aboard that ocean liner, right up until the very end.

I imagine that's a blessing, don't you? Whoever wants to know how it's all going to end before it actually does?

Only poets and madmen, I would think.

Thursday, April 11, 1912
Aboard Titanic

The music wafting through the Café Parisien from the outer chamber nearby might have been chosen specifically to counterpoint the hum of conversation rising from the dining tables, everything tasteful and subtle and full of undercurrents neatly hidden beneath the brighter notes. Madeleine followed those notes even as she didn't mean to, sipping her *café au lait* and pretending not to mind the looks aimed at her, the sound of her name spiking through the air, from mouths to ears and back again.

She had secured a table near one of the windows, brilliant with the late morning sun. She kept her own focus distant, engrossed, gazing out at the ocean view as if sitting alone at this splendid chic table in this splendid ivy-trellised restaurant didn't bother her at all. The wicker back of her chair bit into her shoulders; she had to keep reminding herself not to wrap both hands protectively around her middle.

Her hat, forest felt and chocolate silk wrapping, was rounded and large enough that it blocked a good deal of the chamber. The curved brim was meant to shield her, to protect her from the day, but what it really did was hide her from the intrusive stares.

The scent of her coffee, creamy and rich, filled her nose. The fat pair of croissants on her plate lay spread with jam, red raspberry glistening.

A woman approached the table. From Madeleine's perspective beneath her hat, she consisted entirely of an overskirt of green-and-white serge.

"Am I late for our coffee date?" inquired Margaret, pulling out her chair without waiting to be helped. "I apologize."

"Oh no, I don't think so. I was early, and the waiters kept hovering, so . . ." She shrugged, looked at her *café au lait* and those croissants, buttery and fresh. "My appetite," she added dryly, "seems to have returned."

"That's good news. I'm ready for a real meal myself, taking on all these stairs. Everyone goes on about those fancy elevators, but I haven't seen a moment yet when there isn't a stack of people waiting outside of them."

"I haven't tried the elevators. This is the first time I've been out of our suite since we boarded last night, actually."

Margaret angled a shrewd look around the long, sun-splashed

room, at all the people deliberately glancing away. "Not quite our cozy saloon back on the *dahabiya*, is it?"

"No," Madeleine said, and attempted to smile. "It isn't."

"Where's Jack?"

"He went to the Enquiry Office to post some letters, and then I believe he meant to visit the vendors on the sun deck while we're still anchored. Did you go?"

"I did. Not for long. Nearly as crowded as Khan el-Khalili in Cairo up there, without as many bargains. I have plenty of lace back home."

A waiter appeared, taking in Margaret with an assessing eye. Madeleine supposed this to be a truly authentic Parisian café, as not one of the staff had warmed to her until she'd mentioned her surname. The main dining saloon welcomed every passenger in first class, but the privately owned Café Parisien, along with the à la carte restaurant next door to it, served whom they pleased. Namely, those passengers who could afford yet another charge on their fare.

It was a slender, exclusive space, lined with those white trellises and walls of climbing ivy (real or silk, she couldn't tell), the only shipboard restaurant Madeleine had ever seen with such open ocean views. It was one of the reasons she had chosen it for her late breakfast. Not quite like dining outdoors, but almost.

"Coffee for Mrs. Brown," she said to the waiter, as coolly dismissive as she could manage. Attempting to be friendly had gotten her only churlish looks.

"*Oui,* madame."

"*Excusez-moi,*" interjected Margaret. "*Je préfère le vin rouge.*"

"*Bien sûr.*"

As the waiter bowed and moved off, Margaret sat back, removing her gloves. "How are you feeling?"

"Better. Better than yesterday, at least. I . . . I wanted to tell you how sorry I am about your grandson. I don't remember if I did at the station. I was in something of a state, to be honest, and it's all rather a nightmare to me now. But I hope he's doing well."

"Thank you. I hope so, too. In the end, I know we must surrender everything into the Almighty's hands. But I remember . . ."

Margaret trailed off, lost again. A pair of seagulls hung in the sky beyond their window, tilting and floating.

Madeleine said, "If he's anything like his grandmother, he has the heart of a lion. I'm sure he's very strong."

"Yes. We Browns are tough enough, all right." Margaret nodded, then gave a dazzling smile; in it, Madeleine had a glimpse of the girl she used to be, a girl with a soul like a flame, heroic enough to travel across the country to test her mettle just because she could.

"Tough as nails," Margaret was saying, "and just as stubborn. I'll get there, and everything will already be fine, I'm certain. I'll have raced back home for nothing."

The string trio outside the room shifted into a new piece, softer and even more genteel. A passing waiter placed a glass of red wine exactly between them, as if he could not recall who had ordered it. He walked off without making eye contact.

Margaret's smile turned more sardonic; she reached for the glass.

A new woman swept by in slow, stately steps, pausing by their table as if she had just noticed who sat there.

"Why, Miss Force, Mrs. Brown. I didn't realize you were also on board."

"Mrs. Cardeza," replied Margaret. "Surely you've heard that my friend is Mrs. John Jacob Astor now. It was somewhat in the news."

"Of course. Naturally, one does try to keep up with all of the little tidbits of social happenings, but one becomes so *busy*, you know . . ."

"Quite."

"We are to be shipmates all the way to New York, it seems."

"All the way," drawled Margaret, looking away, trying her wine.

Charlotte turned to Margaret directly, cutting away from Madeleine to get to her point. "Mrs. Brown, as you are here, perhaps you might care to join my son and me at our table for dinner tonight in the dining saloon? Frank Millet is among us, along with Major Butt. The major is always so entertaining with his tales of life at the White House, being such an intimate of President Taft's. Such a handsome, *honorable* man. We've secured the best table in the saloon."

"What a delightful offer. But I've already joined the Astor table, I'm afraid." Margaret examined her etched goblet, the wine inside gleaming liquid garnet against the sun. "Although I'm sure I wouldn't presume to know what's *best*, or even honorable. Merely what is most agreeable."

A small sensation began at the entrance of the restaurant, billowing outward in a hushed verbal ripple. Madeleine glanced around to discover her husband weaving toward them, his bowler in hand.

Charlotte Cardeza made a grimace of a smile, her face puckered. "I see. Enjoy your voyage."

"We assuredly will," said Madeleine, a touch louder than she intended to as the other woman huffed away.

The Astors took a walk on the promenade deck after lunch, because Kitty had needed to escape the suite, and Jack wanted Madeleine to see what she could of the wild Irish coast. By noon, however, what she could see wasn't much. They were stationary at Roche's Point, the narrow mouth of Cork Harbour, still some miles away from the mainland shore.

A thin blue haze had crept in, turning the islands around them into distant dreamscapes, sleeping beasts of rock and green with mysterious stone towers bumping along their spines. The Queenstown traders had already scrambled back down to the tenders and bumboats; a group of passengers stood at the edge of the deck to watch them depart. Madeleine and Jack joined them, gazing down at the boats chugging away, ribbons of pearl trailing behind them, small as toys against *Titanic*'s enormous bulk.

The deck began to vibrate. Or perhaps it didn't; perhaps it was only her imagination, because it was clear now that the great ship was moving, but she heard nothing from the engines. Only the other passengers, laughing and talking, and a thuggery of seagulls that persisted in circles around the mooring cables of the forward funnel, calling out their shrill cries.

"And we're off," said Jack. He lifted his face against the wind flicking at his overcoat, testing the brim of his hat, then glanced back at her with silvered eyes. "Are you pleased to be going home?"

Madeleine answered as honestly as she could. "I am pleased to be with you, no matter where we go."

"A diplomat's response!" He curved an arm around her waist, softened his voice. "It won't be as bad as all that. The press will have moved on to bigger stories by now. New scandals crop up every day, believe me. They might have forgotten all about us."

She couldn't even think of an answer to that, only raised her eyebrows at him.

The corners of his mouth quirked. "Well, maybe not. Tell you what, I've run into at least three acquaintances on board in the company of ladies who are definitely not their wives, including Ben Guggenheim. If any reporters attempt to accost us dockside in New York, we'll just point our fingers in their direction and scurry the other way."

"Golly," she said faintly.

"Don't worry, beloved. We'll weather any storm. You and me and baby Muddington."

She laughed in spite of herself, smacked him lightly on the chest. Kitty whined and pushed between them, her head low, her tail rapping against Madeleine's knees.

"And our dog, too, obviously," Jack said, reaching down to stroke a hand along the Airedale's back. "Our own perfect family. We'll be happy as clams. I guarantee it."

"Yes," Madeleine said, because beneath his tilted smile and easy tone, she knew it was what he wanted to hear. "Yes, Jack. I know we will."

From somewhere on the ship behind them, distant but distinct, came the sound of bagpipes playing a low, mournful lament as they left Ireland behind them.

It seemed to Madeleine that their suite had rooms enough for nearly all of their party, but only Rosalie stayed with them. Carrie had a single cabin across the hall, and Robins had been booked in second class, decks below. Madeleine would have felt badly about it but, as Robins himself had cheerfully pointed out, *Titanic*'s second-class cabins were on par with any of the ones in first on other liners. And perhaps Jack's valet appreciated the space between them, even if he did have to traverse the ship a number of times a day to do his job. Rosalie, in charge of Madeleine's trunks and hatboxes and jewels (whatever wasn't stored in the Purser's Office for the day) had no choice but to remain nearby.

Madeleine made sure several of the vases of flowers ended up in Rosalie's room.

She dressed for dinner slowly that second night, choosing a high-waisted tunic of smoky lilac chiffon over satin, one of her few from Worth that still fit. As Jack and Robins selected his evening coat in the next room, Rosalie stood behind Madeleine at the dressing table, brushing and parting and shaping her hair, creating perfect dark tendrils and curls, all held in place with diamond-encrusted clips.

Madeleine looked at the girl in the mirror and the girl in the mirror looked back at her, gradually transforming into someone Madeleine didn't know, a glossy creature of alabaster skin and parted lips, no hint of her inner qualms revealed.

She slipped out of her silk kimono and into the gown, then sat again as Rosalie added her necklace, a fitted collar of more diamonds, platinum filigree that reached from her jaw to the base of her throat.

Her golden bangles.

The rings to go under her gloves.

"Powder, madame?" Rosalie asked.

"No, I don't think so. I look so pale already."

Her maid replaced the container upon the table, picked up the embossed compact of cream rouge instead.

Madeleine frowned. "All right."

"Scent?"

"Yes. The French jasmine."

"Very good."

Madeleine lifted her wrists, tilted her head, as her maid stroked the glass stopper against her skin. When she rose from her chair, she was fully Mrs. John Jacob Astor, ready to ignore all that displeased her. Ready, on her husband's arm, to glimmer.

She hadn't been back to the Palm Room since boarding, but it seemed to her the same people stood in the very same clusters, drinking their same aperitifs against the same potted plants as they quietly sliced apart reputations.

Outside the ship, the stars were beginning to melt into their river of light. The ocean rippled silver and calm, and the ether became crystalline with ice. Inside, however . . . inside *Titanic,* the celebrated men and women surrounding them lived as if captured in amber. Nothing changed for them, nor would, not ever. The air was perfectly heated, the food was exquisite and fresh, and the gossip fresher still.

The Astors paused for a moment at the wide foot of the grand staircase, allowing themselves to be noticed, and when she looked up at her husband, Madeleine honestly thought there could not be a more attractive man in the room, White House anecdotes or no. Certainly there could be no man more compelling.

Jack's right, she thought. *Everything will be fine.*

The orchestra leapt into a tune from *The Tales of Hoffmann.* They recognized it at the same time, their eyes locking.

That summer night. The paper firefly lanterns, the heady flowers. The moment she'd realized there existed a lovely, tenuous spark between them, unlikely as it might have been.

Jack lowered his gilt lashes, lifted her hand to his lips. Beneath the warm lights, his hair was sandy gold and dark.

"Am I the most fortunate of men?"

She rested her other hand on his upper arm, her glove stark against his sleeve. The music flowed, and they were the only two people in the world.

"You've made me the most fortunate of women. So I'm going to be immodest and say yes."

"Lucky us," he whispered against her hand.

"Yes," she said. "Lucky us."

Dinner awaited.

She made it through, laughing when she should, listening when she should, always remembering the proper fork or knife or glass for each course, because the lessons of her youth were hammered into her, no matter the circumstances, and in the back of her mind was a small, worried voice always reminding her to *be correct, be the public wife he needs.*

In addition to Margaret, Jack had invited a few of the brighter luminaries of his circle: the Wideners from Philadelphia, Eleanor and George, along with practically the entire Fortune family from Winnipeg, which included three lively daughters and a son not much older than Madeleine. Mr. Mark Fortune, like Jack, was involved in real estate. They had a few interests intermingled.

The conversation remained anodyne, consisting mostly of comments about the meal, the accommodations, and had anyone yet ventured into the gymnasium or the Turkish baths?

Despite the voice in her head, despite her many, many lessons in etiquette, by the seventh course (salmon mousse with dilled carrots, lightly roasted), Madeleine's energy was waning. Her attention began to wander.

"I don't care what anyone else says," declared Mabel Fortune, the second (third?) daughter, her voice cutting sharp through Madeleine's stray thoughts. "*I* think your story is fiercely romantic."

She looked up. From her chair three places down, Mabel was leaning toward her, her eyes shining.

"Oh," said Madeleine, putting down her knife and fork.

"We should *all* be able to wed whomever we wish." Mabel threw a fuming glance at her father, who took a bite of carrot off his fork without responding.

"Not this again." Charles Fortune, her younger brother, blond and athletic, covered his mouth on a sham yawn.

"Yes, *this* again. Look at the colonel and Mrs. Astor, after all they had to endure to be together. Clearly marriage has worked out beautifully for them."

"For *them*," enunciated the eldest sister, Ethel. She pursed her lips over her glass of wine. "You, my girl, are not them. And neither is that jazz player fellow from Minnesota."

"Mrs. Astor! Won't you speak for me? *Tell* them how it is."

"I . . ."

Margaret came to her rescue. "Love is a powerful force, Miss Fortune. There's no denying it. But love and common sense don't always go hand in hand."

"I'm afraid that's true," agreed Mrs. Widener. "Hearts may be easily broken, young lady, just as promises made in the heat of the moment may be. It pays to keep a cool head in courtship."

"But my heart is broken *now*," protested Mabel. She shook her head, the tortoiseshell combs in her hair gleaming. "It feels like I'll die without him."

"Mabel," interrupted Mrs. Fortune in a granite voice, "you will bore our companions. No one desires to hear about your heart, broken or not."

Mabel ignored her, leaning forward once more, fervent. "Mrs. Astor! Please! Tell them."

Madeleine glanced at Jack, who had observed the entire exchange with a dispassionate expression. But beneath the table, he took her hand.

"I will say this," she offered cautiously. "I genuinely cannot imagine my life ahead without my husband by my side. He is my rock and my true north and my whole heart. I'm not afraid to say it."

"*There!*" breathed Mabel.

"*But*," Madeleine continued, "I would never hope for anyone else to undergo the ordeal we did to reach this place of happiness, this place where we are now. Especially anyone of a tender disposition. Society can be . . . extremely unforgiving."

For a long moment, no one at the table said anything. There was only the low buzz of conversation from the other diners across the saloon, the stewards hurrying by, the music from the orchestra.

Charles tapped his fork against the china plate. "Speaking of stories. Alice has one, a real lulu, and it only just happened back in Cairo a few weeks ago. Tell them what happened, Alice."

Alice Fortune, young and remarkably pretty, looked flustered for a second, then flashed a smile.

"Oh, it was the silliest thing. We were at Shepheard's, sitting and having drinks one afternoon on the terrace. Do you all know it? No? Well, it's really quite something, very inviting and open, and you can see all the people outside, walking and selling things and trying to get your attention, because they'd like you to buy a mummy or some papyrus or something. Anyway, this one little man in a maroon fez simply would not stop pestering me—"

"Thought I'd have to slug him," Charles offered, concentrating on his mousse.

"He was waving his hands at me and practically hopping in place, so eventually I gave in. We had him brought to our table—I was very much afraid he was going to produce a severed mummy hand from his coat, or one of those pitiful dead cats—but it turns out he was a soothsayer. So he claimed."

"The best one in North Africa, I wager," Ethel said.

"Naturally! And he read my palm for me."

"The right or the left?" asked Margaret, looking serious.

"The left. He was terribly intense about it, scowling and mumbling. Then he looked up at me and told me that I would be in danger every time I traveled on the sea—"

Charles snorted.

"—because he saw me adrift in an open boat on the ocean. He said I was going to lose everything but my life, and that I would be saved but that others would be lost."

She laughed a little, but no one else joined in. A new silence descended over them all, heavy and strained.

"Then what happened?" Madeleine asked.

"Then," said Charles, "I gave the bugger—excuse me!—the man the baksheesh he demanded, and that was the end of it. He went off to fleece someone else."

"An unsettling story, though," said Eleanor Widener, a line of worry creasing her brow. "I swear, you've given me a chill."

And me, Madeleine thought.

Ethel rested an elbow brazenly upon the table, lifting up her wine. "I fancy we're safe enough on this voyage. After all, Charles was right there with you, and the fellow never said a word to *him* about being stranded on a boat or dying."

"That's right," Charles said. "Rather rude of him not to tell me if I'm going to die. I *was* the one who paid him."

The stewards arrived in a spate of snowy jackets to clear their plates, bringing out the next course. The orchestra began a German waltz.

Margaret said lightly, "Has anyone else heard a rooster crowing from time to time? I swear I'm not crazy. I realize *Titanic* is thoroughly modern, but they don't keep live poultry aboard for our meals now, I hope?"

Mark Fortune smiled, obviously relieved at the turn of conversation. "No, Mrs. Brown, you're not crazy, and no, they don't. There's a foursome of prized breeders, roosters and hens, crated and housed by the galley. One of the passengers picked them up in France. Worth a pretty penny, from what I understand, and the lady means to take them back to her estate . . ."

Madeleine gazed down at the *coq au vin* that had been placed before her, fragrant and steaming. Her stomach rumbled.

But she could not stop thinking about what Alice had said, the open boat, the sea. In her mind's eye, she remembered the lifeboat from the *Noma* struggling to reach the stranded men of the *Zingara*, that small shell of wood pitching against the blackened waves.

She looked up and out the windows lining the walls, at the belt of stars caught behind the leaded glass: cold and remote, white as ice.

CHAPTER 23

It was an uncanny dreamworld aboard that ship nearly from the beginning, growing stronger as the days went on. Time seemed suspended; the hours uncounted. There was everything to do and, at the same time, absolutely nothing. You could pace along the decks, compose letters in the reading and writing room, splash around in the swimming bath, or steam yourself like a lobster in the Turkish baths. You could play squash, or chess, or dominoes, or draughts, and there were nearly always card games going on wherever I looked, usually bridge or whist. Charlotte Cardeza's son hosted poker games on the private promenade deck of their suite, raucous affairs that included (from what I understand) a great deal of drinking and smoking, even by the ladies.

(Your father went once. The stakes were a dollar a chip, and he won rather a lot. The cardsharps were not pleased, and after that, they didn't invite him back.)

You could have a meal at practically any time of the day or night, breakfast, luncheon, tea in your rooms, tea in the Palm Court & Veranda Café, the lounge. Dinners of ten scrumptious courses, the most luscious dishes you ever tasted, followed by coffee and port.

Out of boredom, I guess, or just because they could, someone began a betting pool on the number of nautical miles covered by the ship each day, and a good many of the passengers became involved in it. There was always a surge of interest every afternoon outside the Purser's Office when the miles from the previous day were posted. People were happy when *Titanic*'s daily tally bested that of the *Olympic* for the same run.

Everyone expected *Titanic* to be the faster ship, and she was.

Your father got his tour with Bruce Ismay. I declined to go. As he came back grimed with grease and soot—the tour had included the boiler rooms and the engine rooms—it was not a decision I regretted.

At six o'clock, the ship's bugler would play a tune to let us know it was time to dress for dinner. At seven, he reappeared, playing "The Roast Beef of Old England" to let us know it was time to eat.

Titanic was a ship full of sheep, ready to be herded. You hardly had to think about anything at all. All you had to do was enjoy your captivity, and have faith that everything would be well.

Friday, April 12, 1912
Aboard Titanic

Nurse Endres agreed, with trepidation, to a visit to the Turkish baths. The weather had dawned uncertain, with layers of gunmetal clouds blowing in and out, trailing needles of rain. Madeleine had hoped to walk the boat deck with Jack and Kitty, but the rain was slanting cold, the kind designed, according to Jack, to soak through coats and scarves and hats and steal into your heart and lungs.

Thus Carrie had advised against it, and Jack had agreed, and Madeleine was outnumbered.

He went to the Purser's Office to purchase two tickets to the baths instead, handing them over with a bow.

"It's reserved for the ladies in the morning, gents in the afternoon," he said. "So you'll need to be there within the hour."

"But—the Turkish baths, sir?" Carrie had said, with more than a hint of dismay. "Is it decent?"

Madeleine tapped the paper tickets against her palm. "Let's go find out."

The entrance to the baths was on F deck, far lower into the belly of the ship than Madeleine had been before. Down here, she had a much clearer sense of the rhythm of the engines, a constant drumbeat vibrating through the walls and floor. Any trace of natural light, of the rain or clouds, had disappeared; it truly was like being swallowed by a great mechanical beast. But the bath complex itself was extravagant enough, with subdued lighting and a fantastical, Moorish theme. The bath attendant, a slender young woman with downcast eyes, handed them both thick white towels, and directed them to the changing rooms.

"We are to disrobe?" Carrie asked.

"Yes, ma'am, if you please. Right through there, at the end of the cooling room. I will wait out here until you need me."

Carrie said nothing, clutching her towels to her chest, but the look she threw Madeleine was scandalized.

The cooling room, center of the complex, was something to behold. Long and exotic, it had a deeply recessed, blood-red ceiling supported by intricately engraved wooden pillars. Glassy green-and-blue tiled mosaics alternated with fretted wooden screens affixed along the walls. Bronze lanterns glowed from above; metal domes that looked like halved, gilded onions topped the doorways. The chaise lounges were teak and gilt, covered in cream and red pillows and cushions.

The overall effect was one of being cloistered inside in a feverishly contrived harem. All that was missing was the scent of cumin and turmeric peppering the air, and the call to prayers from minarets beyond the screens.

"It's almost like being back in Egypt," Carrie whispered as they walked to the curtained dressing rooms.

"Almost like Egypt," Madeleine whispered back, "but somehow *more*."

There were six other ladies in the chamber, no one Madeleine knew, all of them wrapped in towels and reclining back on the loungers, looking either flushed and frazzled or else peacefully heavy-lidded. Another attendant brought them glasses of water on a tray.

A girl with unbound brown hair, one of the peaceful ones, caught Madeleine's eye. She lifted her glass in salute. On the table beside her was another glass of what appeared to be white wine.

"It's really quite relaxing," the girl offered, smiling.

Madeleine did not go so far as to release her hair, but she did strip all the way down—dress, underdress, corset, linen combinations, shoes and garters and silk stockings; the attendant had to step in to help—emerging from the curtained room in her towels, both embarrassed and curious at what would come next.

The attendant lifted her hand. "Will you sit for the weighing machine chair, ma'am?"

A canvas-covered chair set inside a gilded bench had been placed near one of the walls, strange and mysterious.

"What does it do?"

"It will print out a ticket with your weight, ma'am. So that afterwards, if you like, you may see the results of your bath."

Madeleine took a step back, thinking of her thickening figure. "No, thank you."

Carrie declined, as well.

"This way, then, if you please. It's best to start in the temperate room."

The temperate room was hot. At least it felt so to Madeleine. They settled together on one of the empty couches and looked at each other. Madeleine began to smile, and then to giggle, eventually cupping both hands over her mouth to hold in the sound. A loop of hair coming free from her pins lay plastered against her temple, limp with the heat. Carrie wiped away the perspiration beading along her forehead.

"Isn't it like the desert?" Madeleine asked when she could, lowering her hands.

"But *more*," replied Carrie, fanning herself with one end of her towel.

After the temperate room, they were to go to the hot room. Carrie opened the door, winced, and shut it again.

"No," she said, emphatic, and turned to the attendant. "What is the temperature in that chamber?"

"Around ninety-three degrees Celsius," the woman said.

Carrie drew in a breath.

"It's very healthful," the attendant added, earnest. "For invigorating the circulation and improving the complexion, ma'am. All the finest physicians will tell you so. You need only hop in and out."

Carrie crossed her arms. "What else is left?"

What was left was the swimming bath or the shampooing room, and Madeleine chose the shampooing room, because the bath—while pleasant enough in its own way, with its high, bright walls and ceiling, filled with warmed saltwater from a storage tank on the boat deck far above—was empty and unexciting and nothing like the serene marble pool back in Cairo, where she had floated with her husband beneath the open night sky.

In the shampooing room, she endured a shower from a series of nozzles attached to tubing, their spray lukewarm and hard. She emerged dripping but cleaner than she'd likely been in months, swathed in more towels. The shampoo left her wreathed in the strong, unmistakable aroma of freesias, which clung to her for hours afterwards, sweet and soapy, a phantom scent trailing her wherever she went.

* * *

Back in the suite, Rosalie took in the state of her hair with astonishment.

That evening before dinner, the brush and comb raked extra hard against Madeleine's scalp.

Saturday, April 13th

The liner steamed along the North Atlantic, and the weather was rapidly cooling. Not enough to tempt Madeleine to return to the Turkish baths, but enough so that when she accompanied Jack outside for their twice-daily walks, she donned a woolen tailor-made suit and a fur coat and muff, and worried that Kitty might soon need a coat of her own. They were well and truly grasped inside the fist of an arctic spring.

The child inside her was growing into a heavy weight, far heavier than her body had before conceded. As they ambled along the boat deck, the dog tugging at her leash, Madeleine felt her baby move for the first time, the barest shifting of her center, just enough to steal her balance. She staggered two steps; by the third, Jack had her by the arm.

"Madeleine?"

She laughed and clutched her hands over his. "Dear me! I'm sorry I'm so clumsy but, oh, Jack! I think she moved!"

His face lit up with a sudden quick delight. She slid his hand down her body over her sable, over her thick Parisian coat and dress, uncaring of who noticed or why, pressing his palm against her. One of the emerald buttons from the fur dug into her stomach.

"She moved," she repeated quietly into the curve of his ear, just for him.

They waited but it didn't happen again, and he dropped his hand. Kitty nudged between them, raising her nose to be petted.

"Next time," Madeleine said. "You'll feel her then."

"Yes," he said. "Next time."

In front of all the other people walking and dawdling nearby,

Jack captured her chin with the curl of his fingers and kissed her on the lips.

The wind shoved by. The sky was so sheer a blue it seemed unreal, an echo of her thoughts, of a memory of salt and sand and sea, as fanciful and pretend as the Moorish baths, decks below.

"Hello! Mrs. Astor, yes? How do you do?"

Madeleine twisted a fraction in her deck chair, wrapped from collar to toes in warm blankets, a mug of hot beef tea steaming between her palms. She was waiting for Jack to come around again on his walk with Kitty; the beef tea was a lovely bonus of sitting on the promenade deck on a chilly afternoon. One of the deck stewards waited nearby, ready to replenish her bouillon whenever she liked.

A young woman in mink and a tall, flowery hat gave a little wave from three chairs away. It was the heavy-lidded girl from the baths, her brown hair now neatly tied up, smiling her same sleepy smile.

Madeleine lowered her mug. "Hello, Miss . . . ?"

"Mrs. Bishop! Mrs. Dickinson Bishop, that is. But, please! Call me Helen."

Helen Bishop pushed out of her chair, resettled in the one right next to Madeleine without waiting for an invitation. This close, Madeleine could see that she was probably the same age as she, with a slyly smiling mouth and those slumberous big eyes.

"I've noticed you walking along the decks with the colonel and your dog. So charming! I admire your devotion to it—the dog, I mean. Dick and I have just gotten one of our own, little Frou Frou. We did receive permission to keep it in our cabin, but mostly it's down in the kennels. I'd *love* to have it around us more, but it's such a bother! Whining and barking all the time, always begging for attention! Needing treats, needing walks and pettings, all that. And the *fur* goes *everywhere*! I declare, I don't know how people tolerate it. At this point, I honestly don't know what we thought it would be like to have a dog, but *certainly* we did not brace ourselves for *this*. I imagined a dog would be more like a baby, you know? Adorable and dear, something you could show to your friends and then put away. Something you could hand off to the help when necessary."

"I see. Forgive me, Mrs. Bishop, I find I'm somewhat weary—"

"Oh, no! I do hope you'll call me Helen! Because I really want to call you Madeleine. I hope you don't mind that! I've read so much about you already, you wouldn't conceive it! I mean, *everyone* has, of course. I'm hardly alone! But I feel as if I've just come across an old bosom confidante, even though I know we've never met before in our lives. As soon as I noticed you in the baths—how *amazing* that we're aboard the same ship!—I knew that we should chat. I'm a newlywed, too, as it happens! How positively *amazing* that we are to be friends!"

Madeleine brought her bouillon closer to her face, lowering her eyes into slits. The steam coiled up and around her, scented of beef and garlic and tender rich leeks. She blew a sigh into it, tearing the tendrils apart.

The real world was rushing in again at last, predictable, inexorable. There were going to be girls like this around every corner from here on out.

"Helen Bishop," Madeleine murmured without looking up, getting the words out. "How do you do."

"A pleasure! You're so kind! I never meant to encroach upon you, Madeleine, I swear. I know you're—why, you're New York. Dickie and I are Dowagiac."

Madeleine lifted her lashes.

"Michigan," Helen clarified, her fingers nervously checking the hooks of her coat, up and down and up.

"Ah. I'm from . . . I'm from a few places, actually," Madeleine said. "But Manhattan and Bar Harbor, mostly, I suppose."

"How fabulous!" Helen Bishop gushed.

"Yes," replied Madeleine, breathing in the scent of the broth. "Yes, I imagine it is."

Sunday, April 14th

She slept through the church service held that morning in the dining saloon. After her encounter with Helen Bishop, Madeleine decided to retreat from *Titanic* for a while, and their stateroom was peaceful, the bed plush and comfortable. Even after the sunlight began to breach the velvet curtains draping the window, changing all the shadows of the room into soft colors, warming the satins and silks, Madeleine pulled the covers over her head and squeezed her eyes shut.

Jack, up and dressed, came to sit at the edge of the mattress. She felt it through the languor dragging her downward, the sudden dip of the bedding. He eased back the covers to stroke the hair from her forehead.

She opened her eyes a little, caught a glimpse of golden cufflinks and starched linen. Closed them again.

"I'm not going," she mumbled into the pillow.

"I know, love. I'll make your excuses."

"Tell them I'm hiding from them," she said. "Tell them I'll come out when they all go away."

He laughed, short and rumbling. "I'll present an excuse a little less porcupine, perhaps. Sleep well. I'll return in a while."

She pulled a second pillow beneath her to support her belly. She was already floating back into her warm, quiet dreams as he closed the door gently behind him.

"Messages for you," Jack said that afternoon, coming back to find her seated by the electric fireplace in the sitting room, enjoying tea and scones, pretty blue-and-white bowls of sliced strawberries, ivory dots of clotted cream.

Kitty, at her feet, followed the movement of Madeleine's fork with unwavering attention.

Jack sat down across from them, began to tick off his fingers. "Margaret says she hopes you are feeling better. Mary Fortune says the same. A woman named Mrs. Bishop—your new friend, I presume?—sends her *very* best regards." He mimicked Helen's inflection exactly and then paused; they exchanged smiles across the table. "Eleanor Widener has invited us to join her table tonight at the Ritz restaurant—the à la carte restaurant, everyone's just calling it the Ritz now—for the dinner she's hosting for Captain Smith. Seven-thirty."

"Oh," Madeleine said, lowering her scone. "Must we? I thought we'd maybe huddle together tonight, rather than wade through a crowd."

"Never fear. I regretfully declined, telling her I had already booked my own table at the Ritz and that I was looking forward to enjoying dinner alone with my beautiful bride too much to cancel it."

She sat back, impressed. "How artful you are, Colonel Astor."

"It was only the truth, Mrs. Astor. We dine at eight."

The sunset that evening was the most lovely of the voyage so far, but the temperature outside had plummeted so severely that Madeleine didn't try to venture abovedeck to admire it. She watched it from the sitting room window instead, already dressed for dinner in a gown of iridescent opal satin and net, rows of silver glass beads flashing and dancing against her ankles along the hem.

It was a Poiret, one of her best; for the rest of her life, she would associate the finest fashion house in Paris with ice and cold and death.

The sky beyond the window burned fuchsia and scarlet, orange and pink, tinting the ship and Madeleine and the suite around her all the same colors. She stood there looking at the world as though through a magical lens of stained glass, all the true hues around her washed away, drowned in the dying light of the sun atop the flat sea.

*   *   *

It was the first time she'd dined in the à la carte restaurant, perhaps because she'd been vaguely put off by all the gilt visible from inside it whenever she'd passed by. But the Louis XVI décor wasn't as overbearing as she'd been afraid it would be. The fluted walnut columns and gold-trimmed boiseries seemed quite tasteful in the half-light, and the table centerpieces of milk-white daisies mixed with pink roses added a simple, delicate touch.

They were seated near one of the alcoves, far enough from the entrance to feel no draft, yet close enough to still hear the strains of Puccini from the string trio in the reception room beyond.

On their way in, they had greeted Eleanor and her group, and that was Madeleine's first glimpse of their ship's captain, as well. He had stood as they were introduced, a silver-bearded, older gentleman with a firm handshake and a kindly smile. *Society's captain,* she had heard him called, as if it were a mark against him. But there was a reason why so many of society's most prominent members preferred to sail with Edward Smith, Jack told her.

Experience, he'd said, dabbing caviar on a narrow point of toast, setting aside the bone spoon. *Experience and comfort. Comfort in his experience.*

The mood inside the restaurant was one of rising gaiety. Wine was poured around the room, the stewards rushing from table to table with fresh bottles. A steady stream of people Madeleine hardly knew stopped by to greet them both; at one point, the ship's surgeon and his assistant pulled up chairs at Jack's insistence—he had made certain to meet them the first day aboard, just in case— and they all toasted the ship.

They dined on grapes and smoked quail from Egypt, on plover's eggs and oysters so fresh they slid along her tongue tasting of nothing but the ocean, of brine and tides.

Without meaning to, she'd kept one hand flattened over her middle for the entirety of the meal, testing that new life that pushed against her gown, protecting it. Jack had watched her throughout with his slight, knowing smile.

Halfway through dessert, he'd put down his sherry, reached for her hand.

Their fingers met, skin to skin, all her rings and bracelets afire like the sunset in the low, flattering light.

CHAPTER 24

I didn't know it would be our last kiss, the last time we ever spoke. I didn't know it would be the last time we ever touched.

Sunday, April 14th, 11:40 p.m.
Aboard Titanic

She awoke briefly from a dream about standing at the edge of a green copper roof—one of Jack's hotels, perhaps—looking down at a busy street far below. In the dream, there came an earthquake, the mildest thing, but it alarmed her to be so close to the edge, and so Madeleine took a step back and opened her eyes. The last faint tremor of the earthquake still rattled her bed, but then it was gone, and she was able to fall back asleep.

"Madeleine. Wake up."
"Father?"
The mattress shifted, dipped. "No, it's me."
She rolled over toward his voice, pushing her hair from her eyes. "Jack? What's wrong?"

He was perched beside her on the bed just as he had been that morning, only now he was silhouetted with light instead of captured in shadow, and his clothing was different, and he smelled of brandy and cigars, and he wasn't smiling.

He ran a hand up and down her arm, his palm bunching the silk of her gown.

"The ship has struck an iceberg."

"What?" she said, bewildered.

"I'm sure it's nothing. Just some scratches along the paint. But the captain has ordered everyone to collect our lifebelts and go abovedeck."

"Our lifebelts?" She noticed now that the door behind him was open—the source of that bright shaft of light—with Rosalie beyond it, moving back and forth, carrying bundles in her arms. Madeleine wondered fuzzily if maybe this was all still part of her dream, but Jack's hand was cold, very cold. It was that, more than anything else, that began to wake her.

"Purely a precaution," he was saying in his soothing low voice. "I told you Smith was experienced, and with experience on a liner like this comes a solid dose of prudence. The insurance companies require all these little steps and measures. We're utterly safe. This is *Titanic*, after all. We'll go upstairs and wait in the lounge for a bit while they sort it all out, and then we'll just come right back here. We were moving ahead at about half speed for a while, but I believe we're now stopped. Maybe it's not too late to catch a glimpse of the berg itself. It'll be a fine story to tell our daughter one day."

She sagged back against her pillows, feeling the heat of the mattress warmed by her body, the softness cushioning her head. The notion of even having to poke her bare feet out from beneath the covers seemed overwhelming.

Jack leaned over, brushed his lips against hers. She tasted the brandy, felt the small pleasant sting of his moustache, and lifted an arm to his shoulder to bring him closer.

"It's only for a bit," he said again, pulling away.

The electric lights overhead switched on, cut glass glinting. Rosalie, in her uniform but yawning widely, came to the bed.

"I will help you dress, madame."

Madeleine yawned with her, sitting up. She ran a hand over her face, then crawled out of the bed.

"The mint woolen tailor-made, madame?"

"Yes, all right."

She stood there swaying some, her body still half-surrendered to slumber, letting the nightgown come off, the combinations on, her corset (not tight), stockings, all the rest. As she slipped her feet into her buckled shoes, Jack entered the chamber again, changed out of his formal evening wear for a lounge suit of blue serge and brown flannel. He carried three lifebelts, handed one of them to the maid.

"Ready?" he asked.

"Yes." She yawned again, unable to help it. "What about Kitty?"

The dog stood between them, her ears pinned back, her head low. Jack bent down to stroke her nose. From outside the suite, Madeleine heard fists pounding on doors, men's voices talking about lifebelts and coats. Kitty didn't even cock an ear to it.

"There's no sense in dragging her out into all this," Jack said. "She'll be warmer and safer in here. We'll be back soon."

Just before they walked out the door, he pivoted to the wardrobe, pulling out her jewelry box. He grabbed a handful of things and returned to her with them: the platinum-and-diamond collar, a necklace of South Sea pearls. Five rings, a pin, and the strand of carnelian.

Madeleine accepted them all wordlessly, wearing what she could, fitting the rest into her pockets. As he opened the door to the hallway, she hurried back into the bedchamber, opened the dressing table drawer containing her Irish lace jacket and the baby blanket.

She yanked the blanket free from its layers of tissue, rolled it into a ball and crammed it on top of the pearls next to her hip.

From the center of the rug, Kitty watched them leave, her head still down, her tail tucked between her legs.

Carrie joined them in the corridor, already wearing her life-belt with a beaver coat on top of it. As the four of them climbed the grand staircase up to A deck, they passed masses of people standing, talking, looking bored or worried or simply impatient. Stewards pushed by, bumping into them without apology, hurry-ing on. The cheerful sounds of the orchestra grew louder and then softer, then louder again. They entered the first-class lounge to find even more people gathered, the carved rococo ceiling fogged with smoke, almost as if a real fire burned in the fireplace and the flue had jammed. Apparently the occupants of the smoke room had spilled outward into the main area, and none of the gentlemen had cared to put out their cigars and pipes.

Everyone seemed to be in various states of dress—or undress. Madeleine saw women with furs tossed over their nightgowns and lifebelts, men in pyjamas and silk scarves and smoking jackets. They were people she knew (or at least had met), leaders of society stripped down to their basics, modish matrons with their faces scrubbed and their hair woven into plaits. Tycoons of industry cradling glasses of cognac between their spread fingers and flap-ping around in velvet slippers.

A glance at her corsage watch told her it was not quite twelve-thirty in the morning.

What an eon has passed, she thought, *between our dinner and now.*

Jack led her to one of the green-pillowed chairs arranged around a small table. She sank into it, Carrie on the other side, Ro-salie still standing. Robins found them eventually, looking some-what disheveled as he wandered through the crowd. He joined them, straightening his tie.

Jack placed the lifebelts on the table but then stood without moving amid the languid commotion all around, his head only just slanted away, the yachtsman in him perhaps attuned to some deep phonic resonance that the rest of them could not discern.

Madeleine ran her fingers over the beads around her neck, tracing their repetitive smooth comfort.

"Madeleine! My gracious, Madeleine! Do you have any idea of what's going on?"

Helen Bishop stood over her, tugging at the tapes of her life preserver.

Madeleine released her beads. "I'm sure they'll tell us soon."

"I should say so! I mean, they should! We've heard the most incredible rumors. They positively rousted us from our cabin and sent us up here. I forgot a few things and sent Dickie back, but still. Such a to-do!"

A group of young men near a mahogany-and-glass bookcase were laughing heartily, passing something from hand to hand. It was a chunk of ice, about as big as cricket ball, melting and dripping along their fingers.

Madeleine was no true sailor, not like her husband. From her summers in Bar Harbor, she knew how to handle a canoe and oars; from her time with Jack, she understood the basics of the *Noma*, a small echo of a mighty ocean liner such as this. But as she sat there in the padded comfort of her chair, she thought she could begin to perceive, like the hint of a suspicion that might turn out to be true or might not, a modest listing of the ship to starboard.

The string orchestra, arranged in a corner, began a cheerful ragtime tune.

She drew in a breath. "Jack, I think we should—"

She broke off as one of the ship's officers clipped by, gold lace stripes flashing. It was Captain Smith. Jack quickly followed him, managing to snare his attention. They conferred together for a moment, the captain speaking in an undertone, Jack nodding. Then it was done; Jack came back to them while the captain moved to the fireplace.

"We're going to have to put on our lifebelts, it seems," he said. "Does everyone have one?"

"No," said Helen. "Oh, no. I sent Dickie down to our cabin and he didn't have his. I'd better go tell him."

Jack turned to his valet. "Robins, be a sport and go back to our suite. Mrs. Astor needs warmer clothes. A hat and gloves with fur, if you can find them. And a coat. One for Miss Bidois, too."

"Yes, sir."

Jack caught him by the arm, dropped his voice. "Try to hurry."

"Yes, sir."

"Jack?" Madeleine reached up a hand to him.

"Sorry, darling, I should have thought of it before. Your frock is very pretty, but if they're likely to move us outside at all, you won't be warm enough."

"It's best to be sensible," Carrie said.

"Precisely."

By the fireplace, Captain Smith had raised both hands without a word, gradually gathering the notice of the crowd. The ragtime song ended with a few abrupt twanging notes.

"Ladies and gentlemen. Thank you. I require now that everyone put on their lifebelts and begin to move up to the boat deck—"

"What the bloody hell is going on?" snarled a man behind Madeleine, but the captain only continued without expression, speaking as if he had not been interrupted.

"—the *boat* deck, if you please, in an orderly fashion, with your lifebelts on."

"Are we sinking?" called out a woman, but Captain Smith didn't answer her, only bent his head and walked away.

"Well," announced a matron to Madeleine's right, plump and red-haired. "We just came from there, and let me tell you, I am not going back! I don't care if it *is* the captain's order! It's like an icebox out in the open up there, and I will not go!"

"But mother—" protested the young woman at her side.

"No. I'm sorry, but *no*. We're going back to our cabin. That's the end of it."

Several others looked around, glowering, but as the captain had vanished, they could only complain to their fellow passengers.

Jack picked up one of the belts, held his hand out to Madeleine. "It will be easier to put them on here, rather than up there. One less thing to worry about. Let me help you."

He worked quickly, obviously familiar with odd rectangular sections of the vest, the long string ties. She held out her arms as he secured the last bow, then readjusted it around her waist, trying to find a way to make it more comfortable. It was heavier than it looked.

The lounge was emptying. Jack turned to Rosalie, secured hers in the same way, and then finally slipped into his own.

They were already outside, walking down the enclosed promenade—it *was* an icebox out in the open air; the plump woman had been right—when Robins caught up to them. A loud hissing sound was coming from somewhere above, and they didn't hear him at all until he shouted.

"Sir! Colonel Astor, sir!"

The valet rushed up carrying a mass of slippery furs, having to pause twice to catch it all up in his arms again.

Jack snapped open one of the deck chairs, and Robins carefully set everything upon it.

As people passed by, Madeleine put on the white cardigan Robins had brought, the fur-lined hat (but no gloves), even the extra pair of stockings he'd somehow found. She struggled into the sable coat (very tight with the added bulk of the lifebelt around her), and Jack finished it all with her fox shawl, wrapping it around her shoulders.

"Sir," said Rosalie, tentative. "I'm sorry, sir, but this is not my coat."

She indicated the mink that was left, spread across the slats of the chair.

"Just put it on," Madeleine said. "For goodness sake, you'll freeze otherwise."

They joined the other passengers trudging up the stairs.

The hissing grew louder, more and more piercing. By the time they reached the boat deck, it had climbed into a shriek, hurting her head. She pressed her hands over her ears and turned in a circle to find the source of it: pipes running along the forward funnels were furiously venting steam, great clouds of vapor ballooning up to the stars.

Titanic's crew swarmed around the lifeboats, ripping off their covers, letting out the ropes, yelling at each other without sound. Groups of passengers stood back and watched them work as if they were watching a play, with looks of detached interest.

The frigid air bit her skin, stung her eyes. Jack touched her elbow, his face close, his lips moving, but even when she lowered her hands, she couldn't hear him over the roar. He nodded his comprehension, took her by her hand, and pulled her along. She glanced back to make certain the rest were following as they threaded through the clumps of people.

He led them all to the gymnasium, a well-heated space that smelled strongly of leather and bleach. But after the door was closed behind them, at least the chill abated, and the scream of the escaping steam lowered to a less painful decibel.

The benches were claimed, so they aimed for the electric horses. She eyed the sidesaddle before her, knew she'd never manage it with the fashionably tight skirts she wore, and sat sideways instead, as if on a very short chair.

More people were coming in, going out, clapping their hands against the cold. The hint of the list became more definite.

"Should we be out there?" she asked, sotto voce. "Prepared to be in line for a boat?"

Jack shook his head. "They're only getting things ready, and really, darling, it's all for naught. This ship will not sink. I've toured her, remember? Every precaution was taken in building her, every innovation employed. We are far safer in here than on one of those little boats out there. Warmer, too," he added.

"All right." She tugged off the shawl, unhooked her coat, and wanted to untie the lifebelt, too, but as she began fiddling with the knots, Jack stopped her.

"Better not. Captain's orders are still captain's orders. I know they're not comfortable, though."

"Whatever are they made of? I feel as if I can hardly bend."

"Ah!" He smiled, produced a penknife from his trouser pocket. "I'll show you."

He lifted the edge of his preserver, sliced carefully along the front of one of the lower rectangular blocks.

"Should you?" she asked, anxious.

"I'm not cutting more than an inch, and only the canvas itself. There. Take a look."

Madeleine and Carrie leaned forward together.

"Why, it's cork!" Carrie said.

"Buoyant as anything. Not a chance of any of us sinking with one of these on."

Madeleine leaned back again, gripping the pommel and cantle of the saddle, rocking a little back and forth. Of all of *Titanic*'s miraculous innovations, it seemed somehow ominous that the very last defense offered to save their lives was something as simple as tree bark.

The list of the ship increased, but it had shifted from starboard to forward, from forward to port.

The roar of the escaping steam finally ceased, which should have reassured her, or at least helped with the ringing in her ears, but it seemed the voices of everyone around them only rose to compensate for its sudden loss.

From her perch on the electric horse, Madeleine watched the lumpish shapes of people moving past the teak-framed windows, bunching together, splitting apart, occasionally coming in or going out.

"Did you hear that?" asked Carrie abruptly. "It sounded like gunfire."

"Just a distress rocket going off," Jack said. "They have to shoot the rockets. It's procedure."

But Madeleine hadn't seen the deck beyond the windows flare with light.

The list grew steeper, the floor of the room slanting toward the bow. It became more troublesome to keep her balance on the horse so she slid off of it, leaned against it, as the figures past the windows grew sparser. Jack came to stand beside her, and she rested her head against his shoulder. Her eyelids drifted closed. It seemed entirely reasonable, in this moment, to go to sleep in his arms standing up.

She resisted that sweet dragging pull. There was a map of the world framed on the wall behind them, the colors of the countries garish. She couldn't look at it without wanting to shut her eyes again, so she turned her head away.

She mumbled, "Shouldn't we go out? To see what's happening?"

"It's better to wait where they tell us. If no one comes for us soon, I'll go find someone in charge."

"Colonel," said Robins, just beside them. "Shall I go investigate?"

"Yes, good man. Thank you."

A pair of older fellows in full evening kit and no life preservers stood nearby, discussing the iceberg and the lifeboats and the unfortunate nature of the weather.

"I'm told the *Olympic* is nearing to assist."

"Is that so?" said the other. "But I'm sure *Titanic* won't founder."

"Of course she won't. In fact, I don't know why we aren't still steaming toward New York right now, even at half speed. Smith is putting the devil of a crimp in my schedule."

A man poked his head in past the gymnasium door. It was George Widener, the collar of his overcoat turned up, his nose and cheeks red.

"They're ordering us below again! We're all to go back to A deck."

A collective grumble rose from the crowd.

When they walked outside, Madeleine was shocked to see the row of lifeboats that had been suspended there before from their davits were all gone, leaving behind only long snakes of ropes that disappeared down the side of the ship. Crewmen and passengers stood clustered at the railing, looking down. She joined them, peering past their shoulders.

Below them—way below—the lifeboats floated atop the black waters, tiny pale cowrie shells dotted with dim lights, slowly rowing away.

She turned to her right, toward the stern of the ship, where there seemed to be a storm of people congregating along the edges of the very end of the deck. Their shouting swept over her but it was tinny distant, like trying to hear a phonograph playing from another room.

She looked to her left, toward the bow, taking a few steps closer to be sure: the ocean was creeping, thick as oil, over the foredeck.

"Port," Jack said grimly, his arm clamped through hers. "We need to get to the other side of the ship."

For all the havoc playing out at the end of the topmost deck, A deck below it was full of people looking as dazed as she felt. All the ladies and gentlemen seemed to be sleepwalking, their eyes glazed. In her hat and coat and shawl, she went from chilled to flushed and back to chilled; several of the glass windows enclosing the promenade had been unlocked and opened, letting in the arctic air. Behind her glowed the warm yellow lights of the ship's interior, still filled with people and chatter and heat. But before her were only windows of stars, one after another, blazing in silence against the ebony night.

But for the fact of the saltwater stealing up the prow, that the yellow light occasionally flickered, she would have cast her faith in everything waiting behind her, rather than that deep soundless sky ahead.

A ship's officer, trim and sweating, crouched atop a high, open windowsill, one foot planted on a stack of steamer chairs made into a ramp that reached to its ledge, the other inside the lifeboat that hung just beyond. He was helping women climb up the chairs to crawl through the frame, with men on either side below, pushing the ladies forward as needed.

Madeleine turned away from the sight. Her breath frosted in front of her, short puffs of silver that flashed and dissolved. Behind her, Rosalie was muttering to herself in French.

The officer steadied himself against the frame of the window, called out to the clutches of people hanging back.

"Women and children! Women and children only! Any more women and children to board?"

No one came forward. The lights dimmed, brightened again. The bowels of the steamship let out a long, metallic groan.

"We must get on that boat," said Carrie calmly. "Don't you agree, colonel?"

"Yes," Jack replied, another shock. "Yes, you must."

Madeleine shook her head. "But—I thought—"

"Listen to me," he said, but then nothing more, only looked at her, that focused look, gray and absolute. She gazed back up at him, his lowered lashes, the straight slash of his brows, the determined set of his lips: half in gold, half in night, just like the rest of them.

She grabbed his hands, holding hard. "I won't go without you."

"It will only be for a while. A few hours, at most. We'll see each other in the morning."

"No!"

"Madeleine, you can't think only of me right now. There are three of us in our family, and at this moment, you comprise the most valuable two of our three. The finest honor I've been given in this world—that I will ever be given—is the task of safeguarding you and our child. Take the boat." He touched her cheek. "You're a mermaid, remember? The sea is your element. You'll be fine, and we'll all be together again soon. New York, at the very latest."

"Last call!" the officer shouted. "For women and children, *please!*"

Her husband said to her, very quiet, "You must. You know that you must, *habibti*."

"Ma'am." Carrie took her by the elbow. "Ma'am, right this way."

Madeleine moved stiffly, her legs and feet numb, but she did move because Carrie was pulling her and Jack was pulling her, and her breath was flashing more quickly now because underneath her veil of acquiescence was a black feeling roiling so deep and dark she had no name for it. It was panic and fear and bleak desperation. It was anger and fear, fear, fear.

She climbed the awkward ramp of chairs, Jack supporting her left arm, another gentleman supporting her right. The officer bent down, reached out for her.

The black thing inside her enlarged, choking, closing her throat. She turned back to Jack.

He met her eyes, smiled. "Nearly there."

The officer seized her right hand, plucking her the rest of the way up. The lifeboat outside dangled and swayed from its slender-thin lines, uneasily tilted, just like *Titanic*. Huddles of women inside it stared back at her as she balanced at the window's edge.

"Step here, madam, and mind the gap. Do you see the plank? Your foot just there, one and then the other. I have you."

Below her, so much closer than it should have been, the ocean whispered and flicked against the side of the ship.

"Don't look down," advised the officer, and thrust her all the way into the boat. She collapsed next to a blond woman clasping a toddler, and then Carrie was beside her, and Rosalie after her.

She heard Jack say, "Ladies, you are next," and two more women climbed in.

Madeleine sat unmoving, the numbness blossoming all the way through her body, freezing not just her legs but her arms and hands and heart.

The ship's officer was assisting the latest woman aboard, helping her to find a place to sit. It was Eleanor Widener, her face reflecting all the quiet horror Maddy was working so hard to keep at bay.

Jack's voice reached her again; she lifted her head. He was standing at the open window adjacent to the one they all had crept through, leaning out.

"Sir. Might I board the boat in order to protect my wife? She is in a delicate condition."

The officer straightened. "No men are allowed in the boats until all the women are loaded."

"What is the number of the boat, then? So that I may find her afterwards?"

"This is Boat Four, sir."

"Thank you."

She wanted to say something. She wanted to say *anything*, his name, a demand to be let off, but the last few women were jostling by her, and someone stepped on her foot, and someone else was crying by the prow, and the officer who had pushed her in had climbed back inside the promenade.

Jack, still leaning out the window, stripped off his gloves.

"Madeleine, catch!"

He tossed them to her one at a time and she did catch them somehow, both of them, the leather still warm from his hands.

Above him, someone called out, "How many women are in that boat?"

"Twenty-four," the officer called back.

"That's enough. Lower away."

"Lower away!" the officer shouted, lifting his arms, and the ropes creaked, and the boat gave a sudden hard jerk, pitching toward the stern before leveling out again.

"Jack," she cried, but the black thing had taken over her voice completely, and the only sound that emerged was a strangled whisper.

The little girl next to her shifted in her mother's arms to examine Madeleine curiously.

Even now he waited, watching the lifeboat descend, resting on his elbows and smiling his warm, slight smile at her until the craft struck the water and began a gradual spin, and the distance between them erased him entirely.

CHAPTER 25

Those next few hours. Those next few wretched hours. Some nights still, I close my eyes and I'm trapped back inside them, flattened between the mirrored line of the ocean and the suffocating stars.

Those are the nights that I don't go back to sleep.

I'm so grateful, son, that you will grow up with no memory of any of it. That by the time you'll read these words, those hours, that godforsaken morning, will be nothing but recorded history.

Despite my nightmares, I am merely an addendum.

Monday, April 15th
Alongside Titanic

Lifeboat Four came out of her spin and Madeleine found herself looking directly into a first-class stateroom, the window almost near enough to touch. The lights blazed inside it, chairs knocked over, water surging over the sculpted feet of the furniture, splashing against the tables and bed. Amid a jumble of long-stemmed fresh flowers, a woman's peach satin slipper danced along its surface, whirling for a moment or two before tipping and sinking down to the rug.

"Hey there, Mr. Perkis!" shouted one of the crewmen manning the oars, his head thrown back, his hands cupped around his mouth. "Quartermaster, hey! We need another hand down here!"

They all looked up. A thickset man appeared on the nearby ropes, descending clumsily hand over hand. His boots hit the lifeboat with a thump, and he turned, tugging at his coat.

"The tiller," said the same sailor.

The quartermaster nodded, bent over the gunwale and shoved away a steamer chair that was knocking against their side. In just the few moments that followed, two more men clambered down the ropes, not sailors. They huddled, wide-eyed, against the keel.

The quartermaster's gaze raked them up and down. He shook his head, his mouth flattened, then looked back at the oarsmen.

"We're to go aft, lads, to the open gangway. We'll pick up more women there."

The men dipped their oars into the sea; the lifeboat gained a steadier compass, gliding gradually away from the ship. A series of crashes still reached them from the inside, china breaking, doors breaking, wood breaking. The deeper innards of the liner grinding, balefully loud, steel against steel.

A dog barked from up above. It took Madeleine at least ten seconds to recognize that it was Kitty. She lurched to her feet, prompting Carrie to latch on to her sleeve.

Oh, God. She'd forgotten about her—in the dreamlike fright and calm of it all, she'd forgotten—

"Down, miss," snapped the quartermaster. "You must sit down."

She sank back to the plank of her bench, her hands over her heart. Kitty was barking from the boat deck, and if she craned her head—yes, Madeleine could see her, her familiar outline, so small and shadowed against the ship's lights. The shape of a tall, spare man standing next to her at the railing, one hand on her head.

Something large hurtled down from the sky. She cringed back only as it barely missed them, landing with an enormous splash that salted her with spray. The thing vanished beneath the surface before popping up again: a huge rolling barrel, *Münchner Bier* stenciled in black on its side.

"Away and *faster*," called out the quartermaster, and the lifeboat began to jerk more quickly along.

Jack and Kitty, her barks still echoing, slid from her view.

Madeleine moaned, thin and anguished. Carrie wrapped an arm around her shoulders to hug her close.

There were no gangway doors to be seen that were open. There was no one aft to pick up, only ghost lights glowing an eerie olive beneath the surface of the water. But as they came closer to *Titanic*'s rising stern, a pair of men leapt from the poop deck high above, managing to entangle themselves in the dangling ropes from the davits and grab on. They began to slither rapidly down towards them.

"Oy! Mind yourselves," thundered the quartermaster, as the men at the oars attempted to maneuver them beneath the ropes.

To the alarmed cries of several ladies, one of the men let go, managing to land heavily against the lifeboat's prow, sending them rocking. The other man released his rope and missed the boat entirely, plunging like a stone into the ocean, hardly even a splash as he went down. The fellow came up again gasping, his hair plastered along his eyes, trying to paddle.

Rosalie was closest to him. She cried, "Here!" and stretched out her arm, hauling him near. The woman behind her joined her, and together they wrestled him aboard.

Both of the new men were dressed only in rough cotton shirts and trousers, covered in grime.

"Blimey, that was close," gasped the drier man, and together they crumpled against the starboard gunwale. Someone tossed a blanket over them both.

"Get us away," commanded the quartermaster, and the oarsmen, both of whom had been goggling open-mouthed up at the listing ship, bent their heads again and began to row.

A new man rose up from the waves without warning, his head

just reaching over the top of the craft; a young girl screeched with fright.

"Give us a hand in!" the man in the water wheezed, and one of the oarsmen stood up, astonished.

"Is that you, Sam?"

"Yes!"

The oarsman reached down, the women around him reached down, and between all of them, the man was dragged to safety, shivering.

As the lifeboat turned again, floating away from the liner, Madeleine tried to find her husband once more. But they were too far aft. All she could see, all any of them could see as they slipped farther out, was *Titanic*'s stern slowly lifting free of the Atlantic, its three monstrous bronze propellers shedding rivers of water, platinum waterfalls against the glittering sky.

A flare shot up from the steamship, the first Madeleine had seen herself, even though in the back of her mind, it seemed she must have been hearing them all along, the hard cannon-crack of rockets or gunshots, or both. As the light streamed skyward, everyone in the lifeboat hung in its brief brilliance, black and white, sliding shadows; for a count of three, the canted top of *Titanic* shone almost as bright as day.

It was only seconds. But when she closed her eyes, the image of the upper deck remained, dark frozen people against a dark tilted ship.

Above the baritone groans of the liner and the cacophony of human cries, she thought she heard the orchestra still playing, sweet melancholy notes, a hymn she almost recognized.

Titanic's lights flickered, came back. Along what must have been the promenade's windows, a sinister red glow began to spread.

"Power's fading," muttered the quartermaster. "Surprised they've kept it going this long."

The stern rose and rose, and the ship's iron groans ticked

louder. People were plummeting alongside her hull, cartwheeling down into the water. Those who didn't fall clung to the boat deck in antlike clusters, pressing against the railings.

She closed her eyes. Opened them. Her breath was coming so fast, she saw it all through a cloud of mist. She could not look away; she could not fill her lungs. Carrie's arm remained tight around her but Madeleine's entire body was shaking, and she realized she couldn't stop that, either.

Another series of whipping cracks, like gunshots. The forward funnel ripped loose from its cables in a blossom of hellish sparks and soot. The funnel teetered along its edge, then collapsed in a tremendous rush along the starboard side.

A woman near the back let out a wail. Madeleine felt her throat tighten, every ounce of her wanting to join in with that pained cry, but she couldn't breathe, and she couldn't yell. She could only watch.

The steamer's lights winked out. The stern of the ship rose so high it seemed like some great, invisible hand beneath the ocean must be pulling the prow straight down. More people fell—as her eyes adjusted to the sudden night, she could see them tumbling, blue and silver, lost to the waves below. A series of explosions began, rumbling booms that sounded like rockslides, like the strafing of bombs against a solid hillside or castle.

Titanic split apart. Just like that, she broke in two, and everything before the aft funnel dropped down in a rush beneath the water. Gone.

Madeleine bent her head, panting, covering her face with both hands. The cry trapped in her throat escaped but only barely, another airy thin moan whistling past Jack's leather gloves.

"Holy God," whispered Eleanor Widener. "Holy, holy God."

When Madeleine could look up again, the aft section of the ship remained practically upright, as if it had been designed to float exactly like that. A shooting star lit a long, fiery path behind it, and as the star sank, so then did the ship: almost gently, almost quietly, except for the splashing and screams.

*   *   *

"There will be suction," announced the quartermaster. "I need you to *pull*, lads. This is the time to put your backs into it."

The boat spun for a moment while the two sailors found their rhythm; then it began to skim along the water, away from the boiling center of the wreckage. With the profile of *Titanic* gone, Madeleine thought she saw the bobbing lights of the other lifeboats around them, hundreds of them, thousands, until logic caught up with her perspective and she realized she was seeing the stars reflecting off the ocean, a boundless looking glass that cast their lights up and down and everywhere else in between.

She felt dizzy, her mouth dry. She shut her eyes and tried to measure out her breaths. When she opened them again, she was gazing downward, forward, at the blades of the oars that dipped and lifted and dipped again, stirring up phosphorus in the water, a golden green glow that spread outward in ripples, softly outlining the boat's path before sinking back into oblivion.

"Do we have a lamp?" asked the quartermaster.

"No, sir," replied one of the sailors. "I searched and found none."

"Very well."

The phosphorus dripped, shattered, dripped. Across the ocean, a terrible new noise began to rise.

She would think, later, that it was the sound of a mortally wounded beast, only if the beast had a thousand-some voices, all of them howling with pain and panic and pleading. The frothing of the water where the stern had gone down had not calmed with its loss. It was full of people, flailing and begging for help.

The blond woman next to Madeleine was quaking, the child on her lap clutched against her chest. Madeleine noticed that she was wrapped only in thin shawls, cotton or something else like it; beneath the starlight, the colors were faded, but she imagined that when touched with wind and sun, they resembled butterfly wings.

She pulled the fox shawl from her shoulders, draped it over the woman. She couldn't fasten the hooks, not while the woman held the child, but she tugged the ends closed as best as she could.

"*Tack så mycket,*" the mother whispered. The little girl squirmed, blinking. She lifted a hand to stroke the fur by her face, her eyes amazed.

The oarsmen had ceased their rowing, blades up, huffing. The lifeboat resumed its slow, aimless spin.

"We have to go back," Madeleine said. It was difficult to get the words out without her teeth chattering. She looked up at the quartermaster, who now stood by the tiller with, oddly, an unlit pipe in one hand. "We have to. Only listen to them."

"Yes," agreed Eleanor. "Yes, she's right."

"The suction," said one of the oarsmen instantly. "We can't."

"Surely it's done by now," said a woman seated on the other side of Eleanor.

"This boat is half empty," added someone else, a matron wrapped in sable like Madeleine. Her voice shook, but Madeleine thought it might be from anger, not cold. "We abandoned ship with seats to spare. We left behind our husbands and sons because *you* told us we had to, and now they're out there dying."

The quartermaster stroked his moustache. "I don't think it's—"

"*They're dying,*" Madeleine shouted, enraged. She stood up, holding her coat closed over her chest, her fingers bent into claws. "And we have the room! Listen to them! *Listen*! We have to go back!"

The quartermaster turned, looked back at the distant chaos, the frantic splashing.

"Sir!" protested the same oarsman. "Sir, think on it! It's madness! They'll swamp us for certain!"

A murmur of assent rose from a pair of women near the front, but the quartermaster spoke over them.

"Not if we're vigilant. We'll circle along the edges to start." He jammed the pipe into his front pocket. "Right, then. We're coming about."

The oarsman dropped his oar. "I'm not doing it."

"Are you refusing a direct order, seaman?"

"Not refusing, sir. I injured my shoulder just now." The man crossed his arms, sullen.

"Well, ain't you just a bloody princess?" sneered one of the men they'd rescued from the aft ropes, the one who hadn't fallen into the water. "Shove off, then, mate. I'll row."

But in the end, it took all of them rowing, Madeleine and Eleanor and any of the other women who could, to stroke back to the flotsam of human souls and debris, to begin the dreadful task of trying to salvage the dying from the glossy black sea.

CHAPTER 26

We pulled eight men from the water that night. Two of them were drunk. Two of them died, one right at my feet. All of them seemed delirious, almost—I can't think of a better word for it. Crazed, perhaps. Even after we'd gotten them aboard, covered them with rugs, they moaned and raved. I believe some of them didn't even realize they were no longer in the water.

All of them were wearing lifebelts, which seemed a godsend at the time.

It was, I guess. For them.

But for all those other souls, those fifteen-hundred or so still thrashing for their lives . . . they, too, were wearing the cork-and-canvas vests that would not save them, nor let them drown. And so that is how they died. Frozen in place.

I looked and looked for him. I looked in the darkness of night; I looked in the dawn. I searched every face I found, first the living, subsequently the dead. Like the ocean and stars, sometimes I still see them floating, one after another, behind my closed lids.

I told myself that he had made it into another boat, that he had to be on another boat.

I never stopped looking.

Monday, April 15th
Adrift

Lifeboat Four was leaking. No one could pinpoint the source of it, but it was. Ice-cold water sloshed along its bottom, leisurely rising no matter how much any of them bailed.

The silence of the night expanded, infinite but for their own hushed voices and the gentle lapping of water against wood. After she and four other women had tugged and pulled the last man aboard, Madeleine realized she no longer heard the ghastly dying-beast sound; in the last twenty minutes or so, she'd noticed it thinning, flattening into a dull monotone. But she'd not noticed until just this moment that it was utterly done.

No one else cried out for help. Nor would they, ever again.

The terrible peace of it rang in her head. They searched a while longer anyway, rowing this way and that, but there was no one alive to save.

A baby whimpered, and the man at Madeleine's feet groaned. He was too weak to sit up on his own, and there wasn't enough space to lie him along the benches, so they'd propped him up against the side as best they could. He seemed insensible, his legs sprawled, pressing against her. The violent shivers that wracked him shook her as well, no matter how she tried to shift away. Every now and then, she'd bend down to chafe her palms against his face and neck. She wasn't sure why beyond a vague notion to let him know that even in his delirium, he wasn't alone.

"He *knew*," said a woman to Madeleine's left, low and vehement.

"What?" said another. Eleanor.

"Mr. Ismay. He knew about the ice. Marian and I ran into him yesterday on the promenade. We'd gone out to look at the sunset, and he walked up. He'd gotten a Marconigram about it from another ship. He showed it to us. He told us we were among the icebergs."

Madeleine gazed out into the darkness, her jaw clenched, listening. All of them were listening now.

"He told us they were going to start up more of the boilers to go faster. That we were going to get to New York early." The woman's voice broke.

"Emily—"

"He *knew*," she said again, louder.

The man at Madeleine's feet had stopped shivering. She folded her hands over her stomach and closed her eyes, tired of looking at the stars.

They tied up to a group of other lifeboats, she wasn't certain how many. Four or five, enough to form a miniature flotilla that revolved in a wide, lazy circle, governed by the cold northern currents; no one bothered now to row. After a burst of greetings, of people calling out names, hopeful, over and over again hopeful, until the lack of answer became their answer, the silence won again.

Far away along the unwrinkled line of the ocean, someone in another lifeboat occasionally launched flares that lifted, exploded, thin green darts of fire that melted into nothing long before they reached the water. Even the shooting stars seemed more bold.

The eastern edge of the sky began to separate itself from the Atlantic, going from black to indigo to wine. As the light lifted, she was able to better see all the people around her, their eyes bloodshot, their faces chapped. A breeze rose, sending the calm water into ripples that broke against meandering small chunks of ice.

The sound of a whistle sliced through the chill. An infant released a startled cry. Madeleine lifted her head, then joined several others standing to discover the source. Just barely in view, a group of about thirty men balanced in two neat rows atop what looked like a floating shelf of ice. The man holding the whistle shrilled it again; some of the other men began waving their arms.

Hope caught at her once more, a hot blazing thing. She turned to the quartermaster, who was already reaching to uncouple their boat.

"We've room for eight or ten," he called to the crewmen in the other boats. "Who else will go?"

A second boat cut loose from their flotilla, and the pair of them began to creep along. Madeleine sat against the port gunwale, leaning out to better see. Before she could make out their faces, she could make out their perch: not ice at all, but an overturned lifeboat, rapidly sinking.

None of the men were Jack. She knew it even before the morning was clear enough to tell. None of them had his lean frame, his posture.

The man with the whistle was the same officer who'd shoved her aboard from the promenade window a lifetime ago. Who'd told her husband that he could not go with her.

"Come and take us off!" the man shouted, hoarse.

Behind him—oh, behind him, bright as sundrops against the purple-pink sky—shone the mast lights of a steamship heading their way.

They did not have room for eight or ten more people. They scarcely had room for five, and then only if everyone stood up. The water was up to Madeleine's ankles; she'd lost feeling in her feet a half hour past. With every new man added to their group, the lifeboat rocked and dipped lower into the waves.

"We'll have to row to her," decided the quartermaster, eyeing the approaching ship. "She's miles out still. We won't be afloat by the time she makes it here."

People rearranged themselves, stood sideways, making room for the pulling oars.

With a sudden brilliance, the sun breached the boundary of the sea, spilling a warm lemon light up and up, bleeding through the pink. It spread across the heavens, all the water, and caught in bright burning lines along the icebergs that had been floating around them all along, unseen in the dark.

They were glass mountains, jagged and pale. They were frozen fairy-tale monsters gleaming like opals, coral and salmon and mauve, scattered near and far.

"Holy God," whispered Eleanor Widener again, crammed against Madeleine's side. Madeleine twisted her wrist, finding the other woman's hand; they held tight.

As the lifeboat inched toward the steamer, the light fell too upon all that was left of *Titanic*: deck chairs and shattered doors; bodies that spun by looking like nothing more than blanched and broken dolls, standing whimsically upright in the ocean with their arms out, fingers curved.

The weight of the dead man pressed against her feet. Inside her, she felt Jack's baby shift.

The steamship was called *Carpathia*; she read its name through a squint against the light. She had a single funnel instead of four, and steep gray-dark sides, and as their lifeboat limped up to her, the ice water inside it was up to Madeleine's shins.

Her thoughts had become feathery and fleeting. She was thirsty and she was not; she was warm and she was not. Every now and then a swarm of spots would begin to burst along the edges of her vision. Whenever that happened, all she could do was hang her head, hoping for the best.

"We must get her aboard," said someone in her ear, urgent. She thought they were likely talking about the crying infant and tried to agree, but her lips wouldn't move. Her tongue was too clickity-dry, anyway.

The boat tossed, and she felt herself falling. Only she couldn't fall. No one could. They were packed in too tightly; the falling was all in her head.

"Here, miss," said a man with an English accent, and to her surprise, Madeleine found herself seated upon a swinging plank that seemed to be rising . . . rising . . .

She was holding onto the ropes beside her with both hands, buckled straps bound across her legs.

There was a ship at her back. There was an ocean ahead.

She was rising without her own will, without having to do any-thing at all to make it happen, the plank and ropes jerking. She rose and looked out over the curve of the earth laid out like a vivid blue cartographer's map, dotted with white, with slow-spinning swirls of ice green and black.

In a shadowed chamber, Madeleine came back to herself, open-ing her eyes to a single electric lightbulb burning naked against the wall—

—that stormy night on the Noma, *her father telling her to wake—*

—but she was looking at that lightbulb and . . . linen. At the high climb of a fat pillow and wrinkled sheets.

It was not her pillow, scented with a fragrance she didn't know. It was not her bed, with its downy wide comfort. This mattress felt too firm. A hard lump nudged up against her ribcage.

A glass of water sat before her on a nightstand. She reached for it, drained it, set it down again.

The bed and floor and all of it beneath her moved, a sluggish lift and fall. She'd spent so many hours at sea, she understood at once what it meant.

I am on a boat. A ship. I'm on—

She remembered. She remembered being guided aboard, the bosun's chair swinging against the topsides of this new steamer until the crew had caught it up, pulling her safely back to the deck. She remembered them freeing her from the straps, helping her to a saloon, where a man who told her three times that he was a physician—she kept asking—gave her a quick examination be-fore telling someone else that she needed hydration and heat and a decent place to rest. Somewhere quiet, and at once.

She'd wanted to protest that. The lack of the wounded-beast noise still haunted her, and she hadn't wanted to dwell in it again.

But a uniformed man with a great deal of gold braid on his sleeves had come to her, along with Eleanor Widener and Carrie and some other women, and they had all led her to this room with its firm bed and plump pillows. Carrie had stripped away her coat and her lifebelt, her dress and corset and shoes, and Madeleine, stupefied, had let her. Had flopped down atop the mattress and surrendered to sleep for who knew how long.

She inched out of the bed now, her feet testing the rug. The seam of the stocking along the end of her right foot had ripped (*hadn't she been wearing two sets of stockings? where had the other gone?*); her big toe poked out. She stood, stretching the sore muscles all along her legs and arms and back.

The wall to her left had a series of curtained portholes, the cloth panels closed, sunlight outlining a pattern of navy chevrons against stripes. She eyed the curtains warily, wanting to part them and look outside. Afraid of what she might see if she did.

The door to the room clicked open. A caramel-haired woman who looked familiar—wasn't she?—came in carrying a tray, balancing it on her hip as she turned to shut the door again. She was wearing a sequined velvet evening dress, despite the fact that it was clearly bright day beyond the portholes.

"Oh, you're awake," she said pleasantly. "Good. I've brought you something to eat. A simple soup for now, nothing too rich."

Madeleine pressed a hand to her forehead. "Yes. I—my husband. I need to go—"

The woman, older and unsmiling, placed the tray on a low table in front of a settee. Her voice was gentle, cautious; she went to Madeleine and lifted her hand. Reflexively, Madeleine accepted it. She noticed that the woman's gown was water-stained all along the hem, sequins missing, the velvet stiff and ruined.

"I am Marian Thayer. Do you remember me? We were introduced once in Newport, a year or so ago. And we spoke on the lifeboat, but I think you were in something of a faint by then."

Madeleine bit her lip, shook her head. Their hands parted.

"That's all right. Here, come sit up in the bed and I'll bring you the tray. Try the soup. It's not bad."

"No. Excuse me. I must get dressed and go look for my husband."

"Colonel Astor is not aboard the *Carpathia*," said Marian, in the same gentle tone. "There are a great many people not aboard, though. There's talk that they may have been picked up by other ships."

"You can't know that for certain. He might be here somewhere. He might be injured—"

"Mrs. Astor. Do you imagine there is a single person of our ilk who would not recognize the colonel?"

"Perhaps he's on a lifeboat that hasn't come in yet! I need to go see!"

"All the lifeboats are in, long in. You've been asleep for nearly twenty-four hours. We've been underway for New York practically the entire time."

She stood paralyzed, trying to comprehend it. This time when Marian took her hand, she allowed herself to be led back to the bed.

"You've had quite a soldier of a nurse guarding you all this while, but as the ship's surgeon was of the opinion that you are out of immediate danger, your Miss Endres is off helping with the other injured passengers. There's a lot of frostbite, broken bones, sprained ankles, matters of that sort to deal with. I suspect the doctor is overwhelmed. So I volunteered to check in on you, to see if I could entice you to eat." She regarded the simple tray with a frown. "There was buttered bread to go with the soup, but it seemed to me the butter had gone off, so I skipped it. We have crackers instead."

Madeleine slumped against the pillows. Marian Thayer got up, found Madeleine's sweater, and arranged it over her shoulders.

"The rest of your clothes will have dried by now, I think, although I'm afraid your fur is beyond repair. We stored your jewelry in the ship's safe, just so you know. Doctor McGee has issued strict orders that you remain in bed, and I really do think you should listen to him."

Madeleine gazed down at the bowl of soup, at the bits of carrot and celery turning in the greasy broth, and felt her stomach pitch. When she picked up the spoon, her hand was trembling.

"I'm afraid I must tell you something more," said the other woman, regretful.

Madeleine put down the spoon, trying to control her nerves.

"Apparently there's a journalist aboard this ship. Maybe two. And at least two people with cameras."

"What?" she said, stunned. "Already?"

"The journalist booked his ticket as a legitimate passenger. He was headed off to Europe for a holiday with his wife before *Carpathia* got our distress call and diverted, so it's really just an unfortunate coincidence. I assume the people with the cameras are merely hobbyists, but they've been snapping shots all the while. I wanted to warn you. I understand that . . . your relationship with the press has been difficult."

Madeleine wanted to laugh at that but couldn't. She could only sit there, blinking at the soup, the wooden tray, the linen napkin so neatly folded.

"The newspaperman has been slipping around, attempting to interview the survivors. A Mr. Hurd, I am told. Carlisle or Carlos, something like that. His wife's name is Katherine. They both continue to inquire about you."

Madeleine flattened her palms against the sheets, her fingers spread, shaking her head.

"My husband is missing, too," said Marian in her gentle, grave voice. "I have a son your age, and by God's good grace he lived through that night. Eleanor Widener's had no word of either her husband or her son." She placed the spoon back into Madeleine's hand. "Think of your baby, Mrs. Astor, and eat."

CHAPTER 27

Carpathia's magnificent Captain Rostron had given over his own cabin to me and Eleanor and Marian. (In the days that followed, he would be hailed as a hero, and indeed he is. Without him, I have no doubt that every single person aboard *Titanic* would have perished, instead of three-quarters. I do not plan to go on an ocean liner again, but if I do, I will find the one he commands.)

If you're thinking that three of us sequestered in a cabin meant for a single occupant was a lot, you're right, but believe me, we were lucky. Nearly everyone had to share rooms or berths (except for Bruce Ismay, hiding away in one of the ship's hospital examination chambers, and *he wasn't even injured*). Had you been offered someone's cabin or their bed, you could at least sleep in relative comfort. But the Cunard liner was a great deal smaller than our own had been, you see, and she had set sail from New York with nearly the same number of passengers as they'd taken in from the lifeboats. We were all of us practically shoulder-to-shoulder.

For the four days it took us to get back to New York, people bedded down wherever they could, on tables, on benches, on the floors of the lounges and saloons. Whenever awake, they formed huddles of misery, sobbing and whispering and repeatedly exchanging their tales of that night.

I've mulled for many an hour on that, the compulsion to discuss what had happened again and again. I think now I've teased it out. If one breaks the horror apart, breaks it into all these little, smaller moments, perhaps it's possible to reconstruct it in such a way as to make everything more . . . manageable.

At any rate, it's a better way to carry on than turning to laudanum.

As we sailed for home, the universe beyond *Carpathia* clamored for the names of *Titanic's* survivors aboard the ship, and to the best of the abilities of *Carpathia's* unhappy, exhausted wireless operator, the universe had slowly been fed them. (My own, I was told, was among the first released, and at least I had that slight comfort in the days that followed: my family knew I was safe.)

But, as hungry as *we* were for news of *our* missing loved ones, we never received a single name wired back to us.

Tuesday, April 16th, 11:59 p.m.
Aboard Carpathia

Madeleine came awake with a jerk. The cabin blazed with light, stark white that plummeted into black. Someone was shooting off rockets. The ship was sinking.

She scrambled up, panicked, and the light flashed again, this time followed by a deep roll of thunder.

She remained upright, catching her breath, waiting for her heart to calm.

Beside her, curled away on the far side of the mattress, Eleanor still slept. Marian, covered in blankets on the settee, also didn't stir.

The lightning flickered again, dimmer now. The thunder rumbled. A thin patter of rainfall struck the glass covering the portholes, small and subtle, like mice scampering inside walls.

Madeleine eased out of the bed, trying to shift the mattress as little as possible. As soon as her toes touched the floor, her left foot cramped, sharply painful, and she had to stop and bend at the knee with her foot stretched behind her in a long, flexed arch until the tendon released.

She opened the wardrobe and found her dress and cardigan and shoes. The tailor-made was impossible to manage without help, so she simply tugged the sweater on over her combinations, long and white, and worked her feet into the shoes. The leather seams scraped hard against her skin and stockings, dried rigid from their hours submerged in salt water. Her sable was there, too, so she took it from the hanger, put it on as quietly as possible.

Neither Eleanor nor Marian woke.

She took up a White Star deck blanket that someone had draped over a chair, wrapped it over her head and around her shoulders as the women from steerage did. She made very certain the door made no sound as she closed it behind her.

She did not know the time. There was a wall clock back inside the cabin, but she hadn't thought to look at it, and they had locked her corsage watch away with the rest of her jewels. But it was dark out, cloudy with no hint of anything but full night beyond the dim lights of the deck. After all her hours confined to the captain's quarters, it was a relief to be outside again, breathing in the rain.

Lightning flashed in the clouds overhead, purple and silver, revealing massive whorls and billows in swift broken instants.

Beneath the storm, *Carpathia* steamed smoothly along.

The fur coat hung from her, clumped and ragged, the lower third of it stiffened with crystals of salt. The crystals winked as she walked, minuscule diamonds that melted and dropped away with her every step. She left them behind her like a trail of bread-crumbs, only she didn't know if or when she'd be retracing her steps.

She found her way onto the main section of the deck. She glanced behind her at the bridge, blue-green lights burning, shadows of men within, then down at the empty deck chairs left unfolded from the day. A few fellows had stretched out along slatted benches beneath an awning portside, their arms pillowing their heads. Despite the falling rain, none of them were awake.

Lights glowed, very weak, past the windows of what she guessed was the dining saloon. She found the entrance, pulled open the door. The smell hit her first: onions and cheese and unwashed humans, more than she could easily count. The illumination was coming from a handful of wall sconces; all the chandeliers had been darkened. She could see why the sconces had been left on: there were so many people spread out across the floor that it would be easy get up in the middle of the night and stumble across a neighbor just trying to get to the lavatory.

She began to pick her way between them. She paused to take in each face, men and women both but certainly every single man, but did not see Jack.

The saloon led to a hallway—he was not there either, squeezed up against the polished wood wall—which led to the smoke room, full of stained glass and even more men. There was a scattering of ladies in here, too, lodged in this sanctuary of masculinity. The women slept atop the sofas, their hats and gloves and shoes arranged neatly nearby.

Madeleine crept among them as if on cat's paws, keeping her blanket tugged close against her chin.

He was not here.

She kept going, not understanding the layout of the ship and not caring to, only walking along as her feet took her, finding more people, their expressions etched with sorrow, even asleep—not him, not him—moving on.

On a wooden bench in another narrow corridor, she passed an older woman covered to her waist in falling furs, a satin cushion beneath her head. One hand rested atop her sternum, clenched into a defiant, spotted fist. Her hair was gray and stringy and unkempt. She was breathing heavily, eyes closed, her features cadaverous.

It was Charlotte Cardeza. The grand Mrs. Cardeza, looking like nothing more than a grizzled fishwife caught napping in the open, her mouth agape, aged and senseless.

Madeleine edged past, paused, went back to her. As carefully as she could, she lifted that bony knotted fist, straightened the furs and slid the top one up further, all the way up to Charlotte's chin, before lowering her hand again.

Kinder hearts are stronger, her mother had once said.

Maddy needed to be strong.

She crept on.

A deck below, in what might have been the second-class lounge, Madeleine at last encountered a pair of women awake, wrapped in blankets and nestled in chairs in a corner, holding hands and conversing in whispers. She paused at the entrance, then turned away to grant them privacy.

"Madeleine."

She turned back, uncertain in the low light. The woman spoke again, her voice scarcely a murmur above the steady thudding of the liner's engines.

"Madeleine, it's me."

"Margaret?"

The woman stood, shedding her blanket. She wore black velvet and diamonds and opened her arms, smiling sadly, and Madeleine, all at once and without warning, lost her courage.

She rushed forward to embrace her, barely missing three people along the way.

"They didn't tell me," she said into her friend's shoulder. Her body trembled; her face felt wet and hot. Margaret's auburn hair was loosely bound into a plait, and Maddy turned her face into the rough silk of it, scented of rosemary and brine. "They didn't tell me you were here. I asked and they said they thought so but didn't know. They said they'd find out for me but didn't know."

Margaret patted her on the back. Maddy hardly felt it through the thick ruin of the coat.

"I'm sorry," Margaret whispered. "I should have come to you before. But the doctor said you were to be left undisturbed, and there's been so much to be done down here with everyone, with all these poor people from steerage. But I should have come. I am sorry."

Maddy was crying now, trying not to, trying not to make any noise at all so that no one around them would wake, her lungs burning and shrinking. She pulled back, scrubbing her hands along her face. She felt the stare of Margaret's companion, candidly curious, and ducked away from it.

"Have you seen Jack? Is Jack here?"

"No, my dear heart. No. I've been up and down this ship, top to bottom. And . . . no."

Madeleine nodded, wiping at her cheeks again. She lifted her gaze to a painting of a Spanish galleon battling lapis-colored waves. It hung just a fraction crooked on the wall, the ormolu frame a peeling glimmer against the darker wood behind it.

"Come on." Margaret touched her arm. "Come with me, little mother. We need to get you back to bed."

The rain turned into fog, and the fog consumed the ship and everything around her, forcing the *Carpathia* to slow. Hours and hours were added to their voyage home.

Madeleine slept more, hidden beneath her blankets. Occasionally she'd wake, either from the booming blasts of the foghorn or else whenever Carrie or Rosalie or the doctor would show up. She'd eat the food they'd brought and answer the physician's questions, and then fall back into her ocean of slumber.

It was Carrie who told her there was no sign of Victor Robins, the valet, either. Madeleine could only nod.

If she suffered any nightmares during those damp gray days, she couldn't remember them, and for that Madeleine was intensely grateful.

Her visitors brought any tidbits of news they could glean about Jack, about what had happened to him after Lifeboat Four had launched.

He had helped load the last boats with frantic women and children.

He had placed a woman's hat atop the head of a boy so that the child would be allowed to board with his mother.

He had sawed tangled ropes free from the davits with his penknife.

He had freed all the dogs from the kennels.

He had stood back calmly amid the pandemonium after all of the lifeboats were gone, smoking a cigarette with two other gentlemen.

Margaret and Carrie and the rest—they must have thought they were comforting her. But the only common thread Madeleine found to connect any of their stories was that no one knew what actually became of her husband. No one saw him again once the ship foundered.

Or, if they had, no one would tell her about it.

Late at night, shrouded in fog, she could go out.

Hardly anyone else did, which meant she mostly walked the decks alone, wrapped in her coat and the concealing blanket, her skin and hair clammy with the cold moisture but not caring, because in these moments no one cried, and no one spoke of drowning or freezing or who was to blame. The only sounds she had to listen to were the ordinary ones of the ship herself. Creaking ropes. Thrumming engines. The water below, soughing past.

In the pre-dawn hours of Thursday, the day they were due to dock at last, Madeleine stood at a railing along the promenade deck, contemplating the smooth misted nothingness that erased the sea and sky. That erased the world that would be waiting for her, clawing for her, scrabbling, such a short while from now.

The mast lights behind her lent the deck and rail and darkness a silvery, prismatic glow.

"Mrs. Astor?"

It was a woman's voice, unfamiliar. Madeleine didn't turn from the railing.

"My name is Katherine Hurd. I'm with—"

"I know who you are," Madeleine said, quiet.

"Oh." The woman paused, then rallied. "I'm very sorry to bother you. I was wondering if you'd—if you'd care to say something. For the record."

Madeleine closed her eyes. "Such as?"

"Anything. Anything at all you'd wish anyone to know, even as a matter of public interest. A number of the other wives have given me statements about that last night, or else messages meant for their loved ones."

Madeleine felt her lips press into a smile, keen as a blade. "And you, of course, will publish those messages purely as a matter of public interest."

"A brief statement of fact can do no harm," countered Mrs. Hurd.

"I believe a statement of fact about me has already been released. I was saved. Surely that's enough."

"But—a more personal note, perhaps? For the sake of your family?"

Madeleine glanced at her. Katherine Hurd, the reporter's wife, was in her middle thirties, maybe, tall and wearing a summer hat, despite the time and the weather. The hat was silk and straw—not nearly warm enough—with large, faux coneflowers fixed to the brim. The petals trembled with the wind.

Madeleine let the blanket fall back from her hair. "You're not a journalist."

Mrs. Hurd pursed her mouth, released a rush of air that lifted and withered into smoke. "No. Not as such."

"But your husband is."

"Yes."

Madeleine faced her squarely. "Do you have any news about any other survivors besides us? Anyone else rescued and taken aboard other ships?"

Mrs. Hurd hesitated, then shook her head. "Captain Rostron has forbidden all wireless communication to, or from, either my husband or myself. He has confiscated all the stationery aboard the ship in the hope that we cannot write without it. He's even had our cabin searched for scraps of paper. We've had no news at all, I'm afraid."

Madeleine looked away again, gripping the railing. The vapor rolled by, devious and blank, devouring everything beyond her.

He might still be out there right this moment, tossed by the waves, another gossamer soul surrendered to the sea.

Or, he might have been saved. Another ship, another rescue, another wild reckless hope, and she'd see him soon again, walking toward her with his fast graceful stride, his hat tipped back. Kitty, too, and why not? Other dogs had survived the sinking; she'd seen them. Kitty never would have left Jack's side.

It was the not knowing, *not knowing*, that was slowly cleaving her heart in two.

From somewhere below, above the perpetual swishing of the waves, rose a hollow, rhythmic note of metal striking metal, like a chain hitting a flagpole, an echoing *ting! ting!*

ting!

Mrs. Hurd covered Madeleine's hand with her own. "Dear child," she said, in a much firmer tone than before. She sounded like a schoolteacher, like a headmistress, in charge even though she really was not. "You must take heart. All is not yet lost."

Very gently, Madeleine freed her hand. "I pray you're right," she said, and walked away.

Back inside the cabin, she found Eleanor on the settee, clutching a pillow to her face, silently weeping in the dark.

Madeleine sat beside her without speaking, slowly stroking her friend's hair.

CHAPTER 28

As headlines about *Titanic*'s sinking became splashed across every newspaper known to man, your half-brother's grief was well-documented. Articles described him ricocheting from the White Star Line offices to the Marconi Company's offices, tear-stained, desperate, offering any amount of money that could be named to the wireless operators in exchange for news of Jack's survival.

None of the wireless men could accept his offer.

By the time Vincent found me aboard the *Carpathia* three days later, his grief had turned to rage.

But then, we were all of us in a state. Tormented by the unknowns.

Too often, I found my thoughts straying as I stared into that wall of gray mist, and in my imagination, the ship that sailed through it wasn't *Carpathia* but *Titanic*: fog surrounding me, surrounding the steamer and the berg and the hundreds of corpses the berg had claimed, caught gelid in the boundary between the sea and the air. Just . . . bobbing along through all that nothingness.

Blank fathoms vaulting above them.

Blank fathoms stretching below.

Thursday, April 18th, 5:25 p.m.
Aboard Carpathia

People began to line the decks, the rescued and the rescuers, spilling out of the fusty confines of the saloons and lounges and overcrowded staterooms. It was raining, but no one seemed to care. Everyone was eager to catch sight of New York.

Mostly what they saw, however, were tugboats, dozens of them swarming the ship. The tugs held reporters, and the reporters held megaphones and money and hand-lettered signs, all of them bawling questions up to the passengers and crew. From inside the cabin, Madeleine could hear their shouts, if not their actual words, a dull sort of roar too close in her memory to the cries of the dying. She sat on the edge of the bed and twisted her hands in her lap.

Carrie and Rosalie stood at the porthole windows, looking out. Madeleine didn't even want to glance up at them.

She was dressed and bejeweled and ready to flee. However that was going to happen.

Marian entered the cabin; the clamor outside acutely amplified until she closed the door again.

"Do not go out there," she warned Madeleine. "We're surrounded. All these beastly newsmen have flashlights and cameras and signs. Some are even offering cash to any of the crew willing to jump overboard and speak with them."

"Well, I never," said Carrie, astonished.

"I saw at least five different men holding up placards," said Marian, "inquiring specifically about Mrs. Astor."

Someone knocked on the door. Marian turned back, opened it cautiously, then stood aside to let the ship's second officer enter.

"Good evening, ladies," he said, removing his cap. "Captain Rostron sent me to inform you that we should be docked by around nine this evening. He would have come himself, but—" The officer grimaced, gestured to the portholes. "After a brief stop at the White Star Line's terminal to lower *Titanic*'s boats"—he paused, looking uncomfortable—"er, her lifeboats, we'll head to Pier 54. That's ours. We'll be disembarking the injured first, but then you. The captain wants to reassure you all that the strictest measures are being employed to keep the press at bay, but, of course, our influence ends at the Cunard terminal."

Madeleine and Marian exchanged a look.

"Mrs. Astor, your stepson has requested permission to come aboard after docking and customs to escort you off. The captain has granted his request."

"I see," she said, confounded.

The officer replaced his cap, gave a nod.

"Wait, please," said Marian, catching him by the arm. "Is there any news? Anything at all?"

The man's gaze slid from hers. "I really cannot say, ma'am."

Night fell. The ship reached the Cunard pier amid bursts of white light that popped and burned beyond the portholes—not lightning now, but camera flashes.

Marian Thayer left on the arm of her son.

Eleanor Widener left sandwiched between two friends.

Madeleine sat. She waited. The cabin grew cooler, and she used her sable as a blanket across her lap.

"If only madame had a veil," brooded Rosalie, seated in the swivel chair by the desk. "*Hélas*, I should have thought. I might have borrowed one."

"It's fine. Don't trouble yourself about it."

There was absolutely no chance, Madeleine knew, of leaving the ship unrecognized, no matter how obscured her face.

The door opened swiftly, without the courtesy of a knock. Vincent stood at the entrance, his hand still on the latch. An officer, not the same one as before, stood behind him, peering in.

Madeleine came to her feet, clutching the coat. Vincent took a step forward, his gaze skittering past her, searching the cabin. His face looked chalky pale, his mouth a thin line.

"He's really not here," he said.

"No," she answered, soft.

He took another step forward, his movements jerky, his eyes full of a strange, savage light. He said to the room, "Excuse me. I wish a minute to speak with Mrs. Astor alone."

Both Carrie and Rosalie looked at Madeleine; she gave a small nod. They filed out.

The door closed. Vincent only stared at her.

She was about to ask him what he'd heard about survivors on other ships, if anything, even though she knew it must be nothing by the way he stood so terrible and still, when he said, his lips barely moving, "You killed him."

The air left her lungs. "What did you say?"

"You. You killed him." His voice was hushed, restrained, the opposite of the light behind his eyes. "You left him behind to die."

"*I* didn't leave him behind! They wouldn't let him on the lifeboat! They were only letting on women and children—"

"There are men *everywhere* out there," he roared. "Men from *Titanic* all over this ship!"

Madeleine fought not to raise her voice in kind. "I don't know anything about them. I don't know who they are, or how they were saved. There were some who stole into the boats by the ropes at the last minute, but Jack would never do that. He would never take someone else's place. He asked to come aboard, and they refused him. That's all I know."

A quiet rapping at the door.

"Mrs. Astor? Is everything all right?"

"Yes," she called. "One moment." She held Vincent's gaze, dropped her arms to her sides to reveal her stomach. "Your father was protecting us, from start to finish. And if he has died, then he died still protecting us, and that was his choice."

She wore the white cardigan over her dress. The swell of her belly stretched the soft knit.

"Because he's a good man, Vincent. You know that. A good husband, and a good father."

Jack's son took in the fact of her pregnancy without expression. The slope of his shoulders, the slant of his jaw, his long lashes: for the first time ever, with the camera lights flaring and fading behind him, gleaming along the pomade in his hair, she saw in him a suggestion of the man she loved.

Then, horribly, he began to laugh.

She brushed past him, opening the door to find Rosalie and Carrie nearby, clearly concerned. The ship's officer who had arrived with Vincent stood opposite them, looking down, adjusting his cuffs.

Madeleine cleared her throat. "Which is the way we should go, sir?"

"This way, ma'am, if you please." He tugged at his cap. "I'm to accompany you all down."

Amid the crush of people who still waited to disembark, Madeleine found a woman in a calico dress wrapped in a blanket, no coat. A young boy with a wet nose clutched at her skirts with both hands, his face pinched.

She broke away from her group, walked up to the woman. She pressed the sable into her arms.

"Here. This is for you."

Then she kept walking without looking back.

The gangway down to the pier was steep, so Carrie took her arm for safety. Vincent, on the other side of her, did not touch her, only stared straight out into the mob gathered below. There were powder flashes exploding all around and bright white lights glaring from above. After all her time secluded in the captain's cabin, in the endless blanket of fog, she was a little blinded by it all, and so didn't see her sister until they were nearly upon her.

"Maddy!" Katherine cried, and pushed past the line of men keeping everyone back, sprinting up the last few steps to embrace her. "Oh, thank God, thank God! We didn't know if you had really survived or not! There've been so many different reports in the papers, and some said you were fine, and some said you were injured, and then—just now, *just now,* people in the crowd were saying that you had *died* as the ship was docking! That you *died!*"

Katherine's tears smeared Madeleine's cheeks. Her fingers dug into her back; her breath was coming in whistles.

"It's all right," Madeleine said, her hand against the nape of Katherine's neck. "I'm all right."

Mrs. Astor, came the murmur of recognition from the thousands of people below them, their faces upturned, their eyes shining and their mouths shaping her name. *Mrs. Astor, Mrs. Astor, look who it is, Mrs. Astor.*

Carrie said mildly, "We should keep moving."

Vincent walked around them. "We don't need the ambulance we brought for her. I'll get the limousine."

They *had* brought an ambulance, along with Mr. Dobbyn and two doctors and two more motorcars. Madeleine kept her group together in one auto, Katherine and Carrie and Rosalie, with Vincent driving. The other automobiles would split up, each taking a different route to meet them back at the Fifth Avenue mansion.

Katherine had seized Madeleine's hands as soon as they were seated and not released them since. The brick and marble façades of the city rushed by ambered with light, sparkling in the falling rain; from inside the plush comfort of the limousine, everything began to take on a hazy, unreal edge.

Despite Vincent's efforts to shake them off, a string of motorcars kept behind them, sleek gleaming sharks that matched their every turn.

"We're going home first," Katherine was saying. "Our home, I mean—Mother and Father are so anxious to see you. They wanted to come, too, but Vincent and I convinced them not to—there were already so many of us, and Father's been so ill—"

Madeleine looked up.

"He broke his leg a few weeks back. I didn't write to tell you, because I didn't want you to stew over it, as there was nothing to be done that wasn't already being done. And it was your honeymoon, after all. But as soon as we heard about *Titanic*—oh, Maddy. We've just been . . ."

Katherine lost her voice. The rain spattered against the windows, clinging to the glass in fiery jeweled dots.

"So worried," finished Vincent, his tone even.

"Father was up all last night, Mother told me. He's hardly slept since the news broke. And Maddy—Madeleine . . ."

Katherine released her hands, lightly touched her sister's stomach.

"Are you . . . ?"

"Yes."

"Oh, God," said Katherine, and started to cry. She stuffed her hands against her mouth. Madeleine leaned against her and Katherine instantly wrapped both arms tight around her, but the tears didn't stop.

CHAPTER 29

The nature of hope is curious to me. It can sustain us through the darkest of times. It can buoy us above every reasonable expectation of despair. Yet hope can shatter us just as readily as the darkness can. People refer to it as false hope, but I think that's misleading, because the feeling itself is painfully true.

It is a treacherous hope, more precisely. A dangerous one.

Your brother would not abandon his hope, even as it tore him to pieces. I watched it happen, day by day. In these private pages, I will admit to you that Vincent and I were never friends. We will never be friends. But witnessing him unravel by degrees stirred nothing but pity in my heart.

Even Captain Roberts, whom I sent in the *Noma* up to Halifax to claim your father's body, told anyone who would listen that it might not be John Jacob Astor in the pine coffin they were returning to us. It might have been someone else in his monogrammed clothing. Poor Mr. Robins, perhaps, wearing castoffs.

Because in all of our fantasies, the indomitable J. J. Astor had not succumbed to the sea. He was out there somewhere still, on some mythical ship, miraculously alive and breathing and on his way home to us.

The difference between everyone else and me, I suppose, was that I knew in my heart that it *was* a fantasy. I had already relinquished any hope for his survival.

I think even before *Carpathia*, I had relinquished it. I'd seen first-hand those scattered, terrible human dolls in the North Atlantic. The glistening mountains of ice lit pink by the dawn.

I understood how barbaric hope could be.

For your sake, Jakey, I could not allow myself to be destroyed by it.

The *Californian* searched the ice fields where *Titanic* went down. The *Virginian*, the *Birma*, the *Parisian*, the *Frankfurt*. Even more steamships offered to come.

But it was a gravesite. The only thing left to do was send in the funeral ships to retrieve the dead.

April 18, 1912
Manhattan

That hazy sense of moving through the unreal stayed with Madeleine even as she walked up the steps of the brownstone. There were reporters already waiting there, naturally, and more poured out of the automobiles that had followed them, but she didn't stop to look at them or say anything, even as they surged close with their pencils and questions and damp pads of paper.

The door to the house flung open. She was inside, back in the old familiar hallway, the solitary appliqué chair, the arched nook holding the telephone. She was in her mother's arms, inhaling her familiar sweet vanilla scent.

Mother was crying and attempting not to, delicate little tears that fell and fell. Everyone stayed bunched in a knot against the front door until Katherine herded them all into the drawing room.

"I'm all right," Madeleine kept saying. It was becoming like a chant; she knew the words were correct, but in this unreal world, they were beginning to lose their meaning. "I'm here. I'm all right."

"Matthews," said Mother, "bring the soup and sandwiches." She faced Madeleine again, dabbing the moisture from beneath her eyes. "We have your bedroom ready."

"No, I'm not staying. I need to go back to—" *Jack's house*, she almost said. "To go back home," she finished.

"My dear! Are you sure? To be in that enormous place all alone . . ."

"I won't be alone. There are dozens of servants, plus I have a nurse now, Miss Endres—she's waiting in the motorcar. Jack hired her. I'll need to see her settled in."

"A nurse?"

Madeleine tilted her head, framed her hands around her middle. Mother gasped.

"You never said! Not once in your letters, you never mentioned—"

"We wanted it to be a surprise."

"Oh, my darling!"

She was pulled into another embrace. Madeleine closed her eyes, yielding momentarily to the solace of it, relaxing against her as she used to do as a child. But then behind her eyelids the fog came, and the white faces against the water, and she eased away.

"I'll stay with her tonight," Katherine volunteered. "And Vincent will be there, too, won't you?"

Vincent Astor, his arms crossed over his chest, only nodded.

"I must go home," Madeleine said. "I've only stopped by for a moment, so that you and Father could see for yourselves that I'm okay."

"He's in the sitting room," Mother said. "Waiting for you."

The sitting room had been transformed into a makeshift bedroom, complete with a brass bed, a chest of drawers, and a night table where the secrétaire and a bronze bust of Antigone used to be. Her father lay propped against a mound of pillows, one leg atop the covers, a plaster cast reaching from his toes to just above his knee.

His beard had started to grow in, more of an iron gray than the silver of his hair, rough and glinting along his cheeks and jowls. His eyes were reddened, but when she walked in, he lifted his head and smiled, and he was suddenly exactly the same as he had always been, the exact same, and so was she.

"Madeleine, my little one."

"Dad." She bent down to kiss him, then dropped into the armchair that had been placed beside the bed.

"How it does me good to see you again. What time is it? You must be so fatigued."

"I'm all—yes, I am," she admitted.

He held her hand, his gaze roaming her face. "I'm sorry. We couldn't get rid of the pressmen outside, not even with bribery."

"They're relentless, I know. There were some aboard the *Carpathia*, too. And back on the pier—well. It's good you didn't go and try to wade through it all."

Her father shook his head. "It is my duty to protect you." His forehead furrowed; his fingers tightened over hers. His eyes took on a sheen. "I should have protected you."

"You have, Daddy. You have protected me."

"No. I failed you in this. The ship, the—those vultures outside. I should have . . ."

"I have been protected by you my entire life," she said quietly. "You, and then Jack. I've been the most fortunate girl in the world my entire life."

He exhaled. His hand trembled. She leaned down to rest her cheek against it, lightly, so that she wouldn't hurt his joints.

"Even now," she whispered. "Even now."

She had expected to find the chateau empty and spectral, shrouded in shadows; in the corners of her mind, that was how it always lingered, day or night. But as the limousine pulled up to the *porte cochère*, she saw rows and rows of windows glowing past their scrolled iron grilles, as if there were one of Lina Astor's famous balls taking place inside, throwing yellow brightness out into the rain and along the throngs of men crammed along the sidewalks.

"Here we go," Katherine said. "Don't try to rush through them. Go only as fast as you can bear."

"I can bear rather a lot," Madeleine said, but as she got out, she kept her gaze level and her pace sedate. Just like before, she didn't look at the reporters or answer any questions. Vincent led the way, and Katherine remained beside her. Footmen rushed down the steps but then only stood by, making certain everyone else remained back.

The lights flashed.

A decade later, she would come across a newspaper clipping with an image of the three of them pegged frozen as they walked in, skirts clutched in fists, feet lifted. The caption beneath it read, THE LAST OF THE HOUSE OF ASTOR?

She would think, holding that clipping between her fingers, *How young we all look, none of us older than twenty. How young and audacious and afraid.*

The stony chill of the mansion swept over her; Madeleine felt it keenly through her tired cardigan and dress. Everything echoed, everything was loud and soft at once, reverberating.

In the bronze-and-glass excess of the atrium, a man in evening wear approached, inclining his head. For a second, she could only stare at him blankly.

The butler, she remembered. But she could not, for the life of her, summon up his name.

"May I say, Mrs. Astor, on behalf of the entire staff, how good it is to see you again."

"Thank you. How kind."

"Doctor Kimball is waiting for you in the southeast salon."

She blinked. "Who?"

"Kimball," said Vincent, handing off his coat. "The physician. You saw him down at the pier."

"I don't think I need—"

"Just go talk to him," Vincent interrupted. "So Dobbyn can go out and give a statement to the press saying you're fine, you're in impeccable health, strong as an ox. Then maybe they'll all go the hell away."

Before she could reply, he was gone, vanished through one of the high stone archways that led into the mansion's interior.

She looked at Katherine, then helplessly back at the butler.

"This way, madam," he offered, and both she and Katherine moved to follow him, their footsteps softly sounding.

At the entrance to the salon, Madeleine turned back to her sister.

"My mind's all muzzy. I completely forgot about Miss Endres. She's never been here before and I just left her stranded by the stairs. If you wouldn't mind, could you see about getting a room prepared for her? She'll need clothing, toiletries—oh, you'll have to ask her exactly what. And would you make certain Rosalie is all right?"

Katherine smiled, quick and confident, a resurrection of her old self. "I will."

The southeast salon had a fire blazing in the green marble hearth; the man seated in the causeuse beside it rose to his feet as she came in. He was white-bearded and pot-bellied, eyeing her warily, as if she might either tip into hysteria or else dissolve into tears, and he had braced himself to be ready for either or both.

But all Madeleine felt was a great empty nothing. Not hysterical. Not tearful. After this long, long day, in this cold and ornate home that was her own, all she felt was a sort of droning emptiness.

And it was a relief.

"Mrs. Astor," he said, lifting his hand to her. Instead of shaking hers, he guided her down to the gilded love seat. "We met briefly last summer. I don't know if you'll recall it, aboard the *Noma*. It was a fine, sunny day along the shoals, late June or early July, I believe—"

"Doctor Kimball, I don't mean to be impolite, but I'm honestly worn through. I've been under the care of the *Carpathia*'s surgeon and my own nurse for days now, so I think I'll be fine for the night. All I really desire in the next hour or so is a hot bath and my bed. Vincent mentioned we need to say something to the reporters outside, to tell them that I'm well enough so they'll leave. So, if you could just . . . ask me what you need to ask me? For the statement?"

The doctor nodded but did not move away. Nor did he ask her anything. He only looked down at her with an interested frown.

She sagged back against the love seat.

He said, "Have you had any headaches, or dizziness?"

"No."

"Any sensation of numbness in your limbs?"

"No."

"Any shortness of breath?"

"Only when I was rowing."

"I beg your pardon?"

She said wearily, "I had to row the lifeboat sometimes. All of us took turns. But I was better at it than most of the other women, so I rowed more. That was the last time I was out of breath."

"Good heavens," he said.

She was getting a neckache looking up at him. Madeleine propped her elbow on the arm of the causeuse and rested her chin upon her hand. This salon was one of the rooms Lina had shrouded in tapestries, towering and priceless, and she let her focus gravitate to the closest one. Cyrus and Croesus, surrounded by grapes and peacocks and courtiers. The cloth lifted and fell in its slow mockery of breath.

The doctor was saying, "Please understand that your health is delicate, no matter how resilient you may feel at the moment. It is not uncommon for women in your condition to experience delayed symptoms of one kind or another after a trauma."

Might I board the boat in order to protect my wife? She is in a delicate condition . . .

Exhaustion began to creep through her, a leaden weight in her bones.

The doctor tugged at his beard. "Forgive my bluntness, but I must inquire about the child. Have you suffered any cramping?"

"No."

"Any pain or bleeding?"

"No."

He regarded her with a considering gaze, as if he didn't quite believe her, but only said, "I'm gladdened to hear it," when it became clear that she would not add anything else. "I will leave you to the comforts of your family and call again tomorrow, if that is agreeable. Do not run the water too hot for your bath."

"I understand." Madeleine made to rise.

"One more thing, please."

She sat down again, stifling a groan. He stood with his back to the fire, his hands clasped behind him. Just over his shoulder, one of the gold-lacquered lion heads topping a pilaster winked at her in the dancing light.

"I would request that, at this time, you do not share any of the more—*distressing* details of your recent experience with Mr. Vincent Astor. Nothing beyond the most basic of facts, and even then only if he asks."

Madeleine tore her gaze from the lion. The doctor was frowning again.

"His mind is in the throes of what I would call extreme nervous agitation. He has spent the last few days in a near manic state, ever since the news of the sinking reached us. He is, from what I understand, quite close to his father."

"Yes," she said. "Jack was his anchor."
Just as he was mine.

Her private bath was of sculpted marble, much like the bathing pool back in Cairo had been, oval and deep and (as she knew well) large enough for two. The wall next to it was marble, as well, with a large seashell carved into it, a nude putto and two curved dolphins forming the faucet and handles. All but one of the walls in this room were paneled in marble, in fact: pearl-white, webbed through with silver and gold. They and the bath and the floor gleamed in the darkened chamber—she'd wanted only candlelight, not the electric—the metallic veins dimly sparkling as she moved, and everything was as serene and calm as the inner sanctum of a church.

But the water was tepid. The doctor must have had a word with Lillian, her second maid, and the girl had not dared to draw it any warmer.

Madeleine wanted her bath hot. She wanted it hot enough to sting her skin (*her soul*), to make her feel every inch of herself. She wanted the realness of that, the pleasure of the painful warmth soaking into her, wiping away the chill of every hour she had lived since *Titanic* had gone down.

She could have turned the tap herself, but instead she only sat there, floated there, and watched the play of light along the walls.

This water did not sting. It did not relax her. It only surrounded her, a cowardly temperature, a neutral solution that allowed her arms and legs to float.

The wall framing the door to the boudoir was papered in oyster damask. A large painting of Bacchus dangling a cluster of grapes over his mouth hung above the door, the exquisite labor of some Pre-Raphaelite master.

The god's eyes met hers, sidelong. He wore a crown of leaves in his hair and had his head slanted back, laughing.

Madeleine slid down beneath the surface of the water.

She allowed her arms and legs to stay floating. She kept her eyes open and held her breath as long as she could, her hair drifting like seaweed all around.

She imagined it was the ocean rocking her. She imagined the water icy cold instead of temperate.

Only when her lungs were screaming for air did she come up again.

CHAPTER 30

I became, overnight, the sweetheart of the world.

From gold-digging social climber, I was transformed into the tragic "girl widow," a fecund symbol of all that had gone wrong with society today. Man's hubris and vice had left me—and other, less recognizable widows than me—stranded upon the shores of . . . I don't know. Islands of hubris and vice, I expect.

I became the face of feminine heroism, doughty yet demure. The newspapers published story after story about me, usually quoting other survivors who claimed they saw me that night, or they saw Jack, or they saw us both, so terribly, romantically star-crossed. According to them, we were all over the ship in her final hours, even down in steerage, helping to comfort the distraught.

They said that we aided others into the lifeboats but jauntily refused to go ourselves, no matter how much they (our dearest, most bosom friends!) implored us to do so.

That Jack had jumped into my boat and then out again no less than four times to make room for more women.

That I had helped furiously row away from the sinking ship, only to collapse daintily afterward.

That, as I covered the men we'd saved from the ocean in woolen rugs, I'd howled out my husband's name, she-wolf-like, into the unforgiving night.

People were inventing all manner of stories about the sinking—because some of the papers would pay for them, you see—and if they dribbled the name "Astor" into any of their accounts, it was like the publisher had been guaranteed a return in gold.

I became the dream of countless dreamers, women from all around who still—*still*—thought that my smashed life was perfect. That the marriage which had taken everyone so aback before had crystallized into the most wondrous, sorrowful fairy tale.

I was young, I was wealthy, and I was famous. That was all they really knew, and that was all they needed to know. It was enough to sustain their fantasies.

At long last, I had managed to gain the world's admiration and respect, and all it took was the loss of my husband. The felling of my heart.

Jack was right when he'd told me that his people would eventually come around.

The taste of this success is like ashes on my tongue.

Those first few days, before they hooked his body from the sea . . . those were the worst, I think. Those were the days I surrendered to my heartache and hid away inside the mansion, mostly beneath my bedcovers. I would not answer anyone's questions. I would not look anyone in the eyes. I lived in dread of the next time someone would walk into my bedchamber, because I was sure they'd lean down close and whisper some version of, *Yes, he is really gone. Now you must tell us what actually happened.*

But I couldn't stay silent forever. The gathering of newsmen beyond the chateau's walls had only grown. They were at the doors at all hours, demanding an interview. They were insatiable, and I had to feed them.

William Dobbyn begged me for a statement he could give them, however vague, however short.

So I gave him one. I told him to tell the reporters that I didn't remember much of it. I was on *Titanic* with my husband; I was in the lifeboat without him; I was aboard *Carpathia* alone. That was all.

There was no force upon this earth that could make me offer up my actual memories.

Not to them.

April 23, 1912
Manhattan

The telephone call from the White Star office came early in the morning. The captain of the *Mackay-Bennett*, a cable ship hired by the company to recover the bodies, could confirm with certainty that they had found the remains of Colonel John Jacob Astor. The ship would spend a few more days at sea before steaming to Halifax, Nova Scotia, where the dead could be collected from the curling rink in town.

Dobbyn came to her with the news, along with Carrie, who stood woodenly behind him with lowered eyes.

Madeleine sat up in her bed with her hands resting over her stomach. She didn't really hear the words Jack's secretary was saying; she knew what they would be, anyway, so she didn't need to hear them.

So sorry . . . dreadful news . . . what we surmised . . .

She gazed down at the diamond on her hand, the gold band against it, then stretched out her arm and ran her palm across the undisturbed left side of the bed. The side where Jack slept—where he used to sleep.

She looked up again. "Have you told Vincent yet?"

"No, ma'am," said Dobbyn. "I thought it best to inform you first."

"Thank you." A sigh escaped her, soul deep. "I'll tell him."

She knocked against his door, softly at first, and then, when there was no answer, a little harder.

"Come in," Vincent called, his voice impatient.

She opened it, stepped into the sunbeams that streamed through the windowpanes, brightening the furniture, the paintings and orange mandarin drapery to tropical brilliance. Vincent was seated at his writing desk, scribbling something with his head down and his shoulders hunched. He didn't turn around to see who had entered.

"Tell Wilton I want the roadster brought up, the Bearcat. I'm going to see a stoker in Queens who claims he saw him in the water after the ship went down."

"Vincent."

His back stiffened. His head lifted. He pivoted slowly in his chair to take her in.

She wore black. She didn't own a black morning dress, so it was a day dress, simple and severe.

"You're out of bed," he said, toneless. "Finally."

"We've had news."

He shoved out of the chair. "I don't want to hear it."

"I know."

He stared at her, so awkward and handsome, that savage light rekindled behind his eyes.

"Perhaps you should sit down again," she suggested.

"No. I'm going out. I'm going to talk to a man who says he saw him—"

Madeleine was shaking her head, her lips pressed tight.

"—*saw* him alive in the water, next to a raft, a life raft that—"

"Vincent—"

"He is *not* dead, damn you! He's out there somewhere! Hurt or lost or—"

"He is aboard a funeral ship. They're bringing his body back in a few days."

Vincent reached up to clutch at his hair with both hands before letting his arms fall loose again. He made a sound deep in his throat, not a word but that low, flat moan of despair that chilled her as nothing else could have: the wounded beast again, here on dry land.

It stripped away the usual wall of reserve she maintained with him. She walked through the bars of light, reached for his hand, and he came back to life, recoiling away from her.

"It could be a mistake!"

She lowered her arm. "It could be, but I doubt it. They described him. They described what he was wearing, the suit and shoes and shirt. His gold watch and belt buckle. His wedding ring."

Outside the house, the April sky shone a celestial blue. Outside, she heard the motors of automobiles and omnibuses filled with people, regular people, going about their regular lives, their errands, as if nothing could ever shatter them. Not on such a pretty spring morning, the clouds pale and fluffed, the light bright as butter.

A pigeon landed on the sill of the window, fanning its wings. It strutted for a moment, its head jerking, then dipped down into the air below.

Vincent had not released her from his stare. His lips drew back; he began to shake his head.

"This is your fault. This is all your fault! You lured him to you. You seduced him. He would have never been on that ship if not for you."

"Oh," she said coldly, "this again. I thought we had already addressed this particular stupidity of yours."

"You're a terrible girl. A terrible wife. You left him behind to die, and I suppose you've gotten your wish now, haven't you?"

Madeleine lost her fragile sense of calm. "Why do you think I insisted we turn back the lifeboat?" she shouted. "Why do you think? We were one of only *two* boats to return to the people pleading for help, and *I* made that happen! I was searching for him in every face! Do you think I cared about any of those other men we saved? I would have tossed them back to the ocean in a *heartbeat* had I come across your father and we needed the room!"

She covered her mouth with her hand, forced herself to lower it again. She shot a quick glance over her shoulder at the open doorway—still empty—then flexed her fingers, closed them into fists.

The silk crêpe of her gown glistened in the sunlight, every shade of ebony, of unforgiving loss.

"So, yes. I may be a terrible person, as you say. I may be selfish and terrible. But I *loved* him. I would have sacrificed my own life for his. I certainly would have sacrificed any of those other men's lives."

He said nothing. He looked carved from stone.

"I didn't even know them," she said, much quieter. "They were nothing to me. They were disappointments. Every time I helped haul them up into the boat, letting them crumple and bleed water along my feet, they were disappointments. I don't care if that makes me a monster. I would have thrown any of them back for him. All of them. Feel free *not* to share that with the papers, and don't you *dare* blab to anyone that I've been crying. Don't you *dare.*"

He sat down heavily into the chair. He propped his elbows against the rosewood desk and dropped his head into his palms, his fingers speared through his hair.

"You don't really mean that, do you?" he muttered to the desk. "That you would have killed another man to save him?"

"I swear to God. I'll swear upon any god you like."

He looked at her aslant. She wiped quickly at her eyes, then turned to the door.

"Wait," he said. She turned back.

"Where will the ship—the ship with him. Where will she dock?"

"Halifax."

"I want to be there."

She hesitated, imagining him splintering apart in public, lashing out. What a feast the pressmen would make of that.

"There'll be paperwork to fill out," he said. "Legal matters. Forms to sign. I can do it instead of you. People will expect me to."

"I've already decided to send Captain Roberts in my stead. The *Noma* will be quicker than the trains. You don't have to go. He can do whatever needs to be done."

"I want to go," Vincent said. "Please."

It was the only time he'd ever said *please* to her.

On the wall above his nightstand there loomed a large, empty space, a rectangle of aqua silk wallpaper just slightly brighter than that surrounding it.

His voice came rough, not quite pleading. "Madeleine."

She hesitated a moment longer, then acquiesced with a nod, exiting the room.

John Jacob Astor IV, America's richest man and newly minted hero, was to be given what amounted to two funeral services. His widow would have preferred only one, but the little church in Rhinebeck-on-the-Hudson, where Jack had been a warden, could not fit all the mourners who wanted to pay their respects, and in any case, the Astor family mausoleum was back in Manhattan.

So, two separate services, one in the church, one graveside, all in the same day, and then he would be interred in the mausoleum above his father. Beside his mother.

Other people made the arrangements. Secretaries, undersecretaries, even Vincent, emerged from his mania into a new, razor-edged composure that alarmed Madeleine some, because it seemed so waxen, so brittle. The complex machinery of the massive Astor estate had clicked into gear, grinding away, and at this juncture, there was no stopping it.

But she did not want to stop it. The truth was, planning the details of Jack's entombment had turned out to be more than she could manage. As Vincent had grown stronger, she had veered the opposite direction, her mind and spirit drained to the point where even the simplest of decisions perplexed her.

They asked her about the flowers, and she had no answer.

They asked her about the eulogies, and she had no answer.

They asked her about the hymns, and she said any but "Nearer, My God, to Thee," because by now everyone knew it was the song the orchestra had been playing as the liner went down. It was that final hymn she had heard from the lifeboat, thin and melancholy and ghostlike, undulating across the water.

He was likely still alive then. She couldn't stop thinking about that. He had likely heard it too. Even ripped apart, they shared this one last bond, and it haunted her, imagining him on the boat deck, in the panic, hearing that hymn. And then her imagination would take her down dark, dark paths: had he tumbled from the deck as the ship split in two? Had he jumped into the ocean? Had he been one of those cartwheeling figures she'd seen? Had he struck his head, had he drowned at once, had he suffered, how terrible was his pain—

All she knew, *likely* knew, was that Jack had heard that hymn with her. And that, however differently they had ended up in the same place, they had still ended up in the same place: adrift beneath the shooting stars.

Ferncliff, that rambling, Italianate mess of a mansion, was where her husband had been born. And here was another odd thought that haunted her—she was surely sleeping now in the same master chamber where he had drawn his first breath.

It was a creaky, drafty room. In the winter, it was a beast to heat, as the stone chimney never seemed to draw well, no matter how often it was cleaned. But it was May now, and the days and nights had warmed into a humid temperance. She slept with two of the windows cracked so that she could smell the grass and trees and a beguiling hint of the Hudson River, flowing wide as the Nile nearby.

Her family was scattered throughout this house, pampering her, preparing her for what was to come. Vincent had wired from Halifax; he and Roberts and the *Noma* would be here this afternoon, and Jack's body would be here, and then, in two days, the service at the church, followed by the one in the city.

She told herself the first service wasn't even going to be a real goodbye, because then they had to go back to Manhattan to do it all again, so she shouldn't . . . break here. She must not break. Not yet.

She walked alone along a dirt trail that wove through the woods, listening to the robins calling from the branches above her. Every now and then, a liquid flash of light would reach her through the trunks and sun-flecked shadows, but from here the river was mostly obscured. The forest was only green grass, green ferns and shrubbery. Thick, green, mossy trees. Even the air tasted green, leafy and dense.

Beneath a hemlock gnarled and bent with time, a long-ago someone had constructed a crude stone bench to face a meadow. Madeleine sat there, listening to the robins, taking in the sloping view. A squirrel chittered at her from two oaks away, its tail twitching. A cluster of wildflowers, she didn't know what kind, swayed near her feet, dainty pink and violet bells on long thready stems.

She'd walked here with him a few times—not often, because it was some distance from the house, but enough for her to remember this particular meadow shaded with a different season, with golden autumn instead of green spring. Wrapped in a shawl, holding his hand. Sitting on this bench together, a bit chilled but not too bad, her head on his shoulder as he told her about the trees, how their leaves soaked in the sun and transformed it into life, how all the rabbits and mice and squirrels would burrow in the winter, curled up and warm beneath the white snow. She'd never mentioned to him that she knew these things already, these facts about trees and snow and woodland creatures; she was spellbound by the molasses of his voice, the cadence of his sentences. Sitting there with him, with the leaves changing and the river flashing, Madeleine could have listened to him forever.

But it was spring now, not autumn. The sky was azure, the world was alive.

She closed her eyes, thinking only of that.

"Ah-ha," said her sister, coming up on soft feet. "I've found you at last."

"It's a good hiding spot," Madeleine said, not opening her eyes. "Although not too good, I guess."

"One of the policemen on the patrol told me which way you went. I lost the path a few times. But what an idyllic place to become lost."

Katherine dusted the debris of old leaves from the stone slab, eased down beside her.

With the breeze bumping up against them, they sat without speaking, and at last even the squirrel gave up its scold. Far away, as far as the river perhaps, geese began to honk, a brief, harsh fluster of noise that quickly faded.

Katherine said, "Mr. Dobbyn and his associates asked me to tell you that the arrangements for the private train have been completed. It will leave Manhattan Saturday morning with the mourners for the service in town here, and take us all back to the city for the service at the cemetery in the afternoon. No one has to come here, to the house, unless you wish them to."

Madeleine opened her eyes. "All right."

"But . . . we could have a buffet or something prepared, if you like. Just in case. If you do want to pause a while to have people over. It's a lovely old house."

"It's a rickety old firetrap," she said. "We'll go straight to the train station from the church. That's all there'll be time for, in any case. How many limousines will there be?"

"Twenty."

"That should be enough, I think. Isn't it?"

"Yes, I think so."

The belled flowers swayed in place, left, right. Katherine had plucked an acorn from the grass at their feet and was slowly rolling it between her index finger and thumb.

"It's a rickety old firetrap," Madeleine said again, "but it's one I thought I would be sharing with him for the rest of our lives."

Her sister threw the acorn across the meadow, a hard, clean arc that scored the sky and ended in a patch of brambles.

"I know, Maddy. I know."

CHAPTER 31

The first time I met your half-sister was the morning of the funeral in Rhinebeck. Isn't that peculiar, that I'd never seen your father's daughter before? She endured the entire ordeal swaddled in mounds of black taffeta and ruffles, one elfin hand emerging from the folds of her dress to clutch the hand of her governess. Ava herself had not bothered to attend.

(They'd arrived from England a few days earlier on a German liner. When a reporter sent a note to Ava's cabin asking for an interview, she sent it back, writing on the reverse of it that she had nothing to say and signing it *Mrs. John Astor*, which burns at me still.)

To this day, I have not met her. I expect I never will.

Alice was ten. Vincent sat beside her throughout the service, once or twice murmuring something into her ear; I suspect he was telling her to stop swinging her feet. She wore a constant pout. Her brother's face, as ever, remained inscrutable.

So many people. So many of the Four Hundred and the locals pouring into that pretty country church, overflowing it, offering their words of comfort. For the sake of tradition, I'd come in my widow's weeds and installed myself in the front pew, ready to be seen. Mourners pressed my hands in theirs and went on and on about God's will and redemption and fate and whenever that happened I honestly don't know how I managed to hold my tongue.

God, I wanted to snap at them, *had had nothing to do with* Titanic. *Jack's death was entirely the work of men.*

But I kept silent. I only sat in my designated place and let my mouth curve into a downward bow, twisting my wedding band around and around, waiting for the damned service to end.

Ah, but what bruised me, though, was that one little girl, swinging her feet above the church floor, her bottom lip thrust out.

In other times, under other suns, I would have attempted to lure her into friendship, even if her mother didn't approve. (Maybe especially so.) It pains me to mention it here, but no doubt you'll catch wind of it sooner or later, anyway—there are rumors that Alice isn't Jack's child at all. Which I suspect made me search her features extra carefully, although I tried to conceal it.

Perhaps she had his nose. Perhaps she'd been graced with the extravagant length of his eyelashes. But mostly, I think, she just looked like herself.

Beneath her floppy black hat, Alice Astor had the sweetest, saddest scowl. I couldn't believe her mother wouldn't accompany her to either of Jack's services, but she didn't.

We managed it ourselves.

May 4, 1912
Manhattan

She would learn later that over six thousand people lined the funeral route from the train station to the cemetery, tenuously restrained by squads of policemen. It was only a handful at first, people stopped and staring at the polished hearse, the five horse-drawn carriages strung behind it in a solemn line as they left the 158th Street Station. Men removed their hats. Women held handkerchiefs to their hearts.

Madeleine, in the first carriage, sat beside Alice, both of them trying not to slide around on the slippery leather squabs. Vincent and Dobbyn sat opposite. None of them spoke.

The scent of lilies seemed to hang over her, trapped behind her long lace veil. She felt suffocated with it, had to flip the material back over the brim of her hat (*like a bride, a bride at a funeral*) to take a clean breath.

The baby kicked, just once, against her ribs.

"Who are all those people?" Alice asked, peering out the window.

Madeleine and Vincent glanced at each other.

Voyeurs, she wanted to say.

"Voyeurs," said Vincent.

Alice turned her big, dark eyes to him.

"Those are people who have come to let us know that they admired your father," Madeleine said, as the carriage crept along.

"But why are they here? Why are they staring at *us*?"

"Because we are as close to him as they will ever get," replied Vincent.

The nearer they came to the Trinity Cemetery gates, the thicker the crowd grew. The carriage's windows were not tinted; Madeleine replaced her veil. She'd rather suffer through the reek of lilies than lose the thin protection of the black lace.

"Look!" Alice began to wave at the window. "They're up on the rooftops, too. Some of them have climbed the trees!"

Madeleine raised her eyebrows at Dobbyn.

"They won't get in," he assured her. "No one will be allowed in without an admission card. Captain Kreuscher has assured me he has enough men assigned to keep control."

He was correct. The horses drew them past the gates, and suddenly all the people on foot around them were gone—although, as she exited the carriage, she could still see the ones on the neighborhood roofs beyond the walls, stick figures gawping.

She moved away from the carriage, from the horses, standing

in the shade of a large elm. The other carriages rolled up, her family, Jack's family and friends climbing out one by one in their funeral attire, a procession of ebony crows. They made their way as a group toward the mausoleum, walking along a wide gravel path.

A choir began to sing from the chapel nearby, low minor tones that lifted and fell; a flock of birds abandoned the elm at the same time, scattering against the blue.

The iron doors marking the entrance to the vault already stood open, gaping.

Like it's hungry, Madeleine thought, involuntary. *Eager for its latest meal.*

She stared down at the ground, repulsed, a little dizzy, as Jack's coffin was removed from the hearse. Mother came up, took her arm and led her to one of the folding chairs set up in rows along the grass. She sat, still not looking up, wreathed in lilies, always lilies, and tried not to retch.

In her hands, she carried a black handkerchief—also lace; it did nothing to absorb tears, actually—and her strand of carnelian. She kept her chin tucked, ran her fingers over the stones.

People settled in beside her, behind her, the Vanderbilts, the Huntingtons, the Rockefellers. People who, before *Titanic*, were loath to even shake her hand.

The rector began to speak.

Reluctantly, Madeleine lifted her eyes. The casket was right before her, trapped in a mountain of flowers, a rich show of mahogany and brass blazing in the late afternoon sun.

She found she couldn't look away from it.

He was in there. He was *inside* there. She hadn't been brave enough to view his body, but others had, and Jack was in there, when he had been right beside her only just days ago, warm and alive and smiling at her, teasing her about the name of their baby, kissing her lips and neck and belly. Filling her with his taste and scent and soul.

How could he be gone now? How could it be that she would never see him again?

How could a life so giant, so strong and bold, just . . . end?

The rector had fallen silent. Everyone was looking at Madeleine. She rose out of the chair, walked the few steps it took to stand before the coffin. With the carnelian necklace wrapped around her hand like a rosary, she rested her palm against the lid. The stone beads made the tiniest, tiniest clacking sound as they met the wood.

She bent over. Through the fabric of her veil, she touched her lips to the mahogany.

"Asalamu alaykum," Madeleine whispered. "Goodbye, my heart, my guide. Goodbye, beloved."

She could not sleep. It was amazing that she couldn't; as she'd prepared for bed that evening, she felt as if she struggled through air as thick as cotton wool, dragging her slower and slower, pushing her down toward the center of the earth. Her eyes burned red and dry. Her skin felt too tender, the flannel of her nightgown rough as burlap.

But she'd thought at least that after the long, long day of ritual farewells to her husband, *at least* at the end of it, she could rest her head against her pillow and finally be released into unconsciousness.

Every time she closed her eyes, the visions came. The falling stars, the darkened ship tipped upright. The bodies. The casket.

Doctor Kimball had left her a tincture for moments like this, but she didn't want to take it. She didn't want drugs, only sleep.

Madeleine sat up, pushed back the covers. She found her kimono and slippers and crossed the moonlit chamber out into the hall. She came to the stairs at the end of it and went up instead of down, to the third floor, where Carrie was sleeping, and Vincent, too. She walked the long corridor until she reached the oak doors of the library. She pushed them open, just enough to slip inside, then closed them silently behind her.

Like most of the chambers in the mansion, the library was chilled and gilded and tremendous. There were lamps wired for electricity and wall sconces for gas, but she left them all off, moving through the shadows, trailing a hand along the chairs, the spines of the books, the knee-hole writing desk, until she reached the fireplace.

It was mottled red marble, scrolled with sculpted leaves. A pair of carved lion's heads snarled from the columned ends. She rubbed her thumb over the open mouth of one of the lions, pressed the pad against its pointed teeth, then looked up at his portrait, hung just above her.

Bonnat had painted Jack life-sized, seated, his legs crossed, gazing back at her with his calm winter look. He had his right arm slung along the back of a blue satin chair, his left hand resting on his lap, his pose relaxed, his outfit formal, and even though it had been painted over a decade before they'd ever met, the resemblance to the man she had married was so crisp and true, she felt her heart squeeze.

The bay tree in its Ming jar by the desk gave a dry, rustling sigh; nothing ever stopped the drafts in this place. Madeleine turned away from Jack's painted face and went back to the desk, sitting down before it as he used to do, drawing herself close. The entire surface was bare. Even the jasperware canopic vase he used to hold his pens had been removed.

She opened the top drawer, finding the pens rolling, blank sheets of stationery neatly stacked.

She opened the next and found a series of letters and invoices, some still in their envelopes, from the managers of his various hotels and properties.

She opened the next and found Kitty's spare collar, heavy brown leather with a dangling brass tag. The tag had been engraved:

KITTY
J. J. Astor
840 5th Ave.
N.Y.

Madeleine hunched over it, the collar cradled in her hands. She didn't even realize that she was weeping until her tears began to spatter the leather.

CHAPTER 32

I hid in the mansion. Society began to caper on without me. At first, it was a relief; I'd had my fill of people already at the services, and honestly, it's no great hardship to hide in here. You'll find out about that. It's rather like being a princess locked in a tower, only the tower is made of money and bereavement, and the dragon keeping you inside it is the unending obsession of everyone else in the world.

Instead of the masses forgetting about me, as a teenaged-widowed-almost-mother, I became even more of a fascination. There were still so many articles being printed about me, about unborn you, about Jack. I received letters and telegrams practically every day from absolute strangers. Some were genuinely offering their condolences and good wishes.

Some were worse. Some were from other survivors (so they said), usually people from *Titanic*'s third-class, telling me that they, too, had lost their loved ones. That they had lost everything. These letters would invariably conclude with the authors begging me for financial support.

Some were worse still. At least three different sailors claimed to have found a piece of *Titanic*'s drifting debris—a plank of wood, a portion of a deck chair—incised (perhaps by a knife or a nail) with a final message from Jack to me, or to his children, which they would be pleased to deliver to me in person for only a modest fee.

I told Vincent it was a waste of time. That it was ridiculous to suppose any of these stories to be true and that, if Vincent gave in, he would be handing money to the most vile of men. Frauds, hucksters. Opportunists willing to blackmail our grief.

I told him the night had been too dark for scratching out messages. The deaths had come too relentlessly quick.

But Vincent, you know . . .

I do believe our shared sorrow has changed us both, reshaped us. Linked us, even, in a way neither of us anticipated. I don't think your brother despises me quite as he used to do.

But neither was he willing to listen.

Of course the messages were hoaxes. One was signed "John." One spelled "heaven" as "hevin." And one addressed me as "Madie," which your father never would have written, not even while dying.

There was one day that I did not hide, and that was the one during which I hosted a luncheon for Captain Rostron and Doctor McGee from the *Carpathia*, to thank them for all they'd done. I have to admit that it was not my idea, but it was a good one. Marian Thayer telephoned me, suggesting that she be the hostess and I one of the guests. But I told her candidly that I wasn't up for leaving the house yet, and that there was still an army of newspapermen camped outside, so that anywhere I went, I would be towing chaos directly behind me. I suggested my home as an alternative, and she readily agreed.

It was to be an informal affair, just our guests, me, Marian, Eleanor Widener, and another widow who had been in our lifeboat, a friend of Marian's. At the last moment, Eleanor pleaded illness and had to cancel. She had lost both her husband and her son to the ocean, and no one minded the abrupt change of plans.

I sent her flowers afterwards.

May 31, 1912
Manhattan

At some point after his divorce, Jack had decided to renovate the Fifth Avenue chateau. When he and Ava had lived in it with Jack's mother, it was actually two separate residences, two separate households, that shared a common exterior. They also shared the entranceway, but once inside the main hall, it was necessary to aim either right or left, depending on who was visiting whom. Twin grand staircases curled up opposite walls, leading to either *the* Mrs. Astor, or else to her son and daughter-in-law.

After Lina's death, Jack had combined the homes, replacing the twin staircases with just one, even more grand and frilled. But it wasn't until after Ava moved out that he'd added the finishing touch, a ten-foot-high marble fountain situated in the middle of the bronze-and-glass entrance hall, constantly, softly splashing.

Dolphins danced on their tails at the top, spat water from their mouths. Fat baby sea nymphs, complete with golden tridents, frolicked in rows below them, shiny and dripping.

In the wide bottom basin, goldfish swam in silent circles around and around, slender orange wisps with translucent long tails, fed twice daily by a dutiful kitchen boy.

Madeleine stood beside the goldfish to receive her guests. She was not the late Mrs. Astor; she didn't need to greet anyone while lurking beneath a giant portrait of herself—there was no portrait of her, anyway, giant or otherwise.

Nor was she Mrs. Astor the first, that glamorous Roman goddess who would never step foot in this house again.

She was merely herself, smaller than these rooms, larger in girth than the girl she used to be, a woman with a fresh bleeding wound to her soul that could never be healed . . . but that could at least be understood by the ladies coming to visit her today.

Madeleine thought Jack's goldfish were welcoming enough, with their small colorful grace.

Marian and her friend, Florence Cumings, arrived first. About a week ago, Madeleine had finally realized that the most brawny footmen in the household needed to remain by the entrance gates to keep the peace. It was especially true today, because the insect swarm of reporters and photographers outside had been joined by an entirely new nuisance: moving-picture operators, filming everything in sight.

The news of Madeleine's luncheon starring the heroic Rostron and some of *Titanic*'s most famous widows had already been leaked to the press, and the press was ready to pounce.

The butler spotted the limousine carrying Marian and Florence; by the time the auto reached the lower steps, the footmen were already hurrying out the doors to escort them inside. Both women exited quickly from the automobile, garbed in solid black and heavy veils.

They came in, glancing around, and Madeleine was so happy to see Marian, she simply walked up to her and wrapped her arms around her.

"Thank you for coming," she said, and broke away, surprised at herself.

Marian tossed back her veil. She had the same gentle, grave smile she'd worn back on the ship. "It's good to see you again. You look well, Madeleine."

"I've been tucked away for weeks. I think it's helped."

Marian nodded. "You remember Mrs. John Cumings?"

"Yes, of course."

Florence Cumings was the matron in sable from Lifeboat Four, the one who had joined her voice with Madeleine's in insisting they row back for the survivors.

Madeleine smiled. "Welcome. Welcome to you both. Please, come in. We're still waiting for the captain and doctor."

"There's a snarl of traffic out there," said Marian. "They're likely caught in it."

"There is always," said Madeleine, leading them to the southwest salon, "a snarl of traffic out there. Traffic of one kind or another, I'm afraid."

The salon was flooded with light; Madeleine had chosen it over the southeast because it seemed less somber. But as she watched Marian and her friend discreetly take in the ivory lacquered walls, the tall Japanese urns and marble statues of robed girls playing lyres and holding roses, she realized suddenly that this room was more like a mausoleum than any other in the house. For a second, it crippled her—how had she not seen it before?—but then Marian and Mrs. Cumings were settled in their chairs, and Madeleine was pouring tea, wondering in quiet, simmering embarrassment if they had noticed what she had noticed, the funeral feel of it all.

If the oil painting of Venus riding a dolphin that stretched across the ceiling was *too* marine, too nautical. Too much ocean.

Marian accepted her cup with a murmur of thanks. She tasted it, replaced it to its saucer, and tipped her head.

"What a fine room," she said. "I don't think you've done much to it since Caroline's time?"

"No," Madeleine admitted, uncomfortable. "I haven't really had much of a chance to do anything here. Not yet."

"Your own time will come." Marian took another sip. "Lina always did have a mighty preference for gilt."

Captain Rostron and Doctor McGee had taken a taxicab from the Cunard pier, but it had thrown a wheel on the way over. Luckily, no one had been injured, but it had delayed them sufficiently enough that the pressmen were in a mood by the time they appeared. Madeleine was alerted to their arrival not by the butler, but by the rising volume of shouting outside.

"Is it always like this?" asked Mrs. Cumings. "Those horrible people all around you?"

Madeleine lifted a shoulder, forcing a smile. "So far."

Mrs. Cumings shook her head. "Oh, my dear. I had no idea."

"I don't think anyone could have had," said Marian. "Madeleine is forging her way through an upside-down world."

"It is," agreed Mrs. Cumings sadly. "It is upside-down."

* * *

Madeleine hadn't thought that she would recognize the *Carpathia*'s captain. She had only a muddled recollection of boarding the ship, and once he had made certain that she was safely inside his cabin, she hadn't encountered Arthur Rostron again. Doctor McGee, who had visited twice a day, was a much more familiar face.

(She was ashamed to realize she'd never even considered where the captain might have gone after that, where he had slept since he'd given up his own bed. She had been so wrapped in weariness and misery.)

Yet as soon as she saw him again, she remembered. Like a puzzle piece locking into place to complete a larger image, she knew him: lantern-jawed, sunburned, blue eyes that met hers squarely, squint lines fanning pale from their corners—just like Jack. He wore his uniform, and that was more familiar still; she recalled the rows of gold braid on his jacket sleeves as he'd walked ahead of her on the deck of the steamer, the threaded insignia of his cap badge catching the sun as he'd glanced back at her from over his shoulder to see if she was still there.

Madeleine had trimmed the dining room table with vases of wildflowers and pink roses, anchors to the earth. She had ordered a simple series of courses, only five, because the women were still in deep mourning, and anything more elaborate might be considered frivolous, at least by the papers. The conversation remained genial but subdued, consisting mostly of the weather, the route of the *Carpathia*, which port of call was a favorite of the gentlemen.

At a particular lull, after the grilled lamb chops were cleared, Madeleine turned to the captain.

"I was told that you had all the ship's stationery hidden away during our voyage home. All the paper confiscated. To stop the reporters on board from writing about us."

He frowned in a thoughtful way, looking down at his water goblet. "As it happens, Mrs. Astor, I did. I didn't want them pestering anyone. Matters were unpleasant enough, as you know. They were paying passengers, however, so that was about all I could do."

She leaned forward. "Thank you for that."

"Yes, thank you," echoed Marian.

Madeleine rose to her feet—a little awkwardly these days, with her growing baby—and instantly, both men did as well.

"No, no," she said, indicating they should sit again. "Please. I'm only fetching something from over here."

She crossed to the fireplace, took the pair of small wrapped boxes waiting there from the mantelpiece. There was a mirror above the hearth, a great silvery rectangle that bounced light around the room. She faced herself in it briefly, her cheeks slightly rounder than they had been a year before, her hair much more elegantly upswept. Now that Jack was gone, she didn't bother with so many gemstones, only her engagement ring and two simple diamond clips at her ears. She was all black and silver and sparks, though. At least in the mirror she was. Black and sparks, and haunted pale eyes.

She returned to the table, handing each man a box.

"The smallest of tokens," she said, "representing our infinite gratitude."

She had rehearsed the phrasing in her head, hoping that it didn't sound mawkish, that she'd chosen the right words. Both men seemed caught off-guard.

"We hope you like them," Marian added, when neither of them moved to unwrap the boxes.

The captain rubbed his chin. "Mrs. Thayer, we were only—"

"Of course," said Marian. "You were only *saving our lives.*"

"Please do accept our thanks," said Mrs. Cumings.

They had commissioned a pocket watch for the captain, a cigarette case for the doctor. And although they were of solid gold and crafted by the finest artisans in the city, right now they really did seem to Madeleine to be nothing more than tokens, shiny things wrapped in expensive tissue paper.

Spoken words could never fully express what had passed through her that morning, how it had felt to see the mast lights of the ship coming toward them through the dawn. Golden trinkets could not measure up as thanks enough. A mountain of gold would not measure it.

"We know we can never really repay you—" Madeleine began, but her voice caught in her throat, and she couldn't finish.

Captain Rostron touched a finger to the cover of the watch, where his initials had been emblazoned in dark blue enamel, then looked up at her.

"There, now," he said quietly. "It was only my duty, and my honor. Knowing you're safe at home again is thanks enough for me."

June came, and her birthday. She had at last turned nineteen, which seemed only a step away from something better than all the years before, something more mature and stable and less prone to heartache.

Vincent left for Europe with his mother and sister, and the Fifth Avenue residence seemed to take on an even keener echo. Madeleine retreated to Beechwood for a while, the home she liked best. She would eat her meals outside when she could, watching the shifting blue waters of the cove. Sometimes she would entertain Katherine or Mother or Father, or any of her girlhood friends who dared to trickle by. But mostly she remained alone, because that usually felt better than not.

She wondered if the locals would end up spinning morbid legends about her, the solitary young widow always in black, walking through the salt wind with her hair streaking madly behind her. After she died, they could whisper about her ghost still stalking the grounds, eternally searching Sheep Point Cove for her lost love.

As her time grew more near, however, Madeleine realized she needed to return to the city. Mother was especially adamant that the baby be born in Manhattan, closer to hospitals and competent care.

(Carrie, who overheard that particular remark, said nothing, only narrowed her eyes.)

So Madeleine gave in. One amethyst twilight, she paced a last loop along the expanse of Beechwood's rear lawn with her hair entirely loose—why not give the legend an extra little kick?—then went back inside and did not come out again except to motor away.

But the Manhattan chateau had not surrendered its emptiness. Even after it began to fill with doctors, with nurses, with Mother and Katherine, everyone at the ready for the moment Jack Astor's baby decided to arrive . . . the house was empty.

Like Madeleine, its heart—whatever heart it might have once possessed, beneath its stylish public shell—had been felled.

She began to steal out the servants' door once a day to be chauffeured around the park, around a maze of random streets. Away from everyone else, she would lean her head out the open window and let the smoke and fumes of the city flow over her, clinging to her hair and clothing and skin. She imagined herself an ordinary girl then, no one special, just a girl going out somewhere. Maybe meeting friends for an ice cream soda, or going to a concert uptown.

Maybe driving away, far, far away, never turning back.

The limousine always turned back.

One early gray dawn in the middle of August, she awoke to find her nightgown soaked hot between her legs, and for a confused moment thought her courses had come, finally, at last. But then the pain rolled through her, a great tidal wave of pain, and, gasping, she rang for Carrie, who gathered up the doctor and the other nurses like a bossy hen rounding up her errant chicks. Mother arrived in her dressing robe to hover near the headboard, telling Madeleine how brave she was, how brave her daughter was, but Madeleine really only wished that no one would talk to her at all, because the pain was a volcano now, a continent, the entire world, and it was all she could do not to scream, and she was afraid of *what* she might scream if she opened her mouth.

Jack's name, a curse, a plea. She didn't know. They were all there inside of her, violently pushing to come out.

Their son entered the world with a final cresting rush of agony and, after a few seconds, an indignant bawl.

They cleaned him up and placed him in the cradle of her arms, against her sweaty skin, her heaving chest. He felt heavy and foreign, like nothing that could have actually just come from inside her own body.

How awful that was, she thought, exhausted, remote. *How wonderful. How awful and wonderful to feel him like this, above my heart, just where his father used to rest his head.*

She didn't look at him at first, that tiny, weighted thing. She was still trying to align her senses, to hold back words or tears or anything else she didn't want to share with this roomful of people, in this fresh crack of morning with its bright warming light.

With his head against her collarbone, her baby made a questioning noise, a cross between a whimper and a cry. Madeleine lifted her hand to his face. She stroked his perfect new skin, smooth beneath his sticky heat; the creases of his eyes and mouth; the delicate seashell shape of his ear.

She brushed a kiss to his forehead, then dropped back to her pillows. They breathed together, chest to chest. Through the resonance of flesh and bone, she imagined she felt his heartbeat, a faint hammering simultaneously fragile yet certain, so desperately swift it might belong to a hummingbird darting across the sky.

EPILOGUE

I would not attempt to guess at the nature of true love, except to say that when I was immersed in it—swimming through it, breathing it in, holding that breath, exhaling—in those short, extraordinary days and nights I shared with your father, true love was absolutely clear to me.

Jack was clear to me. Jack was me, and I was him, and you, sweet child, are now us both.

Such crystalline perspective, and gained at such a price. It is Survival's gift to me, I must assume. It is the gift I will cling to, holding my breath to keep it safe and alive inside me.

Only exhaling at the very, very end, when I know I'll see him smiling at me once more.

ACKNOWLEDGMENTS

⁓⦅───────⦆⁓

This book began with a phone call. My wonderful agent, Annelise Robey, wanted to know if I'd be willing to pitch a story about *Titanic* to Kensington Publishing. I said, "Yes!" and quickly settled upon Madeleine Astor as my protagonist, a 1912 version of a young Princess Diana if there ever was one. I thought to myself, "This'll be easy!" Then I set about researching.

And researching.

And researching.

There is a *lot* of information out in the wilds regarding *Titanic*, its passengers and crew, and not all of it is credible, to put it mildly. There was far less information about Madeleine herself. For the most part, I was able to trace the footprints of her life through archived newspaper articles, nearly all of them period. The *New York Times* was a particularly valuable resource in this regard, as it was essentially her hometown paper. Here are some others, in no particular order:

For a closer look at the first-class world of the passengers aboard *Titanic*, try *Gilded Lives, Fatal Voyage* by Hugh Brewster.

Encyclopedia Titanica (encyclopedia-titanica.org) is an exhaustively detailed, fascinating site dedicated to all facts *Titanic*. Fair warning: it's very easy to lose hours and hours there.

Another interesting site is the Titanic Inquiry Project (titanicinquiry.org), where you can read actual transcripts of both the American and the British *Titanic* inquiries, including verbatim survivors' testimonies.

In 1926, Vincent Astor decided to auction off practically everything in the Fifth Avenue chateau (the mansion itself was subsequently demolished). The Internet Archive (archive.org/details /paintingsfurnish00amer) has a searchable file of the auction catalog, if you'd like to get a peek at how the really, *really* rich decorated.

Interested in the fashion of the era? Take a look at *Titanic Style*, by Grace Evans.

Research is the blood and bones of *The Second Mrs. Astor*, but the heart of it is the living, breathing people who helped me out, over and over. I want to thank Annelise and everyone at the Jane Rotrosen Agency for their many years of encouragement and support.

And I am lucky enough to have the hardworking and talented Wendy McCurdy—who was actually my very first editor for my very first book, so long ago!—return as my editor once more.

My friend Bev Allen gave me a great big happy surprise when she directed me to the Missouri Historical Society's Frances Hurd Stadler *Titanic* Collection. Bev's first job out of grad school had her working with Frances, the daughter of Carlos and Katherine Hurd. It's through Bev that I know someone who knew someone who knew someone who was aboard the *Carpathia* with Madeleine!

And, of course, I must acknowledge all the love and strength provided by my incredible husband Sean: my sounding board, my steady anchor, my true north.

The Second Mrs. Astor

About This Guide

The suggested questions are included to enhance your group's reading of Shana Abé's *The Second Mrs. Astor*.

Discussion Questions

1. At the beginning of the story, Madeleine is a sheltered seventeen-year-old socialite who has just graduated from finishing school. By the end of the novel, just two years later, her world is radically different. Do you think she handled the transition from relative obscurity to fame well? What would you have done differently?

2. Jack Astor was a man far more complex than the press portrayed, yet he was still incredibly wealthy, powerful, and renowned. Was he walking a morally ambiguous line by courting a teenaged girl nearly thirty years his junior? Do you believe he actually loved her, or was it just libido? Does the time period help excuse the age difference between them?

3. One of the biggest impediments to the potential marriage of Madeleine and Jack was the fact of his divorce. In the end, the minister who performed the ceremony had to be paid a staggering sum to overcome his qualms about the union. Do you think it was fair to punish both Madeleine and Jack for the perceived moral failing of his divorce from Ava? Have our views of divorce since then changed for the better or worse?

4. Their wedding ceremony took place just over a month after their engagement was publicly announced. Were Madeleine and Jack right to insist upon a swift, small wedding, instead of the huge social blowout that was more typical of their time and station? Do you think the primary motivator behind it all was their growing love for each other, or more a fear of the escalating scandal?

5. "I wish I were as brave as you," Madeleine confesses to her sister. Do you think bravery was one of Madeleine's inherent

traits, or not? What does her comment tell you about her in-sight into herself? When Katherine replies that she wishes she were as strong as Madeleine, do you agree that Madeleine is strong?

6. Madeleine's relationship with the press evolves over the course of the story. Do you think how she treated them was justified? Do you think how she was treated *by* them was justified?

7. While sipping bouillon one afternoon on the deck of the *Titanic*, Madeleine encounters a fan and realizes: "The real world was rushing in again at last, predictable, inexorable. There were going to be girls like this around every corner from here on out." Was Madeleine being snobbish to Helen Bishop when Helen tried to befriend her? If so, why do you think she acted like that?

8. Madeleine never interacted with anyone from steerage while aboard *Titanic*. Were you surprised when she gave away her fur shawl, and later her sable coat, to the two steerage survivors?

9. As *Titanic* was sinking, no one in the Astor party had any way of knowing that Lifeboat Four was going to be one of the last to leave the ship, although it was. Should Madeleine have argued more forcibly to stay with Jack once it was clear he would not be allowed in the lifeboat? Or was she right to leave him behind?

10. Madeleine's interaction with Vincent was contentious from the beginning. As his future stepmother, should she have tried harder to befriend him? Or do you think it was always a hopeless cause?

11. Madeleine says of Jack: "He is my rock and my true north and my whole heart." How do you think she changed after suf-

fering his death? Did her grief force her to grow as a human being, as a soul, or did she perhaps shrink? Or both?

12. Bonus question: Are you in a book club meeting right now? If so, what kind of wine are you holding in your hand? Extra points if it's champagne!

Don't miss *An American Beauty,* Shana Abé's stunning next novel based on the life of Arabella Huntington, who rose from poverty-stricken obscurity to become the richest woman in America during the Gilded Age.

Read on for a preview.

CHAPTER 1

Journal entry of Arabella Duvall Yarrington
June 1st, 1867

I just suffered the most wretched dream. I found myself in a room
of gold, a room so grand and exquisite it surely belonged in a palace.
The tables and chairs and settees were all gilded and scrolled, inset
with precious gems and pearls. Curtains and tapestries adorned the
walls, every one of them cloth of gold, and a fire burned in a great
cream marble hearth. (A wood fire, mind you, not coal.)

Beyond the windows shone sky, only sky; deep blue, flat and brilliant as a slab of polished turquoise.

In the center of the room was a banquet table, all laid out. There
were dishes such as I've never seen before, never even imagined.
Dream dishes, I suppose, roasted meats and nuts and soft cheeses,
fresh fruits and confections, everything so mouthwatering, and I
could not wait to dine.

I walked toward that table, saw my own arm reaching out. The
sleeve of my gown was as fine and golden as my surroundings; I wore
a link bracelet inset with carved cameos, exactly like the one in the
window at Monsieur Monroe's on Broad Street.

It looked so *right* around my wrist.

I reached for an iced petit four—chocolate, with little pink frosted roses—no gloves or fork, nothing so civilized, just my bare hand, and I picked it up and brought it to my lips and knew—oh, I *knew* how it was going to taste; *knew* how that delicious dark bite would melt across my tongue; *knew* how I would lick my fingers after I'd finished it all, sucking the very last hint of chocolate from my skin . . .

And that, of course, is when I awoke.

I cannot recall the last time I tasted chocolate. Or a petit four.

Today is my seventeenth birthday. And the clock is chiming downstairs, and I must hurry to work.

Arabella
Richmond, 1867

The best part about working for Johnny Worsham, aside from the fact that he paid reliably, and in cold Yankee cash, was that he insisted she never wear her spectacles while on the floor. Which meant that Belle never had to really *see* any of the men she served, not unless they came quite close, which some of them did. It was a blessing in disguise, although she could certainly smell Johnny's customers well enough, and feel their hands, and still had to laugh coyly at their drunken (and usually filthy) jokes.

Most nights she was the Champagne Girl, a position which sounded both joyful and amusing, but in fact meant a great deal of meandering around the faro parlors balancing a heavy silver platter along one arm, loaded with cut-crystal flutes. By dawn, her back and legs would be afire.

Some nights, the Tuesdays and Sundays Franny had off, Belle was the Piano Girl, playing a series of tunes carefully selected by Johnny himself. There were thirty-two in total. She had memorized them all.

She couldn't advance to the position of Dealer, the girls who received the best tips, because that would require her spectacles again. She'd tried to convince Johnny that she could read the cards well enough without them; the world was only *slightly* blurred, really, but he refused to take the risk. Johnny was flamboyant and debonair and deeply committed to one thing and one thing only, and that was his income.

She supposed she couldn't blame him. Worsham's illicit gaming saloon was the most popular in Richmond, not in the least because of the beautiful young women he hired to work in it. Currency of all sorts—cash, credit, conversation—drifted thick as cigar smoke through these ornate chambers, but it wasn't so very long ago that Richmond had been in flames, Richmond had been beaten and shamed and starving, and no one had forgotten that.

Money meant everything now. Maybe it always had.

So, yes, really, being paid was the best part of her job. Clutching those coins in her fist when Johnny first handed them over, the weight of them in her pocket. The sound they made as she walked home with them, a silvery clinking song, barely there but there if you listened.

It was the finest song she knew. It was a song that meant *today the earth spins on and still carries you with it. Today you will survive.*

Jam 2024

Visit our website at
KensingtonBooks.com
to sign up for our newsletters, read
more from your favorite authors, see
books by series, view reading group
guides, and more!

BOOK CLUB
BETWEEN THE CHAPTERS

Become a Part of Our
Between the Chapters Book Club
Community and Join the Conversation

Betweenthechapters.net